THE DECEPTION

THE DECEPTION

MAUREEN MYANT

This edition produced in Great Britain in 2023

by Hobeck Books Limited, 24 Brookside Business Park, Stone, Staffordshire ST15 0RZ

www.hobeck.net

A CIP catalogue for this book is available from the British Library.

ISBN 978-1-915-817-16-7 (pbk)

ISBN 978-1-915-817-15-0 (ebook)

Cover design by Jayne Mapp Design

Printed and bound in Great Britain

Are you a thriller seeker?

Hobeck Books is an independent publisher of crime, thrillers and suspense fiction and we have one aim – to bring you the books you want to read.

For more details about our books, our authors and our plans, plus the chance to download free novellas, sign up for our newsletter at **www.hobeck.net**.

You can also find us on Twitter **@hobeckbooks** or on Facebook **www.facebook.com/hobeckbooks10**.

In loving memory of my parents, Agnes and Eddie Cummins

ONE

Glasgow

DI ALEX SCRIMGEOUR put down his phone and unclenched his jaw. He closed his eyes and counted to ten. This was too much. He was exhausted. His mother hadn't settled into the home he'd chosen for her, and every day – every single fucking day – the manager phoned to give him an update on her 'challenging behaviour'. Even though she rarely recognised him, never knew what day of the week it was, hadn't a clue who the prime minister was, somehow she understood that she'd been taken from her beloved bungalow with its carefully tended garden and dumped in a nursing home. And she was never done shouting at the staff who cared for her. He hated that he'd put her there, but there was no other option. She wasn't able to look after herself and he couldn't do it alone. It would be different if he had someone to share the burden, but he had no wife, no partner and no siblings. His only brother, Billy, had died from cancer two years ago. Not that he'd been much help anyway. He'd used his family as an excuse to avoid visiting their mother too often.

Billy's daughter, a police officer, was Alex's only relative apart from his mother, and she visited even less. Yet last time he saw her she'd had the nerve to tell Alex he shouldn't have put his mother in a home. 'Poor Gran, she hates it there. You've got a huge flat, Uncle Alex, she could live with you.' Christ, she was a sanctimonious little bitch. Thank fuck she no longer worked in the same division. And how would she know what his mother thought of the home? She'd visited Mum only once in the six months she'd been there.

He picked up his cup of coffee and took a sip. It was cold. The call had taken longer than he thought. He'd get another. Before he could move though, Mark Nicholson, his DS, popped his head round the door.

'You got a second, sir?'

'Aye, what is it?'

Mark came into his office and pulled the door closed behind him. 'It's a wee bit awkward, I don't want anyone earwigging.'

Alex tried and failed to put on a sympathetic expression. No doubt it was about Mark's relationship, which was going south fast after Mark's affair last year. What an idiot. From Alex's point of view, Mark had everything. Youth, a lovely partner, three beautiful children. And yet, he'd as good as thrown it away for a fling. Worse, he nearly lost his family when a deranged killer had set fire to his house. Mark had a lucky escape there. Alex knew what it was to lose a family. He'd found it hard enough to cope, and God knows, he'd done nothing to risk it.

'How can I help you?'

'I hate to do this. I know how busy we are, but is there any chance I could have some time off?' He must have seen the expression on Alex's face – they were in the middle of an investigation into corruption that had the potential to go apeshit as it

2

involved a local councillor – and he rushed on, the words tumbling out of his mouth. 'It's... Karen has found a last-minute deal for Lanzarote and we haven't had a holiday, well, since Emma was born, and you know, after...' He tailed off.

Alex twirled the ballpoint between his fingers. He liked Mark, he really did, though he was careful not to show it. If he'd had a son, he would have liked him to be like Mark. Easygoing, good with people, and intelligent. He was a good guy all round, but with a wild temper, which, thank goodness, he'd managed to tame. 'And if I say no?'

Mark's face fell enough for Alex to understand that ultimatums had been made. 'Is everything OK, Mark?'

'I... No, not really. Karen's going off on one. I don't know what to do. She keeps going on about... you know...'

'Suzanne Yates?' Mark nodded and Alex thought quickly; he could spare Mark for a few days. 'Look, take next week off. But that's it for the time being, right? You'd better not be sick or late or anything after this. And you'll work your arse off until you go. Comprenez?'

'Thank fuck,' breathed Mark. 'I mean, thank you. It... You've no idea. You've saved my life.'

Alex waved him away. He had a fair idea how much of a big deal it was. It was bad enough that Mark had had an affair at all, but to have chosen the sister of that deranged woman; that was a fucking disaster. Julie Campbell had led them all such a merry dance, going on a killing spree when she was supposed to be fucking dead. Christ, thank fuck she was out of the picture now; she'd killed herself in Suzanne's flat. Something about Julie's death niggled Alex though. Suzanne had been the one to find her sister – a little too convenient maybe – and Alex sometimes wondered if Suzanne had helped her sister on her way. But there was no evidence, though he'd searched hard enough for it. He shook his head. Enough of this. With Mark off next week, he had to be sure he was absolutely on top of everything. One thing was good though. Mark's interruption meant he hadn't thought about his mother for oh, at least five minutes. He turned back to his screen, coffee forgotten, and got on with opening his emails.

'Shite, shite and more fucking shite,' he recited as he binned one email after another. One of his pet hates was people who insisted on replying to the mainly banal emails. Inane little messages saying *thank you, message received, kind regards, I'm on it* and so on. He fucking knew when they read it, he had 'read replies' set up in Outlook. Maybe he should send a message requesting that people didn't reply to his emails unless there was a specific question. No doubt some fucking eejit would miss the point though and send back an email with a thumbs up emoji.

The next message was from an unknown address, a string of numbers and letters. His heart sank. In his experience these came from nutters. He clicked to open it.

X1CO99rrCOpupt2@gmail.com
RE: You're consceince
To: DI A.Scrimgeour@PoliceScotland

How do you sleep at night? You lying cunt.

That was it. Nine words. He was about to delete the email when it vanished. Alex looked at his finger. Had he actually touched the keyboard? He didn't think so. He looked in the deleted folder but there was nothing there. Damn it. He'd heard of emails that vanished; one of his younger colleagues had been threatened that way last year. No one had believed he was getting threats by email because nobody else ever saw them. Then he was badly beaten up and they'd had to change their tune. The PC had left the service. Why would he stay, after all, when his reward was a battering and colleagues who'd been sceptical about the vanishing emails, to say the least? Alex pushed the thought aside; no point dwelling on it.

He closed his eyes and tried to visualise the email address. It began with an X and had upper case, lower case and numbers in it. It was a Gmail address; he remembered that much, but that was all. The subject line was something like *you're conscious*. No, that wasn't it? Shit. He scribbled down the message before he forgot it. *How do you sleep at night? You lying cunt.* He was pretty sure that was it. Your conscience – that's what the illiterate wee shite must have been trying to say in the subject line. Your conscience. What did it mean? He thought hard, wishing he'd paid more attention to the email address. After a few seconds he put it out of his mind. Some bastard trying to mess with him. Well, he'd be fucked if he let anything like that bother him. He settled down to the report he needed to write before he left work today and put it out of his mind.

TWO

Buckinghamshire

THE INSISTENT RING of her mother's phone startled Kate. It was ten days since Mirren's death, so who was calling her? Kate had contacted all of her mum's friends. She was sure she hadn't missed anyone. Kate looked at the screen – number unknown; it must be a cold caller. She ignored it and turned back to the To-Do list she was making, a sad affair of contacting lawyers, utility companies and financial institutions. A few seconds later, the phone buzzed again – a voicemail. Damn, maybe she'd missed someone after all. She picked up the phone, keyed in 123 and put it on speaker to listen.

'You there? I'll phone again in a few minutes and you'd fucking better pick up this time. I'm warning you.'

Kate pressed the end call button. It was a warm day but the voice had chilled her. The voice was rough, his accent pretty much incomprehensible. Scottish, she thought. Like Mum's, though hers had been much softer. Sure enough, after a few seconds the phone rang again. Kate picked it up, holding it by the edge as though it might bite her.

'Yes.' She spat out the word.

'Who's that? I want to speak to that bitch.'

Kate looked at the phone in disbelief. No one ever described Mirren in that way. She was, had been (when would she get used to using the past tense in relation to Mum?) gentle and kind and never argued with anyone.

'You have the wrong number. To whom do you wish to speak?' Her voice was clipped and cold.

He repeated what she said, mimicking her home counties accent before adding, 'No, I haven't. Muirrean fucking Fallon, put her on.' He mispronounced Mirren's real name.

Kate considered hanging up but decided against it. He'd only keep phoning. He sounded the persistent type, and somehow he knew Mum's name was Muireann and not Mirren, as she preferred to be known. 'Ms Fallon died ten days ago.'

Silence, then she heard his breathing, ragged and angry. 'You fucking what?'

'She died. Ten days ago.' It was hard to keep her voice from shaking.

'I don't fucking believe you. I spoke to her last week.'

Her voice was tight with rage. 'Nonetheless, she died.'

'You're a fucking liar. I want that twenty grand or I go to the papers.' He cut her off.

Kate's hands shook as she put the phone to one side. His voice had been venomous. She imagined her mother being spoken to in that way and tears pricked her eyes. Best block the number and forget it but when she looked on her phone, it had been withheld. She scrolled back through the last few calls made to her mother, and sure enough there they were: two calls from an unknown number on the day she had died.

It had been a shock to come home from work and find her. She was lying on her bed, sleeping, or so Kate thought. Only when she had reached out to wake her did she realise. Mirren had had only a few weeks left to live. Nine months she'd been given in November, when she was diagnosed. That was seven months ago. Kate's throat tightened as she thought about Mum dying alone. She should have been with her. She should have been there to protect her from the poison in that man's voice. Had this helped to kill her? It took an hour to stop shaking, two hours to stop thinking about him. What the hell was he after? Money evidently. Twenty thousand pounds. It sounded as though he'd been blackmailing her mother. But that was ridiculous. Mum had lived a quiet life, never doing anything to draw attention to herself except where it concerned advertising her embroideries. The idea that she had done something worthy of blackmail? Inconceivable. No, she had to stop thinking about it. Other things were more pressing.

Two days later, the day she'd been dreading arrived. Her mother's funeral. She'd had little sleep. In spite of her attempts not to think about the phone call and possible blackmail, it wouldn't go away. Yesterday a man in a silver car had appeared outside the house, well, a few doors down. Was it the man who'd phoned? Common sense told her it was unlikely, but it worried her nonetheless. The funeral wasn't until three o'clock, so she went out for a run, hoping to forget about him. She ran along the main road to the roundabout and crossed over to get to the other side. It wasn't far to the golf course and the woods where she loved to run.

The exercise helped. She was calmer as she ran back along the road that led to their house, her house now. But when she turned the corner, her heart beat faster. The small, silver Fiat was there again, same place as the day before. Kate paused at her gate to stretch out, using this as a chance to get a good look at it. There was a man in the front seat, his face in shadow. She was sure it was the same guy, his bulky outline filling up the car. A bear of a man. Who the fuck was he? For a moment she considered confronting him, but that would be foolish. She opened the gate and hurried up the path, moving faster as his gaze scalded her neck. Her hands shook as she put the key in the door. The lock was stiff but she persevered until it opened. She stumbled through the open door and slammed it behind her. For a moment she stood with her back against it, slowing her breathing, calming herself down. After two or three breaths her heart rate settled. She blinked to adjust to the lack of light in the hallway. Kate shivered, unable to shake off her unease. 'Get a grip,' she muttered. 'He'll be another bloody double glazing salesman.' But as she was thinking this, she couldn't remember the last time she'd opened the door to any sort of salesperson who hadn't had an appointment.

After her shower, she ate lunch and then checked to see that everything was ready for the service. She picked up the bundle of pamphlets she'd had printed and read through the order of service. She and Mirren had planned it together. Kate smiled as she remembered the arguments over the choice of poems and music.

'Not Auden,' Mirren had said. 'Completely ruined since that bloody awful film. And Rossetti's way too corny.' Eventually they'd agreed on a poem by Liz Lochhead about going through her mother's wardrobe after she'd died. They sobbed together while reading it.

Music was no easier. Kate suggested something classical – her mother was always listening to Radio 3 – but Mirren insisted on going back to her early days with songs from the late sixties and seventies and refused to consider anything else.

Kate went into to the living room, a comforting, homely place with a low ceiling and white, painted beams. There was a small redbrick fireplace, which wasn't original but nonetheless suited the wood burning stove they'd put in a few years ago. On either side of the fireplace were chimney recesses with built-in bookshelves from floor to ceiling. Throughout the cottage every spare corner was crammed with either shelves or bookcases.

Kate wandered round the room, drawn to the window but at the same time knowing she should avoid it. After a few seconds, she peeped out from behind the curtains and saw that the car was in the same place. Her fear vanished, to be replaced by rage. She should be thinking only of her mother, instead of letting this cretin dominate her thoughts. She rushed to the front door, determined to put an end to this, whatever it was. By the time she got there though, he'd driven off, leaving only a puff of exhaust in the air. She cursed herself for letting him get to her.

She looked at her watch. Two hours before the undertakers were due. Enough time to make the cottage clean and tidy so that if friends came back to the house after the funeral, the mess wouldn't embarrass her. She ran a finger along the mantelpiece, leaving a clear trail in the dust. She and her mother had kept the house tidy and clean enough to scare off major germs, but there was always something more urgent or interesting to do than iron or dust, and even by Kate's admittedly low standards it had been neglected over the past few weeks. Books were stuffed into every corner, and there were piles of paper everywhere waiting for Kate to deal with them.

Five minutes to go and she had finished. The sun beamed in through sparkling windows looking in vain for dust to highlight. Books had been put back onto shelves and the mess of papers was hidden in drawers for her to sort through later. She'd done a good job. Time to get ready. Upstairs she applied mascara and lipstick and then went outside to wait for the undertaker.

The garden, Mirren's pride, was at its best. Hollyhocks, flanked by delphiniums and foxgloves, lined a border beneath the window. She'd have to pull up the fading foxgloves soon or they'd seed everywhere. Kate picked up the trowel that rested in a pot by the doorway and dug up a couple of dandelions, taking care to keep her hands clean. The biggest of the dandelions defeated her, so she put the trowel back and sat down on the steps to the front door. Mr Harris from across the road scuttled over.

He smiled at her. 'Are you locked out, dear?'

Kate shook her head. 'No, I'm waiting for the undertakers.'

'Oh, I hadn't realised the funeral was today,'

Kate felt a pang of guilt at his reply. Perhaps she should have told the neighbours. But Mirren had always kept them at arm's length. Thankfully, the undertakers' car drew up at that moment and she made her excuses and left.

It was only a few minutes' drive to the undertakers' rooms where the service would be held. Mirren hadn't wanted a church service, but she did want to be buried and had found an environmentally friendly cemetery in the Chiltern woods. 'I'll be at peace here,' she'd said.

Kate got out of the car and looked round. A group of colleagues from work came over to greet her. Her Head of Department, Gus, was first to speak. 'Bearing up?' As if he cared. Kate nodded, not trusting herself to speak. Sheena, who was her ally and helped her bear the trials of working in Higher Education, rolled her eyes. The others, ageing men with a yearning for the good old days of journalism when women made the tea, hovered in the background. Kate smiled at them all and turned to Laura, her closest friend. Laura squeezed her arm. 'Shall we go in?'

They packed into the small room where the willow casket lay on a trestle. Kate bit her lower lip. The strains of Pink Floyd's 'Wish You Were Here' rang out and she blinked back tears. Mirren's friend Josie read the eulogy and Kate recited the Liz Lochhead poem. After that, everything was a blur until Sandy Denny's voice rang out with 'Who Knows Where the Time Goes?'.

Mirren's favourite song, the perfect ending. Kate bowed her head and whispered goodbye. After a short pause, she stood up to go. When she turned round, she gasped. The man from the silver car was there at the back of the room. She was sure it was him. He was tall, with the same broad outline that had filled up the Fiat. He stared at her for a moment and then slipped out the door. Kate pushed past everyone, desperate to confront him, but by the time she got outside, he was nowhere to be seen.

On the way to the woodland cemetery her eyes staked every pedestrian, scrutinised every passing car. Josie, who had insisted on accompanying her, noticed. 'Are you OK?'

'Not really. There's this man I keep seeing. He even turned up at the service but he disappeared as soon as it finished.'

'You keep seeing him where?'

Kate grimaced. 'Outside the house. He was there two days running. I've never seen him before. I told myself it was nothing, a double glazing salesman or something.' She forced a smile. 'Don't think that now, though. Any thoughts?'

'One of your mother's lovers?' Josie went straight to the point.

'Do you think it is? She never mentioned any men recently. Did she say something to you?' Her mother hadn't had a partner, but that didn't mean she'd been a nun. She'd had men friends, all of them single, divorced mainly, with whom she remained on good terms after they'd failed to persuade her to marry them. When Kate asked her why, she was succinct: *Men are good for company, and for sex, but you don't want to be living with the smelly creatures.*

But Josie shook her head. 'Sorry, no. I haven't a clue.'

'There's something else.' Kate told Josie about the phone call, omitting the part where he'd mentioned money. 'Do you think it's the same person?'

Josie was lost in thought. She sighed and told Kate to forget it. 'If it's important he'll be in touch again.'

'Mm,' said Kate. 'That's what worries me.'

Once the burial was over, they went to a local hotel, which served a disgusting meal of congealing steak pie, tinned peas and watery boiled potatoes. It was the last straw for Kate. The irony of such bad food being served at her mother's funeral when Mirren was such a superb cook. A tear rolled down her cheek and she brushed it away. She put down her knife and fork, defeated by the rubbery meat, and turned to Laura. 'You will come back to the house, won't you?'

Laura hugged her. 'Of course I will.'

Once home, Kate relaxed. She wandered round the small group who had come back with her, dispensing drinks and snacks from Marks and Spencer. Some people were drinking too much, mainly Kate's colleagues. Hard drinkers every one of them, Gus especially. He pulled her over as she passed.

'Kate, poor Kate. I know how you feel. I lost my dog last year,' he slurred.

Kate couldn't think of anything to say that wasn't rude. She excused herself, hissing to Sheena to keep him away from her as she went into the kitchen to get more drinks. At least he tried to empathise, she told herself. And some people were very attached to their pets. It was no comfort. She took Laura aside, 'Is it very bad of me to want people to go? Not you, of course, but the boozers.' She nodded towards Gus who was regaling people with tales of when he used to write for the *Glasgow Herald*. By the looks on their faces they'd heard them many times before.

'I'll get rid of them,' said Laura and true to her word she started chivvying people to leave.

By eight o'clock only Kate, Josie and Laura were left. Kate made scrambled eggs for supper. Afterwards, they opened a bottle of chilled Chablis and reminisced about Mirren. 'Do you remember how she used to have about ten books on the go at one time?' said Laura. 'All in piles or scattered across the floor.'

'God, yes. All sorts of books. I never knew how she managed to keep all those plots in her head. She was very selective about what she read too,' said Josie.

Kate laughed. Sometimes she thought Josie hadn't known Mum at all. 'No, she wasn't! She read everything. Chick lit even.'

'No! I didn't know that.'

'Yep, chick lit was her secret vice; it infuriated her but she found it entertaining too,' said Kate. 'I can see her now. She'd throw the latest offering across the room, shouting, *Why do these feeble women always have to weep into pillows with a 600 thread count? What's wrong with polycotton? It's good enough for me!*' They all laughed.

'And she didn't get fashion, did she? All that obsession with shoes.' Kate imitated her mother's Scottish accent. 'For fuck's sake, you'd never see Charlotte Bronte in a pair of Manolo

Blahniks. Good stout walking boots, that's what these girls need. Or a pair of Doc Martens. They'd soon catch their man then.' Kate fell silent, wishing more than anything else that Mirren would call from the kitchen, *I'm making some tea, any takers?*

At quarter to twelve, Josie and Laura got up to leave. Kate wanted them to stay, scared of being alone with her memories, but she was too proud to ask. When the doorbell rang two minutes later, Kate flung open the door, thrilled they'd come back. But it wasn't Josie and Laura. She pulled the door half in front of her. It was nearly midnight and a stranger was standing on her doorstep.

THREE

Buckinghamshire

'WHAT DO YOU WANT?' It was the man who had been lurking around her house for the past two days. Her voice was sharp, her muscles tense, ready for flight or fight.

He took a step back. 'I'm sorry, I'm intruding.' His accent was Scottish, and rage rushed to Kate's head.

She was too angry now to be scared. 'How dare you? You phone me, calling my mother a bitch, and then turn up here on the day of her funeral. What's wrong with you? Did you not believe me when I said she was dead? You think you can blackmail her but you're wrong. She's dead. Did you not see her coffin today?'

His hands were up in front of him, palms outward. 'I'm sorry, I've no idea what you're talking about. I would never, never,' he emphasized the repetition, 'use that word to describe any woman. And as for blackmail...'

She'd made a mistake. The person on the phone had sounded much rougher. Terrifying. She thought of how threatening he'd been, how he'd demanded twenty thousand pounds.

This wasn't the same person. Didn't mean he was to be trusted though.

'Who are you? You were at my mother's funeral. Are you a friend of hers?'

He scratched his nose. 'This is very difficult. I don't suppose... May I come in?'

Kate stepped out from behind the door and onto the doorstep. She looked around and saw Mr. Harris watching from his bedroom window.

'Excuse me?' she said. 'You have the nerve to turn up here late at night, a complete stranger, and ask to come into my house?' Her voice rose. 'Move right back, away from me, and say what you have to. And I'm warning you, my neighbour across the road is watching your every move.'

'Ah, Jesus, I'm sorry. What was I thinking? You're right, I shouldn't be here. I'll come back in the morning.'

'No, you bloody well won't! Spit it out, whatever it is.'

He took a deep breath. When he spoke again his voice was shaky. 'I'm your uncle,' he said, 'your mother's older brother. I've been searching for her since she went missing in June 1992.'

Kate stared at him. She took in his large frame, his worn but kind face. Her head was swimming with disbelief. 'No,' she replied. 'Mum was an only child. Her parents both died when she was a teenager. She had no brothers and sisters.'

He blinked. 'I'm sorry. This must be a shock to you. As well as me, she has two sisters. Her... our parents are dead. They passed away a few years after she disappeared.' His eyes glistened with unshed tears. 'They died within a year of each other, worn out from trying to find her.'

Kate tasted bile in her mouth. This couldn't be true. It

wasn't possible. It must be horrible to have someone in your family vanish, but her mother was an only child. Her voice softened. 'Look,' she said, 'this is obviously a terrible mistake, my—'

He interrupted her, his stare unwavering. 'She was born on the twelfth of May, 1951. Surname Fallon, Christian name Muireann, spelled the Irish way, like all our names.'

The date of birth was right and her name, the fact that it was Irish Gaelic. She was forever having to spell it out to people when she was a child, she'd told Kate, so she chose to be known as Mirren. Kate shook her head. 'You could have got her name and date of birth from anywhere,' she said. 'It doesn't mean a thing. It was in the announcement I put in the *Guardian.*'

'Yes. That's where I saw it. I didn't believe it when I spotted her name.'

Kate didn't believe it either. He was after something. It had to be a scam. A sick bastard who attends funerals, pretending to know people. She'd heard of such things. Time to get rid of him and his lies. Now. 'Well, if that's all...'

He took out a wallet from his inside pocket and slid a photograph out. He handed it over. It was black and white and creased. Old. A group of four children lined up in order of size. Kate glanced at it and shrugged. 'So?'

'That's us when we were children. Look, that's Muireann there.' He pointed to the child on the right, the smallest. Kate examined it for a second or two – it wasn't even clear if the child was a boy or a girl – and handed it back.

'Honestly? *That's* your evidence? It could be anyone.'

'There's more,' he said. 'Please, all I ask is an hour of your time. I'm sure it's her.'

Kate hesitated, torn between telling him to get lost and hearing him out. The poor man appeared to genuinely believe her mother was his long-lost sister, but he was wrong and she ought to try to convince him.

'All right,' she said. 'Tomorrow, ten thirty at The Coffee Grounds, it's the new café in the High Street.'

'I don't know it,' he said. 'I'm not from round here.' For the first time he smiled. 'Maybe you noticed.'

'Where are you staying?'

He wasn't staying in the village but at a hotel in Beaconsfield, so she gave him directions. 'It's small for a High Street. You can't miss it.'

He left and Kate went inside, shivering though the night was warm. She made cocoa and took it upstairs. Three hours later, she was still awake, eyes burning with fatigue, mind racing round the details of the day: had she said too much at the funeral; was she too upbeat; what would she do with Mum's things; where was her will? And at the back of her mind, the stranger and his claims. At four a.m. she decided she'd have nothing more to do with him. Decision made, she slid into a deep, dreamless sleep.

FOUR

Buckinghamshire

KATE AWOKE at three minutes to nine. She stretched her legs out across the bed and considered spending the day there. It took a few seconds to change her mind. She'd meet the stranger and be done with it. He was wrong and she needed to convince him. At the very least, meeting him would stop her worrying about the phone calls. Every time her own phone had rung for the past two days she'd jumped, terrified it would be the unknown caller again. Had his calls hastened her mother's death? Mum had been fine when she left that morning. Well, as fine as you could be with terminal cancer, but even the Macmillan nurse had been surprised she'd gone so soon. 'I thought she had another month or two in her yet,' she said in her lilting Welsh accent.

Kate walked to the café. On the way there, she tried to remember what her mother had told her about her childhood. It wasn't much. Mirren's parents were Irish and she was their only child. They lived on the south side of Glasgow, where the majority of Irish immigrants had gathered. She attended primary school there; St Bride's or St Bridget's, something like that. After primary school she went to an all-girls' school, which she hated. All Kate had were the barest of facts. There were no stories about Mirren's childhood. Kate's grandparents were shadowy figures, Mirren had told her so little about them. They came from the west of Ireland – Connemara – and not Donegal like the parents of most of her schoolfriends. And that was it.

He was already there, sitting at a table for two by the window. She joined him.

'Thank you for coming.' He looked exhausted and much older in the harsh morning light. His thick grey hair needed a trim. He was more of a teddy bear than the grizzly Kate had feared. Not a threat at all. 'I didn't think you would,' he added.

Kate shrugged. 'If I'm honest, I don't really know why I'm here. My mother can't be your sister, and I thought if I could at least convince you of that...'

The waitress arrived to take their order. She was the daughter of a neighbour and Kate didn't want her to know any of her business, so she fell silent. After accepting the girl's stuttered condolences, she ordered a flat white and the stranger asked for tea. 'The scones are good here, if you're hungry,' said Kate. He shook his head.

Kate looked out of the window at the traffic rumbling past. It was out of place here in the main street, where the buildings were all built in the nineteenth century or earlier; tiny buildings, many with leaded glass windows and low ceilings like her mother's cottage. Kate's cottage now. She'd have to get used to that. The village had been campaigning for a bypass for years with little success. She watched as a huge lorry destined for the Tesco in the neighbouring town squeezed past one of the four-wheel drive monsters that people round here claimed to find necessary. It made it with centimetres to spare. She turned to her companion. 'Before we start, why have you been hanging about my house? You scared the life out of me.'

He shook his head. 'I'm sorry, I didn't mean to. I wanted to be sure it really was Muireann before I approached you. I thought it was best maybe to wait until after the funeral.'

'And you were finally convinced late at night?'

'I lost track of time. I'd been waiting for everyone to leave. It's hardly the sort of thing you discuss in public. I knew it would be a shock to you.'

Kate thought of the fright he'd given her. Her voice was sharp. 'But to come to my house so late at night? It's not right. You're lucky I didn't call the police.'

'I know, I'm sorry. I should have come before the funeral or at least left it until today, but I have to catch a train at four so there isn't much time. I don't know what got into me. I'm an eejit, so I am.'

His apology sounded genuine. 'So, tell me why you're so sure that my mother is your sister.'

'Well to start with, everything that was said in the eulogy checks out and—'

She held a hand up. 'That's not going to convince me, I'm afraid. You'll have to do better than that.'

He blinked and paused for a second. 'I've checked the Registry of Births in Scotland. There was only one Muireann Fallon born in Glasgow on that date, and in any case, as I'm sure you know, Muireann is not a common name. The only other ones I found were all born in the last twenty years or so.'

Kate had brought her mother's birth certificate with her. She opened her handbag and took it out. 'Even if you know the answer to this question, it proves nothing. What are the names of my grandparents?'

He didn't hesitate. 'Michael and Mary Katherine Fallon, née O'Neill, married in Galway in 1943, on May the third.'

Kate's hand shook. She didn't need to look at the paper. He was right. 'And their occupations?'

'Clerical worker and shop assistant. They came to Scotland after the war. He trained to be a draughtsman and got a job in the shipyards.'

Her mouth was dry. Where the hell was that coffee? 'OK. What's going on? Is this a joke? Because if it is, it's pretty sick.' To her dismay, a tear rolled down her cheek. 'You've obviously gone to the trouble of finding out about my mother. And of course if you've seen the Registry of Births you'll have seen a copy of her birth certificate, but I don't understand why you're doing this.'

The waitress came over with their order. Kate looked resolutely out of the window, determined not to let the girl see her cry.

'I am sorry,' he said. 'I didn't want to upset you.'

Kate sipped her coffee; it was too hot and burned the roof of her mouth. 'My mother had no family. She told me over and over again. No family.'

He reached into his pocket and pulled out an envelope. He pushed it towards Kate. 'I brought this along to show you.'

She took out the paper and unfolded it; another birth certificate, for Aodhan Daithi Fallon, male, born 23rd July, 1949. Except for those three details it was identical to her mother's. 'What is this?'

'My birth certificate. To prove to you who I am.'

'What are these names? I've never seen them before.'

'They're Irish. Aodhan, it's the Irish spelling of Aidan. The other is pronounced Dahee. As I said, we were all given Gaelic names. Bane of our lives.' He raised his eyebrows. 'You can imagine the slagging we got at school. A lot of kids had Irish parents where we lived, so Irish names were common. But they were all anglicised: Brendan, Kathleen, Bridget, that sort of thing.'

A chance to trap him. 'School? Where was that then?'

He didn't miss a beat. 'St Bride's Primary in Govanhill on the Southside of Glasgow. And then St Mungo's boys' school for me, but your mum and my other sisters went to Notre Dame, an all girls' school in the west end.'

Everything Kate took for granted was being overturned. She stood up. 'This is too much for me to take in. I'm sorry. I have to go.'

'Wait! Please. Kate, isn't it? Did Muireann name you for my mother? She was Kate too, Mary Kate.'

'Look, give me a few days. I need to think about this. I'll give you my phone number.' She managed a smile. 'And no, I wasn't named after your mother. My name is Caitlin, actually, but everyone calls me Kate.'

The colour drained from his face. 'Caitlin?' he repeated in a whisper. 'Caitlin. Are you sure?'

She raised her eyebrows. 'Well, yeah.'

'Where and when were you born?'

Why on earth did he want to know? Kate frowned. 'I was born in Glasgow on the first of October 1991. Mum told me she left Glasgow when I was a few months old.'

He got up from the table, grey and older looking, his forehead studded with beads of sweat. God, was he having a heart attack? 'Aodhan? Are you all right? What's wrong?'

He pushed the table back. 'Nothing. I'm sorry. This is all a mistake. You were right. Your mother can't be my sister.' He rushed from the cafe without another word.

Kate sat down, stunned. What the hell was that about?

Why on earth did he run away like that? It took a minute or two to attract the attention of the waitress, and by the time she paid the bill and ran out into the street he was nowhere to be seen. She kicked the wall of the café, earning a bruised toe and some disapproving looks. Damn. Where did he get all that information about Mum? Too many details were right for her to dismiss him as a crank, much as she wanted to. She fingered her phone and considered calling the police, but what would she say? *I met an old man who thought my dead mother was his long-lost sister, but when I told him my name he ran away.* It was nothing to go on. It was tempting though, if only on the off chance of seeing Jack again.

She sat down on a nearby bench, closed her eyes and pictured Jack's face. His blue eyes, the way the skin around them crinkled when he smiled. The full lips, the six o'clock shadow. The rasp of his stubble on her fingers. She'd hoped he would come round to see her when he heard about her mother, but no doubt his wife had one of those tracking devices put on him. There was a time when Kate thought they had a future together. Christ, she was naïve. Instead, his wife got pregnant.

Mirren had been so good about it. She didn't moralise, didn't say *I told you so*, didn't bad mouth anyone. Kate was so shattered with grief after the split that she moved back home. It was meant to be temporary, but a few weeks later, Mirren was diagnosed with terminal cancer and it was Kate's turn to look after her. Now she was gone. Kate opened her eyes and faced reality. There was too much to do to spend time dreaming about the past and what might have been. And she had to find out more about Aodhan Fallon. She set off on the walk home.

Once there, she googled the name of his hotel. It wasn't yet noon so there was a chance he hadn't checked out. She hadn't held out much hope, so was surprised when the receptionist asked who was calling. 'It's his wife,' said Kate and waited to be put through to his room.

'Margaret? How did you get—?'

She interrupted. 'It's Kate, Aodhan. Why did you run off like that?'

He was defensive. 'I told you, I made a mistake.'

'I don't believe you. You hang around my house for two days, appear on my doorstep late at night, beg me to meet you and then turn up with all that evidence, photographs, birth certificates. But as soon as you hear my name you disappear. What the hell is going on?'

'Please, forget you ever met me. Please.' His voice broke, and despite everything Kate felt sorry for him. 'Your mother isn't my sister.'

'But you were so sure. What's changed?' She was talking to dead air; he'd hung up. Kate tried the hotel again but the receptionist said he wasn't available.

FIVE

Glasgow

THE DAYS WERE DRAGGING and their ongoing cases were uninteresting after the excitement of nailing the corrupt councillor. The Procurator Fiscal was sure they had enough evidence to convict her. The emails to her brother giving him information about sealed bids for a contract that his company won had done it. That the woman was a Tory was an added bonus to Alex. But everything else since had been an anticlimax. There had been no more dodgy emails to taunt him, and they were far from his mind when the second one came.

X1CO99rrCOpupt2@gmail.com
RE: Your to blame
To: DI A.Scrimgeour@PoliceScotland

You'd better watch your back.

What the fuck was this? Once again, he was too slow to get the address. He'd been taken off guard, sleepy after a restless night. A worm of unease was squirming through him at the numbers he had noticed. Put together they made 1992. A year he wanted to forget. He wondered if he should mention it to tech support – try to get it blocked. He was surprised it got through the firewall, to be honest.

Half an hour later, he'd reported it and was settling down to finish a report he was writing when his phone rang.

'There's a woman on the phone for you. Says it's important.'

'Aye, that's what they all say. What is it this time? Dog shit on the pavements in Newlands?'

'She says it has to be you she speaks to.'

Alex rolled his eyes. 'Did she give a name?'

'Nope, just said it was a matter of life and death.'

'Oh well, if it's that important...'

The call came through. 'DI Scrimgeour. How can I help?'

'You should know what's going on at that nursing home.' Her voice was strained.

'Right. And your name is?'

'Never mind that. There's been a death there.'

Alex refrained from saying what he was thinking, which was *what do you expect? They go there to die.* Instead he said, 'Was it an unexpected death?'

'Too right it was.'

Silence. 'Can you tell me more?'

'It's the third in a fortnight.'

Three deaths in two weeks; that did sound a lot even for a nursing home. Perhaps this was important after all.

'I see. How many residents are there in – what did you say the name of the home was?'

'I didn't.'

28

Christ, blood and stones had nothing on this woman. He waited. Nothing.

'Look, you'll have to give me more than that. There's more than one nursing home in Glasgow.' He'd personally visited fifteen before settling on Rosebank for his mother.

Alex listened to her ragged breathing and waited for her reply. Nothing. 'I need to know the name of the nursing home,' he insisted.

'Rosebank Nursing Home,' she whispered. Her voice was so low, he wasn't sure he'd heard right.

'Sorry, did you say Rosebank?' but there was no answer.

———

At first, he didn't know what to do. Whoever it was, they had hidden their tracks well. They'd withheld their name and number. Presumably it was someone who worked there, or a relative of one of the patients. How could he find out? It might be a hoax, an ex-employee with a grudge, something like that. He decided to find out first whether there was any truth in it at all.

That evening when he visited his mother he stopped and spoke to the manager. If she was surprised by this – usually he sneaked past her room to avoid being harried by her – she kept it well hidden. After he'd endured five minutes of complaints, he turned the conversation round. 'And how are things generally with you? I heard you'd had a run of deaths recently.'

There was no emotion in her face as she spoke. 'I'm afraid so, yes. Three in the past two weeks.'

'Is that unusual?'

'Sadly, no. You know how frail our clients are. Their average age is eighty-eight.'

'Is it?' Alex was surprised then cursed himself for being so stupid. Of course it would be high. This was no retirement home where jolly residents played bridge and took trips out to matinees at the theatre. This was somewhere where an intense amount of nursing care was given, where half the residents had Alzheimer's or another form of dementia and the other half were too frail to get out of bed. Of course they were old.

'Anything to worry about with any of them?'

'What?' A red flush crept up from her chest, covering her neck and face. 'No, of course not.'

'Are you sure?'

'Why do you ask?'

'We've had a complaint.'

'Who from? A relative?'

He shrugged. 'Maybe, they didn't leave a name.'

Was that relief he saw in her eyes? 'Oh, right,' she said. 'It'll be one of our rivals then. We've had to take legal action against one because they kept posting negative reviews.'

'What did they die of, these last three deaths you had?'

'I can't tell you that.' The steely tone was back. 'That's confidential medical information.'

He was tempted to remind her of his status as a police officer but refrained. He'd do some digging on the side. 'Of course,' he said. 'Sorry to have bothered you.'

He contacted an old acquaintance, someone who'd been at school with him and who now worked as a pathologist. After the usual catch-ups that Alex always dreaded – anyone he spoke to from that era always had children they never failed to boast about, a loving wife or husband, a stellar career, all the things missing from his life – they got down to business.

'Not much to go on there, an anonymous phone call, three deaths in a fortnight,' said Gordon. 'It's par for the course in these places.'

'So, not worth following up then?'

'That's up to you, mate. But they rarely bother with PMs for these folk. They're old, death is to be expected. I checked the records and we've done no PMs on anyone from a home since May. And that was only because the family insisted.'

'Right. Do you remember any more details?'

Gordon grinned. 'Thought you might ask that so I've noted them down.' He took out a piece of paper from his back pocket and passed it to Alex. 'Think you owe me another pint, mate.'

Alex took the paper and shoved it in his jacket pocket without reading it. He'd do that later. For now, he settled down to an evening of reminiscing with his old school pal.

———

There wasn't much to go on: name and address of the person who had complained; the name of the deceased; a resume of the post mortem. Natural causes was the verdict. Nonetheless it was worth following up, he thought.

The next day he decided to carry out an interview. He should have sent someone junior but thought it best to see it through himself, so he drove to Croftfoot, where the complainant lived, phoning beforehand to ensure someone was at home.

It was a bungalow, not unlike the one he'd sold on behalf of his mother last year. The bell was one of these modern ones that you couldn't hear and he pressed it twice. An irate woman answered the door. 'All right, all right. Give me a chance to answer.'

'Sorry. I didn't hear whether it rang or not.'

'I know. They're bloody hopeless, these things.' She ushered him into an immaculate kitchen diner. An extension had been built onto the house and light flooded in through the bi-folding doors, which were open to the garden. His mother would have loved a room like this. She'd always complained about her poky wee kitchen, but Alex's father, who spent little time in the kitchen, didn't see any point in doing anything about it. By the time he died ten years ago, his mother didn't have the energy for a big project.

'Lovely room,' he said.

'Thank you. I've just made some coffee if you'd like some?'

'Not for me, thanks.'

She poured herself a coffee and sat down on a modern white chair at the table – one of those plastic moulded things that were based on a mid-century design – and indicated to Alex to do the same. He sat down carefully, worried the delicate chair wouldn't support his bulk.

'So, what's this all about then? The death of my mother? How did you learn about it?'

Alex sidestepped the question. 'I understand you weren't...' He hesitated; he'd been about to say *happy about her death*. What an idiot. He started again. 'What made you ask for a post mortem?'

She took a sip of her coffee. 'I don't know, really. I had a feeling that something wasn't right. I'd seen her the night before, you see, and she was fine. Lively even. Full of chat about when she'd been young. And she knew who I was, which wasn't all that common. So, when they phoned the next morning to say she'd gone... I didn't believe it. The GP who covers Rosebank was on holiday at the time and the locum I saw said I was overreacting when I asked for a PM. Snooty little madam she was. Just made me all the more determined.'

Christ! He hadn't expected that. 'Wait, your mother was a resident of Rosebank?'

'Yes, why?'

He didn't want to tell her about the anonymous phone call. He was as sure as he could be that she wasn't the caller. The timbre of her voice was all wrong. 'Oh, it's... well, my mother lives there.'

'I thought I recognised you. Your mother moved in a few months ago, right? She narrowed her eyes. 'Why are you really here?' she asked. 'Why does a detective inspector come to ask me about why I requested a post mortem?

He dodged the question. 'Were you satisfied with the outcome?'

'I... um, well yes. I suppose so.' She pushed her coffee aside. 'Actually, to tell the truth, no. The pathologist was so sure of herself. Dismissed all our questions.' She gave a half laugh. 'You know what doctors can be like. Paul, my husband, he wanted to go for a second opinion and I thought about it, I really did, but then, well it didn't feel right to keep pressing on when she should have been safely buried.' She rubbed her nose. 'Are you saying we should have made more noise about this?'

'No, not at all. Thank you, Mrs Crawford, you've been very helpful. I'll be back in touch if I think of anything else.' Alex got up to go.

'Please, if there is something funny going on in that place, let me know.'

'At the moment there's no real evidence...'

'But there's something, isn't there? It's fine. You don't have to say anything. I know you're bound by protocol but...'

'As I said, I'll let you know.'

He got into his car and sat there for a few moments before driving off. He had some digging to do.

SIX

Buckinghamshire

KATE PUT ASIDE her concerns about Aodhan Fallon. He'd made it clear he didn't want to talk to her; she wasn't going to waste time on him. She had a list of things to do before going back to work. She was taking four weeks off so wasn't due back until the end of July but she knew it would take most of that to get everything done. She decided she'd sort out her mother's clothes first. She called Josie and asked if there was anything she would like.

'What?' shrieked Josie. 'No thank you. Give them to Oxfam, darling,' she stretched out the vowels, *Oxfaahm, daahling*, 'but only the outer layers. Ditch the undies and anything old. If you must give me something, give me a piece of jewellery. I always liked that Art Nouveau pendant of hers.'

Kate rang off, subdued by the put down and by Josie's final comment. It was typical of Josie to want that beautiful necklace. But it belonged to Kate. Her mother had given it to her years ago, and if she remembered rightly, Josie had been there at the time.

She shook her head. Forget Josie; she had to get on with the task in hand. Two hours later, she had three piles of clothes. Older ones for the textile bin at the local supermarket; she wouldn't throw them out like Josie suggested – Mirren would have been horrified at the waste. The biggest pile was for the Cancer Research shop on the High Street, and the smallest pile she'd keep. An original Biba dress, a couple of Laura Ashley dresses from the seventies, a sumptuous black velvet evening coat and a few scarves. She took them through to her room, hung up the dresses and coat and put the scarves away in a drawer. It was like burying her mother all over again. Kate sat down on her bed, overcome. Heaving sobs, snotters, eyes swollen as if stung by wasps, the lot. After a while she stood up to get some tissues and caught her reflection in the mirror. It was a horrible sight; she was all red and blotchy. Kate laughed. It didn't help her appearance but it made her feel better. She blew her nose and picked up her make-up bag from the dressing table, but before she could do anything with it the doorbell rang. Shit! The state of her. She considered hiding under the bed; she looked like something that had risen from the grave. The bell rang again, insistent. Damn it, she thought, if she couldn't look like shit now, when could she? She ran downstairs.

'Jack.' Her voice was flat but inside she was shaking. She yearned to reach out and touch him but kept her arms at her side.

He thrust a bunch of chrysanthemums at her. She hated them; she'd told him often enough. 'I heard about your mother. I'm so sorry.' He stood on the doorstep shifting from foot to foot. His hair was shorter than when Kate had last seen him. He looked good.

'Thank you.'

'Any chance of a coffee?' His smile stabbed at her heart.

She hesitated, then, 'Of course, come in.'

She put the flowers on the kitchen table. There was a time when he would have brought her red roses, beautifully hand tied, from a florist. These were from a supermarket and were past their best. An earwig crawled out of one of the flowers and she flicked it onto the floor. Jack took a seat and watched her grind coffee beans. Although she had longed for him, prayed he would come round, she was dismayed by the strong feelings it stirred up. They should have diminished by now; it was over nine months since she'd broken up with him. The knowledge that he would drink his coffee and leave, destroyed her. She busied herself with the kettle and cafetière as he mumbled platitudes.

'How are you?'

She wanted to tell him the truth, that she was desolate. Dumped by him and then her mother died. She wanted to yell in his face, *How do you think I am?* Instead, she handed him a cup of coffee and said, 'Oh, you know. Up and down.'

He sipped his coffee. 'I liked your mum.'

She busied herself pouring milk into her cup. He was waiting for her to say *yes, Mum liked you too*, but the truth was, she didn't. She'd hated that he was married and how he hadn't had the decency to tell Kate.

Kate had been in John Lewis browsing through the various boutiques when she spotted them. He'd told her he was on a business trip. A woman was hanging on to his arm, laughing up at him. What the...? Rage surged through her at the betrayal. She followed them, hiding behind pillars and racks of clothes, sucking up snatches of conversation as if they were lollipops.

Banal at first: *is this my colour; I need a coffee; oh, they don't have it in my size, what a shame.* Then the killer: *we'll have to go soon, what time did you say Jim and Sue are coming round?* Kate knew what that meant. She came out from her hiding place and willed him to see her. On cue he looked up. His eyes opened wide; a warning.

If she'd confronted him then instead of melting into the crowd it would have been over and she wouldn't have wasted another year waiting for him to leave his wife, his 'dead marriage'.

It had been a source of stress between her and Mirren. She didn't nag about Jack, but when Kate told her how she found out he was married she said, 'Kate, you're a grown woman so I won't go on about it, but I have to say this before you get in too deep with this man. He's married. He has lied to both you and his wife. And there's no winning with a married man. Either he stays with his wife and your heart will be broken or he leaves her and you're stuck with a man who has already left one wife. And you will never be sure he won't do the same to you. All I ask is that you take that into consideration before seeing him again.'

Kate listened but didn't hear. *They* were different; he had married his wife because he didn't know what love was until he met Kate, or so he said. It was the age-old tale, and like a fool, she believed in it. For over a year after that chance meeting he swore he would end it with his wife. But it was never the right time. He had been going to tell Vicky but then she announced her pregnancy. They spoke at the same time. She said, *I've got something to tell you*, and Jack, always the gentleman (or coward, putting it off) said, *no, it's all right, on you go.* Sometimes Kate asked herself what would have happened if he'd gone first. Would it have made a difference? She hated herself for thinking this way. What sort of person had she become that she'd deprive a child of his father?

But all that was in the past. It had been wrong to have a relationship with a married man, she recognised that. But, oh, how she'd paid for it. The sleepless nights, the tears she'd cried. They stared at each other. The silence was uncomfortable but Kate wouldn't make it easy for him. She was the bereaved one; she didn't have to make an effort.

'When are you going back to work?'

'Not for a while yet.'

'Of course, it's summer. Are you going anywhere on holiday?' He had the grace to look embarrassed at the banality of the question.

Kate ignored it. 'How is your wife?'

He didn't look at her. 'She's fine. She was dep...' He stopped, no doubt remembering who he was talking to.

'And the baby?' This was worse than sticking pins into her eyes.

'Oh, Alfie's great.' His face lit up.

'Good.' Kate drained her coffee, scalding the roof of her mouth, and stood up. 'Well, I've got things to do.'

'What things?' His bluntness took her by surprise. She'd expected him to say something pacifying like *time heals*, give her a peck on the cheek and vanish.

'Jack, I have things to do,' she repeated, 'and it's none of your business what they are.'

'Kate, please. Don't be like this.'

'Go, Jack.'

'I don't want to.'

His sulky tone made her want to laugh, but she kept her face straight as she opened the door.

He stood up. 'You hate me, don't you?'

She shrugged, her turn to be petty, but stopped herself saying *whatever*. No point in both of them reverting to their teens. 'No, Jack, I don't hate you, but please, I really am busy.' She relented. 'I have to go through Mum's stuff and I need to do that alone.'

That got through to him, and after a couple of minutes of the usual clichés he went, and Kate sat down and wept until she had no tears left.

She dragged herself upstairs to the piles of clothes and thought about what she still had to do. She had to make an appointment to see the lawyer about the will. It should be straightforward as she was Mirren's only relative, but even as she thought this, the visit from Aodhan came to mind. There was no denying that his behaviour was odd. The evidence all pointed to him being Mirren's brother. The photograph, his birth certificate. He had made a convincing case but then he'd withdrawn. She went over the scene in her mind, trying to remember exactly what had happened. He'd paled when she'd said her name, but thinking back over it, it was the place and date of birth that had freaked him out. Why? She'd probably never know. She heaved the bags of clothes outside and piled them into her car wishing she had relatives, a brother or sister to share this with. It was too scary being alone.

It was harder than she had imagined, going through her mother's belongings. At times, Kate felt Mirren's presence and she'd look round expecting to see her in her chair, sewing or reading. Once, she swore she caught sight of her in the kitchen reaching into the oven. But when she blinked, the kitchen was empty as it always was.

The clothes were the easy part. The rest was more difficult. There were papers to go through. Mirren hated to let go of things. There were receipts, bills from years ago, even shopping lists. It was strange finding these, as if her mother had popped out leaving the list behind and any minute now the phone would ring and Mirren would say: *I'm a right eejit, so I am. I've forgotten the shopping list.* There was even a folder full of newspaper cuttings from the 1990s about Romanian orphanages. Typical Mum, she was so soft hearted. Kate read everything to decide what to keep and what to throw out. She threw out very little.

In general, Mirren's papers were in surprisingly good order – for someone who was naturally untidy they were very well organised – but as Kate went through them, something bothered her. There was nothing from her mother's childhood. No photographs, no copies of her parents' death certificates, no school reports. No letters. That wasn't all that unusual these days, was it? After all, Kate hadn't sent a personal letter since she was a small child and her mum forced her to send thank you letters to Josie every Christmas and birthday. But Mirren was forty years older and Kate did have every email and text Jack ever sent her. She had printed them out when they split up, and when she did, she understood why people keep these remnants of their past. So yes, on balance it was unusual. It was as if Mirren hadn't existed before the age of forty or so, in fact from about the time Kate was born.

Mirren had been hiding something. Now Kate thought about it, it had been obvious all along. An argument from her childhood came to her. Kate had been about eight at the time.

'Mummy,' she said. 'We have to take in photographs to school.'

Mirren's eyes narrowed. 'What sort of photographs?' There was a wariness to her tone.

'Of me, when I was a baby. And you too. Family photos. We're looking at family semblances.'

'Resemblances,' Mirren corrected her. 'I'm sorry, but I don't have any of me or my family. There's a few of you but not as a baby.'

'Why not?' Kate's lower lip trembled. She was a model pupil, always wanting to be the best at everything, and hated the thought of having nothing to take into school the next day.

'Kate, I've told you there's nothing. This is not something I want to talk about.'

The warning in Mirren's voice was too subtle for Kate. 'But I have to take something in. There must be something; you must have a photo somewhere. What am I going to tell Miss McMillan?'

Mirren muttered something under her breath that Kate didn't catch and carried on putting the washing away. Kate followed her upstairs. 'Well, what am I going to say?'

Mirren dropped the washing on her bedroom floor and turned round. Her face was pinched and white. 'Listen to me, Kate. I have no photos of you as a baby and none of me as a child, so say sorry to your teacher and get over it.'

'But what happened to them?'

She took a step towards Kate, her fists clenched. Kate moved back, shocked, and her mother took a deep breath. 'Sit down, Kate.'

Kate sat down on the edge of the bed beside her, keeping her distance. Mirren reached over and took Kate's hand. Hers was shaking. 'When you were very little there was a bad fire and I lost everything then.'

'Is that when you lost my daddy?'

A flash of irritation. 'No.'

Kate had never before dared to ask about her father. 'When then?'

'Long ago,' she said. 'Long ago, and listen to me, Kate, listen to me very carefully. It was a bad fire and upset me a lot. I don't want to talk about it.'

Kate had cried herself to sleep that night. It wasn't the lack of photographs that got to her, but because her mother had spoken so harshly. She rarely raised her voice.

It was years before Mirren spoke about her family again. When Kate was seventeen, Mirren revealed that her parents had been killed in a car crash when she was a young woman and she'd been left alone in the world. Her parents had been in their forties when they had her, a late baby after years of trying. They also had been only children, so she had no cousins, no aunts and uncles. 'I find it very upsetting to talk about,' she'd said, 'so I don't. Anyway, I have you and that's all that matters.'

Kate asked about her father then and Mirren laughed. 'Oh well, you're old enough now to know I suppose. He was a one-night stand, Kate. At a party. I don't even know his name.'

Kate was shocked. No teenager wants to know about their parents' sex life, let alone one-night stands. She wasn't stupid; she knew her mother had sex, but a one-night stand? That was something else. Now that she thought about it, it wasn't all that surprising. Her mother always kept her distance from her men, never got emotionally involved. It was fitting that Kate was the product of a one-night stand. A father would have been nice though.

Kate wished she'd tried to find out more. It was too late now, but she was baffled as to why there was nothing in her mother's belongings. Surely everything wasn't lost in that fire? It saddened her. There were photos of the two of them but none of Kate as a child, none of her parents or grandparents. Perhaps one day when she had time, she'd do some research into her family history. She had her birth certificate after all.

A birth certificate that wasn't destroyed in the fire. Had there even been a fire?

Kate felt cold as she remembered a conversation not long before her mother died. It was a sentimental conversation, the kind that is best kept private. But one thing Mirren had said had struck Kate. 'We've never had a cross word, Kate.'

'We had our moments.' Kate laughed. 'Have you forgotten the fight over baby photographs we had when I was a child?'

Mirren stiffened. 'I don't remember.'

Kate hastened to reassure her. 'It's OK. You don't need to talk about it. It must have been so awful for you to lose everything in that fire.'

'What fire?' said Mirren.

At the time, Kate put it down to fatigue or the drugs. But perhaps there was another explanation. Her mother had lied.

Kate didn't want to think too deeply about it. What did it matter? She must have had her reasons. She carried on, sifting her papers. Filed those that were important, shredded those that weren't. She sorted out the papers in her filing cabinet, apart from a huge file of bank statements, but that was too much to face today, so she turned to her mother's desk to see what was in there.

The top drawer was stuck. Kate had crammed so much stuff into it when she was tidying up on the day of the funeral that it stuck when she tried to pull it out. Something was catching on the bottom of the drawer, so she took out the ones beneath and looked up at it. A photo was taped to the underside. Kate loosened the tape, carefully, but even so it ripped.

Kate put the two pieces together. It was identical to the one Aodhan had shown her.

What was going on? Had he broken in, hidden this photograph? She stared at it as if that would give her an answer. Her mind froze, unable to process this information, but her heart knew the truth and it made her sick. Her mother had lied to her about her family and Aodhan Fallon *was* her uncle. She needed to talk to someone about this. But who? There was only one possibility. Josie. Her mother's closest friend. She must know something.

She handed the photograph to Josie and watched her study it. Josie squinted at it for a while and then handed it back. 'I don't know,' she said. 'It's hard to see any family resemblance when the photo is so blurred. If only we had the negative.'

'That wouldn't do much good. We'd have a large blurry photo instead of a small one.' Kate put it in her handbag. 'What should I do?'

Josie thought for a moment. 'Well, you have two alternatives: try to find this man who says he's your uncle, speak to him and find out why he ran off the way he did, or forget about it. Put it behind you and forget it.'

Kate ran her finger round the edge of her wine glass. 'What would *you* do?'

'Honestly, darling? I'd let sleeping dogs lie. You don't know this man. He turned up after your mother's death. He's after something, and I'd be prepared to bet it isn't getting to know his niece. Money, that's what'll it be. After all, Mirren was worth a bob or two.' She filled up their glasses.

Kate sipped her wine. Aodhan hadn't struck her as 'after'

anything. He had given her the impression of being sincere. It was a mistake to discuss this with Josie; she was too cynical, too quick to see ulterior motives in other people's actions. Truth was, Kate had never really liked her. She only put up with her because she and Mum were so close.

'No, that can't be the case. If he was after money, why would he run off when he heard my name and date of birth? There's something else going on here and I want to know what it is. Are you sure she never said anything about her family?'

Josie drained her glass; the woman drank wine like someone coming out of the desert in a drought. She'd had three large glasses to Kate's one. 'No, she never said a thing. Are we going to open another bottle or what?'

Kate suppressed a sigh as she went into the kitchen and fetched another bottle of Pinot Grigio from the fridge. When she returned, Josie was smoking an e-cigarette. Kate waved the perfumed vapour aside and opened the bottle.

Josie held out her glass. 'Thank you, darling. Well, it's up to you, but it might help to think about it from your mother's point of view. Why was she estranged from them? What had they done to her?'

It was a good point. Mirren must have left her family behind for a reason. Perhaps it was better to let things lie.

The post was late the following day. Kate had already eaten lunch by the time she heard the letterbox rattle. She went to have a look. There was the usual junk mail, a circular from a wine company and a leaflet from the local Conservative MP that went straight into recycling. There were also cards, three of them, and she put them aside to read later, knowing there would be a scrawled *Thinking of you* or *You're in my prayers* inside. She knew why. It was hard to say the right thing in these circumstances, but oh, for something personal, a little anecdote to remind her of Mirren instead of these facile phrases. The remaining letter was addressed to Mirren. It was light, as if it contained nothing. When she opened it, there was only a flimsy piece of paper, torn from a cheap notebook. Her heart beat faster; something wasn't right here. She looked at the note. The writing was untidy and she saw immediately it wasn't signed. It was brief and to the point.

Do you ever think about what you done to Robert Taylor? You'll pay, you wait and see.

Kate put it down on the table. What the hell did it mean? She turned to her laptop and typed in Robert Taylor. As she feared, there were millions of matches even when she put it in inverted commas. She thought about the man who'd phoned and Aodhan Fallon, who claimed to be Mirren's brother. Was one of them behind this? She dismissed Aodhan right away. Unless she was a terrible judge of character, he had nothing to do with this. It must be linked to the call she'd received on Mirren's phone. There hadn't been another and yesterday she'd contacted the mobile phone company to cancel the contract so there wouldn't be any more.

She added Glasgow to her search, but even so there were over half a million matches. She scanned the first few pages but found nothing that linked this man with her mother. What did Mirren have to do with this? What had she done to make someone think she could be blackmailed? The man who'd phoned her sounded angry, dangerous even. One possibility was to take it to the police, but there was nothing really there for them to follow up. A veiled threat? She didn't think they'd take it seriously. She had to put it out of her mind.

Easier said than done. It was impossible to forget it. The next two days were hell. From the moment she woke up until she fell asleep, it was there, niggling at her. *Do you ever think about what you done to Robert Taylor? You'll pay, you wait and see.* The writer blamed Mirren for something, something to do with someone Kate had never heard of. But who? She knew so little about Mirren's life, especially what she'd done before she'd had Kate. She ran various scenarios through her mind. Had Mirren harmed this man in some way? Knocked him down? Stolen from him? Mirren had worked briefly as a social worker; Kate remembered her mentioning it once. Maybe Robert Taylor was an ex-client, a child she'd had taken into care, something like that. She'd never know. What did she know about her mother when it came down to it? She was single, her parents were dead, she had no siblings (or three, if Aodhan was to be believed), she loved music and she loved art.

For as long as she remembered, her mother had produced beautiful tapestries, collages, she wasn't sure what to call them. They were like paintings. Landscapes but with texture and depth. There was one on the wall in the living room, and she went through to look at it, leaving the accusatory note on the kitchen table.

It calmed her to look at it. Like much of Mirren's work it was a seascape, but it was unusual in that the sea was rough. Most of her work portrayed calm seas, but this showed a violent, dark side of the sea and stormy skies. She'd used a grey silk for the sea, which she'd ruffled so as to give the impression of large waves. The waves were topped with intricately sewn stitches in different shades of white, giving the effect of a turbulent boiling sea. Kate loved it and had begged Mirren not to sell it but to keep it, and reluctantly Mirren had agreed. Reluctantly, because if Kate remembered correctly, they'd had little money at the time, but the nine-year-old Kate had been so insistent, her mother gave in. And here it was. And here it would stay.

She sighed. She wasn't going to find any answers here. And she didn't know what to do or where to look. There were two mysteries in her life now, both connected to Mirren. They must be linked.

SEVEN

Buckinghamshire

THAT NIGHT KATE tossed and turned, limbs tangled in sweaty sheets. When she fell asleep it was to a theatrical show of dark dreams. A man without a face was threatening her mother, who held out her hands to Kate, pleading *save me*. Kate woke up, her heart pounding, sweat lining her forehead. She took a drink of water from the bottle on her bedside table and breathed slowly to calm herself down. She needed to take control of this. The obvious place to start was with Aodhan Fallon. At least he had a name. The anonymous caller was just that. Unknown.

After breakfast she dealt with a few chores, all the time mulling over what to do. She'd have to find Aodhan, she decided. And where better to start than the internet? She typed in his name on Google, thinking it would be easy to find him with such an unusual first name, but she scrolled through several pages without finding anything. There were Aidan Fallons aplenty but no Aodhans. Five minutes later, Kate slammed the lid shut in disbelief. No footprint on the internet? It was impossible. Only criminals on the run and very old people were invisible online. And Aodhan wasn't that old. She re-opened her laptop and tried a people finder site. Useless. Entering A. Fallon gave around a hundred results, but when she looked through them there were Alans and Andrews and an abundance of Annes but no Aodhans. Her doubts flooded back. She was right to be suspicious. He didn't exist. She'd been taken for a fool. His birth certificate was a forgery. She searched online for the Scottish Registry of Births, Deaths and Marriages and typed in his name. It came up immediately with the same details he had shown her.

Kate put her head in her hands. Why wasn't she able to find him? Of course. He had two first names and she'd only tried one of them. She added Daithi to the search. Nothing. So she tried his initials: A.D. Fallon. Success. Fifteen hits, but only three in the right age range; the others were too young. She paid the fee demanded. And there it was. The information she needed. Two lived in London, the other in Glasgow. It had to be the Glasgow one. He'd stayed in a hotel and spoke about catching a train home. His accent was strong, much more so than Mirren's, which had been moderated by her time in England. Kate noted the addresses and phone numbers and made a coffee to give her time. She tried the Glasgow number first. After half a dozen rings the impersonal tones of an answering machine cut in. Kate hung up, not wanting to leave a message.

She dialled one of the London numbers next. A woman answered with a curt 'Yes?' and Kate asked to speak to Aodhan. Wrong number. The other London number was a dead end too. Kate put on a cardigan and decided to walk to the village. Anything other than hanging round here waiting for the right time to phone Glasgow again.

Outside it was cooler than it had been for some time. She

pulled her cardigan tight to protect against the breeze that had sprung up. To pass the time she treated herself to lunch in one of the cafes, and an hour later, poorer by ten pounds for a lunch that would have cost less than a pound to make, she returned home.

Kate opened the door and froze. Empty houses have a deadness to them, the air always thick and unstirred even after a short absence. The air in the house had been disturbed since she left little over an hour ago. She stood at the threshold, unwilling to go any further. Adrenalin rushed through her; fight or flight? She'd be damned if she fled. This was her house. She took in a deep breath to calm herself and listened for tell-tale noises. Then she smelled it. It was elusive, gone before she fully processed it, so she moved further into the hall and breathed in deeply. The scent was stronger here. Mirren's perfume, Clinique's Elixir. She closed her eyes and saw her, in the kitchen, wooden spoon in hand. She waved it at Kate in greeting, sauce spilling on to the floor. She beckoned and Kate moved forward, her heart full of joy. Her mother was back, the past few weeks nothing more than a dream.

A cough from the living room brought her out of her reverie. Her mouth was dry as she opened the door. The agony of disappointment made her sharp. 'How did you get in?'

Josie smiled at Kate from Mirren's chair. 'Same way I always do, with the keys your mother gave me.'

'I want them back.'

'Are you all right, Kate?' Josie frowned.

'Get out,' snapped Kate, not caring that she was being rude. Her eyes were wet.

'But—' Josie stopped as it dawned on her what she'd done. She covered her mouth with her hand. 'Shit, I'm wearing the perfume she always wore. Oh Christ, Kate. I'm so sorry. You must have thought...' She stuttered to a standstill. Kate stood there, not saying a word. Josie took the hint and left, her apologies becoming more and more effusive. Only after she'd gone did Kate realise she hadn't left the keys. It didn't matter. She would change the locks. Maybe she had overreacted, but Kate was furious that Josie had walked into her house when she was out. How dare she?

She looked round to check that nothing was disturbed. Josie had helped herself to coffee; the half-full cup was on the side table beside Mirren's chair. Kate picked it up and took it through to the kitchen. Her phone beeped, and she went through the menu options until she reached the recorded voice that told her she had two messages. The first was from Laura about lunch. Kate had missed her call by a few minutes – what a shame. It would have been good to talk to someone. She calmed down as she listened to Laura's long rambling message. Then the other message played. It was Aodhan. His voice was harsher than she remembered.

'Don't phone me again, I have nothing to say to you. I made a mistake.'

Kate put the phone down. He must have dialled 1471. She'd forgotten to conceal her own phone number. She started to punch in his number, her stomach churning. Halfway through she stopped. For several minutes she stood there and tried to decide what to do. What was the worst that could happen? She dialled again and it was answered at once. His breathing was rapid and heavy.

'Aodhan?'

'Leave me alone.'

'Please, I need to talk to you. I found a photograph in Mum's desk. It was the same as the one you had.'

'Oh, Christ.'

Silence. 'Are you there, Aodhan?' ventured Kate.

'Don't phone again. I have nothing to say to you.' He hung up.

Kate put the phone down. What the fuck was going on? He might think he could stop her looking into this, but he had started it and she was going to find out the truth if it killed her.

There was nothing for it but to get back to going through Mirren's stuff. Although there was nothing in the house that predated Kate's birth, Mirren had been a hell of a hoarder. In a writing bureau in Mirren's work room, Kate found a drawer stuffed full of her own drawings. Fair enough if she'd been artistic, but only a mother would see any merit in these childish scribblings. She picked out one or two of the better ones to show to her own children if she was ever lucky enough to have any, and the rest went straight to recycling. Another drawer had jotters from primary school. God knows why Mirren had kept the maths jotters: page after page of addition and subtraction did not make interesting reading. The language jotters were more significant though. Kate read through them, and the first thing that struck her was that there was never any mention of any other adult than her mother nor of any children. A typical entry read *Last night I watched television with Mummy and then she read me a story.* Near the end of the jotter, the teacher, no doubt exasperated by the lack of variety in Kate's life, had written: *Don't you ever go out to play, Caitlin?* The childishly formed *Mummy doesn't want me to* brought unexpected tears to her eyes. It wasn't right to keep a child in such isolation. She'd never given any thought to it before, because it was what was normal for her. Now she saw how wrong it was.

She pushed the uneasy feeling aside before it had time to take root. She threw out the maths jotters and the language ones too. They were too depressing to keep.

Kate was fed up, really sorry for herself. For a second she wondered about contacting Josie to see whether she'd help with this horrible task but immediately dismissed the idea. She didn't trust Josie. Little things came to mind. Digs she made when Kate came back to live with Mirren: *What is it they call your generation, the boomerang generation, that's it – what age are you now, Kate? Isn't it time you found your own place?* Josie frequently borrowed money from Mirren and never, to Kate's knowledge, paid her back. Her mother didn't mind but Kate was pissed off about it. Especially when it kept on going when Mirren became ill. She'd tried speaking to Mirren about it once, but her mother was too tired to talk about it.

'Don't worry,' she said. 'There's plenty for you.' And according to her will, which Kate found stuffed in a drawer, there was. Apart from some charity donations, everything was left to Kate.

As Kate worked her way through the rest of the drawers, pulling each one out in turn, she noticed that one looked shallower than the rest. It appeared identical on the outside, but Kate was sure it didn't hold the same amount as the others. She measured it roughly with two fingers. It wasn't as deep as the other drawers. Her heart pounded as she hauled all the papers out of it, convinced she was going to find a secret compartment, but there was nothing. She had imagined the difference. She shook it to make sure. Disappointed, she returned it to its place.

She couldn't rest though. Thinking that there had been a secret compartment niggled at her. Why did she think it was possible?

The answer came to her early the next day as she was lying

in bed trying to squeeze a couple more minutes of sleep. A memory of a hot summer's day when she was seven.

She was reading in the garden, lying on a rug on the grass. Mirren stole up behind her. 'Still reading that book?' she'd said.

'Yes,' said Kate as Mirren sat down beside her on the grass.

'What is it this time?'

'The Treasure Seekers. It's about children who find treasure.' Kate gabbled on for several minutes, happy to share the story.

'Mmn,' said Mirren. 'Do you know, there's meant to be treasure buried here?'

Kate was bursting with excitement. 'What do you mean?'

'Well.' Mirren leaned towards her. 'When I bought this house, the lady who sold it left some of the furniture. She told me the desk had a secret compartment. She'd never been able to find it but she said there was a story in her family that a treasure map was hidden in the secret compartment and that it showed where treasure was buried in the garden.'

Kate hadn't been able to contain herself. She rushed into the house and rummaged through the desk, looking for the secret compartment. It didn't take long to find the map and Kate ran back out to show Mirren.

'That's amazing! Let's see if we can work it out.'

They spent the afternoon deciphering it. The paper was old and crumbling, and it looked as though the map had been drawn with a fountain pen or perhaps even a quill. The lettering was old fashioned and shaky, the letter f looked like an s, the grammar was from another age. *Here lieth treafure.* They worked out the clues and discovered where in the garden it had been buried. They went outside – it was raining – and dug for what seemed like hours until Kate's garden trowel hit something metal.

56

'It's the treasure,' she breathed, imagining the box crammed full of gold coins and jewels. She pulled it out of the earth, squealing as a worm came with it. But when she looked closer she frowned. 'This isn't treasure, Mummy. It's too light.'

Mirren took the box. 'This is exciting, isn't it? Shall we open it?'

Kate might only have been seven but she was bright and observant. The box was similar to one that stood on a shelf high up on one of the bookshelves. A little silver box, with flowers carved on the outside and a red velvet interior. She shrugged a sulky, 'All right.'

It opened easily. Surely it would be rusty and hard to open? Kate's misgivings deepened when she spotted the piece of jewellery. 'That's not treasure,' she shouted and threw it as far as she could. It clattered onto the garden path, a bracelet belonging to her mother, gold links studded with garnets. Kate used to play with it in secret, pretending to be a princess. Mirren never suspected because she rarely wore jewellery, and in any case, Kate was always careful to put it back.

Her mother got up and retrieved the bracelet from the path. She came back and sat beside Kate while the rain soaked them. 'I'm sorry,' she said. 'I thought the fun was in looking for it, not the actual treasure itself.'

'You've spoiled everything!' yelled Kate as she ran into the house, sobbing.

Why had she been so angry? Mirren was right. It had been fun and she'd only been trying to bring joy into her daughter's life.

With these thoughts in mind, Kate ran downstairs to the study and stood in front of the desk, trying to remember where the compartment was. She visualised herself as an excited seven-year-old, rummaging through the drawers – no! It wasn't a drawer. She opened the lid of the desk and looked at the fitted interior. There were two pilasters the full height of the interior, made from carved wood. Kate pulled at the right hand one. It didn't move. She tried the other one and it slid out, revealing a folded piece of paper. Kate opened it up every bit as excited as she'd been all those years ago when she discovered the 'treasure map'.

This was no treasure map, however. Kate stared at it bemused, unable to take it in. Her stomach twisted. It wasn't possible. She looked again, praying she was mistaken. But no. It was a death certificate. The name of the deceased jumped out at her – Caitlin Fallon. Her legs gave way and she slumped against the wall.

After a few seconds she pulled herself together. It was a coincidence, nothing more. It was a relative's, her grandmother's perhaps. Yes, that's what it was. Relieved, she stood up, feeling like an idiot for her overreaction. She read through it. The date of death was 25th December 1991, not long after Kate was born. What a shame they never had the chance to get to know one another. Then doubts assailed her, sharp as arrows. Why on earth would her mother keep the certificate hidden? Moments later, she had the answer. There, under cause of death, was written 'Sudden Infant Death Syndrome'. Kate looked at the date of birth: 1st October 1991, same as hers. In her hands was her death certificate. What the fuck was going on?

Kate stared at the piece of paper in her hand, mouth open, stupidly gaping. Her death certificate. According to this she had been dead for almost twenty eight years. She put it back into the compartment and closed up the desk, then changed her mind and took it out again. Folk wisdom flooded her mind – let sleeping dogs lie – don't let the cat out of the bag – leave well alone. She had unleashed a monster, opened Pandora's box. Her legs were unsteady as she walked through to the kitchen and put the certificate on the table. She went over to the cupboard where she stored alcohol and took out a malt whisky. She poured out an inch and a half, put it on the table and sat down with it in front of her. For several seconds she studied the oily liquid slicking round the glass before picking it up and taking a gulp. It was a Bowmore, one of the Islay malts, eighteen years old, smoother than your normal blended whisky, but even so, it caught the back of her throat and her eyes watered. Her head swam as the alcohol reached her bloodstream; drinking so early in the day was always a mistake, but that was good, she wanted to forget what she'd found. Maybe if she drank enough, she would. She lifted the glass once more. This time she sipped the whisky, but it didn't hit the spot so she diluted it with water and swallowed it all. Now her head was spinning; it was too heavy to hold up so she rested it on the table. Before long she was asleep.

When she awoke, she felt as though someone had placed an iron band round her head and was slowly tightening it. Her face was beaded with sweat and her hands were clammy. Her legs trembled as she went upstairs to the bathroom, where she vomited yellow bile into the toilet bowl. What the fuck had she been thinking, downing whisky like that so early in the day? She doubted she'd ever touch the stuff again.

After a long, hot shower she felt a little better. She dressed in clean clothes, brushed her teeth and went downstairs, where she made some tea and toast. Her stomach wouldn't take anything stronger. Her mind refused to contemplate the death certificate. She couldn't begin to fathom what it meant. If Caitlin Fallon was dead – and the evidence was there on the table in front of her – what the hell did it mean? She stared at the kitchen ceiling, convinced the cracks were getting wider, wishing her mother hadn't died. She had so many questions for her. But she was dead, so that was not going to happen.

She closed her eyes and thought about everything that had happened since her mother had died. That phone call the day before the funeral. What was that about? And the anonymous letter. They had to be linked. Aodhan Fallon too. He knew more than he was telling her, she'd swear to it. He'd told her not to contact him again, but damn him, she had a right to know. She picked up her phone and keyed in his number. She stiffened as she listened to a disembodied voice. Her number had been blocked.

She still had her landline though. She wouldn't make the same mistake twice, she thought, as she dialled 141 to withhold her number.

A woman answered. 'Can I speak to Aodhan, please?'

'Who is this, please?' There was no warmth in the woman's voice.

Kate spoke firmly, trying to effect a confidence she didn't feel. 'I believe I may be Aodhan's niece. My name is Kate Fallon. My mother was Mirren Fallon and Aodhan turned up at her funeral last week. He told me how his sister disappeared all those years ago, but when he learned that my name was Caitlin and not Kate, he left without explaining why.'

There was a gasp from the other end of the line. 'Can you say that again, please?'

Kate repeated herself. There was a long silence, then, 'Jesus, Mary and Joseph. I don't believe it.'

'Neither did I,' said Kate. 'My mother always told me she was an only child. But Aodhan showed me a photo of his family when they were children. I was going through Mum's things and I found the same photo taped to the underside of a drawer in her desk. I can't think of any reason why she'd have that unless Aodhan was her brother.'

'Dear God, I'm sorry. I'm finding this hard to take in,' said the woman, her voice shaky. 'I know nothing about this. I thought Aodhan was away golfing last week but he was at Muireann's funeral?' Her voice rose. She sounded close to tears. 'He's out at the moment. I'll speak to him and we'll get back to you later this evening.'

Kate hesitated. She was worried they wouldn't phone back. 'There's something else you should know,' she said. 'I phoned your husband earlier and he's refusing to speak to me.'

The woman was suspicious now. 'Why?'

Kate found it hard to keep the frustration from her voice. 'I don't know. Perhaps it's something to do with the death certificate I found hidden in my mother's desk. The details on it are mine. Except the date of death, obviously. As far as I'm aware I'm still alive.'

There was a long silence then, 'Dear God, I don't know what to say. That must have been a terrible shock for you.'

'That's one way of putting it.' Kate's voice trembled.

'You poor thing. I'll make sure he phones you.' The woman sounded determined and this reassured Kate.

'Can we Skype?' she asked. 'It would be good to speak face to face.'

'You're not local, then?'

'No, I live in Buckinghamshire.'

'Ah, right. Well, I don't know. I'll need to ask Aodhan, see what he thinks.'

Kate suspected the answer would be no. 'Please,' she said. 'It would be better to speak face to face and I don't want to have to come up to Glasgow.'

'No, I can see that. All right then, let's do Skype.

'Thank you,' said Kate. 'What's your Skype name?'

'It's Margaret Fallon 54.'

'And mine is Caitlin Fallon. Shall we say seven o'clock?'

They said their goodbyes. It was done. Maybe now, she'd get some answers.

EIGHT

Buckinghamshire

KATE CALLED Margaret and Aodhan on Skype at seven o'clock. They answered immediately, their faces tense. The two of them were squeezed up on a grey sofa. Their room was decorated in a shade of off-white. Behind them was a watercolour painting. It reminded Kate of something, but she couldn't think what.

Margaret spoke first. 'Well,' she said, 'I'm not sure what to say. I'm sure you have a lot of questions. Perhaps it's best if you go first.'

'Yes,' said Kate. 'I have many questions, but the one that bothers me most is why is there a death certificate with my name on it? I don't understand it. I mean, look at me. I'm clearly not dead.' She attempted a smile but neither of them smiled in return. 'Do you have any idea what's going on? Is it a forgery, a joke, a mistake? It must be one of those things, surely.'

'It would have been best if you'd let things be,' said Aodhan. 'If I'd let things be, I should say. I wish I'd never seen that death notice in the *Guardian*.'

'But you did. And here we are,' said Kate. 'So...'

Aodhan cast a desperate look at his wife. 'This isn't easy,' he began.

Before he could say anything else, Margaret spoke up. Her voice shook as she talked. 'Like my husband said, there's no easy way of saying this. Muireann had a baby in 1991. She and Tommy waited years for that baby. Muireann was very young when she moved in with Tommy and our parents didn't approve. They didn't like him and of course they hated the fact that they weren't married. They weren't estranged from Muireann but there was a coolness in the relationship. The baby was very much wanted and it was also a chance for Muireann and her parents to be reconciled.'

Another shock, her father must be this Tommy person. 'She never mentioned him to me,' said Kate.

Aodhan took up the story. 'Tommy was a lot older than she was, fifteen years older. They met at art school. He was her tutor. And if that wasn't bad enough, he was an atheist. Our parents were Irish Catholics and very traditional, but I'm sure Muireann will have told you that.'

'She never told me much about my grandparents.'

Aodhan cast a brief look at Margaret before he carried on. 'My parents were thrilled with the baby. We all were. Any animosity between Muireann and them disappeared. It helped that Muireann insisted on Caitlin being registered as Fallon. She was a feminist and determined that the baby would carry her name. Anyway, that's beside the point. She and Tommy were thrilled. The wee lassie had everything a baby needed. She was like a wee doll, so she was.'

'And that was me,' said Kate. Why was Aodhan referring to her in the third person when she was right there in front of them? 'Caitlin. But why did she leave you all? Especially if she was so happy.'

Aodhan and Margaret exchanged a look. 'I'm so sorry, pet,' said Margaret. 'But you're not Caitlin. Surely you must realise that?'

Kate blinked. 'What do you mean? Of course I'm Caitlin. The death certificate, it's a mistake, it must be.'

'Caitlin was twelve weeks old when she died. It was a cot death, they said. Nobody's fault, could have happened to anyone. All the usual platitudes. Muireann was distraught. Tommy was too, but for Muireann it went way beyond grief. There was no comforting her.' Aodhan had tears in his eyes as he spoke.

Margaret nodded. 'You've no idea. It was a terrible time. We had three children by then and I was expecting again. I felt guilty for having children when she had none. We would have done anything to help her, but all she wanted was her baby.'

Kate's throat tightened. 'I don't understand,' she said. 'Who the f— Who the hell am I then?'

'We don't know,' said Aodhan. 'Six months after Caitlin died, Muireann disappeared. Her car was found in Troon, that's a town down by the sea, and several people reported seeing a woman walking alone on the beach that day, crying. A dog walker found her shoes and coat the next day. There wasn't a note. The police assumed she'd killed herself but they never found her body.' Aodhan kneaded the sides of his forehead. 'I didn't believe she'd killed herself. I lived in hope that one day I'd find her. And I did, but this, sweet Jesus, I never expected this.'

Kate wanted to shut down the meeting, block their phone number and forget everything, but she had to see this through. If only Aodhan had never seen the death notice in the

Guardian. She'd be at peace now, safe with her memories of the woman she thought was her mother. She broke the silence. 'So, do you have any idea what happened? Is there *any* chance I am her child?' she asked. 'I mean, maybe she was pregnant when she left. She wasn't able to reconcile the fact of losing one child and gaining another, and then when I was born, she named me after Caitlin...' She tailed off.

Aodhan was blunt. 'There is no possibility that you are her child. It was a difficult delivery. Muireann had an emergency hysterectomy.'

A simple statement and Kate's hopes were thrown to the wind. How stupid to think she was Mirren's child. She was devastated, bereft for a second time. She had loved her so much. She lowered her head to hide her tears.

Margaret stepped in. 'There is another possibility. Maybe it's not Muireann at all. You hear about it all the time. Someone with a young baby fleeing a violent partner. Perhaps someone took on her identity.'

Aodhan looked baffled. 'You're making it too complicated,' he said. 'How could anyone have stolen her identity?'

'But this is so out of character for her, you said so yourself. And you hear of stolen identity all the time.'

'I know, I know, but...'

'We have to accept that Mirren was who she said she was. I'm the one with no identity, no family that I know of.' Kate was crying now; tears ran down her face unchecked. She took out a tissue from her bag and wiped her face.

'Oh, Kate, you poor thing.' Margaret paused. 'Look, Muireann thought of you as her daughter, so as far as I'm concerned, that's what you are. It's clear you loved her very much.'

Kate caught the look of dismay on Aodhan's face and

winced. 'Wait a minute,' he said. 'We don't know for sure that this woman was my sister.'

Margaret flushed. 'Two seconds ago, you were convinced she was.'

'Yes, well. Oh God, I don't know any more.' He put his head in his hands and sighed.

Kate's eyes were drooping. Skype calls drained her, and this had been a difficult and emotional session. 'Thank you for listening to me but I need to go now. I won't bother you again.'

'No, don't go. There's an easy way to solve this.' Margaret broke in. 'You must have photographs of your mother... of the woman who claimed to be your mother.'

Kate hadn't thought of this. She was more tired than she thought. 'Hang on a second. I'll get one.' She ran through to the living room and dug out her mobile. Back in front of the laptop screen she held it up. Aodhan looked at it as though it was a hand grenade, indecision in his eyes.

'Can you send it to me?' He read out his mobile number.

Kate shared the photo and waited. She watched as he and his wife studied the photo, their faces creased in concentration.

She let it go for a few seconds before demanding, 'Well?'

Aodhan gave a brief nod. 'It's her. I'm sure of it. What do you think, Margaret?'

'Yes, it's her all right. The way her two front teeth cross over slightly at the front. That's unmistakeable. She's hardly changed.' She turned to her husband. 'I meant what I said you know, about Kate. She was Muirrean's daughter. She brought happiness into your poor sister's life. As far as I'm concerned, she's family.'

Aodhan didn't look up. 'I don't know,' he mumbled. 'We need to consider this carefully, not rush into anything.'

Kate rubbed her eyes. She hadn't expected this, for anyone

in this family to welcome her. It was too much. All she wanted was to talk about what might have happened. After all, they had known Mirren. They must have theories.

'Please, stay in touch,' said Margaret.

Aodhan's mouth was turned down and he was frowning. 'That's very kind,' Kate said. 'But you don't have to. You don't owe me anything.'

'Please,' Margaret repeated. 'Muireann's disappearance tore this family apart. We need to know what happened to her. How she lived her life. You must see that.'

Kate was unsure how to respond. On the one hand, she wasn't related to this family. On the other, the possibility of discovering more about the woman she thought of as her mother was tempting. 'I don't know,' she said after a second or two.

'Sleep on it,' said Margaret.

Beside her, Aodhan shrugged and he added, 'We can talk again next week when we've all had time to process this.'

'OK,' agreed Kate. 'We can do another Skype call next week. I'll be in touch.' She cut off the call. For several minutes she sat in front of the screen, unable to move. Inside though, her stomach churned as though she had a bellyful of squirming eels. If she wasn't Caitlin, then who was she and how was she going to find out?

NINE

Buckinghamshire

DESPITE HAVING SO much to do, Kate couldn't help brooding about what had happened. She wasn't sure how she felt. Sad? Yes. Mirren's story was a desperate one. Kate couldn't begin to imagine what it felt like to lose a child. And after so many years of trying. Angry? Yes, that too. Why had her mother not told her who she was. It was no big deal to be adopted. No doubt there was some horrible background, abusive parents maybe, but she'd rather know than not. How dare Mirren not tell her? She felt sad for Mirren's family too. All those years of wondering what had happened, of trying to find their daughter and sister. Most of all she felt betrayed. She'd always prided herself on their relationship; they'd been so close. Not close enough for her mother to tell her she was adopted though.

Kate continued to go through her mother's belongings, hoping to find something, anything, to tell her who she was. Mirren must have adopted her; it was the only explanation, but why hadn't she told her and why did she have a dead baby's name and date of birth? She'd go crazy if she didn't find out. She would be back at work soon, didn't need this hanging over her. There was also the problem of the Fallons. Margaret was lovely, so warm and welcoming – Kate would have loved to have had an aunt like her – but Aodhan was more cautious, that much was clear. She hoped they would keep in touch, maybe meet up, but perhaps it would be too hard for him. Well, there was no point worrying about it before their next Skype call and she did her best to put it out of her mind. It flooded back though, when she got home one day after she'd been shopping and another letter to her mother was lying in the hallway. She recognised the handwriting. Another anonymous letter.

Her first instinct was to throw it away. No good was going to come of opening a letter from someone who was too cowardly to sign it. She stared at the envelope. Fuck it, she had to know.

Another note scribbled on a torn piece of paper. This time though, there was also a photocopy of a newspaper cutting. She looked at the note first.

I know what you done.

Christ! It was like being in a bad teen movie. One with poor grammar. She opened the folded press cutting. There was no date on it, nothing to say what newspaper it was from.

Missing Woman Thought to Have Drowned

Muirrean Fallon, missing for several days, is thought to have drowned after a witness said he saw a woman wading out to sea. She left several items of clothing on Troon beach. Police are not looking for anyone else in connection with the incident. Ms Fallon is believed to be depressed and in an unstable frame of mind, following the death of her three-month-old daughter last year.

Oh God, what the hell was this about? Maybe this Robert Taylor was a discarded lover, or maybe she'd pretended to drown herself because she owed him money. A knock on the window startled her and Kate shoved the cutting and the note back into the envelope. She looked over and saw it was Jack. She closed her eyes, unable to cope with him right now.

'Kate, are you all right?'

'Go away.'

'Let me in or I'll break the window.'

She stayed put. He wouldn't break the window. He was a policeman, there to uphold the law.

'Kate! Speak to me.'

Without thinking, she opened the door and he was in. She pulled him towards her. It was wrong but she wanted him so much. His wife, his child, the sinister notes, the newspaper cutting – all of them forgotten. He was hers. She kissed him, hard, and he responded, pulling her close to his chest. Her hands moved to the belt of his trousers and unbuckled it. He pressed himself against her. He pulled down her knickers, knelt down and lifted up her skirt, kissing his way up her thighs. It was over far too quickly.

'I have to go.' Jack put a finger on her lips to stop her protest. 'My shift starts in ten minutes, I'm going to be late. But I'll be back. Is that all right?'

She nodded, too emotional to speak. He kissed her again and left. Kate watched him walk down the path to the gate in the back garden that led to the lane behind the house. It was crazy to let him into her life again but she didn't care.

Exhausted and satiated, she climbed the stairs to her bedroom, the newspaper cutting forgotten. She needed sleep.

The insistent ringing of the doorbell woke her. Her mouth was dry and her head throbbed. She stared at the ceiling and thought about what had happened. Jack was back in her life, but it was the anonymous letters that preoccupied her. The bell rang again, accompanied by banging on the door.

'Kate, Kate. Are you in there?'

Shit. She'd forgotten Laura was coming over. She hauled on her dressing gown and ran downstairs.

'What's up with you?' Laura held out a bottle of wine and came in. 'Did you forget I was coming?' She settled herself into Mirren's chair. 'Don't tell me you're not well. Let me make you a cup of tea.' She moved as if to get up.

'No, no. I'm fine.' Kate's knickers were in the middle of the kitchen floor; she had to get to them before Laura saw them.

'You sure?'

Kate nodded. 'I'll make us a cup of tea.'

'Make mine a gin,' said Laura, 'and make one for yourself too.'

Kate decided tea would be a better choice for her. She poured Laura's drink and waited for the kettle to boil. Her knickers were nowhere to be seen. She must have taken them upstairs after all.

'Aren't you going to get dressed?' Impatient as ever, Laura had come into the kitchen to fetch her drink.

'Can't be bothered.'

'For heaven's sake, Kate. You need to look after yourself. Go upstairs and put your clothes on right now. And make up too. You look awful.'

Kate thought about arguing but decided against it. Once she'd washed her face and put on some make up she felt better. Maybe she'd have that drink after all.

Laura helped herself to another drink and looked in the

fridge. 'You really aren't looking after yourself, are you? I'll phone for pizza.'

'Thanks,' said Kate.

'How have you been doing?'

Kate hesitated. 'Oh, you know. Up and down.' She decided not to mention the letters. Not until she'd had the chance to think about what the latest one meant.

'More down than up by the look of you.'

'It's not been the best day, but it's good to see you. Tell me the gossip, cheer me up.'

Over pizza, Laura launched into a story about her neighbour who had bankrupted himself because of his gambling debts. 'He's borrowed on the house and everything,' she said. 'Re-mortgaged up to his eyeballs. So, the house is up for sale and they're having to move into a tiny flat. His poor wife, and those children. They're devastated at having to move school.'

'At least he'll still have his job.'

Laura shook her head. 'No, that's the worst of it. He's been caught embezzling money from his firm. That's how it all came out. He's facing a prison sentence.'

Kate topped up their drinks. 'That's awful. Any other news?' She was desperate to keep Laura away from how she was doing. She was tempted to tell her everything, including her affair with Jack, and that would not be a good idea. No one knew about him and it was more important than ever to keep it that way. But before Laura could say anything, her mobile rang.

'Hello?'

'Are you alone?' It was Jack.

'It's not convenient at the moment, no.'

Laura concentrated on her pizza, pretending not to listen.

'When then?'

'I'm not sure.' She glanced at Laura, who mouthed *your dinner's getting cold*.

'I'll come round after work, about half past ten. Is that OK?'

'Yes.'

'Who was that?' asked Laura.

'One of those opinion polls, wanting to know who I'll vote for.'

It took over an hour to get Laura to leave. Lots of yawns and *shit, how tired I am*. At last, she took the hint and phoned for a taxi. Kate stood at the door to wave her off; she was jangling with nerves.

He didn't come. For three hours Kate paced the floor. She dialled 1471 in case she had somehow missed a call, though she knew she hadn't. She checked her email and mobile like someone with obsessive compulsive disorder. At half past one she gave up and went to bed where she lay sleepless, on edge, seething with rage. She had to put an end to this now. Before she got hurt again.

TEN

Buckinghamshire

KATE WAS furious with herself for letting Jack trick her in that way. This time, he wasn't going to get away with it. She refused to make excuses for him. When they'd been together, this sort of thing happened all the time. They'd make an arrangement to meet and he'd fail to turn up. If she was lucky, she'd get a phone call or a text message to apologise, but most times she'd be left hanging, like tonight. Well, it was over now. She wouldn't make that mistake again.

The following evening she had arranged to meet some of her work colleagues for a drink. It was late when she arrived back at the cottage. The sky was velvety black, stars spread across it as if a child had been let loose with glitter. There was a warm breeze, which was like a comforting hand stroking her hair. Kate stood outside in the garden and breathed in the fragrant air. Every year, her mother planted night-scented stock, and its perfume was prominent tonight. Her key was in the door when Jack approached. Kate stifled a scream.

'What the hell are you doing?'

'I'm sorry, but I had to see if you were all right. I phoned earlier, but you didn't answer.'

Kate opened the door and they went inside. She had turned off her mobile in the pub. When she turned it on there were six missed calls and two messages. For once he was telling the truth. 'You didn't come round when you said you would.'

'Alfie was ill. We were scared it was meningitis.' He looked tired.

'Is he all right?'

'Fine, it was a virus. Vicky tends to panic when he has a temperature.'

'Vicky must have a sixth sense to be able to come up with a drama whenever it's necessary. Are you sure she hasn't put a tracking device on your phone?' said Kate.

'What do you mean?' His voice was tight, always a danger sign, but to hell with it. Kate was tired, fed up and more than a little jealous.

'Well, let's see. There was the time we were going to the Lake District for the weekend. Didn't she break a bone in her foot? And what about my birthday? That was a great day, me left alone in the restaurant while you went home to fix the flood that had appeared in your kitchen. And I can't count the number of times you were meant to come round and some little crisis arose at home.' Kate was raging now at how near she'd been to falling into the same trap. 'You know what, Jack? I bet you anything Vicky knows all about us, but instead of confronting you, she's gone into passive aggressive mode. This will go on for the rest of your life. Poor, needy little Vicky, and now she's got an ally in baby Alfie.' Her voice was full of spite. It was foolish to demean herself like this. Jack stared at her with narrowed eyes, then turned and left.

She wasn't sorry he'd gone, but she hated herself for maligning a baby. As she brushed her teeth, she couldn't look at herself in the mirror.

———————————

Kate thrashed around in bed trying to find a cool spot. Her mind was as agitated as her body; it wouldn't leave the fight with Jack alone. She should have said nothing. What a bitch she was. If she'd kept her mouth shut, he'd be here now. She heard her mother saying *perhaps it's for the best*. Mirren's voice was so clear Kate put on her bedside light and looked round the room. Christ, how she missed her. If she was here Kate could talk about Jack, ask her what she thought. More than that, Kate wanted to know why Mirren left her family in that horrible way. If she was here, Kate could find out who she was. But she was alone.

She sat up in bed and read for a while but found it too hard to concentrate. At two thirty she got up and made herself a cup of tea and watched three episodes of a Netflix series on her iPad. It was nearly six o'clock when she at last felt tired enough to go back to bed and eleven o'clock before she woke up. Her mind immediately went to the anonymous letter. Why did someone think they could blackmail Mirren?

Downstairs, she made coffee and toast. The house was full of papers, she thought. Maybe she'd find something in there to help her solve this mystery. Perhaps there would be something that would point towards her true identity. When she finished her breakfast, she started her search.

An hour later, she had found two diaries, 1991 and 1992, on a shelf amongst Mirren's vast collection of novels. Ordinary

Lett's diaries, a page to a day. Kate picked up 1991 and skimmed through it. It was a work diary, filled with appointments for meetings with clients. Kate knew her mother had been a social worker for a time, but Mirren had never elaborated on it, saying only that she had given it up after Kate was born and had found a way to make money through her embroidery. There was a scribbled note on February 4th in tiny writing at the bottom of the page.

I'm pregnant! Tommy's thrilled. He broke down in tears when I told him. Everyone's so happy for me. It's happened at last, after all these years of trying. I can't wait for the baby to be born. I hope it's a boy.

Kate put down the diary. Now she'd found it she didn't like the idea of reading it. But there it was on the coffee table, tempting her. She picked it up and continued to read.

Mirren had made lots of notes like this. Always in tiny writing in the space left after her work commitments had been noted. It didn't make for great reading. Sickness early on, swollen ankles later. A short spell in hospital after some bleeding. The way it was described made Kate hope she'd never be pregnant. In early September Mirren stopped work and the entries were longer. Ruminations on what to call the baby, Sean if it was a boy, Caitlin for a girl. In October there was little except on the day of Caitlin's birth. A brief but joyful note. *It's a girl and I love her! Why did I think I wanted a boy? She's simply perfect.* After that there was the occasional marking of a milestone – *smiled for the first time, held up her head* – then she came to Christmas Eve, the day before Caitlin's death. Kate's hand shook as she turned the page. It was blank.

Kate breathed out slowly, relieved. She didn't want to read

about Mirren's sorrow. There was nothing written in the remaining pages. Kate picked up 1992 and flicked through it in a despondent way, hoping to find something about her adoption. It was totally blank. She put the diaries back on the shelf.

She'd been so sure they would hold the key. Kate looked round the room, rage bubbling up inside her. She picked up her cup and threw it at the wall. It bounced off without breaking. She couldn't even lose her temper properly. Maybe it was best that way. Mirren always said anger wasn't a good way to react. She was wise. Or was she? Kate didn't know what she was like, not really. She'd kept an enormous secret from Kate, all the while instructing her to be calm, to be truthful, to live by the golden rule. That was a laugh. Do as you would be done by. No, Kate didn't know her at all. The urge to search for adoption papers left her. There was so much to do and she had no energy to do any of it.

Kate arranged another Skype call with Margaret and Aodhan. She was sure now she had been adopted but couldn't think how to find out about it. When she mentioned it to Aodhan and Margaret, they looked sceptical.

'They were too old to adopt,' said Aodhan. 'I mean Tommy was in his mid-fifties by then and Muireann was forty. I think the upper age limit for adopting at that time was thirty-eight.'

'Are you sure?' asked Kate.

'I wouldn't want to swear to it, but friends of ours adopted a wee boy and I remember them talking about it at the time and saying how they'd almost missed out. They were thirty four and thirty six at the time.'

The call ended soon after with Kate feeling more bereft than ever. She'd been so sure about an adoption and had hoped to ask if Aodhan and Margaret could help her look into it. The conversation had ended any hope of that.

Two days later, Kate went into work for a staff meeting. She didn't have to as she was still on leave but she thought it might help her forget her troubles for a few hours.

The team meeting was hell, as always. Kate hoped that for once there would be no argument over whose turn it was to take minutes, that Mick, the oldest, most cynical member of the department would turn up on time and that Sheena wouldn't fall asleep. But as usual she was disappointed. No one offered to take the minutes, so Kate agreed to do them but only if it was going to be by alphabetical order thereafter. She saw by their faces they were thinking *mug* but she was prepared for that: at the end of the minutes she'd name the next minute taker so there could be no argument about it.

They were halfway through the meeting by the time Mick arrived, bringing with him an unappealing aroma of smoke and beer. He sat down without an apology next to Kate. She moved her seat away from him, hoping he wouldn't notice.

Sheena opened an eye and glared at him. 'Sleeping again, Sheena?' he said. She raised a lazy middle finger.

The meeting rambled on until past lunch time as was customary. Gus, the head of department, was oblivious to the mutterings. Like many hard drinkers he had little appetite. At last, they came to the final item on the agenda.

'New acquisitions. Well, there's not a lot of these. But we do have one exciting development. The Principal has agreed to pay for a subscription to a number of newspaper back catalogues. So, in addition to the *Guardian* and the *Times*, we're adding the *Mail*. I know, I know,' he said to the chorus of groans, 'but they do fund a scholarship.' He shuffled his papers together to show he'd finished and added, 'Oh, and we've got the *Glasgow Herald* too.'

Sheena woke up at that. 'How provincial. If we have to have a Scottish newspaper why not the *Scotsman*?'

Mick knew the answer to that, the old cynic. 'It's where the old man did his apprenticeship, isn't it, Gus?' He was the only member of staff who called the head of department by his first name. Everyone else called him Mr McDonald, and behind his back, the cheeseburger.

The cheeseburger flushed an unseemly red, showing that Mick, as ever, had hit a sore spot. He left the room without a word. Kate ran after him, taking no notice of Mick's muttered *don't crawl too far up his arse, now*, and caught him as he was about to go into the Gents. He moved his hand away from his fly and glared at her. But he must have remembered she was in mourning because he changed it quickly to a lukewarm smile. 'Yes, Kate, what is it?'

'When will we get access to these newspapers?'

'They're available now. Jane,' he was referring to the departmental secretary, 'should have sent round details of how to log on.' He stared at Kate. 'You're keen. I like that. You'll go far.'

Kate smiled and thanked him.

Sheena caught her as she was going in to her room. 'Do you fancy lunch?'

Kate was about to refuse because she was desperate to get into the back catalogue of the *Glasgow Herald*, but she was pretty hungry and she never concentrated well when her stomach was rumbling, so she agreed to a quick trip to the local sandwich bar.

Two hours later, her head was full of Sheena's troubles

with her teenage son, whom she had spoiled rotten from the day he was born. Now she was reaping the rewards of indulging his every whim. Kate gave her some advice that she knew Sheena would ignore. Why wouldn't she? What did Kate know about teenagers? Finally, Kate extracted herself and returned to her room to get on with what she was desperate to do. She switched on her computer and the kettle at the same time. Her work computer was so ancient she always made tea while waiting for it to wind up. Cuts at the college over the last few years meant her requests for a new one went unheeded. There were times when she was tempted to spill coffee over the hard drive, but she refrained mainly because she feared it wouldn't have the desired effect and she'd end up with something even worse. At last, she was into the system and she logged in to her email to find Jane's detailed and excellent instructions.

Kate wasn't sure of the exact date of Mirren's disappearance, but Aodhan had mentioned June 1992, about six months after the baby died, so she started there. Immediately it was clear from the font that the cutting hadn't come from this paper. She scoured the 1st June edition but there was nothing about a missing woman. The next few days were the same – perhaps she had the wrong month – then she found it, on the fifth page of 7th June. It merited only a small paragraph headed: *Fears grow for missing woman*. Kate read it quickly. It had the barest of details. Muireann Fallon, aged forty-one, car found in car park in the town. Not seen since the previous Thursday. Thought to be in unstable frame of mind following the death of her daughter. It was all as Aodhan had said and pretty much what was in the anonymous newspaper clipping. She went through the following days' archives, but the only other mention of Mirren was on the sixteenth where there was a stark paragraph stating that police were assuming she'd committed suicide in a period of deep grief after the death of her baby daughter. A brief quote from her father concluded the article: *Muireann would never kill herself. I know she's out there and I'm begging her to come home.*

Kate printed out both stories. It wasn't much to go on. Perhaps Aodhan or one of his family had kept newspaper cuttings. She'd ask them when she next spoke to them. She was about to exit the site when a headline caught her eye. It was on the front page, not a banner headline but large nonetheless: Man Questioned Over Missing Baby Case.

Kate read the article, her mouth dry. She looked at the details, the baby's date of birth, her address on the Southside of Glasgow. At first the police thought she'd been abducted from her pram, but something changed their minds, because a week after she went missing, her father was arrested. The father's name was Robert Taylor. Robert Taylor, the name on the cutting she'd been sent. Kate stared at the computer screen, trying to process this information. She began another search and found reports of the trial six months later. As she read on her heart beat slowed. A coincidence, that's all it was. There was a cast iron case against the man; he'd confessed. But a few seconds later, she was worried again. The baby's body was never found.

Kate shut down the computer, deep in thought. A woman distraught with grief disappeared around the same time as a baby similar in age to the one she lost. She faked her death and ended up in the south of England far from friends and family. Somehow, she procured a young child. Kate had to face the possibility that she was Danielle Taylor, an abducted baby whose father was tried and jailed for her murder. It explained the phone calls, it explained the anonymous notes and the newspaper cutting. She found she was holding her breath. She was terrified. Someone had found out Mirren had stolen her, but who, and what did they want?

ELEVEN

Glasgow 1992

It was after midnight when the call came in. That was one of the things that made him suspicious. Newly promoted and with a young baby of his own, DS Alex Scrimgeour was nobody's fool. 'For fuck's sake,' he'd said to anyone who'd listen, 'the wean goes missing in the afternoon and they don't tell us until now? There's something not right there. Any normal person, their wean disappears and they're going doolally.' They'd planned how to handle it as they drove over to Pollok. 'You need to be all tea and sympathy,' he said to the PC with him, a young woman called Debbie. 'But keep your eyes and ears open. Something's not right here.

More information came over the police radio as they drew up in front of the house in Old Pollok. The father was known to the police. 'Robert Taylor, answers to Robbie. We thought we had him last year for drug dealing,' said the voice on the radio, 'but the case was dropped because no one would testify. Word on the street is that he intimidated witnesses. Though of course nobody'll say anything official.'

Alex and Debbie walked up the path and rang the doorbell. That was another thing. You'd have thought they'd be outside waiting for them, desperate to see the people who were going to help them find their baby. Instead, the police were the ones waiting for the door to be answered. Alex counted silently, *one elephant, two elephants, three elephants*. He'd rung the bell another twice and counted to seventy-two before they answered. What did that say, other than that they were in there still trying to get their story straight?

He almost changed his mind when Brenda Taylor answered the door. A tiny woman, she only weighed seven stone, if that. Her cheekbones were prominent and her blonde hair was cut short, giving her an otherworldly look. Peter Pan maybe, or an elf. 'Mrs Taylor?' he said.

'Aye. What kept you?' There was nothing sprite-like about her voice. It was gravelly, a sixty-fags-a-day voice. Not surprising she was so thin with a habit like that. He ignored her question and they followed her into the house.

Robbie Taylor was huge. His tight t-shirt showed off a body built by steroids. Muscles bulged. Alex mentally cursed the PC who'd told him he was a 'wee ned'. He'd envisaged someone only a couple of inches taller than Brenda, and thin to boot. This guy was over six foot and stacked. Sixteen stone if he was an ounce.

They introduced themselves. There was an awkward moment when Alex held out his hand to Taylor. It was ignored in favour of a fag. The air was already thick with smoke and Alex's lungs tightened in protest. There was a hint of dope in the air but he said nothing. This wasn't the time. He sat down on the leather sofa that dominated the room. Debbie did as she was told and offered to make tea. When Brenda and Robbie said they didn't want any she ignored them and went through to the kitchen anyway. She was smart, Debbie, knew this was a fishing expedition. He got out his notebook. 'I'll take a few details.'

'Never mind that. You should be out there looking for her,' said Robbie.

Alex put on his sympathetic face. 'I assure you, there are officers out there right now looking for her, Mr Taylor. First things first though. 'Your baby daughter's missing. Danielle, is that right? I'm so sorry. This must be a very difficult time for you. When did you last see her?'

Brenda looked at Robbie. If he wasn't wrong, she was asking for permission. A barely perceptible nod from Robbie and she answered. 'I put her out in her pram for a nap in the afternoon. I thought the fresh air would be good for her. You know, help her sleep better.'

'What time was that exactly?'

'Another glance at her husband. Another nod from him. 'I'm not sure.'

'You must have an idea, surely?'

'What the fuck's this about? It doesn't matter when she went missing. She's gone and you're sitting here harassing us.' Robbie's knees jiggled up and down as he spoke.

He'd go in heavy later if he had to. For the time being the important thing was to get them on side. Alex spoke with a calmness he didn't feel. 'It's important to get a timeline and then we'll ask neighbours if they were about at that time. It will help. It will tell us if there were any strangers in the area at the time, any cars that were out of place.'

Robbie muttered something under his breath. Alex wasn't sure but hazarded a guess at *fucking nosy cunts*. He let it go and continued with his questioning. It took two hours to get something like a coherent statement out of them. He and Debbie left at three a.m. promising to be back in the morning with a family liaison officer. No way was he leaving Debbie in that house with that brute. Liam Fisher, he was the man for the job. Six foot six and a karate expert. He'd do fine.

He let Debbie drive back. 'So?' he asked. 'Anything in the kitchen?'

'There was stuff in the washing machine. All dirty but nothing suspicious. All adult clothes and a couple of tea towels. No baby clothes and nothing that looked like blood.'

'Any sign of drugs, anything like that?'

'Nope. I had a poke around in a few of the more obvious hiding places, freezer, packets of flour etcetera, but not a sniff. It was pretty much spotless in there.'

'Right.' He scratched his nose. 'What did you make of the pair of them?'

'One of them did it, for sure. All that looking at each other, checking each other out. They'd been using all those hours to come up with a story.'

'Fucking useless story though!'

Brenda had told them she thought her mother had the baby, that she'd taken her to give them a break. 'You know what it's like with a wean screaming all the time.' Alex did know. He had one at home. But screaming or not, she was the joy of his and his wife's life and they'd die sooner than see harm come to her. If his wean went missing he'd be onto it before anyone else thought about calling the police.

Robbie had no explanation, couldn't think of anyone who would've taken her, denied having any enemies. He barely listened to their questions or his wife's responses. Not that they were much use either.

Brenda had no answers for his more probing questions about why her mother had left Jamie, the older brother, to play in the garden, or why they'd not reported her missing until nine hours later and what they'd been doing in that time.

'They're hiding something,' he said to Debbie. 'And I bet it's murder. Sure as fuck it's not Easter eggs.'

TWELVE

Glasgow 1992

THE NEXT DAY they started to search the nearby Pollok Country Park. It was one of Alex's favourite places, where he loved to walk with his family. He hoped the body wasn't there. He prayed his instincts were wrong in his suspicion of the parents.

He wasn't holding out much hope for the search. The park was big and it was too obvious a place to have hidden the body, too near their house. Judging by the way he'd avoided any serious charges sticking to him, Taylor was no idiot. They needed to see what they'd get out of the neighbours.

Alex briefed the team of police officers who had been sent from all over Glasgow. 'Gentle probing, that's what does it. No promises of anonymity. We want someone willing to testify. Find out if anyone saw either of the Taylors leave the house. Or if there was anyone strange hanging about. Concentrate on the houses closest by at first before going on to those further afield. Appeal to their consciences. This is a baby, for Christ's sake.'

He took a deep breath before walking up the path to the Taylors' front door. Liam had been there since first thing that morning, and although it was now only nudging ten o'clock, he'd had enough. 'What did I do, Sarge? Why me?' he said as he opened the door. 'We're supposed to be mates.'

Alex gave him a friendly punch. 'You were the biggest bastard available. They up?'

Liam nodded towards the living room door. 'Aye, and in a foul mood too. Barely speaking to each other.'

Alex went through. Brenda was in a terrible state, and despite his doubts, his heart went out to her. She was suffering, no doubt about it, whether from guilt or desperation he couldn't tell. He needed to get her away from Robbie so as to get more out of her, but judging by the way he was jammed into his armchair, Robbie wasn't going anywhere soon. If only they had a reason to take him down the station.

Their chance came sooner than he'd dared to hope. One of the officers from the north of the city who was doing door to doors spoke to a neighbour who had contacted social work with her concerns about Taylor and how he treated his children. Alex followed up on her initial statement. She lived two doors down, an elderly woman with a kind face.

'He's always shouting at his wee boy, so he is. Day in, day out. And the other week, he had this bruise on him, so he did. Right across his right cheek, so I called the social work. Of course they had a story ready for them, but I'm not fooled even if they were.'

'And were they fooled? Social work I mean,' Alex asked.

She shrugged. 'You'd have to ask them. But nothing happened and now that poor baby's gone missing.'

'Were you ever worried about the baby? Or about Mrs Taylor?'

The woman took her time before answering, lit a fag to give her time to think. 'Brenda can look after herself so no, I wasn't worried about her, but the baby, aye of course I was. Weans being brought up by scum like Taylor, it's not right.' She took a drag of her cigarette and coughed violently. 'You know,' she gasped when the coughing subsided, 'we're all feart of him. He should have been done for drug dealing last year but he got to the witnesses and threatened them. Nobody'll speak out against him. But killing a wean? Nobody's going to stand for that.'

Alex frowned. 'Nobody knows if the baby's dead.' He left it at that, to see what she'd say. In his experience people didn't cope well with silence.

She shook her head, refusing to look at him until at last, she broke. 'I can't say, I promised.'

Alex looked down at his notebook for her name. 'Mrs Walker. This is a serious matter. If you know anything you have to tell us.'

Tears came to her eyes. 'I'm sorry, no. I promised.'

'Did one of your other neighbours see something?'

After a few seconds she nodded, a movement so slight he thought he imagined it.

'Who was it?'

'Listen, son, if it was up to me, I wouldn't hesitate, but it was a wean who seen something. The parents are terrified of Taylor, so they are.' Her voice rose. 'People like you have no idea what it's like living here. This was a great wee spot until that family moved in. Now it's overrun with the thugs he gets to do his dirty work. And there's drugs everywhere, bringing misery to everyone.'

He couldn't argue with that. Alex got up from his seat. 'I'm going to ask you to nod or shake your head in response to my questions. That way you'll be able to say with a clear conscience you didn't say anything. Do you understand?'

For a few moments she stared at him, then at last she nodded.

'It's a child who saw something?'

A slow nod.

'A boy?'

Shake of the head. For five minutes this farce went on until he had the address of the child who could be a valuable witness. This would take sensitive handling. Debbie was the best woman for the job. He called her on his radio.

They were at the address within ten minutes. It wasn't within the immediate area of the Taylor house, so he doubted she'd have seen much, but they had to follow it up. It was all they had. They knocked on the door. A girl of about thirteen answered.

'Are your parents in?'

She shook her head and went to shut the door. Before he knew what he was doing, Alex had a foot in the door. He caught Debbie's horrified look and gave her a reassuring smile. 'It's really important that we speak to you.'

'My mum says I've not to speak to anyone. Least of all the polis.' She nibbled at her thumbnail.

He already knew but he asked anyway. 'What's your name, pet?'

'Pauline,' she mumbled. Her thumb was now fully in her mouth.

'Pauline, have you heard about the baby that's gone missing?'

The girl blinked back tears.

'It's a terrible thing. A baby going missing. Do you have a wee brother or sister? Can you imagine what it'd be like if it was one of them?'

Pauline sniffed and wiped her nose with the sleeve of her cardigan.

'Look, can we come in? We won't take long.'

Pauline opened the door wider and they followed her into the house. It was well furnished and very tidy for a house with three children. A toddler of about two was playing with Duplo and another child was sitting on a sofa watching TV.

'Where did you say your parents are?'

'Dad's out helping to look for the baby and Mum's gone to the shops. She'll be back soon.'

Alex gave Debbie a look that said *get on with it*. It was a stroke of luck finding the girl as good as alone and they needed to make the best of this opportunity. Debbie smiled at Pauline. 'Do you know the Taylor family?'

'Only to see them. They're a bad lot, Dad says I've to stay well clear.'

'OK, well we're asking everyone in the area whether they saw anyone strange in the streets round here, any cars that didn't belong, that sort of thing. Did you see anything?'

Pauline hesitated. She opened her mouth to speak then closed it again. 'No.'

She was lying. Her face reddened and she was close to tears.

'I don't want you to get upset,' said Debbie. 'Perhaps you saw something and you're frightened to say, is that it?'

Silence. This was getting them nowhere. Alex sighed. He shouldn't be here interviewing a child without an adult present. He stood up. 'Well, thank you anyway, Pauline. Come on, Debbie, we need to go.'

'Is it true the baby's been killed?' Her voice was a whisper.

They stopped dead. Debbie held up her hand, warning

him not to say anything. Her voice was soft. 'We don't know what's happened, Pauline. We're trying to find out.'

The words tumbled out of Pauline in a tangled rush. 'I was at my pal's house. She lives in the same street as them, by the way. He came out of the house, carrying a bag, you know the kind people take to the gym, or maybe the swimming except he doesn't go to a gym, or so my pal says. Mrs Taylor was standing at the window, crying, and we thought they'd maybe had a fight and he'd left her, but then an hour later, he comes back.'

'I see,' said Debbie. 'Is there anything else?'

'No, please don't tell anyone I told you. Please, my dad'll kill me.'

Alex shot Debbie a warning look. He'd swear she was about to give Pauline a promise she couldn't keep. 'Don't worry about that, Pauline. You've done the right thing. Thank you. We'd better go now.'

'He didn't bring the bag back, or at least not that we saw.'

The hairs stood up on the back of his neck. 'We really need to go now. Thanks, Pauline you've been really helpful.' It would be Taylor's stash of drugs, he told himself. He'd want anything incriminating out of the house before they called in the police. But as they left the house, he was on the radio to HQ asking them to arrange for a search warrant.

THIRTEEN

Glasgow 1992

THEY CAME CLOSE to missing the blood-stained Babygro. It was in the wardrobe in the Taylors' bedroom, stuffed in a plastic bag underneath other baby clothes. It was dirty, whereas the other things were clean, and that raised suspicions. If they'd shoved it in the washing basket, they might have got away with it, because at first glance the stain looked like chocolate. He shook it out to look at it and was about to put it away again when he saw Brenda's reaction. She froze and turned white. He studied it more closely before he bagged and labelled it. She wouldn't react like that if it was chocolate. 'Is this Danielle's?' he asked. She didn't answer. It didn't matter; forensic testing would soon tell them if it was hers or not.

'Why's it in a plastic bag? Looks like you're trying to hide it.'

Her eyes were darting back and forth. 'I was going to give it away.'

'Give it away? It's dirty, look.' He thrust it under her nose. She winced.

'This looks like blood to me. Can you explain it?'

96

'I... I don't know. Oh, I mind it now. I cut myself, that was it.' She looked over at her husband for approval. He didn't react.

'I see, and when was this?'

'I don't know, about a week ago?' She was the worst liar he'd met.

'Show me.'

She frowned. 'Show you what?'

'The cut.'

She hadn't expected that. It took her several seconds to recover enough to answer. 'It was a scratch, that's all. It's healed now.'

It was time to act; he needed to question them separately to break her down. 'We need to carry on this conversation at the police station.'

Her statement never changed: *I was at home the day Danielle disappeared. I thought my mother had taken her to give me a break. She does that sometimes. I have been very tired since she was born. I didn't call the police because I hadn't been able to contact my mother. I thought she'd taken Danielle to my gran's and my gran doesn't have a phone. It was only when my mother phoned me at midnight that I realised Danielle was missing.*

Alex had no doubt she knew her daughter was dead but she was doing everything to protect her husband. He interviewed her again and again, pressed every button – *do you take us for idiots, Mrs Taylor? You waited nine hours before contacting us, plenty of time for your husband to get rid of your daughter's body* – but she didn't react. She continued to stare in front of her, her face the picture of desperation.

Meanwhile the evidence continued to mount up against Taylor. Forensic tests revealed that the blood on the Babygro was Danielle's; another witness came forward to say he'd seen Taylor walking into the woods surrounding a local golf course with a sports bag and returning without it. The prosecution wasn't satisfied it was enough to get a conviction. A body was needed.

And then Taylor confessed.

Alex wasn't sure what had done it. The relentless interviews? The appeals to Taylor as a father? Or was he tired of all the lies? In the end, Alex didn't give a toss what it was that had prompted the confession.

It wasn't much. A brief statement was all they ever got from him. *I killed the wean. It was an accident. I dropped her on the floor.* They tried over and over to get him to add to it, to tell them where the body was. *Why didn't you call an ambulance? How did you know she was dead? Was your wife there? Where is the body? Where is the body? Where is the body?* But Taylor wouldn't budge.

Brenda said nothing when they told her. Afterwards, Alex wondered if maybe Taylor thought she'd confess too, confuse the prosecution. But she didn't. She looked at him with dead eyes.

'How could you?' Alex said to her. 'How could you let him kill your child?' She didn't blink, gave him nothing but that same blank stare.

Alex was desperate to have her charged too. But the Procurator Fiscal was having none of it. 'Now listen, we've got a confession from your man, that's an end to it. You've done your job, so.' His accent danced with the rhythms of Dublin, where he'd spent his early years. He'd added that he thought Brenda was innocent and that Alex had the wrong end of the stick.

He was wrong. Alex would swear on the life of his child that she knew something, but the PF was not convinced. Even the fact that she'd lied about the blood on the Babygro that they now knew to be Danielle's didn't shake him. The big daftie. Knowing he was beaten, Alex had dropped it. Brenda was released and a pre-trial date was set.

He hadn't seen it coming. None of them had. They'd all expected Taylor to submit a guilty plea. The shock resonated in the courtroom when he stood in the dock and said *Not Guilty*. 'It doesn't matter,' the PF said, 'not unless you beat a confession out of him and you didn't, did you?'

Of course he hadn't. God knows he'd wanted to, in the early days when Taylor sat in front of him with that smirk on his face, but he'd refrained. No point in giving the defence anything. No, the confession was sound, but it was a bugger that the trial would go ahead. He'd promised Sandra, his wife, they'd go away soon. A trial meant going over and over every bit of evidence to make sure that the charge would stick, and Sandra was sick of him doing overtime. He dreaded telling her.

'But you promised, Alex. You said we'd go away next weekend.' Sandra's face was pink with annoyance. She banged and clattered saucepans as she tidied up the kitchen. 'I need to get away. Mum and Dad have offered to take Mairi.'

'I know, I know. But the wee shit's gone and put in a not guilty plea. We've got to go through all the evidence again. Make sure we're not missing anything.' He was talking to himself. She'd left the room, slamming the door behind her. Upstairs a thin cry emitted from Mairi. He waited for a few seconds for her to quieten down, but when it didn't happen, he trudged upstairs. His mood lifted when he saw her lying in her cot. She beamed at him through her tears. 'You poor wee thing,' he said as he lifted her out, 'are you hungry?' Sandra came into the room behind him and he saw she'd been crying. Damn Taylor. He'd been looking forward to a break too.

'Why don't you go with one of your friends if your parents are happy to take Mairi? I'll be fine here.'

She didn't meet his eye. 'Maybe,' she said. 'I'll think about it.'

He knew she was mollified though when she turned to him in bed later that night. That didn't happen much these days.

The next weekend she drove to her parents' house with Mairi and left her there while she went off to meet her pals from university. Alex didn't know them well and that suited him fine. He'd met a couple of them at their wedding and found them to be stuck up and pretentious. Not that he said anything to Sandra. All that chat about film studies. You watched a film and either liked it or not as far as he was concerned, but they dissected films, talking about things like the use of montage in *The Godfather* (excellent, apparently) and how revolutionary *Citizen Kane* had been in its use of mise-en-scène. Even now he blushed when he remembered their reaction to his attempt to join in the conversation. *Citizen Kane? Isn't that a dusty old black and white film?* Their looks of scorn had been excoriating. He'd learned that word from his wife. Ah shit. Who cared? Good action films, that's what he liked, so tough luck. It didn't bother him, not really, but it was galling nonetheless to see her so carefree, running out to the car. She'd looked happier than she'd done for a while. Alex waved them off, cursing Taylor and whatever it was had changed his mind. He went back inside and settled down to work, wishing with all his heart they had found the poor wean's body. He wanted Taylor safe in jail.

He got what he wanted right enough. The jury found him guilty, a unanimous decision. A life sentence. Alex wasn't able to contain himself; his grin would have lit up Glasgow. Taylor saw him and yelled, 'I'll get you for this, you cunt. I know where you and your wife live. Aye, and your wean and all.'

No one watching knew the effect Taylor's words had on him. They chilled him even as he kept on grinning. He got up from where he was sitting and left the courtroom, the vicious words ringing in his ears.

FOURTEEN

Buckinghamshire

KATE COULDN'T STOP THINKING about what she'd read. She'd immediately assumed the two cases were linked. But there was one thing that puzzled her, making her think she was wrong. Danielle Taylor was abducted on 4th June and it was the 7th June when Mirren disappeared. No one had seen her with a baby in Troon. She could have hidden the baby in the cottage, but surely Mirren wouldn't have left her alone while she wandered along the shore line staging her disappearance. It was too risky. No, it was a coincidence, that's all. The more mundane explanation would be the truth; Robert Taylor had murdered and hidden the body of his baby daughter. Try as she did to believe this though, it niggled her. Why was someone threatening Mirren if indeed she had nothing to do with it?

She had to find out more. There had to be a way of settling this. Kate opened her laptop and typed in Danielle Taylor. Immediately an article in one of the Scottish tabloids from two years ago popped up.

. . .

Family Sorrow Unabated

Brenda Taylor looks years older than the fifty-three she owns up to. She sits in the living room of the house she's lived in for the past thirty-five years, her two remaining children by her side. Prominent on the wall is a portrait of a baby in oils. The frilly pink nylon dress tells us this is not a recent picture of one of her four grandchildren. It is of her daughter, Danielle, who disappeared from her pram in the garden twenty-five years ago today.

'I think about her every day, pray she'll be returned to me,' she said, her voice barely audible. 'I've never moved house because I want her to come back here, where she belongs. Her son, sitting beside her, nods in agreement.

'We all do,' he adds. 'I was only four when she disappeared but I remember it well.' He looks down at his hands. 'For years I blamed myself.' His mother shakes her head but he is adamant. 'I was in the garden too, playing. I don't understand why I didn't see anything.'

'Is that why suspicion fell on Danielle's father?' I ask. Brenda agrees it played a part. 'The main thing though was he'd been in trouble before. When he was a young boy. Fighting in gangs, that sort of thing. So he was known to the police.' Her eyes fill up with tears. 'It was so unfair and it killed him in the end. He never got over being sent to the jail.'

Danielle Taylor was four months old when she disappeared from the family garden. Little Jamie, her brother, was playing nearby yet saw no one enter the garden. When questioned by the police, all he remembered was his mother bending over the pram and shouting out to his father, who was inside the house. The rest was a blur.

Robbie Taylor was arrested for the murder of his daughter a few days after she disappeared. There was circumstantial evidence against him, which, along with his confession, helped to convict

MAUREEN MYANT

him. He claimed it was an accident, that he'd dropped the baby on her head. Despite this, some thought he was innocent, including his wife. After all, Danielle's body was never recovered. The defence did their best to throw doubt on the confession, but the tapes proved there was no pressure on him. It had come out of the blue, during routine questioning. Suspicion first fell on him, and Brenda too, because they waited nine hours before reporting her missing. I ask Brenda about this.

'I told the police at the time... I thought my mum had taken her to her house to let us have a rest.' I'm unable to hide my scepticism and Brenda breaks off when she sees my face.

'You're all the same,' she snaps. 'There's women like me rely on their mothers to help them. If I'd been a lady (she put air quotes round the word) and all lah-di-dah and said I thought the nanny had her, nobody would have blinked an eye.'

I interrupt her. 'But you must admit, even if you did think your mother had taken her, to wait nine hours before telling anyone she's missing is suspicious.'

Brenda's eyes narrow, and she looks at me with hatred. For the first time I see the hard, unfeeling woman she was made out to be at her husband's trial. 'Monster Mum stands by her man,' was one of the kinder headlines. The press had been tougher on her than on the man who was actually convicted of killing his daughter. 'Aye well, the PF (procurator fiscal) was satisfied with my explanation so that's all that matters, isn't it?'

In order not to antagonise her further, I move on to what I hope is a safer topic. Taylor himself. 'And your husband? You're sure he was innocent?'

She avoids the question. 'He doted on Danielle. He was a good man.'

It's far from what was said at the time. Taylor was, to be blunt, a well-known thug, a career criminal. In spite of his wife's claims that he had been victimised by police, he was known to be a gang leader and suspected to be dealing in drugs. He was no angel.

I spoke to neighbours from the time, who told me about his terrible rages. One woman, who doesn't wish to be named, admitted to phoning social work about how he shouted at his son. 'He was always yelling at Jamie, once I heard him call him an f***ing wee b******d. It was horrible.' It was evidence like this along with the confession (which he withdrew before the trial) and unexplained blood on Danielle's Babygro that led to his eventual conviction.

I put this to Brenda Taylor and her face darkens. She swears before saying, 'I know who told you that. Lying bitch. Let me tell you, she has her reasons for doing him down and they're not the ones she'd have you believe.'

Nonetheless that particular neighbour was not the only one to condemn Robbie Taylor. No one I spoke to had a good word to say about him. But the atmosphere has turned chilly so I change the subject. 'Jamie, how has this affected you and your family?'

'Well, I'm very protective of my own children. I've seen at first hand what it does to a family to lose a child. It's something you never get over. It drives my wife mad that I pick them up from everywhere, but she doesn't understand...' He tails off. His mother takes his hand.

It's touching to see this family, who have been through so much, support each other. But in the end, I am left with several unanswered questions about Robbie Taylor, the man with the violent temper who took his own life five years after his child's disappearance. He was found hanged in his cell in Barlinnie prison. His wife claims it was depression brought on by media persecution, but perhaps it was brought on by guilt. From what I've read and heard about Taylor though, he wasn't the type to feel remorse. One thing is certain, however. Until her body is found we'll never know for sure.

Kate closed her laptop. Was this her family? They sounded... well, different to what she was used to. Rougher. They must have been furious about the article. It was a stitch up job. She imagined the journalist going into their house, full of bonhomie, and then returning to the office to write the poisonous article. It was illustrated by several photographs: one of Danielle, cradled in her brother's arms, another of the extended family, Brenda in the middle, cushioned by Jamie and a woman who must be his wife. There was also one of Robbie Taylor. A police photograph. A bold stare from a handsome but cold face. The face of a killer?

Kate googled his name, using Robbie this time instead of Robert and adding Barlinnie to the search terms. Success. The hits were mainly about his arrest and trial, but there were also several articles about his death. He had hanged himself with bed sheets. One of the more interesting articles speculated that taking one's own life by hanging is an indication of guilt. Perhaps Kate was wrong about this being her birth family and it was nothing but coincidence that this baby disappeared from Glasgow about the same time as Mirren disappeared from Troon, only thirty-four miles away. She closed the lid of her laptop. It was too much to take in; it was past two in the morning and she needed to sleep.

When she awoke it was after eleven o'clock and she was more refreshed than she'd been for weeks. Sleep had brought with it a resolve to go up to Glasgow. She had questions for Mirren's family and she was determined to meet the Taylors. She was in the middle of booking a flight to Scotland when Laura called round.

'Why Scotland? Make it France and I'll come with you. I have several days' leave to take.'

Kate didn't want to tell Laura the real reason. Her emotions were too raw. 'I've never been,' she said, 'and after all, Mum was Scottish. It's time I saw what it's like.'

'I'll tell you what it's like,' said Laura. 'Wet. Oh, and windy too. And if you do get any sun and decide to go for a walk in the country, well, count on the company of several million midges all wanting to get up close and personal.'

Kate laughed. 'I don't believe it's that bad.'

'It's worse, I'm telling you. We used to go on camping holidays there when I was a child. I needed therapy for years to get over it. Why would any parent torture their child like that?'

'I won't be going camping and I won't be near the countryside either. It's culture I'm after. The art galleries, museums, architecture.'

Laura raised an eyebrow. She hated visiting art galleries and museums. 'Well, I suppose the shopping's good.'

'So I've heard.' Kate had no intention of shopping. She had much more important things to do.

That evening after Laura left, she phoned the Fallons. To her relief, Margaret answered. Kate wasn't sure how they'd take this latest development but she thought Margaret would be easier to deal with than Aodhan. She took a deep breath. 'Margaret, it's Kate. I'm coming up to Glasgow at the weekend and I'd be really grateful if I could meet you and Aodhan. I may have found out who I am and what might have happened.'

Margaret's voice was warm. 'Of course, and please, you must stay with us.'

Kate refused. She was about to blow their world apart; no way could she accept their hospitality. 'That's very kind but I've already booked a hotel.'

'Cancel it, then.'

Kate thought quickly. 'No really, I've already paid and it's one of those deals you can't cancel.'

'Well, next time then. Did you find the adoption papers?'

Kate made a non-committal sound. 'I found out some things, yes, but I need to see you face to face because, well... .' She tailed off, unsure of what to say.

'Is everything all right? It sounds very mysterious.'

Kate tried to reassure her but her voice was stressed and their farewells were awkward.

'Well, we'll see you tomorrow, then? Where and when do you want to meet? What about lunch, there's a lovely little Italian restaurant near us.'

Kate hesitated. 'Would it be possible to come to your house? It would be better to have some privacy.' She grimaced into the phone, aware of how ominous her words sounded.

Margaret's voice sharpened. 'Kate, I'm getting worried about all this.'

'No, no. Nothing to worry about.' Kate hastened to reassure her before hanging up. She had handled this badly.

The flight was delayed. Kate wandered round the bookshop trying to find something to read; her Kindle was beside her bed. Eventually she chose a best seller, the current number two, knowing she wouldn't be able to concentrate on anything too literary.

She settled back in her seat and waited for the plane to taxi. Impossible to relax until it was safely in the air. Kate was a nervous flyer and normally would have taken the train, but a train seat booked at the last moment was twice the price of a flight. At last, they were in the air and she could stop worrying, at least until it was time to land.

The book was terrible. She had prebooked a meal – if a burger and chips counts as nourishment – and when it was served, she put the book away in the seat pocket in front of her and concentrated on her food. It wasn't as bad as she feared, and she was so hungry, she finished it all. The man next to her tried to strike up a conversation, but after two monosyllabic answers from her, he gave up. She ditched the book for the rest of the flight and tried to sleep In the little time that was left.

The hotel was stuck in the last century. Kate entered her room with trepidation. The carpet was dark blue with small rust coloured fleur-de-lys scattered across it, and the walls were papered with two different designs separated by a border at waist height. The curtains were ostentatious. The had been the height of fashion thirty years ago and they looked ridiculous. But the room was clean, and when she turned on the shower, the water thundered out.

Kate unpacked and looked at her watch. She'd told Margaret she'd be round at seven o'clock. It was two minutes past five. Too early to call a taxi, and her nerves were too jangled to read or watch television. She googled the distance. It was further than she liked but she'd decided. She'd walk.

The road outside was busy with rush hour traffic. Kate brought up Google Maps on her phone and headed off in the direction of King's Park. A drunk lurched towards her and she crossed to the other side of the main road, earning an angry toot of the horn from a speeding driver. The pavement was hard beneath her feet, and soon they were aching and there was the beginning of a blister on her right heel. She reached a bus shelter, but there was no timetable and no one waiting to ask, so she wandered on, hoping a taxi would come along the road.

Fifteen minutes later, she stopped. She was in the middle of suburbia with not a shop in sight. It was all very grand. Large detached houses, Victorian by the look of them. She looked at the Google map. Three miles to go.

Kate quickened her step. When she reached Queen's Park, she decided to get off the busy road and walk through it. There was a pond with grebes, eider ducks and far too many seagulls and pigeons for her liking. Glasgow must be nearer to the coast than she thought. Or maybe there were good pickings here. Further up the path she jumped to avoid some grey squirrels, who, she'd swear, were sitting up begging for food. Once through the park she passed a building site that had the remains of Victorian buildings in it and a new hospital, and then there were more tenements before she arrived in a suburban area. The houses were more modest than the ones she'd passed earlier. Built in the nineteen thirties from the look of them, not red-brick like London semis but roughcast and painted white. The gardens on one side of the road were steep and most had been terraced or turned into rock gardens. Another few minutes and she'd be there; she looked at the numbers, 139, 137. She was looking for 117.

The steep garden had been partly dug into to make room for a car. A white BMW, spotlessly clean, was parked there.

Kate steadied herself and climbed the steps up to the front door. She glanced at her watch. One minute to seven; perfect timing. There was no doorbell but a brass knocker. She took it in her hand and knocked four times.

It was several seconds before a young man answered the door. He introduced himself.

'Hi, you must be Kate. Come in. I'm Conor, the youngest in the family and still living at home for my sins.' His smile was genuine and Kate smiled in return, even though her stomach was churning with nerves. 'They're all agog, wondering what you've found out.'

Kate followed him into the living room, all too aware that what she was about to say would shatter them.

FIFTEEN

Glasgow

KATE WATCHED the second hand go round on the clock on the mantelpiece. Fifteen seconds before they spoke. No,' said Aodhan. 'She would never have done anything like that. She knew what it was like to lose a child. She would never have inflicted that pain on anyone else.'

Kate wanted to believe him. She did believe him. These actions were not compatible with the woman she thought of as her mother. Yet she had to know for sure. 'Tell me about her disappearance. Everything you remember. Please.'

Margaret sighed. 'She took a cottage in Troon. Tommy was meant to go with her but at the last minute she told him to stay away. I wanted to go and keep her company but she was adamant she had to be on her own.'

It wasn't what Kate wanted to hear. She longed for them to say they'd seen her every day before she disappeared, that there was no chance at all she'd stolen a baby, taken it to Troon and hidden it in the cottage she was renting there. 'Did anyone see her in the week before she disappeared?'

They looked at one another. Aodhan sighed. 'None of us

did, that's for sure. We thought of driving down one evening, just to check on her, you know, but she'd been so sure she wanted to be alone.' He shook his head.

'So, no one saw her for several days before?' said Kate.

Margaret's tone harshened. 'We must've gone over this a thousand times. The guilt we felt. It was agonising. If only we'd gone down to see her, if only we hadn't let her go alone, if only we'd looked in on her... but she wouldn't budge; she wanted to be alone.' She tucked a loose strand of hair behind her ear. 'We blame ourselves. Her parents blamed themselves. Tommy... he never got over it.'

Kate had forgotten about Tommy. Perhaps he might know something. 'Where is he now?'

'He's dead. Lung cancer, five years ago.' Margaret exchanged a glance with Aodhan. 'We didn't really keep in touch after Muireann's disappearance.' From the look of it there had been no love lost between them.

'Weren't there people who saw her? Do you know what they said?'

'The newspaper reports said that several people had seen her that day but they didn't have more to say than that.'

'Didn't I read that one man said she'd been seen walking into the sea?'

'Yes, but that was an exaggeration. We managed to speak to him ourselves. He had seen her on the beach, late in the evening. She was distressed, crying. He'd tried to speak to her but she ignored him and he thought it best to let her be. He was worried though, and went back later to have a look. There was no sign of her. He thought she'd gone home.' There were tears in Margaret's eyes. Kate was sorry to bring such pain into their lives but she had to keep probing.

'And when did you realise something was wrong?'

'When she didn't return from Troon as we expected, we went down to the cottage she'd rented.' Aodhan jumped up from the sofa and paced the floor, narrowly missing the family cat, a huge tabby that shed hairs everywhere from the look of Kate's trousers. 'The owner was there, getting it ready for the next rental. She was furious because Muireann's belongings were still there.'

'What had she left?'

'Oh, you know. Clothes, food, a book she'd been reading.'

'Nothing to hint she'd had a baby there? Disposable nappies, baby milk, that sort of thing?'

Margaret shook her head. 'There was nothing of that sort. Only what we've told you.'

'And then what?'

'We went to the police. There was a little publicity and the man who'd tried to speak to her on the beach came forward. The police decided she'd killed herself and that was that,' said Aodhan. 'My parents never got over it. For them, taking your own life was a mortal sin.' He put his head in his hands. 'The stress killed them. And this, what you're suggesting. It's not possible. Muireann would never do something like that.'

Kate rose from her chair, brushing cat hairs off her trousers. 'I'm sorry. I've upset you. I should go.' No one tried to stop her.

In the street outside she looked for a taxi. It was a main road so there should be the possibility of one, but ten minutes later she was still walking. Christ, her feet would be in shreds if she had to walk all the way back to the hotel. Behind her she heard footsteps, and mindful of all she knew about self-defence, she pulled herself up to her full height and strode ahead, showing a confidence she didn't feel. Women were more likely to be attacked if they seemed nervous, or so she'd been told at the self-defence classes

Mirren insisted on. She needn't have worried though. It was Conor running to catch up with her. His fists were clenched and his jaw tense.

'What the hell were you doing there?' he shouted. Someone across the road looked over.

Kate put up a hand in front of her in a stop motion. 'Hey. Calm down.'

'Do you know what you've done to my parents? My father is devastated. He has heart problems, this could kill him.'

'I'm sorry, Conor. I'm only trying to find out the truth.'

'My aunt spent the best years of her life bringing you up and this is how you repay her? By slandering her?'

Kate chose her words with care. 'It is an odd coincidence though.'

'People go missing every day. So what if Muireann and a baby vanished at around the same time? Around the same time, mind. Not even the same day. That doesn't make her a kidnapper.'

'She was grieving for her own child. Not in her right mind. You don't know what she was capable of, what anyone is capable of when they're in that state.'

'And you do?' He spat out the words.

Kate knew how determined Mirren was at times. Memories of sitting for hours at mealtimes over the last forkful of food, memories of trying to bargain over bedtime, memories of never getting her own way, rose to the surface like the scum on a bubbling pan of home-made jam. She pushed them down. She loved the woman she called mother, even if she had been difficult at times. As Kate grew older the difficulties got fewer and they'd had a close, loving relationship. When she was a child though, it hadn't always been easy. 'I knew her better than anyone,' said Kate. 'Better than your father, better than your mother. I don't want to believe it, I swear to you, but she might have been capable of this.'

He turned away so his face was in shadow. 'I wish you'd never come near here.'

Kate walked on. There was no point in prolonging this. She was sorry to have upset this family who had been nothing but kind, but she had things to do and only a short time in which to do them. He followed her and grabbed her arm. 'Let go,' she hissed. 'Let go or I'll scream and that bear of a man across the road who's been watching us for the past few minutes will be over like a shot.' He loosened his grip.

Kate carried on, with Conor at her side. 'You're wasting your time. I'm going to contact them.'

'Then let me come with you. You don't know these people. For God's sake, Kate, you said the man was a criminal.'

'He's dead. It's only his wife and son left.'

'I know but even so...'

At last. A taxi came into view on the other side of the road and she flagged it down. 'Oh, for heaven's sake, I'm a grown woman. I am able to look after myself.'

'Are you? I'm not so sure.'

Once in the taxi she looked out of the back window as it moved away, but he had started walking back to his home, his shoulders hunched up against the night.

SIXTEEN

Glasgow

IN THE MORNING Kate was sorry she'd dismissed his help. She didn't have the first idea about how to approach this. How *do* you tell a family you might be their long-lost daughter? She rummaged in her handbag for the article she'd downloaded from the web. It showed a picture of the house where Brenda Taylor had been living at the time. No address, but it gave the name of the area. With any luck she'd still be living there. Kate had her NUJ card and several twenty-pound notes. She reckoned some of the younger generation in the housing estate wouldn't be too resistant to bribery and she'd find out from them where Danielle Taylor's family lived.

Such ideas were always all right in theory. When she got there courtesy of an Uber, the only young people around were far too terrifying to approach, being a group of young teenage girls, straightened dyed hair falling like curtains on either side of their highly contoured faces, eyebrows like caterpillars. Maybe they looked good in their selfies, but in real life they looked like actors who'd lost their stage. Kate gave them a wide berth, but in truth she was of the wrong age and gender to attract their attention. That was kept for the two boys swaggering down the middle of the road, giving the finger to a car that was trying to get past.

Well, at least it had saved her some money. Kate started at the edge of the estate. She had the photo from the article with her, which was helpful because it showed the house was on a corner site, at the bottom of a hill, so she ruled out this particular street, which was flat. Ahead though, there was a road that looked promising. Now she was away from the terrifying teenagers, Kate took the time to study the area. It was pleasant. Semi-detached houses with small gardens. The gardens were mostly well kept, with only the occasional one scattered with rubbish. For the greater part they were neat, with mown lawns and trimmed hedges. A little unimaginative perhaps, but who was she to talk? She wasn't a gardener. Mirren would be turning in her grave at the weeds that had sprung up since her death.

In one of the tidier gardens an old man was weeding. He knelt on a yellow cushion to protect his knees. Kate watched him for a few moments then decided it was now or never.

'Lovely day for gardening, isn't it?'

He looked up, smiling. 'It is that. Are you a gardener yourself?'

'Not a very good one, I'm afraid.'

'So you'll not want to talk to me about leaf mould then?' His voice was amused. There would be no fooling him.

'I don't even know what it is,' said Kate.

'How can I help you then? I'm hoping you're going to say you need a man.' His smile broadened.

Kate resisted joining in with further banter. Best get

straight to the point. 'I'm looking for the Taylors' house. You know, the baby that was stolen all those years ago.'

'I knew you were a journalist.' He got up slowly. His pain was palpable. One of his knees cracked and he looked down at it. 'Bloody awful, this arthritis.'

Kate smiled and waited.

'So, what's the story then this time?'

'This time? What do you mean?'

'Got something to prove Robbie's innocence, have you? Because I'm telling you now, if you haven't, then forget about talking to Brenda. She swore she'd never speak to journalists again after the last one was so snidey.'

Of course! She didn't need to confront them outright with who she was. She'd tell them about the missing woman, about Mirren, and see how it went from there. And that way she'd see them close up without committing herself. She could make up her mind whether or not her theory was right before saying anything to them.

'I may have exactly that. Do you happen to know where they live?'

He raised his eyebrows. 'It's only Brenda there now, though her son and daughter-in-law live nearby. That's it across there.' He nodded towards a house a few doors up on the other side of the road.

'Thank you. You've been very helpful.' She strolled across the road, trying not to look as if she was in a hurry. The garden here was not so well kept. There was a pram in the garden, which gave Kate a frisson, but it was empty; the child must be safely inside.

The front door was ajar. Kate looked for a doorbell, but there was none. The door was one of those white plastic ones.

There was a knocker, but it might as well be made of paper for all the noise that came from it. 'Hello!' she called. 'Is anybody in?'

The subsequent stillness told Kate she was being watched. Not that she'd been aware of any noise coming from the house, but it was even quieter now. Sure enough a curtain twitched and she saw a pale face behind. She smiled her friendliest smile. 'Mrs Taylor?'

The curtain was released and she heard steps coming down the hallway, clicking on what sounded like laminate flooring.

She was in front of Kate, a tiny woman, frail and much older looking than the photo in the article Kate had found on the internet. Kate stared at her, looking for any resemblance. There was none that she could see.

'What do you want?'

Kate decided to stick to the truth as far as possible. 'My name's Kate. I'm a journalist.'

She moved to shut the door. 'I don't speak to journalists. Not since the last one stitched me up.'

'Wait!' Kate moved towards her. 'I have a theory about what happened to your daughter.'

A flash of something on her face. Fear? It was gone before Kate identified it. The door opened slowly. 'Is that right? How do I know you're not going to set me up?'

'You don't know,' she said, 'but please let me talk to you. I won't ask you any questions, at least not until I've said what I have to say.'

'All right, you've got five minutes.' She beckoned her inside. Kate followed her into the narrow hallway. It was pleasant inside. Everything very neat and tidy. Too tidy. Mrs Taylor sat down on one of two leather sofas. Kate fidgeted with her bag, unsure how to begin. 'Well?' said Mrs Taylor.

Kate took out her NUJ card. 'This is my union card. It proves I'm a journalist.'

Mrs Taylor waved it aside without looking at it. 'Who do you work for?'

'I'm freelance. I write articles and then try to sell them to magazines or newspapers. I've written for the *Guardian*, the *Independent*. Broadsheets mainly.'

Her face was blank. Kate hastened to reassure her. 'I don't write for the tabloids, the *Sun*, papers like that. It's more serious stuff I do.' It wasn't all lies. Kate occasionally wrote for these papers, though not so much now she was teaching rather than practising journalism.

Kate's mouth had dried up and her lips were cracked. She tried to moisten them with little success. Now they were face to face, she didn't know what to say. 'I know it must be very upsetting for you to talk about how your daughter went missing and what happened as a result.' She stopped, unsure how to go on. 'I'm researching for a book I hope to write about children who've disappeared, and when I was reading the articles about your daughter, I came across this.' She took out a photocopy of the *Herald* article about Mirren's disappearance and handed it to her.

Mrs Taylor got up and opened a drawer in a sideboard. She took out a pair of reading glasses. Kate watched as she read. 'I don't understand,' she said. 'What has this got to do with Danielle vanishing? This poor soul took her own life after she lost her daughter. Well, I understand that. I came close to it myself after Danielle.'

Kate was puzzled as to why she hadn't made the link and then realised. The article made no mention of the fact that it was a baby who died. She put the paper back in her bag. 'I'm sorry, I haven't made it clear. This woman who vanished, the daughter she lost, well, she was a baby. She was three months old when she died. And she disappeared three days after Danielle.'

Brenda Taylor stared at her for what seemed like hours. At last, she spoke. 'What are you saying? She took my Danielle. This... what was her name again? I've never seen a name like it.'

'It's an Irish name. You pronounce it Mirren.'

'This cunt took my Danielle?' Her voice rose. 'How do you know this?'

Kate felt there was something 'off' about the way she reacted. Almost as though she was acting.

Brenda glared at Kate. 'I'll ask you once again. How do you know this?'

Christ, she might be acting but she was damn scary. Could she be related to this woman? Kate loathed the very idea. The Fallons had been so kind and this could blow their world apart. What had she been thinking, going ahead in spite of their worries? She should have left well alone. She backtracked. 'I don't know for sure.'

'Fuck's sake. What the fuck do you mean? Did she take her or not?'

Kate didn't answer. She wanted to leave and pretend the last few minutes hadn't happened.

'You can't just walk in here and tell me someone took my baby. Does this mean Danielle might be alive?'

Surely she'd sound happier at this possibility? This was Kate's chance to tell Brenda who she suspected she was, but it was too soon, she wasn't ready, so she smiled and said, 'Yes, it's a possibility.' Her stomach was alive with squirming insects.

From upstairs there was the sound of a baby crying. Brenda

stood up. 'That's Callum awake. I'll have to go and see to him. You wait here.' She ran off to get the baby.

What the fuck was she doing? Kate had to leave now, while she had the chance. She'd return to the hotel, pack and be on her way back to London within two or three hours. Brenda wouldn't be able to track her down.

There was the sound of a key in the lock. Kate braced herself. Heavy footsteps echoed down the hallway; they sounded like a man's tread. The door opened and he entered the room. He was tall. At least six foot three. It was unbelievable that Brenda Taylor's tiny frame had produced this huge man. Kate spoke without thinking. 'Jamie.'

His eyes locked onto Kate's. He glared at her. 'How do you know my name?'

His voice – she'd swear to it – it was the voice of the man who'd phoned her dead mother. Of course it was. It all made sense now.

He took a step towards her. Kate stood up. 'I... I'm here to see your mother.'

'Oh yeah? What about?' He moved closer. He was face to face with her, way too close. He'd smell her fear. Then Mrs Taylor called out.

'Jamie, is that you? Can you come up and help me with Callum? Bring a nappy up with you. They're at the bottom of the stairs.'

The tension broke as he moved away from Kate. 'Stay there. Don't leave.'

Fuck, and she'd thought the mother was intimidating. This was ten times worse. The guy oozed danger. He didn't look like his mother, must have taken after his father. He didn't look like Kate either. She was tall like him, that was true, but his chin was weak and his eyes were brown, not blue. It didn't matter.

Kate had seen and heard enough. No way was she staying to find out what he was capable of. As soon as he was out of sight, she snatched her handbag and in two seconds was out of the door, running fast, her heart pounding so hard she felt it beating in her head. She had to get away from here. All the way to the main road she kept glancing behind, expecting to see one of them running after her. But she reached the main road and thank God, there was an empty black cab passing.

Kate couldn't face telling the Fallons how horrible Brenda Taylor had been. Instead, she sent a brief text message to Aodhan saying she'd changed her flight and was going back to her hotel to pick up her luggage. He phoned back immediately but she let the call go to voicemail where he left a message offering her a lift. Damn, she couldn't ignore that.

'Thanks for the offer, Aodhan but I've already ordered the taxi.'

'It's no problem.' He hesitated for a moment. 'Are you ok? You sound a bit subdued.'

'I'll phone next week and tell you all about it.' She wasn't being fair, he must be desperate to know what had happened. 'I didn't tell them anything in the end about what I suspect. I have to think more about what my next steps should be.'

Back at home she saw how crazy her behaviour had been. Truth was, she hadn't thought things through before going to Glasgow and she'd behaved like an idiot. Charging in on what might/might not be her birth family, ruining another family's memories of their loved one by making a wild claim that Mirren had snatched a baby when grieving for her own. The main thing that worried her was Jamie. What was he after apart from twenty thousand pounds; a nice family reunion? She doubted it. She should never have gone near them.

SEVENTEEN

Buckinghamshire

It hadn't been the best of evenings for Kate. Her work colleague, Sheena, had asked her round for a drink but Kate wasn't in the mood for small talk. She was finding it hard to get the Taylors out of her head. Several times during the evening she thought about confiding in Sheena but it was all too raw. Eventually she made her excuses and left early. Driving home, Kate agonised about whether or not to tell Brenda Taylor she might be her daughter. Her conscience told her she ought to but there was something unsettling about Brenda. There was also her son to consider. A man who walked through life surrounded by a miasma of violence. How she wished it was the Fallons she was related to. She was going to have to discuss this with someone or she'd go mad. Josie was the obvious choice. She knew and loved Mirren and wouldn't judge her, but Kate was still angry with her and didn't want to talk to her yet. She put the thoughts aside and drove into her street determined not to spend any more time fretting. When she pulled up outside the cottage however, Jack was there, sitting in his car, waiting. For a second she considered turning round but he was already out of the car walking towards her.

Kate ignored him and pushed open the garden gate. He slipped in behind her. Surely he wouldn't dare come into the house? At the door she stopped and turned round. 'What do you want?'

He raised an eyebrow. 'You,' he said without smiling, and like that, she was lost.

There was no excuse for what came next. They barely made it to her bedroom before their clothes were off, strewn on the carpet, and they were in bed, Kate on top.

Afterwards, they lay in silence for several minutes before he said, 'Is it true?'

Kate rolled round to look at him. 'Is what true?'

'That there's a new man in your life.'

She frowned. 'Where did you hear that?' There was only one person he could have heard it from and that was Laura. When Kate had come back from Glasgow she'd been upset. Laura had asked about this and Kate, not wanting to worry her, had said she'd met someone she liked but that she couldn't see a future for them.

'Your friend, Laura. So it is true then?'

'How do you even know her?' Kate had been careful not to let anyone know of the affair with Jack and he'd never met any of her friends, or so she thought.

'Through work. I have a new post in community police and she's a social worker, as you know. I see a lot of her, at case conferences and the like. She started talking about you one day, saying how you'd lost your mother and she was worried about you, that you'd been acting strangely. A cup of coffee after a case conference and I had the full story.'

Kate was furious that Laura was gossiping about her. She started to get up from the bed.

Jack tried to pull her back, but she pushed him away. 'Hey, hey. What's wrong? Have I put my foot in it?'

Kate got dressed, not looking at him. What enraged her most was that he wasn't bothered that she might be with someone else. Far from it; he was excited. She'd seen it in his eyes when he put the question to her.

'Is that why you're here? You've heard I have a new man so you decide, like the fucking alpha male you think you are, that no one else has the right to any of your women, so you fuck me to stake your claim.' Kate was on the verge of tears. She cursed her weakness in letting him in. It was hardly any time since she'd decided never to see him again. Well, this time she'd put an end to it once and for all.

'I'm sorry, it's none of my business,' he said, his voice soft.

Kate was on the point of weakening until she remembered all the nights spent on her own when they were together. She was worth more than that, as Mirren had told her several times. She stood up. 'Get up, get dressed and fuck off. It's over and I mean it this time. If you come anywhere near me, I'll tell your wife about our affair.'

He paled at that, but it was nothing compared to his reaction to her next words. 'And make sure those knickers you stole from me are back here by tomorrow. I won't be part of your fantasies when you have a sly little wank.' His reaction confirmed her suspicions and she added, 'Put them through my door in a plain white envelope, and if you don't, well, your wife will get a matching pair through the post along with an explanatory note.'

His face was rigid as he got dressed. 'I never thought you were such a bitch.'

'Well, now you know. Fuck off.'

He was out of the door in under two minutes. She locked it behind him, thanking all the powers that be that she hadn't cried in front of him. When she was sure he'd gone, she lay on her bed and howled.

After a few minutes she came to her senses. She was better off without him. She'd had a narrow escape from a relationship that was one-sided and that was on the way to destroying her. He'd never leave his wife and child and she'd been a fool to hope for so long. With shaking hands, she dialled Laura's number.

'Kate! I was about—'

'Never, ever discuss me or my business with anyone else.'

'I... what?' Laura stuttered.

'You've been gossiping about me, telling people you're worried about me since Mum died. Well, don't.'

'But I haven't—'

'Don't make it worse by lying to me, Laura.' Her voice had as much warmth in it as a bag of frozen peas.

Kate hung up when Laura began to cry. She felt guilty, but then Jack's behaviour came to mind and she was angry again. The phone rang and she let it go on to the answering machine. It was Laura, crying through an apology.

'Kate? Kate, are you there? I'm sorry, I haven't been gossiping. I was genuinely worried about you and there was this really nice police officer who I met the other day at a case conference. We had coffee after and he was so understanding that before I knew it, I was talking about you, and he asked all the right questions and it was so comforting...' She broke off and took a deep breath. 'I really needed to talk to someone and he was there. In fact, it was him who brought you up first, said he knew you slightly through work and he'd been really sorry to hear about your loss and how were you doing. I'm so sorry, I shouldn't have told him anything about you.'

Kate had talked to Jack about her friends, how her best friend was Laura and she was a social worker, what she looked like, how funny she was. The bastard had known who Laura was all along and had charmed her into betraying her. Kate closed her eyes, picked up the phone and dialled Laura's number for the second time. Laura picked it up immediately, her *hello* soft, wary.

'Laura. I'm so sorry,' she said. 'I should never have spoken to you like that. I've been had for a mug and you're right, I'm not coping. Can you come over?'

Bless her, she agreed immediately even though it was late. Kate checked there was wine in her drink cupboard. This was going to be a long night. She'd tell Laura everything. She was sick of secrets.

By the time Laura came, Kate was in bits, unable to believe how she'd treated her best friend. Why did she speak to her in that horrible way? She expected Laura to be cool with her, it was the least she deserved, but Laura never bore grudges. She breezed into the cottage as though the first telephone conversation hadn't taken place. Kate stammered out an apology.

Laura broke in. 'We'll be having none of that. I've forgotten it. You're not yourself, you need to talk about whatever's going on.' She looked round the kitchen. 'First of all, food. Good, you've got pizza. There's always room for pizza. When did you last eat?'

She'd had a skimpy ham sandwich for lunch. God knows when she last had a decent meal. Kate shrugged. 'Lunchtime?'

'Not good enough, Kate. You've got to look after yourself better than that. Let's sit down, reheat that pizza and get some nourishment into us before you start on your story.' Laura took charge of everything, getting out wine glasses, plates, cutlery, while Kate sat and watched, grateful to have someone look after her. Laura even put together a salad from the scraps in Kate's fridge. Pizza served, wine poured, she sat down. 'Eat first then talk.'

Once they'd finished eating, Kate opened another bottle of wine. 'Let's go through to the living room, make ourselves comfortable while I tell you my tale of woe.'

Laura was a good listener. She didn't interrupt in the way Josie would. She sat quietly, nodding at the right places, asking questions only to clarify things. When Kate finished, she looked at Laura.

Laura held out her arms. 'Come here, you. What a hell of a time you've had.'

Kate let herself sink into the warmth of her hug. 'It's not been the best. But what am I going to do now? Should I tell the Taylors?' Her voice caught as she said this.

Laura let her go. She didn't answer immediately but prodded at a little drop of wine that had fallen onto the side table, swirling it round until it disappeared. 'What do you want to do?'

Of course, the counsellor's response. Kate had forgotten she'd done training in counselling recently. Ask them for advice and they fling the question right back at you. The trouble was she hadn't a clue what to do, that's why she was asking Laura. Laura must have seen the irritation on her face because she said, 'I know that's not what you want to hear. You want someone to tell you what to do, the way your mother always did. And then you'd ignore my advice, like

131

you always ignored your mum's, and do what you want anyway.'

Kate opened her mouth to protest but closed it again as she realised Laura was absolutely right.

Laura continued. 'You have to work this out for yourself. It sounds as though you know what to do about Jack.'

'Yes,' agreed Kate. 'It's over. I've finally seen sense.'

'Would you have listened to me months ago if I'd told you it was going nowhere?'

'You didn't know months ago.'

'Not that it was him, but I'd worked out there was someone, and that as you never mentioned him, he must be married. I thought of saying something but reckoned you'd come to your senses in the end.'

'Oh.' Kate was chastened. 'I hadn't realised anyone suspected. Does anyone else know?'

Laura's eyes narrowed. 'I haven't said anything, if that's what you mean.'

'I'm sorry. I know you wouldn't.'

Laura didn't point out that only a couple of hours ago Kate had been yelling down the phone accusing her of that. They sat in silence for a few moments before she added, 'So you see, you'll do what you have to when the time is right.'

'Let me talk through the pros and cons with you, please.' Kate didn't wait for an answer but instead launched into trying to verbalise all the thoughts that had been churning around inside her. 'As I see it, the cons outweigh the pros. This is a violent family, criminal even. I don't know if I want to acknowledge them or not. They could harm me, claim damages from Mirren's estate.' She stopped. This made her sound petty, as though she'd forswear justice being done, so as to keep her inheritance. And like that, in that instant, it was crystal clear.

An injustice might have been done. It didn't matter if Robbie Taylor was a criminal, he didn't necessarily kill his daughter and Kate could well be Danielle Taylor. She didn't like it but if that's how it was, she had to find out.

'What are you thinking?' asked Laura.

Kate sighed. 'I have to do it, don't I? I have to tell them my suspicions. Otherwise, I'll never have peace.'

Now she'd made her decision she felt better. Laura phoned for a taxi about one in the morning, having declined an invitation to stay. They'd finished that second bottle of wine, and if Laura stayed, they'd no doubt open a third. Once she left, Kate washed the dishes before going up to bed. She was sure she wouldn't sleep, but she was wrung out by all the ups and downs of the last few hours and fell into bed, exhausted. A few seconds later, she was asleep.

When she woke up, she felt more alive than she'd done for months. She knew she'd have to plan how she was going to do this. The thought of going back to see Brenda and Jamie Taylor was not in the least appealing. And she wanted to make her peace with the Fallons. They deserved to know what she'd decided to do. It was not going to be easy, but doing the right thing is never without its difficulties.

The first thing to do was to contact Aodhan and tell him her decision.

EIGHTEEN

Buckinghamshire

MARGARET ANSWERED THE PHONE, but it was Aodhan Kate wanted to speak to. He was Mirren's brother after all. She watched the seconds tick round on the kitchen clock while she waited for him to come to the phone. His greeting was cautious.

'I'm sorry to have brought all this trouble onto you,' she began.

'Mm. I'd say it was the other way round. It was me started all this after all.'

It was good of him to say that, even if it wasn't strictly true. Jamie Taylor started it. Or it might have been Mirren, all those years ago. On impulse Kate blurted out, 'Oh Aodhan, I wish you were my uncle and Margaret my auntie. I always wanted relatives. At school I was the odd one out, no cousins, no grand-parents, no one except Mum.'

His voice was warmer now. 'It sounds hard.'

She didn't want his pity. 'No, it was fine. She was a good mother to me even if she didn't give birth to me.'

'Is that what you're phoning about, the Taylor family?'

'Yes, it is. I'm sorry but I'm going to have to go to the police. I don't know if they're my family, I don't want them to be my family, but what if they are and Robbie Taylor was sent to prison for nothing? I can't ignore that.'

'He did confess though, Kate. Why in the name of God would he have done that if he wasn't guilty?'

'I don't know. Maybe it was beaten out of him?'

'The defence tried that line but there was no evidence. It was a freely given confession made in the middle of questioning. There was a tape recording of it and the defence had it forensically examined to see if it had been tampered with. It hadn't.'

'You've been doing your research.'

His reply was exasperated. 'Of course I've been doing my research! You're not a blood relative, Kate, and I know we only met recently, but my sister loved you. You were her daughter, no matter what, and I feel responsible for you.' He took a deep breath. 'How did they react when you saw them?'

She was torn. The Taylors could be her family, but then she thought of the menace she had felt coming from both of them. 'Not great,' she admitted. 'Jamie, the son, was aggressive, and to be honest I was frightened of him so I ran away.' She told him everything then, including the calls to Mirren's phone.

'Oh, Kate, Kate. Promise me you'll go to the police first and not back to them. Or at least let me and Conor come with you.'

She shuddered at the thought. 'It's OK, Aodhan. I've already decided to go to the police. One of the things I wanted to ask you about is how to do that. Is there a local police station I should contact?'

'No, no. Everything's centralised with Police Scotland. It's all one big police force now, but back in the day it would have been Strathclyde Police. You'll need to go through their head-quarters now to get anywhere.'

'Should I phone, do you think?'

'To be honest, I wouldn't. A phone call is too easily fobbed off. Send an email or better still, a letter. That way, there's a paper trail.'

They chatted on for half an hour. Kate felt as though she'd known him all her life. There were patterns in his speech that reminded her of Mirren, frequent religious references that she recognised, which must have come from their parents: *sweet Jesus, in the name of God, mother of God.* It had always baffled Kate when Mirren had resorted to saying things like *God willing* when she never set foot in a church, but now she knew their origins, it was oddly comforting. Eventually they rang off and Kate set about thinking what to do next. She decided to write to Scotland's chief constable, stating her case. Then she thought again. Perhaps her original idea of saying she was a journalist writing a book about missing children was better. She might even get access to someone who had worked on the case originally. A quick Google search revealed that going through the courts takes forever and she wanted this settled as soon as possible.

It would be even better if she had a commission from a newspaper to write an article. That would give her greater leverage with the police. There'd been a lot in the press this summer about a child who went missing years ago and a recent breakthrough in the case. The papers never had enough stories about missing children, especially if they were white and female.

It didn't take long to cobble together a pitch: a comparison of three cases, one where the child was found after a few days missing, one where the mystery had never been solved and one where there had been a conviction. It wasn't Kate's usual style and she was unsure where it would be best placed, but in the end she approached one of the Sunday broadsheets with an idea for a substantial article for their magazine. The editor was someone she'd worked with before and she emailed her before she got cold feet. Her response was swift. A rejection.

Kate read through the editor's email, looking for signs of encouragement. Apart from a lukewarm *nice to hear from you*, there were none. Instead, phrases like *out of your comfort zone; nothing in your CV to indicate that you can do this; haven't seen any recent work of yours*, jumped out, assaulting her with their bluntness. And at the end, a stinging *why don't you try one of the tabloids?* Kate didn't hesitate to delete it permanently; if she kept it in her inbox, she'd read it over and over, picking at the scab.

It was disappointing, but there were other papers, and perhaps one of the tabloids would be a better place to look. It would need a different pitch though, something more tantalising. They wouldn't be interested in a comparison of cases. A conspiracy theory would be good if only she could think of one.

Someone knocked at the door. Kate ran to it, a smile on her face. It was sure to be Laura. The smile vanished when she saw Jamie Taylor on the doorstep. She tried to shut the door but he shoved his foot in. He looked as shocked as she felt.

'You? You were at my mother's house. What the fuck?'

'Move your foot.'

'Where is she? Muirrean Fallon. I need to speak to her. Who the fuck are you?'

Kate noticed curtains twitching in the house across the road. She shouted as hard as she could. 'Mr Harris, please, phone the police. This man is trying to break in.' She prayed he'd heard her. He must have done because he disappeared right away.

'I don't know who you are. Please go away.'

He looked her up and down. 'You know that might have worked if you hadn't come to my mother's house with a story about some woman who disappeared the same time as our Danielle. That confirmed what I was already thinking. For years I've been wondering what happened to her so I started researching. Read everything I could about the case. Did you know my da died in prison, killed himself because he was so miserable in there? There was no evidence against him, the polis beat a confession out of him. Fucking corrupt bastards.'

The venom in his voice frightened Kate. 'I... I don't know what you're talking about. Please go away.'

'Not until I get to speak to that Fallon woman. As soon as I saw that newspaper article about her going missing at the same time as Dani I knew she'd taken her. There was a big spread about her in the *Daily Record*. All about her baby dying and how depressed she was. You hear about it all the time, how women who've lost babies steal others. And then when I contacted her, she got all defensive. Now you've proved her guilt I'd say. I'm asking you again. Who are you and where's Muirrean Fallon?'

Kate cried out with relief when she saw Mr Harris coming out of his house. He shouted over, 'I've called the police. Are you OK?'

She didn't get a chance to reply. Taylor shoved her hard so she fell backwards into her hallway and ran off down the path. He was gone before Mr Harris reached her.

Mr Harris and his wife sat with Kate until the police came. They made her a cup of tea and talked about their grandchildren, telling her stories that made her laugh and forget for a moment about Taylor. The police were not long in coming. Kate had half dreaded their arrival because she feared Jack might be one of them, but she was safe from that at least.

They took the details from her, but she didn't give them his name. Perhaps she was wrong but she didn't want to discuss her suspicions about Mirren.

'Do you have somewhere else to stay tonight?'

Before she could reply, Mr Harris, or Tim as she'd been instructed to call him, interrupted with an offer to put her up.

'Oh Tim, thank you, that's very kind but I'll call my friend, Laura.'

It was over half an hour before they all left. Kate was frightened Taylor hadn't left the area so she phoned Laura and arranged to leave at the same time as the police. As she drove to Laura's she wondered if she'd managed to scare him off.

NINETEEN

Glasgow

ALEX HADN'T BEEN sure what to do about the anonymous phone call. His first instinct had been that there was nothing to go on, but after mulling it over for a while, he decided to check with his line manager, DCI Pamela Ferguson. She was a smooth-talking woman twenty years younger than him. They weren't always on the best of terms. Last year, she'd called him in to discuss his 'forthcoming retirement'. Alex smiled as he remembered the look on her face when he said he had no intention of leaving. She looked like a cat that had been expecting cream but had lapped up sour milk instead. Since then, however, she'd managed on the whole to hide her dislike. Sometimes though, she couldn't help having a dig at him, reminding him of his age. Once, she'd caught him with his eyes closed during a particularly long briefing. *Are you sure you wouldn't rather be at home watching Bargain Hunt or whatever it is people of your age do?* He hadn't dignified it with a response. He'd been up all night on a murder case and she knew it but that hadn't stopped her.

He knocked on her door and went in.

'Alex, sit down. Can I get you a coffee, a tea?'

'No thanks, Ma'am. This won't take long.' Alex told her what he had so far, which as he outlined it, seemed remarkably little. When he'd finished, they sat in silence for a few moments. He was in for a roasting for wasting her time, he could tell.

For once, his instincts were wrong. Pamela played with her pen as she talked but her face was serious. 'People in care homes are amongst the most vulnerable in our society. Leave it with me, Alex, while I think how to proceed. I'm not sure we can do anything without a formal complaint, but I'd like to discuss it further with those upstairs.'

Not what he'd been expecting. He'd just have to wait and see what happened. He strolled back to his desk, feeling a bit more optimistic. Once there, he opened up his laptop and started to scroll through his emails. His heart thumped uncomfortably in his chest when he saw it. There in the inbox was another unusual email, but this time he was ready for it. He used his mobile phone to take a photo when he opened the email. The format was the same as before.

X1CO99rrCOpupt2 @gmail.com
RE: Murderer
To: DI A.Scrimgeour@IScotland

Your all the same. Putting the blame on innocent people. Watch you're back.

Once again it disappeared within seconds of him opening it, but now he had a record. He marvelled for a moment at someone who had the ability to do such a thing but who couldn't differentiate between your and you're. He studied the email address. It was an anagram of '1992 corrupt cop'. He was right to have been uneasy. It must be to do with the Danielle Taylor case.

The problem now was what to do about it. At least now tech support should be able to block it. When he'd reported it last time they'd laughed when he told them he didn't have the email address. He probably ought to tell DCI Ferguson but he didn't want her rummaging around in his past. Maybe he'd email the anonymous sender, tell them to fuck off. Or maybe do nothing. He'd take Mark for a pint and chew the fat about it.

'Know what, Alex?' said Mark after he'd downed the best part of a pint of lemonade. 'I'd forget about it, don't tell Ferguson. Ignore it. Definitely don't reply. Whoever it is, they want a reaction.'

'You're probably right.'

'Any idea what it's about?'

'No,' lied Alex. He had no intention of spoiling a good night out by bringing up that time again. 'Haven't a clue. It'll be some nutter out there. Anyway, how are things?'

They chatted on for an hour or so before Mark got up. 'Can't take any more of these soft drinks. Next time we'll go somewhere where I can walk home and you can drive. Right?'

Alex nodded. His flat was a fifteen-minute walk away, whereas Mark's home was a fifteen-minute drive. It had been a bit sneaky of him to suggest this place knowing Mark would have to drive. Mark offered him a lift, but Alex felt it would be good for him to get a bit of exercise. He walked up Battlefield Road past the flats that were being built on the site of the old hospital. More than four hundred of them. He hoped there were going to be enough parking spaces. It was wild trying to park round here. Ach well, it was the same all over Glasgow. No point in worrying about it and people had to live somewhere.

It was a fine clear night. What a shame there was so much light pollution. It was years since he'd had a good look at the night sky. Perhaps he should take a trip up north somewhere. Far north. Iceland maybe, see the Northern Lights. He was so lost in a dream of starry nights that he didn't see the bloke walking towards him until it was too late. Whoever it was, he was in a hurry and shouldered Alex as he rushed by.

'Hoi, watch it!' shouted Alex. But the only response was a muttered *fuck off, cunt*.

He had no wish to get into a fracas so let it go. Well, if he was honest, he was too old to chase after the man, so there was little option open to him other than to carry on. It had been a vicious shove, almost knocking him off his feet, and he thought uneasily of the threatening emails. No, he was imagining things. He was only a few minutes from home now. He increased his pace, thinking of the bottle of malt he'd opened the other day. A nightcap was what he wanted, not a fight.

Alex had shaken off the feeling of unease by the time he reached home. But as soon as he opened his door it was back again. It was the smell that hit him first. Someone had posted a fucking dog turd through his letter box. Fuck, what a shitty end to an evening. It was a long time before he settled to sleep.

TWENTY

Buckinghamshire

KATE WAS DITHERING over contacting Police Scotland. She told herself she didn't know how to go about it but the truth was that now she'd had close contact with the man who could be her brother, she regretted her decision to dig into her past. She buried herself in work instead. Although term didn't start until next month she had to update lectures and deal with various administration tasks that a new term brought. The cheeseburger had given her permission to work from home on the days when she had no lectures. It saved her two hours of commuting time each day, giving her six extra precious hours. She used the time wisely, going through Mirren's belongings and sorting out papers, still hoping to find something to convince her she wasn't Danielle Taylor. She didn't want to be related to that family. Every so often, though, her conscience twinged. Could she live with herself if there had been a miscarriage of justice and she did nothing about it?

There was an air of violence about Jamie Taylor that she'd never come across before. When he'd come to her house, she'd been frightened he was going to attack her. She wished she'd never found out about her mother. She should be getting on with life, finding a partner, doing up this cottage, securing her career. Above all she ought to be grieving for the woman who had raised her, but it was hard to do so when she was so angry with her.

She made a cup of tea and settled down to read through her notes for her first-year course. She was so engrossed by them she didn't hear the telephone at first. She reached it as it went to voicemail. It was Aodhan. She snatched up the receiver.

'Ah Kate, it's good to hear your voice. How are you?' He didn't allow her time to answer before going on. 'Listen, I'm phoning because, well... I've made a breakthrough.'

'Oh,' said Kate. 'How so?'

Aodhan laughed. 'Mother of God, Kate. You sounded like Muireann there. She always said *how so*, in the exact same way. Our mammie used to say it all the time. You even have a hint of an Irish accent in there.'

Kate put on her best Dublin accent. 'Is that right, so?' It came out badly, a parody. 'Sorry,' she said. 'I won't do that again. What was it you were going to tell me?'

'Aye, you're needing to practise that.' He laughed before continuing. 'I've been doing research. There's a few old guys in the golf club used to be policemen, so I've been asking around to see what they remember about the Danielle Taylor case. A couple of them remember it well. One of them, Colin, was involved in the search for the baby's body, and get this,' he's put me in touch with the guy who was running the show.'

Kate was slow to catch on. 'What show?'

'He was in charge of the investigation at the time. Scrimgeour's his name.'

'Oh.' This was all going way too fast for her.

'Is that all you can say?'

She tried again. 'That's good.' It came out like a question.

'So, should I arrange a meeting with him?'

'Um, I don't know. Maybe?'

'It's too much, isn't it? Margaret said I should ask you first before I started meddling, but I thought...' He tailed off.

Kate came to her senses. She had to see this through. 'Aodhan, it's brilliant. It will save me so much hassle, because to be honest I didn't know where to start. Should I write to the Chief Constable, go through a lawyer or what? I hadn't a clue. So, this is great. Are you sure he'll speak to me, though?'

'Aye, of course he will. He's already agreed. We need to make a date to meet him. It's off the record, mind.'

'But will he have access to the files, the case against Robbie Taylor?'

'He says that's not a problem. So, what do you say?'

She still had some annual leave so it could be done if she went to Glasgow at the weekend and came back the following Tuesday or Wednesday. 'Yes,' she said. 'Let's meet him, ask him if he's available on Monday.'

'Will do. Margaret wants to speak to you, hold on.'

Margaret came to the phone with an offer for Kate to stay with them. She wasn't sure as she didn't know them all that well and wasn't used to staying overnight with people. It wasn't something she and Mirren ever did, as there were no relatives and few friends. Kate preferred the anonymity of hotels. She started to say no, but when she heard the disappointment in Margaret's voice, she changed her mind. 'Do you know what, Margaret? That would be lovely. If you're sure it's no trouble?'

'None at all. It'll be great craic. The rest of the family's dying to meet you and this'll make it so much easier. The weather's going to be good at the weekend so we'll have a barbecue.'

Kate already regretted saying yes. Meeting a houseful of strangers filled her with dread. But it was done now and she rang off, promising to phone later with details of her travel plans.

TWENTY-ONE

Glasgow

Every day the news was full of heatwaves in France, heatwaves in the south of England, forest fires, drought and climate change. Alex could do with some climate change here. They'd had a few nice days at the end of May and he managed to get away for a day or two and climb a couple of Munros. He'd been doing that for years but was still nowhere near the full Munro bag of 282 peaks. Ben Lawers and Beinn Glais. Two for the price of one. They were deserted the day he climbed them, surprising given the weather and the lucid blue skies, but he didn't mind. Little chance of seeing anyone he knew up here and the walk cleared his mind even though he was out of breath when he was climbing up the steep slope. But after that, the weather was its usual mediocre self. Every day was 19 degrees, or so it seemed, with the sky covered in cloud. Sometimes it would brighten up around five in the evening for a couple of hours and he'd wander round Queen's Park for half an hour trying to catch the sun and top up his vitamin D. All in all, it was a dreary, dreich summer.

There had been no more nasty emails, no more aggressive

encounters and, thank fuck, no more dog shit. He didn't fancy cleaning that up again. There had also been no progress with the nursing home. He continued to visit his mother at least twice a week. Some days she recognised him, others she recoiled from him. He never knew what to expect when he went to see her and it depressed him. What sort of life was it for her? Sometimes when she was particularly unresponsive he wondered if there was any point, but inevitably after one of these sessions she'd rally round and they'd have two, sometimes three visits with no problems at all.

He'd kept his ear close to the ground; there were no further deaths in the nursing home. Pamela had got back to him after discussing the phone call incident with her bosses.

'There's nothing to go on,' she said, no doubt parroting what the Chief Superintendent had said to her.

'What about Mrs Crawford?'

'Who's that again?'

'She's the woman who asked for a second post mortem on her mother.'

'Oh, right. Wasn't that months ago?

'Yes, but—'

Pamela started typing. 'No, there's nothing to go on. Three deaths in June. One post mortem which showed nothing. You know what I'm going to say, Alex. Leave it. There's no evidence that a crime has even been committed and we have plenty to do on actual real crimes. I can't spare anyone to look at this when there's so much else to do. And that includes you.'

She was right of course. Nonetheless he'd keep an eye on Rosebank nursing home. Step up his visits to his mother.

The phone call came as a shock. Out of the blue, someone he'd worked with years ago. 'Colin Finlay, well I never. How's it going, big man?'

'Fine, fine. Enjoying my retirement. How about you, Alex? Any thoughts of giving it up yet?'

'No. I'll stick it as long as I can.' Alex wondered as he said this whether it was true. He was fed up with the same old, same old but feared that if he left his job, he'd have nothing to do but drink. And that was not a happy prospect. 'Anyway, Colin. What can I do for you?'

He listened in disbelief as Colin told him about a young woman down south who thought she might be Robbie Taylor's missing daughter. Fucking Taylor.

'No, I don't think it's a good idea,' he said when Colin asked if he'd meet the woman.

'Well, it's up to you, of course,' said Colin. 'But the guy who told me says she's pretty determined. And the bad news is she's a journalist. She'll have pals in the press. She's mouthing off about miscarriage of justice, that sort of thing. Best have a word, see if you can head her off at the pass.'

He had a point. Meet her face to face to kill this before it grew legs. He wrote down the phone number he'd been given. He'd arrange this later, send her off with a flea in her ear.

He put down his phone feeling depressed. He'd hoped to forget about Taylor, about that awful case and its aftermath, but it seemed that fate had something else in store for him. Ah well, not much he could do about it now. He picked up a telephone message that had come in for him while he'd been talking to Colin. It was from his mother's nursing home. Shit. What now?

It was four o'clock before he managed to get to Rosebank. He parked his car. Instead of getting out though he waited for a moment to compose himself. Ms Jenkins had demanded he come immediately, that his mother was creating 'havoc'. He'd explained that it was impossible for him to drop everything and that he'd be there as soon as he could. That had turned out to be five hours later. He was in for a difficult meeting.

She was waiting in the reception area for him and summoned him to her office. Her first words were, 'I told you this was an emergency.'

He held his hands up in a placatory gesture. 'I know, I know. What can I do? We're up to our eyes in it.'

'I'm sorry to hear that but I really do need to talk to you about Mrs Scrimgeour.'

'Of course.' Alex was surprised by the mildness of her tone. Presumably she'd calmed down since this morning, or his mother had.

'Your mother has made a very serious allegation against one of the staff.'

'I see.' Alex waited.

'She claimed that one of them tried to poison her.'

Alex's thoughts immediately went to the anonymous phone call. Would this provide him with the evidence he needed? 'What did she say, exactly?'

'Nothing. She hit her, all the time screaming that she was a murderer. I've had to send the woman home. She may want to press charges.'

Alex ignored the last sentence. No point in worrying about it yet. 'Can I see my mother now, please?'

'You can, but she's been sedated.'

'I'll go along to her room anyway.' Alex was determined to see whether his mother was in fact all right. He didn't like the sound of her being sedated, although he understood why they'd done it.

'I'm going to phone social work and ask for a case conference,' she called out to him as he walked out the door.

'Make sure you give me plenty of notice so I can get time off,' he replied.

His mother was lying on her bed, but she wasn't asleep like he thought she would be. Her eyes were open but at least she wasn't agitated.

'Liz?' He tried using her first name. Sometimes this got a better response than calling her 'Mum'.

'Is that you, Ian?' Her voice quavered, reminding him that she was in her late eighties. Where had the voice of her youth gone? That strong, authoritative voice that he had respected so much. He didn't correct her. He'd found that if he did, it made her even more confused, so he made a non-committal noise.

'Oh, thank God you're here. Where have you been? The boys will be in from school soon and we need to talk about this place.'

'What place?'

'This.' She waved a hand at the room. 'This hospital or whatever it is. Why am I here?'

'You've not been well, Liz.'

'Rubbish, I'm fine, but I won't be if you keep me here any longer.'

'What do you mean?'

'They're all dying here and soon they'll get me too. One of them tried to kill me today but I punched her and she backed off.' She pulled at the cloth on her skirt, plucking at it to remove imaginary threads.

Alex sat down beside her and took one of her hands in his,

to stop her agitated movements. 'Why do you think she was trying to kill you.'

'She had a fucking needle!'

He winced at the swear word. He'd never get used to her using profanities. Hypocritical of him, he knew, with every sentence sprinkled with fuck and worse, but she was still the woman who'd washed his mouth out with soap and water when he'd been nine years old and made the mistake of swearing in her hearing. 'OK, I'll ask about it on the way out.'

'No, you bloody won't. You'll see to it now.' She half rose from her bed then sank back down, exhausted. Her eyes closed and in a few seconds she was asleep

What to do? These accusations towards care staff were nothing new. She'd made them before and she'd struck someone too. That was why she'd ended up here instead of at home where she wanted to be. That particular carer had wanted to press charges and it had taken all his diplomatic skills to stop it happening. Christ, she'd been a piece of work. She'd had the cheek to demand two grand in compensation. Luckily her son was often on the wrong side of the law and a gentle reminder of this fact stopped her in her tracks. He wasn't proud of what he'd done, but in his defence the woman concerned wasn't the only one to have bruises. His mother was covered in them. Could be she bruised easily, as the GP suggested, or perhaps she wasn't lying when she complained about the carer pinching her and hitting her. He'd been one click off buying a surveillance camera when the care package blew up in his face.

Was he wrong though to assume his mother was to blame here? What if there was someone killing old people? He had to do something.

He stayed by his mother's side for the rest of the evening,

unhappy about leaving her alone. Fortunately, he had his Kindle with him, but the thriller he was reading didn't hold his attention. The noises from outside didn't help. There was much more activity than normal, people rushing up and down the corridor. He risked a peep, and sure enough there were paramedics going into a room down the corridor. He made a note of the number of the room.

At half past six he decided to go home. His mother hadn't stirred since falling asleep, and in spite of his attempts to wake her up she remained stubbornly asleep. He stopped by the manager's room on his way out but she was nowhere to be seen. A passing worker told him she was busy because there had been an unfortunate death.

'I'm sorry to hear that,' said Alex. 'Was it expected?'

The woman, Pauline, according to her lanyard, shrugged. 'I don't know, I'm new here. But his daughter's making a fuss, says he was fine earlier.' She moved away, her face red as if she realised how indiscreet she'd been. Alex stood for a moment and looked after her. She disappeared into a room. He looked round. The door to the manager's office was ajar. Did he dare? Before he had time to talk himself out of it, he slipped inside.

He wanted to find out who was in room 10, who were their relatives. Perhaps this was one way of finding out what was going on. In a few seconds he had the information he needed. If the old man's daughter was kicking up a fuss, then... shit! What was that noise? Someone was coming down the corridor. He shoved the folder back into the filing cabinet. He sat down in the chair looking at his phone, acting bored. When Ms Jenkins entered the room, he glanced at his watch. 'I was hoping for a word,' he said.

'Not now, Mr Scrimgeour. May I ask what you're doing in my room?'

'Waiting for you,' he said, an injured expression on his face. 'I wanted to know if the woman my mother hit was OK.'

'She's fine,' said Ms Jenkins. She looked round her office. Alex could swear her nose was twitching. 'The notice on the door is pretty clear.' Her mouth was like a prune. 'Wait outside if the door is closed.'

'It wasn't closed.'

She didn't believe him but he didn't care. He had what he wanted. 'I'll see you tomorrow then, Ms. Jenkins.'

Outside he waited in the car. He knew that the deceased's daughter was in there and would be coming out soon. Now he had to think how to approach her.

In the end he had to wait over an hour for her to come out. When she did, she was alone. He had begun to fear that someone from the home would accompany her to her car. Thank goodness it was still light, and better still, he recognised her as someone he'd often spoken to in the home. A pleasant middle-aged woman, she had a kind face and an even kinder manner. What was her name again? He got out of the car as if he had just arrived and started walking towards her. Feeling like a heel, he addressed her with a cheery, 'Lovely evening,' and then when she gave him a bleak look, added, 'Are you all right? Sarah, isn't it?'

She nodded. 'Actually no, I'm not great. My dad died a couple of hours ago.'

'Oh, God. I'm so sorry. Had he been ill?'

'No, that's the thing. I mean he was old and he had Alzheimer's, but his physical health was great. I can't believe it.' A tear rolled down her face.

Alex shook his head. 'I'm so sorry.' He paused before adding, 'Maybe you should ask for a post mortem?'

'Oh, that's already arranged. The doctor who came said he wasn't happy about signing the death certificate when Dad had been so physically strong. The funny thing was, Ms Jenkins argued against it. Tried to persuade the doctor and me that it wasn't necessary.' She took out her car key from her handbag and pressed it to open. 'I'm glad the doctor insisted.'

Why would the manager try to stop a post mortem? 'I wonder, Sarah... You know I'm a detective?'

A suspicious look, then a drawn out, 'Yes.'

'I'd be grateful if you'd let me know the outcome of the PM?'

'Why?'

'My mother claimed one of the staff attacked her today. I'm a little worried about the standard of care, you know? Lack of supervision, that sort of thing.' He couldn't tell her there had been an anonymous report of murder.

'Oh, well, I hope there's nothing to worry about. I've always been happy about the care Dad received, but better be safe than sorry.' She climbed into her car. 'But I'll let you know.'

Alex was careful not to show the relief he felt. At last, there might be a way into this morass. In the meantime, he had to worry about how to keep his mother safe. He had some leave due to him. He'd contact a private care company and see if he could arrange for his mother to stay with him for a few days.

TWENTY-TWO

Glasgow

On Saturday morning, Kate settled into her seat on the London to Glasgow train and closed her eyes. This, not flying, was the way to travel. She had managed to buy a ticket that wasn't too expensive and was looking forward to a relaxing journey. She had plenty of things to do: her Kindle, the *Guardian* and a stock of food from Marks and Spencers in Euston Station. She'd brought a small piece of embroidery to work on as well. A sampler. Mirren would have been pleased, she thought. She was always trying to get Kate to share her interest in arts and crafts. It was a poor thing compared to what Mirren used to produce, but Kate was pleased with how it was shaping up nonetheless.

The train was only half full, although the reservation windows lit up on the side showed there would be plenty of people waiting to join at Preston. But that was two and a half hours away and until then she had a table for four to herself. The train jolted and they were off.

Kate hadn't thought properly about Mirren for some time. The past month had been so traumatic with one revelation after another that she hadn't processed what she thought about the possibility that Mirren was a child abductor. It was out of character. Mirren had always been so full of empathy for other people. How could she have put someone through that experience? Maybe she'd been a do-gooder, a passer-by who heard Taylor shout at his little boy and who seized the opportunity (and a baby) with both hands. She'd hated child abuse of any kind and would turn off the TV whenever anything like that came on.

A few years ago, Kate had watched a drama series on the BBC called *The Missing*. It was about a child who'd disappeared from a French bar on the night of the world cup final. His father had turned away from him for a second to watch a goal being scored, and when he looked again for the boy, he was gone. It was agonising. The anguish of the parents, the mystery surrounding the child who vanished, the inability of the father to accept the truth that his son was dead and the haunting vision of him trudging through the snow near a Russian apartment block convinced he'd found his son. It was harrowing and Kate wanted to talk about it to anyone who'd listen. Mirren wouldn't. 'What do you want to watch that sort of stuff for?' she demanded when Kate told her, for the twentieth time, she'd regret not seeing it. 'It's morbid.'

She tried to justify it, talked at length about the compassion shown by the writer for the parents' torment.

'Torment? Huh. If they'd been looking after their child properly, he wouldn't have disappeared.'

Kate had been horrified. They argued for ten minutes before Kate reined herself in. They shouldn't be fighting over a fictional family. But even after Kate apologised, Mirren muttered under her breath, 'A proper mother would look after their child, always.'

'It was the father who lost him, Mum. Not the mother.'

'Whatever. She should have known better than to let them out of her sight.'

At the time Kate had laughed it off. Mirren was winding her up, as she was prone to do on any subject, *to hone your debating skills*, she claimed. Now, with the benefit of hindsight it was more sinister, and with all Kate knew about the Taylor family it was entirely possible Mirren thought she was rescuing the baby from a horrendous life. Maybe she had. The thought was comforting for all of five minutes.

It wasn't right though, was it? No one has the right to steal someone else's child, even if their intentions are good. If Mirren had been concerned about any child's welfare, then the thing to do was to go to the authorities, to social work or the police. She'd been a social worker so she would have known exactly what to do. She would have known how wrong it was to take things into your own hands. And if she had done that, it looked as though it had led to Robbie Taylor being wrongly imprisoned for the worst of crimes. That brought Kate full circle to her doubts. Why would Robert Taylor confess – even if he did later retract it – if he was innocent?

She shoved all these thoughts aside and tried to read for a while, but concentration was beyond her. Instead, she thought about the present she'd chosen for the Fallons. It was a wall hanging that Mirren had made. She was a brilliant embroiderer, fashioning tapestries, wall hangings and bedcovers out of all sorts of materials. Kate loved this particular one and knew it was one of Mirren's favourites. It had been hanging in her bedroom.

She opened her suitcase, took it out and laid it on the table to examine it. She had taken it down from the wall last night and hadn't inspected it properly. For all she knew it was damaged or dusty and not fit to give anyone as a present. She looked at it closely. The backing was a piece of hessian about seventy centimetres by thirty centimetres. It was fashioned to be hung in landscape orientation, so it needed two lengths of thin dowelling to keep it rigid. The only thing that worried her was that it was a representation of a beach. Was that a tad tactless given where Mirren was last seen? She hoped not.

It was indubitably beautiful, part collage, part embroidery. The mountainous background was built up from felts that Mirren had made herself, dying the wool to get exactly the right shades of purple and green. The sea was silk, a greyish green the colour of the sea glass she collected. Waves were embroidered on top in silver thread. The foreground of the work was a shore; sand was sprinkled there (real with tiny fragments of shells), grass that was sewn in chainstitch, and best of all, an embroidered profusion of flowers: sea pinks, sea campion, sea bindweed with its pink and white flowers, and golden samphire. It was perfect. Kate would miss it, but it was the ideal present for Aodhan and his family.

They were coming into Preston and Kate put it away. There would be crowds joining here and she didn't want it damaged by a child's sticky fingers.

The rest of the journey passed quickly. Kate ate her sandwiches, drank tea, played peek a boo with the baby opposite and hangman with his bored older sister while their mother studied her phone with an intensity she should have been devoting to her children. When the tannoy announced they were approaching Glasgow Central, Kate gathered her things together. Her stomach was tight with anticipation. She was really looking forward to seeing the Fallon family.

TWENTY-THREE

Glasgow

As PROMISED, Margaret was waiting for her under the clock in Central Station. They left by a side door that led into a street, thronged with shoppers, as busy as any London street on a Saturday afternoon. They walked for about fifteen minutes before coming to a car park on what looked like waste ground.

'Sorry about the walk, this car park is half the price of the nearest one. You used to be able to go right into the station to pick someone up, but that stopped after those eejits tried to blow up Glasgow Airport with their car bomb.'

Kate smiled, remembering the press coverage at the time, how they'd been foiled by members of the public taking them down. Mirren had been so proud of how the locals had reacted. She hastened to reassure Margaret. 'Honestly, it's fine. I've been sitting doing nothing for five hours. It's great to get some exercise.'

Kate looked out of the window as they passed inner city waste ground and tenements before reaching the suburb where the Fallons lived. This route wasn't as pleasant as the one she'd taken when she last visited. It wasn't inspiring; the streets were dirty and tired looking and it wasn't at all like the pretty little village where Kate lived. But as they went further out it improved. Ten minutes later, they arrived at the house. They climbed up the steps to the front door where Aodhan was waiting for them. To Kate's surprise and a little discomfort, he enveloped her in a huge hug. She stood loosely in his arms, unsure what to do. She had never been a hugging sort of person.

'Sorry I wasn't there to pick you up, Kate. I'm on barbecue duty. Takes all day to get the damn thing going.'

'I've been on at him for years to get a gas one, but some people say it isn't the same.' Margaret gave him the side-eye.

'It isn't and you know it.'

The good-natured bickering went on for a few minutes, with Kate resisting both of their efforts to get her onside. 'I know nothing about barbecues,' she said. 'It's not something we went in for much. I think we had one barbecue where we invited other people. Mum, Mirren I mean, served everyone charred sausages with raw interiors.'

Margaret laughed. 'You'll get none of that here. Aodhan's the king of grilling. His kebabs are to die for, you wait. But come on, let's get you settled in your room.'

Kate followed her upstairs to a spacious attic room. It was pretty, with a stunning patchwork quilt on the king size bed. 'This is lovely,' she said. 'So much nicer than a hotel room. And that quilt. You didn't make it, did you?'

'Yes, I did. It's mainly old dresses of the girls that I cut up and kept for years until I had the time to put it together.'

Kate looked at it more closely. 'But it all matches so well.'

'Mm, yes. I have to confess that I made a lot of their clothes and I did try to buy material that I thought would go well together. So there's an awful lot of Liberty prints in there. I always intended to make a quilt one day. And twenty years on I finally did.

'Gosh. That must have cost you a fortune.'

She smiled. 'It's the most expensive bed cover known to humanity. Now, look, in here's the en suite. It's an electric shower, I'm afraid, as the water pressure wasn't good enough up here for a normal one. You work it like this.' She pressed a couple of buttons. 'Why don't you take a shower and lie down for half an hour? I'll come up and get you in time for one of Conor's famous gin and tonics before the others arrive. It'll give us a little chance to catch up.'

'That sounds perfect,' said Kate.

Once she left, Kate started unpacking. She took out the wall hanging and put it on the bed to look at. Margaret, with her sewing skills, was bound to appreciate it, and Aodhan, well, it was a memento of his sister so he was sure to like it too.

After her shower she put on clean clothes; a pair of navy linen trousers and a white top. To Kate's surprise she felt better than she had since Mirren died. She decided to have a nap and then do her make up, but as soon as she lay down, she no longer felt tired. Her anxieties about meeting new people rose to the surface. No way was she going to sleep now. She put on her make up, taking care to emphasise her eyes, her best feature, and gave a quick spin in front of the mirror. She'd do.

They were all in the garden. Margaret was weeding while Aodhan tended the barbecue. Conor was setting out plastic glasses on a trestle table. He spotted Kate and gave her a wary nod. Of course. Their last meeting was less than smooth. Kate smiled at him in return. She turned to Margaret. 'Is there anything I can do?'

'No, no. You take a seat right there. You didn't have a nap, then?'

'I'm not tired, honestly. Would you like some help with the weeding?'

She gave Kate a quick look. 'That's too good an outfit to be doing the garden in. Why don't you help Conor lay out the tables?'

Conor didn't look best pleased at this. Kate wanted to say no, but she'd offered so she approached him and said, 'Is this the drinks table then?'

'Looks like it.'

Margaret looked up at his tone of voice and glared. He tried again. 'Yes, it is. Maybe you could continue setting these out and I'll bring out the beer.' He turned and went inside. Kate took over and set out the glasses. There were a lot of them, and once again her stomach twisted at the thought of the night to come. Conor joined her. She gave him a tentative smile.

'Look, I'm really sorry about last time we met. But this is something I have to do.'

'Yeah, sure.' He handed her a pile of paper napkins. 'No hard feelings, only it's...'

'It's hard on your parents. I know.'

His mouth was set in a straight line. She was going to have to work hard with this one. She changed the subject. 'Who's going to be here tonight, then?'

He frowned. 'Only immediate family. So Auntie Roisín and Auntie Sinead. They're what's left of my dad's family. They'll bring along their husbands too. Then there's my brother Michael and the twins, Clare and Franny.'

'Oh, are they identical?'

'No, far from it. Clare's tall and blonde and Franny is small with red hair. And their personalities are the complete opposite of each other.'

It didn't sound too difficult to manage, another seven people on top of the three already here. She'd cope.

He continued, 'And of course they'll be bringing their partners.'

More people. Her face gave her away.

'It's too much, isn't it? I did say to Mum, but she was adamant you had to be presented to everyone, so they'll all be here. Along with the great aunts.'

'Great aunts?'

'Yes. They're my grandfather's younger sisters. It was a huge family. He was the oldest, would be over a hundred now, but he died, oh it must be twenty odd years ago now. I don't really remember him. Annie and Bridget were the youngest of the family. There were eleven children and they're about twenty years younger than he was. They're in their eighties now. Neither of them married. They were both school teachers back in the day. I used to be terrified of them, to tell you the truth.'

Kate smiled at him, glad to see him relaxing more. 'I am sorry, you know, for coming into your life and totally disrupting it.'

He took a swig of the beer he'd opened. 'It's been hard. I'm not going to lie. Mum and Dad have done nothing but talk about it and they are fretting about what will happen when the Taylor family find out.' He put the bottle back on the table. 'I'm sorry if I was grumpy when you first came in, but it's been worrying me.'

'It's fine,' said Kate. He was right to be apprehensive. She was worried about the Taylors too, but decided to say nothing more about them and to concentrate on the night to come. 'Tell me more about the formidable great aunts.'

He grinned. 'You'll need to wait and see, but they're one of a kind. Don't get into an argument about religion with them. I made the mistake of telling them I'm an atheist. Shit, do I wish I'd kept my mouth shut. They must have had about a hundred masses said for my soul now. And they remind me of it every time I see them, which isn't too often, thank goodness. Last time I caught Annie adding holy water to my tea.'

'What's holy water?'

'Ah, so you weren't brought up in the faith then? Good for Muireann, shaking off the shackles of religion. I wish my parents had.'

'Your parents are lovely.'

'Yeah, except when they get started on religion. I suppose it's understandable, having been brought up the way they were. Dad's worse with his Irish parents. Mum's more liberal, but still...'

'You haven't told me what holy water is.'

He made a face. 'It's water that's been blessed by a priest. It's used for baptism and also it's in little fonts at the entrance to churches. You dip your hand in it then make the sign of the cross.'

'Sign of the cross?' Kate laughed at the expression on his face. 'No, don't tell me. It sounds ritualistic.'

The doorbell rang and he moved to the window, 'Shit! It's Annie and Bridget. They're early and we're only half ready. If you take the rest of the stuff out into the garden, I'll settle them in. I promise they don't bite.' It was Kate's turn to make a face and he reached out and touched her arm. 'This is all too much for you, isn't it?'

'I'll be fine. But please don't leave me alone with them. I know nothing about religion and I'm frightened they'll exorcise me.'

The doorbell rang again and she told him to go. She was

happier now he'd thawed out more. Outside in the garden, Margaret had stopped weeding. She looked flustered and Kate overhead her hissing at Aodhan about his aunts' timekeeping. 'Don't they have watches? I said six o'clock and it's not even five thirty!' He shushed her as two elderly women joined them. 'Where is she then?' said one of them, and Margaret beckoned to Kate.

Two women, neither of them taller than five feet, stood by her side. Kate suppressed a smile at the thought of six foot three Conor being terrified of them. They looked like sweet little old ladies. White hair, gentle faces. 'Annie, Bridget, this is Kate.'

Kate held out her hand but they ignored it. One of them turned to Margaret. 'She's no relation of ours. She doesn't look in the least like Muireann.'

'Annie, I've told you a hundred times. This is Muireann's adopted daughter.'

'Adopted? What would she need to adopt one for? Especially a great big gallumphing girl like this. Sure, hasn't she got that dote of a baby?'

Margaret raised an eyebrow at Bridget, who mouthed *sorry*. Margaret took Annie by the arm and led her to a chair, all the while talking to her in a soft voice. Kate was left with Bridget.

'I'm so sorry,' said Bridget. 'Alzheimer's is a terrible thing, so it is. I thought she was having a good day but I was wrong.'

Kate swallowed. 'It must be very hard for you,' she said.

'Ah, it is, it is. But God sends these things to try us.'

Conor came over with two drinks. 'Here we go, Auntie Bridget, ninety percent gin, just as you like it.' He gave Kate the other one.

Bridget took the drink from him and downed half of it in one go. 'Jesus, Mary and Joseph, I feckin needed that, so I did.

Your auntie Annie'll be the death of me, I swear to God.' She took another gulp. 'Honest to God, Conor, I never know where I am with her. One minute she's here with me in the present, the other she's back in Galway, a babby wanting her mammy and daddy, and then she's jumping forward thirty years, thinks she's back in the classroom. There's no keeping up with her. She was fine earlier. I explained all about Kate to her and I thought she'd taken in all in but no, not at all.' She smiled at Kate. 'She's only gone and told your woman here she wasn't part of the family.'

'Honestly, it's fine,' said Kate. 'And after all, I'm not part of the family.'

Bridget frowned. 'Nonsense, of course you are. Sure and didn't Muireann go and adopt you, so?'

Conor shot Kate a warning look. Kate nodded, not trusting herself to say anything else.

'Come on, Auntie Bridget. Let's find you a seat. Conor guided her over to where her sister was seated, eyes closed.

'Jesus, Mary and Joseph,' she said. 'Don't put me with that one. Sure, and don't I see enough of her every day. Leave me with Kate.'

'Kate's helping me with the food. You'll catch up with her later. And if there's no one else to speak to, well, you shouldn't turn up half an hour early and catch us on the hop.' He pretended to duck as she took a friendly swipe at him.

Conor re-joined Kate and they went into the kitchen. Kate put her untouched drink on the worktop. 'They don't know, do they? Not the full story.'

Conor shook his head. 'God, no. Mum and Dad were arguing about it for days, but in the end, they agreed it was best not to tell them the full story. You've seen how Annie is, she doesn't know what day it is, and Bridget, well she has enough to worry about.'

'Everyone else though, they know?'

'Oh yes. Sworn to secrecy in front of the old aunties though. But yes, they know it all.'

Kate picked up her drink and sipped it. It was far too strong and she looked round for the tonic water. Conor handed it to her.

'Sorry. Bridget's a fiend for her G and T. I'm used to making them nuclear strength for her.'

They settled down to preparing a fruit salad for dessert. Margaret came in at one point to check on their work before slipping upstairs for a quick shower before the rest of the family were due to arrive. When she came back downstairs fifteen minutes later, she took the knife from Kate's hand. 'I was going to do that. It's shocking the way we've put you to work. And you our guest.'

Kate was touched that they had welcomed her into their house and entrusted her with helping with the food, and wanted to say so, but she wasn't good at expressing these sorts of thoughts, so she mumbled that she was fine, which Margaret ignored, pushing her out into the garden with Conor. 'Go, circulate, and keep an eye open for the doorbell.'

'Not sure you've got that one right, Mum, but we'll do our best.'

The garden was laid out with a mish mash of tables and chairs. The patio was too small to take them all, so some were on the lawn. Conor steered Kate towards the back of the garden, ignoring Bridget's imperious hand beckoning them towards her and her sister. There was a camping table there with four garden chairs set out around it. It was beneath a rowan tree where it was pleasantly cool. Kate sat down.

'Ah, there's the door. Stay here and I'll be back in a minute.' Conor ran off.

Kate studied her drink, sensing the two older women watching her. She was terrified they'd come over and she'd be stuck with them for the evening, trying to avoid saying anything out of turn, but Conor returned with a child under each arm, followed by a man who was obviously his brother, along with a harassed looking young woman. 'Kate, this is my brother, Michael, his partner Isabelle, and these two little monsters,' he set down the squiggling toddlers, who immediately ran off indoors to their gran, 'are Theo and Max.'

Kate's tongue was stuck to the roof of her mouth. An evening of small talk ahead of her. Why had she agreed to this?

Isabelle broke the awkward silence. 'Kate, great to meet you. I have a lot to thank you for. You have single-handedly made the entire Fallon clan forget their mission in life.'

Kate tried a smile. 'Oh?'

'Yup. Before you breezed into their lives with what frankly is an *amazing* story, it was all, *Michael when are you going to make an honest woman of Isabelle? You can't go on living in sin forever.* Honestly, you'd think we were child murderers the way they go on, especially the two old witches. And it's me that won't get married, not Michael. He'd be down the aisle in a shot. But since you've been around – not a fucking word.'

'Izzy! The children will hear you.' Michael hushed her.

'Oh, fuck that! They don't understand and Kate doesn't mind, do you?'

'Fuck, no.'

'I do believe we're going to get on,' said Isabelle, pouring herself another drink.

From then on, the evening sped up in the mysterious way that happens when everyone is having a good time. One minute you're having your first drink and the next everyone is getting up to go. Kate looked at her watch and saw that five hours had passed. She was surprised at how much she'd enjoyed herself despite her earlier fears. Everyone had been so welcoming and even the old aunties turned out to be not half as intimidating as Conor had made out. Michael and Izzy left first as they had to get the children to bed. Not long after, Clare and her partner Lorna went, and shortly after them Franny headed off home saying she was on an early shift in the morning. She worked as a hospital registrar and was very serious compared to the rest of her family.

Kate sucked up the atmosphere. The affection the family had for each other was palpable, even though Bridget sighed with impatience every time Annie asked about Kate.

'This is Kate, Muireann's adopted daughter.' And each time she said it, they had the same argument they had when they arrived. Out of nowhere Bridget launched into an out of tune version of 'I'll take you home again, Kathleen'. It reminded Kate of an episode of *The Royle Family*, but she found it very touching listening to the elderly woman's quavering voice.

All in all, Kate was happy to have met the family but it made it even harder to understand why Mirren had left them the way she did. Aodhan came over with another drink.

'Are you OK? You look very sad.'

'I was thinking about Mirren. Leaving you all behind. She must have been very disturbed after the death of her baby.'

'Oh you've no idea,' said Margaret, who had pulled over a chair to join them. There were only the four of them left now that Aodhan had managed to get a taxi for his aunts. 'I've never seen anything like it. Inconsolable, that's what she was. And I understand why. She'd waited years for a baby, then there was the trauma of the birth and being told she'd never have any more children. So she was in a vulnerable state anyway...' She tailed off.

Aodhan took up the story. 'She was that. To be honest I was never that convinced that she hadn't taken her life—'

'Really? You never said.'

'Ah well, you know what my parents were like. They wouldn't countenance the thought and so I never dared say anything.'

'But they've been dead, what? Twenty years?'

'I know, I know, but it was too painful to talk about.' He fell silent.

'It must have been awful for her to lose a baby like that. For the whole family. And losing your sister too.'

Aodhan nodded, his lined face filled with sadness. 'It was a terrible time. I—'

Margaret interrupted. 'Now let's not get maudlin. Tell us about Muireann, Kate. Was she happy? Did she ever meet anyone else? What did she do for a living? I imagine she carried on painting.'

'Whoah, Mum. What's with all the questions?'

'It's OK. I'm more than happy to talk about her, but first I have something for you. It's upstairs, I'll go and get it.'

By the time Kate returned, someone had lit the chimenea, and flames flickered as the kindling came to life. 'I've brought you this,' she said, handing over the tissue-wrapped wall hanging to Aodhan. If you like it, I'll send you more. You asked how Mirren made a living. Well, she made these.'

He opened the loosely wrapped parcel and took out the wall hanging. 'We need light to see this by,' he said, going inside and putting on the outside light. He laid it on the table and studied it. 'Ah she was an artist, right enough.' He turned to Margaret. 'This is as good as if not better than her paintings, don't you think?'

She examined it closely for a few moments. 'It's stunning. I love it.'

'Her work was very popular,' said Kate. 'They were sold in some of the better galleries in London. I knew she was an artist but I always thought of her as a textile artist, not a painter. I never saw her paint.'

'Oh, she was beginning to make a name for herself, all right. It was always seascapes she did, similar to this but in acrylic mostly, although she did watercolours too. I think I remember her doing a textile course at some point but I never saw her embroider—'

Margaret interrupted him. 'Look, she's even sewn in a tiny mermaid, like the ones she put beside her signature on her paintings.'

Margaret pointed it out to Kate. It was tiny, no more than a centimetre. The fish tail was done in silver thread like the waves, so it was easy to miss. 'I've never noticed that before,' Kate said.

'She did it because of her name, you know.'

'What do you mean?'

'Muireann means 'of the sea', so she used the mermaid to identify herself along with her signature. As I said, she was beginning to be known for her paintings, on the verge of success. Much to Tommy's chagrin.'

'She never mentioned him to me. I used to ask about my father but she always avoided the question, at least when I was young. Although of course, he couldn't have been my father.' Kate was confused now. Too much to drink. 'When I was old enough, she told me I was the result of a one-night stand and she didn't know his name.'

'Didn't that bother you? I mean I know you weren't her child, but you didn't know that at the time.'

Kate considered this for a moment before answering. It hadn't worried her at the time because they'd been so close, but now she questioned why Mirren didn't tell her she'd had a long-term partner. She'd been with him for over twenty years. The answer was obvious; she didn't want Kate rifling around in her past. 'No,' she said, 'it didn't worry me. You have to understand, we were very close and I adored her, even though there were times when she was difficult. I did ask about my father, especially when I was younger, but she always closed off the subject and eventually I took the hint. Later, she told me she didn't know his name and didn't care because she had what she wanted. She gave me the impression she had set out to get pregnant and that the means and the man were irrelevant, so after a while we didn't talk about it.'

'But surely it was on your birth certificate?'

'I've never seen the full certificate. I only have the short-form one and that only shows my details.'

'What! But you must have seen it when you applied for a passport. You need the full certificate for that.'

'Oh, Mum did that for me.' As Kate said the words, she realised how naïve she'd been. When she first applied for an adult passport, Mirren had avoided giving her the certificate, eventually saying she'd take care of it. Kate had been busy at the time and was happy to let Mirren do all the work. She steered them back to the subject of Tommy.

'Tommy was her art tutor. She was a first-year student at Glasgow School of Art when they got together. It caused a scandal at the time, but nothing to what it would be these days.

He got away with it because in those days you did. Nowadays he would be fired for gross moral turpitude.' Aodhan paused to sip his beer. 'People were unhappy about it, my parents especially. She was only seventeen and he was thirty- two when they moved in together.'

'Were they happy?'

'Yes, up to a point. But he was jealous of her success, and then there was all the strain over trying to get pregnant. He'd tell her she was working too hard and that was why they'd never conceived. She stopped painting so much and he was certainly happier. He hated it that she was more successful than him.'

'Did he have any success?'

'A little, but he never made it into the big time. His paintings sold, but for very little and certainly not enough for him to make a living. It bugged him that her paintings were successful even though she wasn't a fulltime artist.'

'It's odd though that she gave up painting when she left Scotland.'

Margaret shrugged. 'I imagine it was because she didn't want to be found. She had a very distinctive style, and an art specialist might have recognised her work. I don't understand why no-one recognised her name though.'

'She worked under the name Mirren O'Neill. Told me it was her mother's maiden name. That at least was true.'

'If only we'd thought to look for her under different names. But any searches we did focused on her real name,' said Aodhan.

This was a lot for Kate to take in. What a shame that her partner had been jealous of her work and that she had to stop doing the painting she loved. Whether the embroidery was an adequate substitute or not, she'd never know. Mirren certainly had made enough money from them and the workshops she sometimes held in the cottage and she never complained, but was it enough for her? She hoped the Fallons had some of her paintings. She'd love to see them but wasn't going to ask tonight. She stood up and made her excuses. Something flashed in Conor's eyes. If she wasn't wrong, it was disappointment. That was a complication she wasn't looking for. Time for bed.

TWENTY-FOUR

Glasgow

KATE WOKE at six to the sound of birdsong. She picked out the chirping of sparrows and the more tuneful song of a blackbird, but the rest were beyond her. It was too early to get up; she didn't want to go downstairs before everyone else was awake, so she picked up her book. The story didn't engage her and before long she drifted off to sleep. When she awoke for the second time there were definite sounds of movement from below, so she got up and showered.

Downstairs there was only Conor, messing about in the kitchen. Her stomach tensed as she remembered the look he had given her last night, but she must have imagined it, for he greeted her with a cheery grin and waved a frying pan at her.

'I'm going for the full heart attack, what about you?'

Kate's normal breakfast was Greek yoghurt, muesli and blueberries, but she nodded, thinking something more substantial would help soak up yesterday's alcohol. 'That would be great.'

He set to work. There was no sign of his parents. 'Are your parents still in bed?'

'Shit, no. They're away to church. Be thankful you weren't up earlier or they would have invited you along.'

'Oh, that's a shame. I'd have loved to have gone.'

His face. She laughed. 'Gotcha.'

He flicked a tea towel at her and missed.

'Not a very good shot, are you?' Kate was flirting, a big mistake. She stopped. 'It was really nice meeting all your family. You're very lucky, you know.'

He concentrated on breaking an egg into a cup. 'One egg or two?'

'One please.'

Eggs sorted, he turned his attention to Kate. 'There are disadvantages, you know.'

'Such as?'

His expression darkened. 'Too many people meddling in your life. Instead of saying things straight to my face my parents go to the aunts, complain about me and get them to do the dirty work.'

'What do you mean?'

'Well, you know. When are you getting married, when are you getting your own place to live, why don't you get a proper job, that sort of thing.'

'Oh, do you have a girlfriend then?' Kate kept her voice casual.

He shook his head. 'Broke up a year ago. They all thought it was my fault.'

'And was it?'

A shrug. 'She didn't want children. I do.' He got plates out of the cupboard and piled the food onto them. It smelled delicious. 'They all assumed I was a commitment-phobe, and you've no idea the grief I got about it.'

Kate sliced into her egg and it oozed beautifully over the sausage. 'Why didn't you say something?'

He sighed. 'Stupid male pride, I suppose. I didn't want them to know she didn't want children, and I didn't want to discuss it with them. Everyone assumes it's always women who get broody. Well, men do too, and when Michael's two came along, well—' He broke off.

'You don't need to tell me if you don't want to.'

'No, it's fine. I'm over it now. But there are times I wish... Anyway, she's with someone else now and they're getting married so that's that. No doubt she'll be pregnant within the year.'

The hurt was there in his eyes even now. Kate knew what it was to be rejected, but telling him would reveal too much. She didn't want one of the first things he learned about her to be that she'd been involved with a married man, so she carried on eating. 'This is delicious.'

He turned away. 'All in the ingredients,' he said.

Her lack of response put an end to his confidences. They finished eating in silence and he put everything away in the dishwasher, leaving the kitchen spotless. Jack never offered, not once, to either cook or clean up afterwards, happy to leave it all to Kate. She opened her mouth to say something more sympathetic, but Conor got in first.

'Well, if it's OK, I'll leave you. I'm off to see friends for the day. Maybe see you later, if I don't get waylaid into the pub.'

Kate smiled, already regretting the things she should have said. 'Great, yes. Maybe see you later.'

179

It was after twelve when Margaret and Aodhan returned. Kate didn't want anything to eat, but she sat with them as they ate a light lunch in the garden. It was a beautiful day, warm but not too hot in the sun, and windless. She took a photo to send to Laura, who was always full of doom and gloom about the weather in Scotland. They suggested a walk, so she changed into something more suitable.

They went to Loch Lomond, less than an hour's drive away. They drove through the city for about thirty minutes, but once they left the suburbs behind, they were in beautiful countryside to the north. They stopped briefly at the Queen's View, which overlooked the hills round the loch.

'Next time we're here, we'll take you to the Whangie, which is not far from here. It's a rock formation that legend will have you believe was formed by the devil's tail slicing into the hillside.'

The name was like something a porn star would call his penis, thought Kate, but she kept it to herself. This couple were a little more conservative than Mirren had been. She would have enjoyed the joke though.

Twenty minutes later, they arrived at Balmaha, a small village on the loch. A short climb took them to the top of Conic Hill, part of the West Highland Way.

'You're lucky to have all this so near you.'

Margaret looked a little smug as she smiled her agreement. 'It is nice, isn't it? What's it like where you live?'

'Nice is exactly how I would describe it. Blake probably had it in mind when he wrote 'Jerusalem'. England's green and pleasant land. But it doesn't compare to this. This, this is gorgeous.'

They stopped for coffee and scones on the way back and arrived home around six o'clock. Kate was disappointed that

Conor was nowhere to be seen but told herself it was for the best. He was very attractive and Kate was pretty sure he liked her, but she wasn't going there. Too complicated.

After supper she asked them what was going to happen the next day. 'Where are we going to meet this police officer?'

'In a café in town. At ten o'clock. We thought it was best to keep it informal at this point.'

Fair enough, but a café sounded too casual. What if he didn't take her seriously? She wanted to say something, but they'd done so much already it seemed churlish to criticise their choice of venue. She was nervous about the next day and tired from the walk and the socialising the day before. An early night was in order. She made her way upstairs and cursed as the front door opened and Conor came in. A nightcap with him would have been the perfect end to the day. But it wasn't to be. She undressed and got into bed. For once she had no trouble falling asleep.

TWENTY-FIVE

Glasgow

HE WAS WAITING outside the café. An overweight man in his late fifties. There was a grey tinge to his complexion that suggested a poor diet.

He nodded as they approached. 'Alex Scrimgeour.'

His unsmiling greeting unsettled Kate and immediately she was on edge. She mumbled her name, and Aodhan and Margaret introduced themselves.

'Shall we go in?' He pushed open the door. The café was minimalist and cool inside. The seats had been built in around the sides and were made of plywood. A few cushions were scattered around. It was less than comfortable and had an air of desolation about it. Once the waiter had taken their order Scrimgeour turned to Kate. Not a hint of a smile.

'You already know, I presume, that I was the chief investigating officer in the Danielle Taylor case. What did you say your name was?'

Kate's hackles rose but she managed to mumble her name.

'So, how can I help you, Miss Fallon?'

She decided to charm him, smiling her prettiest smile,

'Please, call me Kate.' It had no effect on him whatsoever. He stared at her, waiting for an answer. She told him what she'd found out so far. He listened patiently enough, not interrupting until she finished. When she'd done, he pressed the tips of his fingers together making an archway.

'I see. And what are you expecting from this meeting?' His voice was as far from encouraging as Novoskobirsk was from Glasgow and equally cold.

Kate's own voice wouldn't have warmed up a one-person tent. 'In my opinion, Mr Scrimgeour, a miscarriage of justice has been carried out, and I expect you to re-open the case.' Christ, what was she doing? She sounded like an entitled, middle-class bitch. His answering smile stopped short of his eyes.

'It's Detective Inspector, and as for re-opening the case, no chance. It's a waste of time.'

Kate sat back in the uncomfortable seat. The plywood was cold on her thighs. She wished she'd worn trousers. 'What do you mean?'

'I don't have to explain myself to you. The case is closed. We got a conviction.'

'But what if he was innocent? My mother, Mirren, she disappeared at about the same time as Danielle. She was grief stricken, out of her mind. I think she may have taken—'

'I know what you think but you're wrong.' He sipped his tea. 'Look, Miss Fallon, please believe me when I say I'm one hundred percent sure that Danielle Taylor was killed by her father. He was a right nasty piece of work.'

'That could be said about thousands of people, it doesn't mean they're murderers.'

'I worked on this case day and night. Let me go through it with you.' He started on the tale of how his suspicions were raised because the parents waited so long to report her missing. Kate interrupted him, arguing what she'd read in the magazine article, that Mrs Taylor thought her mother had taken her. He shook his head. 'I've been involved in too many missing children cases in my career. In only one other case did I ever come across parents who waited hours before reporting their child gone. We found the wee boy buried in their garden.'

Kate made her voice as neutral as possible. 'Perhaps people were ready to see the parents' guilt because of their background.'

'You mean because he was a convicted criminal. Nice try, but in the other case the parents were as middle class as they come and arrogant with it. Thought they were smarter than us. No, as I said, every parent who loses a child like that is frantic.' A pained look passed over his face but it quickly disappeared and he pulled himself together. 'In both of those cases that urgency wasn't there. It was obvious the parents knew what had happened.' He leaned towards her. 'You should leave well alone. You don't know what you're meddling with.' Kate reeled back, stunned by the hardness of his tone.

Margaret came to her aid. 'But surely a DNA test...?'

'Out of the question.'

'But—'

'You're wasting your time. Go and see Mrs Taylor, see for yourself what she's like. See how she reacts when you ask for her DNA. She'll not agree. I can guarantee it.'

'What makes you so sure?' asked Aodhan.

'Look, the evidence was circumstantial, I'll give you that.' He started to go through it bit by bit. Kate listened, her certainty lessening with each piece of evidence.

'And then we found the Babygro. Stuffed in a plastic bag. It had blood on it. Danielle's blood, as it turned out.'

'But there might be an innocent explanation for that.'

The look Scrimgeour gave Kate was pitying. 'Mrs Taylor lied about it. Said it was her blood, that she'd cut her finger and forgotten about it. Well, we tested it for DNA of course and it was Danielle's. No doubt about it. If there had been an innocent explanation, why would she do that?'

Margaret touched Kate's arm, 'Are you OK?'

Far from it, she was close to tears. 'I'm fine. Well, thank you for your time, DI Scrimgeour, but I assume there's nothing to stop me asking the Taylors to do a DNA test?'

'You're free to do as you wish, but I would be wrong not to warn you about them. They are not good people.'

There was no point in discussing it further. Kate thanked him for his time and he surprised her with his response. 'I'm sorry not to be more encouraging, Miss Fallon... Kate. I understand how you must feel, not knowing who you are, who your parents are.' He left without a backward glance.

Kate blinked back tears. Despite everything he'd said earlier, the unexpected kindness touched her. She played with her tea.

'What do you want to do now?' asked Margaret.

'I don't know. He was... very sure of himself.'

'Maybe he's right though? Taylor did confess after all.'

'He retracted it.'

'Hmm.'

Kate needed to be alone. 'If it's all right with you, I'd like some time to myself?'

Aodhan and Margaret looked at each other. 'Of course, how long do you need?'

'I honestly don't know. I want to walk around and absorb what Detective Inspector Scrimgeour said. Maybe take a look at the shops too. Listen, why don't you go home? If you tell me what bus to get, I'll manage fine.'

'Well, if you're sure.' Aodhan had the air of a man given a get out of jail card. Kate knew Margaret was itching to go with her, but she didn't push it. 'It's easiest if you get the train to King's Park Station. They're every half hour or so. Do you remember the way to Central Station?'

'Yes, I'll be fine. You go on home. I'll call you when I'm on the train. And thank you for coming with me this morning.'

Kate paid the bill and left the café and its uncomfortable seating behind. Once out in the street she looked around. She was in a side street, but up ahead there was a wider street that looked promising. She was dithering about which way to go when Margaret ran up.

'Buchanan Street, Princes Square, you have to go there. It's that way. John Lewis is at the top of the street. And they're all near the station.' She pointed to the left.

Kate thanked her and made her way along the street until she found herself in the pedestrianised area of Buchanan Street. She picked out Princes Square without too much trouble. It was a small, beautiful shopping centre, filled with exclusive shops that were too expensive for Kate, but the art nouveau style décor was stunning. She left the square and made her way towards John Lewis. It was in another centre, this one much more mundane but with useful shops like Boots in it. Kate went in and browsed the offers, buying some make up. As she wandered round, she spotted something that stopped her in her tracks. She picked it up, heart beating as fast as the wings of a sparrow in flight. A DNA test. Did she have the nerve to contact the Taylors again?

TWENTY-SIX

Glasgow

ALEX LEFT THE CAFÉ, his mind in a turmoil. The meeting with Kate Fallon had unsettled him. He'd thought he'd cope, but seeing her face to face, hearing her defending that fucking, sick bastard; it was too much. The meeting, which he should never have agreed to, had brought back bad memories. Memories he thought he had under control. But now they came flooding back in such detail it was as if he was reliving it. Fuck, he needed a drink. He walked into the nearest pub and ordered a double whisky. He looked around to make sure there was nobody he knew and then ordered another before finding a seat as far from the bar as possible. Two doubles, that was his limit these days. He sat down and allowed himself to remember.

It had been hot that May. He was worn out from so much overtime. Sandra had refused to return to work after her maternity leave and it meant that their finances were strained. He'd broached the subject one evening, asked her if she had thought about maybe taking some part-time work. 'You could job-share,' he said.

She'd barely looked up from her magazine. 'No, I don't think so.'

'Sandra,' he said. 'We're skint. We bought this house when we had two salaries.'

She'd insisted on moving because a flat was apparently no place for a baby. Now they were stuck with a money pit. It was a beautiful house, no doubt about it. Red sandstone, in the catchment area for Jordanhill School and near Victoria Park. But, and it was a big but, it needed everything done to it. Mortgage rates were at an all-time high Over fifteen percent now. Bloody Thatcher. And the day before he'd spotted a thick, white mushroom in the attic.

'We've got dry rot, he said. 'That could cost thousands to fix. We just don't have the money.'

'Do more overtime,' she said and turned back to her magazine.

The row that followed was spectacular. She'd smashed a whole dinner set. They weren't speaking when he went to work the next day. So it was a surprise when the duty sergeant buzzed through to say she was on the telephone. 'It's Sandra, he said. 'She sounds a bit upset.'

He was abrupt with her when he answered. 'What is it? I'm busy.'

He wasn't able to make out what she was saying. Her sobs were terrifying; Mairi was the only thing he heard. Bile rose to his throat; he swallowed it. 'What about Mairi? Is she all right? For God's sake, Sandra, tell me.'

He'd got it out of her bit by bit. She'd been tired, needed to nap. They'd been out in the garden. Mairi was asleep; she didn't want to disturb her so she left her in her pram. 'I set the alarm to go off in fifteen minutes,' she cried. 'But when I got up, she was gone.'

'What do you mean, gone?' He could scarcely say the words. His hands were shaking and he thought he might vomit.

'Someone's taken her, Alex.'

His immediate feeling was one of relief. He'd thought she meant that their precious child had died. But that feeling lasted only seconds. She might not be dead but she had gone. Who could have taken her? Who would steal a sleeping child? It wasn't long before Danielle Taylor came to mind. Was he wrong about Robbie Taylor having killed his baby daughter? Was there a pattern here? Two babies taken from their prams within a year. Maybe Taylor was innocent after all. Or perhaps there was another explanation. Taylor's chilling words at the end of his trial came to him: *I know where you and your wife live. Oh, and your wee lassie too.* Taylor was behind this, he knew it in his bones.

They wouldn't let him have anything to do with the case. Sent him home to take care of his wife. That was a joke. He couldn't bear the sight of her. What the fuck had she been doing leaving Mairi alone in the garden like that? *I was tired,* she kept saying between sobs. As if that was an excuse, as if he cared. All that mattered was his missing child. He should try to comfort her but *I was tired?* That was no excuse. There were police everywhere, questioning him, his wife. Now he understood the frustration of parents in cases like this.

His DCI came to see him. This was it, he thought. She'd been found. Dead? Alive? The DCI was stony faced. Alex braced himself.

'Sit down, Alex.'

Sandra was in bed. She should be here. 'I... should I get my wi—'

Nick cut him off. 'This concerns your wife.'

'What? What do you mean?'

'Did you know Sandra was having an affair?'

Alex stared at him. 'What? No of course she wasn't. Where did you get that from?'

'Your neighbour across the road. Says she's seen a man coming and going for the best part of a year now. Always in the afternoons. He was there at the time Mairi disappeared.' Nick scratched his nose. 'Thing is, Alex. She identified him.'

'I don't understand. So, has this man taken my daughter?'

It was Nick's turn to look baffled. 'No. No, definitely not.'

'Why are you so fucking sure?' Alex was shouting now. 'Taylor put him on to it. Got him embroiled with my wife, got him to take Mairi. He threatened me. You know he did.'

'The affair's been going on since before Taylor was convicted. Alex, I'm sorry to have to tell you this, but the man is one of ours.'

There were words coming out of Nick's mouth but they weren't making sense. 'What do you mean, one of ours?'

'He's a police officer, Alex. It's... it's Jimmy.'

'Jimmy,' he repeated like an eejit. 'Jimmy who?' Nick said nothing, let him work it out for himself. 'Not Jimmy Macfarlane? My best mate?'

Nick looked away and nodded.

It was impossible, a mistake. 'Get Jimmy in here. He'll tell you there's nothing in it.'

'I've already spoken to him and he's admitted it. He's home, suspended pending an investigation. He'll lose his job because he was on duty at the time, when—'

'When Mairi disappeared. When he was fucking my wife.' Alex got up and left the room. Nick followed him, asking what he was going to do. He told him he was going for a walk, to clear his head.

His marriage was over. That was clear. He'd never forgive

his wife for this. Or his so-called pal. Christ, Jimmy had been his best man. They'd been at school together, joined the police straight from sixth year, although both sets of parents had wanted them to take up the university places they'd been offered. They'd been through so much, the death of Alex's father three years ago, Jimmy's breakup with a girl from school, which had devastated him. They went to football matches together – they both supported Partick Thistle, a lost cause if ever there was one – and they spent Friday night in their local whenever they were both free. When Jimmy got married two years ago, they started seeing him and his wife as a couple. All those Saturday nights at each other's houses. They'd even been on holiday to Spain with them, for fuck's sake.

Did Jimmy's wife know? Alex looked around for a phone box. There was one on the other side of Dumbarton Road if he remembered correctly. His pace stepped up as he walked towards it, feeling in his pocket for the necessary change. He went inside the box, gagged at the smell of urine, and dialled Jimmy's number. He'd hang up if Jimmy answered. But it was Ellen. When she heard his voice, she immediately started expressing her condolences about Mairi's disappearance. He broke into her meanderings. 'Did you know about Jimmy and Sandra?'

Suspicious now, 'Know about what?'

'They've been having an affair. He was in my house, in my bed – the words were choking him – when Mairi was taken.' He heard an intake of breath. She hadn't known then. Another unsuspecting cuckold. He put down the receiver and leaned against the wall of the phone booth. When the phone rang a minute later, he didn't answer it.

He stumbled out of the phone box into the rain-soaked street. It was good it was raining; it helped cover up his tears.

There was a pub nearby, one he didn't frequent, preferring instead to go to the west end for his pints. No one would know him in there. He pushed the door open and walked up to the bar. 'You all right, mate?' asked the barman.

'A whisky, double. Malt if you have it.'

The barman took the hint and laid off the questions. Alex took the drink and knocked it back in one. 'Another, please.' The barman frowned, but the bar was empty at this time of day and he no doubt needed the custom, so he shrugged and poured a decent double. Alex swallowed the drink, turned and left. His head was beginning to swim. He hadn't been eating well since Mairi's disappearance and two double whiskies on an empty stomach was ill advised. He hoped Nick had told Sandra what he had found out. He hoped she had left the house and gone to her parents. He didn't want to have to look at her lying face.

He was out of luck. She was there in the living room, sitting staring ahead. It was hard to tell whether she knew she'd been rumbled or not. He stood in front of her. 'Why?'

'He paid me attention, made me feel I mattered.' So she did know.

'And that's it? That's your excuse? To blame it on me.'

Tears were streaming down her face. 'I'm sorry, I'm sorry.'

Alex left the room, destroyed by the feelings he had. Love turned to hate in an instant. 'You should go,' he said. 'You make me sick.'

He thought she'd gone to her parents. It was only when they phoned looking for an update early the next morning that he realised he had no idea where she was and nor did he care. He told his in-laws what had happened. 'I'm sure she'll be in touch,' he said before putting down the receiver. A small, mean part of him felt vindicated. They'd never liked him; he wasn't good enough for their precious daughter. Well, no doubt that information had changed their mind. Though knowing them, he suspected the narrative would change soon to blame him although he'd done nothing to merit it. True, his lack of attention had led her into Jimmy's arms, but nothing excused her leaving their child unattended while she fucked another man.

Nick came by soon after to update him. 'We've interviewed Taylor in prison, I did it myself. Alex, I don't think he has anything to do with this. He looked genuinely shocked, well, not shocked exactly but surprised. Either he's a brilliant actor or...'

Alex said nothing. He knew he was right. What he would do right now to be in a locked room with the bastard. 'So, any other updates?'

'One of your neighbours reported seeing a woman passing your garden round about the time Mairi went missing. Poor old soul has glaucoma so her description is scanty unfortunately, says she might have been early middle aged, but that's all we got out of her. There's nothing else, no other leads. We'll put out an appeal on TV tonight and see how that goes.' He looked away and Alex waited for the bad news. 'An empty pram was found by the pond in Victoria Park. It fits the description of Mairi's. A navy blue Silver Cross, is that right? I have a photograph here.' He pushed it across the coffee table to Alex.

Alex picked it up. He recognised it immediately. Sandra had wanted the best and that's what they got. The carriage was metal and the wheels were sprung, making it a doddle to push. He'd baulked at the price but gave in and had to admit his wife had been right. They'd got great use out of it. He nodded and handed it back to Nick. 'That's it, all right.'

Nick got up. 'You know what happens now, right? I'm sure we'll find Mairi alive but we have to search the pond.'

Alex gave a bark of a laugh, 'You've broken the first rule of these cases.'

'What do you mean?'

'You don't know what's happened, so don't make any promises. You have no idea whether we'll find her. Alive or dead. And let's face it, Nick, that's what we're looking at here.'

Nick's face reddened. 'You're right. I shouldn't have said that. I'm sorry. But the sighting of a woman makes me optimistic. We've also contacted the hospitals to see if there's any women who have lost a child recently and are you know, depressed.'

He left soon after, leaving Alex alone with his thoughts. It was a lead, he couldn't deny it, so why then did he have this feeling of dread hanging over him?

Sandra came home three days later, after a televised appeal by her parents, who were distraught by now and, as Alex had predicted, blaming him for her disappearance.

'You must have said something terrible to make her go.'

'Nope, only the truth. That she was a cheating liar and didn't deserve to have a daughter.'

His mother-in-law drew in her breath. 'How could you?'

'The question you should be asking is how could she.' He spat out the words. 'She left our daughter in her pram in a garden open to the street while she was upstairs fucking my best friend.'

His father-in-law, who was an elder in the Church of Scotland, hissed at him, 'Mind your language,' and it took all the strength Alex had not to punch him.

194

'You need to get your priorities straight, mate, if that's what outrages you. Just fuck off. Now.'

He'd forgotten the old bastard played golf with the deputy chief constable. It wasn't long before the weasel went whining to him. A phone call ensued.

The deputy chief constable was a smooth talker; he'd give him that. It was all *we know what a difficult time this is for you, terrible. Best put out an appeal for Sandra to come home. What do you say? Present a united front.* There was nothing else for it but to agree, and so the three of them appeared on the Scottish news, begging Sandra to come home, and she did.

She'd been holed up in a hotel in nearby Dumbarton. He hoped it was cheap. An expensive hotel bill was the last thing they needed. She looked terrible, but he was past caring. She wanted to talk, to explain, but he resisted. She insisted on staying even though her parents begged her to come to them. He couldn't bring himself to say anything to her. Didn't reproach her, nothing.

The papers were full of it. The policeman, his wife and her secret lover. Somehow, they'd got wind of it and she was vilified in all the tabloids while he was the long-suffering, devoted father. It wasn't fair, but the fuck if he cared. Then one day there was the headline that tipped her over the edge. *Wife of missing baby's mother's lover loses baby*, it said. Alex had trouble getting his head round it. What the hell was the sub-editor doing, letting such nonsense through? He read the article through. Jimmy's wife had been pregnant, eleven weeks and on the point of telling everyone, when she'd found out about her husband's affair. She'd miscarried three days later. *I'll never forgive them.* Well fine. They didn't deserve forgiveness. He took the paper upstairs to Sandra, who was sleeping, as was her wont these days, and woke her up by throwing it at her.

'Take a look at this. Another two lives destroyed by your selfishness.'

He'd gone back downstairs and thought no more about her while he waited for the daily visit from Nick to update them on the progress of the search. There'd been a breakthrough the day before, with indistinct CCTV footage of a woman in Mothercare carrying a baby. Apparently, the cashier who served her thought her behaviour was dodgy. She kept looking over her shoulder as if she was being hunted. So Nick was going to update them on that. Alex looked at his watch and frowned. Nearly three o'clock. This was ridiculous. She was getting up later and later every day. He stormed upstairs ready to drag her out of bed if necessary.

Something was stopping him getting into his bedroom. He pushed harder at the door and it moved a little. Another hard push and he was in. Sandra was on the floor, one end of a tie round her neck and the other tied to the door handle.

She didn't make it. A mercy, the doctors said, as her brain had been so deprived of oxygen, she would have been a vegetable. If he'd gone up five minutes earlier, she might have been fine. Mentally scarred but physically fine. He didn't tell them how he'd been frozen to the spot, unable to do anything, until at last he freed her and called an ambulance. He had no idea how long it was, five minutes, or a few seconds. He hadn't a clue. And now he had to live with that.

Alex hadn't realised he was crying. He thought he was past all that. He rubbed his stubby fingers over his face, erasing the traces of tears. The barman was staring at him, looked on the point of interfering, so he got up and left. He saw the Fallon woman as he walked up Buchanan Street and thought of speaking to her, impressing on her how wrong she was, how she should stay away from the Taylor family, but he didn't. He watched as she marched along, full of confidence, full of entitlement. Forget her, he told himself. Forget her and her problem; you've enough of your own.

When he got back to work, Pamela called him into her office. Thank fuck he'd had the sense to buy some extra strong mints. With any luck she wouldn't smell the booze off him.

'Where have you been, Alex?'

Shit. Why today of all days? He'd have to tell her. Pamela listened carefully, her eyes never leaving his face, as he stuttered his way through his story.

When he finished she thought for a second. 'From what you've said, it sounds as though she's prepared to go all the way to get this DNA test. I know her type. She's probably on the phone to the Daily Record right now. Let's get it out of the way. Phone the Taylors, phone Kate Fallon and get them in here. Today if possible. Tomorrow at the latest. After all, we've nothing to hide, have we?'

Alex spoke through clenched teeth. 'Taylor was guilty. It's a waste of money.' Pamela was always ranting about budgets.

She waved his protest aside. 'Get it done, Alex.'

Nothing for it but to do as she said. Alex looked up Brenda Taylor's phone number in their records. It was a landline and he felt a surge of hope. No way would she still have the same number. So many people now didn't bother with landlines. He dialled the number, fully expecting to hear the out of service tone so it was a shock when it rang, even more so when he heard her unmistakeable voice. He mumbled his way through an explanation saying there was a possibility of some new evidence and he'd like to see her and her son to talk it through. It hadn't been easy to persuade her, but she'd eventually capitulated. 'This had better not be a waste of my time, man. You've done enough damage to my family.'

Alex rang off. He hoped Kate Fallon would be pleased at least.

TWENTY-SEVEN

Glasgow

IN THE END, Kate didn't buy the DNA kit. She didn't want to go back to that house and face the Taylors alone. It was better to keep trying the official channels. Scrimgeour had turned out to be a dead end but she'd try again – higher up.

When she got back to the Fallons, Margaret rushed to the door to greet her. 'You've to phone Alex Scrimgeour. It's important, he says.'

Kate took the note with his number on it. 'Did he say what it was about?'

'No. I asked but he just repeated that it was important. He sounded flustered.'

'Can't say I have any desire to speak to him again but I suppose I should get it over with.'

'I'm sure it'll be fine,' said Margaret. 'Maybe he's had a change of heart.'

'Huh, the only way that's likely to happen is if he has a transplant.'

'By the look of him, he might need that sooner than later,' said Aodhan.

Kate laughed. 'I'll ring him now. Should only take a minute or so. He didn't give the impression of being one for small talk.' She went upstairs to make the call keying in the numbers as she went. He answered immediately.

'DI Scrimgeour. How can I help you?'

'It's Kate Fallon. You rang me?'

'Ah, yes. Right. Well. It's about what we discussed this morning. I mentioned it to my DCI, just to keep her up to speed, you know and on reflection, we think it best if we make this a police matter.'

'What do you mean?'

'I've asked Mrs Taylor to come and see me tomorrow so she can meet you and have DNA samples taken.' He hesitated. 'Well, to be perfectly honest I haven't told her about the DNA testing. It was hard enough to persuade her as it was. I have to warn you, Kate, Mrs Taylor is not at all keen, but she did agree to come. Does two o'clock suit you?'

Kate's stomach churned at the prospect of seeing the woman again, but she took down the address he gave her. She was stunned. It was the last thing she'd expected.

Downstairs, Margaret and Aodhan were in the kitchen ready with coffee and a smile. 'Everything OK?'

'DI Scrimgeour wants me to meet Mrs Taylor and have our DNA tested.' Kate sat down at the kitchen table and Margaret put a cup of coffee in front of her. She brought over a plate of scones. Her face was pale, worried.

Kate took a scone and buttered it. 'I'm sorry. I know this must be upsetting for you.'

Aodhan sighed. 'I have to be honest, I'd hoped that was an end to it when he was so dismissive this morning.'

'I thought it was,' admitted Kate. 'I don't know what made

him change his mind.' Margaret stood up and started to clear the table. 'When is your meeting?'

'Two p.m. tomorrow.'

'Isn't your train before that?'

'I have an open return, so there's no problem. I'll be able to get a later one.'

The three of them sat in silence round the table. Kate wanted to apologise again but the words wouldn't come.

After a long pause, Aodhan spoke. 'I understand you have to do this, Kate, but I'm worried for you. What if you are Danielle Taylor?'

Kate's stomach twisted at the thought. 'I don't know. I'll deal with that when I have to. But I must find out.'

He sighed. 'Fair enough. At least let me drive you over to Police Scotland.'

'You mustn't let them see you.' Kate didn't want the Fallons involved any more than they had to be.

'Of course. I'll drop you off, wait for you and then take you to Central Station.'

It was more than she deserved but he wouldn't be dissuaded. After five minutes of wrangling, Kate gave in. 'Thank you,' she said.

Margaret had invited Mirren's sisters round for dinner. They weren't at all like Mirren, either in looks or in personality. Mirren had held forthright opinions on everything from Brexit to euthanasia. Kate had thought Scotland was strongly pro-European. If so, she had found the only two Brexiteers north of Carlisle. Fortunately, Margaret and Aodhan were on her side.

An argument started with Roisín moaning about her Polish cleaner.

'She's going back to Krakow, apparently, I don't understand why. I'll not get a cleaner as good or as cheap again.'

Kate bit her tongue. Margaret let hers loose.

'You know perfectly well why, Roisín. I told you this would happen. The no vote led to all the racists coming out of their holes. You *know* what happened the day after the referendum. People telling other Europeans to go home, they weren't welcome.'

Roisín flushed. 'I'm not a racist.'

'Now, now, Margaret didn't say you were,' said Aodhan. She's merely pointing out that it allowed people who are racist to express racist views. We bumped into Kasia last week, and she said she's had so much abuse since the vote she can't stand it any more. She's lived here since 2004. From the day of the referendum result she's had people telling her to go home, to speak proper English, to stop eating foreign muck. Three years of abuse in a place she thought of as home.'

Roisín shook her head. 'Too many of them came, that was the problem. Using up all our resources.'

Margaret sighed. This was an argument that'd been done to death. 'We need immigrants, Roisín. Especially here in Scotland. Don't moan at me about not finding anyone cheap enough. You know fine well you should be paying the minimum wage at least. You've exploited that poor girl for years. And as for using *our* resources. They pay taxes, more than they take out of the system.' She didn't say *so there* at the end, but it hung in the air unspoken, nonetheless.

Kate listened to the argument, enjoying it but not joining in. Sinead turned to her for support. 'You'll have voted to leave.'

Kate shook her head and laughed. 'Definitely not. I'm European first, English second.'

'You're part Irish and Scottish though... Oh wait, I keep forgetting.'

Sinead's mistake broke the tension and the subject changed to Mirren and what she was like as a child and young woman.

'Oh she was a holy terror, that one. Got herself expelled from school for smoking.'

'Excluded,' said Aodhan, raising an eyebrow. 'For one day.'

'The shame of it nearly killed Mammy.'

'It was Mammy started her on the fags and you know it,' said Sinead.

'It was not!' Roisín's voice rose a tone.

'It so was. I came home from school one day to find her and Mammy in the back court both chain smoking.'

'Oh, I know what that was, it was Mammy trying to make her sick. She must have caught her with cigarettes and made her smoke them all. She did the exact same thing with me.'

'I never knew you smoked, Aodhan.'

'I don't. I was as sick as a dog after that experience. Haven't touched a fag since.'

Roisín turned to Kate. 'Was it the lung cancer she had, Kate?'

'No, Roisín. I never saw her with a cigarette, so maybe your mother did some good after all. It was breast cancer.'

They were all silent for a moment, contemplating cancer. The terror of it. Kate broke the silence. 'Tell me more about Mirren. What else did she get up to?'

'Well, she was a very pretty girl, you know. So all the boys were after her from the time she turned, oh what, fifteen? Just as well she was at Notre Dame, no boys to bother her there. But

203

she was having none of it, anyway. Art was everything to her. She spent all her time painting.'

'Do you have any of her work? I'd love to see it.'

'Loads, wait there.' Margaret went upstairs and returned with a large cardboard box. It was stuffed with sketch books and loose papers. 'You should have this. It's all we have bar a couple of paintings each. Tommy sold the best ones after her de... after she went missing.'

Sinead's face darkened. 'Aye and spent it all on drink.'

'Don't be too hard on him, now,' said Margaret. He lost his partner and daughter in the course of a few months.'

Sinead sniffed. 'I never did like him.'

'Why not?' asked Kate.

'I've never told this to anyone before now.' She rubbed the side of her nose. 'About two weeks before Muireann went missing, I saw him with another woman.'

'What?' Roisín glowered at her. 'And you never said?'

'I didn't know what to do. I couldn't tell Muireann. Thought it would kill her.' Her face crumpled. 'And then she went missing.'

'But why didn't you tell us?'

'I thought she'd found out and killed herself. How could I say anything? Mammy and Daddy were so sure she was alive; this gave them another reason to think she was dead. So I kept it to myself. Never thought about it, well not much anyhow, until recently. I was wrong. You all thought she was alive and I was the one who thought she'd killed herself.'

She was close to breaking down, so Kate came to her rescue, pointing to the box. 'May I look?'

'Take them, take them,' repeated Margaret.

'Oh, no, it's too much. But it would be lovely to have one of her sketch books.' Kate looked through the box. There were watercolours there that should be framed and up on a wall being admired instead of locked away in a cupboard or an attic. She picked one up, recognising the view from the hill they'd climbed the day before. 'This is Loch Lomond, isn't it? I'd love to take this if that's OK, and maybe a sketch book.'

Aodhan reached out and took her hand. 'You should have them, Kate. You knew her best. If we pack them all into a suitcase or bag you can take them with you tomorrow.'

'But—'

'But nothing. They've not seen the light of day since we got them. Tommy passed them to us not long before he died. We looked through them briefly, but as I say, we all have one or two of her paintings and that's enough.'

Kate looked at the watercolour. It was beautiful, showing the loch and the hills to the north. She blinked back tears, overwhelmed by their generosity. 'I can't thank you enough. You've been so welcoming to me and I've done nothing to deserve it.' Her voice was close to breaking.

The sound of a key in the lock brought them round. 'Ah that'll be Conor,' said Margaret. The atmosphere lightened when he came in, though not enough to stop him saying, 'Bloody hell, what's going on in here? It's like a wake.'

His father smiled. 'It is that. We've been reminiscing and getting sentimental. Not that it hasn't been lovely. We've told Kate about Muireann when she was young and she's told us about her later years.' He looked at his watch and exclaimed. 'Half past eleven. Come on you two, I'll run you home.'

There was a general bustling as he hustled his sisters out and then it was all quiet, with only Kate and Conor left as Margaret excused herself and went off to bed. They looked at each other. 'Good night out?' asked Kate.

'I was working,' he replied. 'Local pub. One of the three jobs I do while I decide what to do next.'

'Do you know what you want to do?'

'I have some ideas.'

Before she could ask what they were, he asked her what she did. Kate swithered between pressing him further or answering his question before saying, 'I lecture in journalism.'

'Really? How did you get into that?'

Kate shrugged. 'I did an English degree, then a Masters in journalism. Got lucky and managed to get a few decent stories that the *Guardian* and the *Independent* took. I had hoped one of them would offer me full-time work, but it didn't happen, and then this job came up. I applied because I needed a steady income. I was living in London at the time and the rental market is crazy there. I was paying one thousand two hundred quid for a poky studio flat. It was grim.'

'Yeah, I know. Ridiculous, isn't it?'

'Oh, have you lived in London then?'

'Mm. When I left university I got a graduate trainee post with a bank, lived there for a couple of years. Hated it. Sorry.'

'Don't apologise to me. I loathed it too. Way too busy for me. I was so glad to get out of there.' Kate sipped her wine. 'So, what happened with the bank then? I got the impression that —' She stopped, aware she'd been about to say something rude.

He raised an eyebrow. 'I wonder what your impression was. Not good from the looks of things.'

Kate blushed. 'Sorry, it's just that you said earlier you were trying to decide what to do career wise, so I thought—' She ground to a halt. 'I'm sorry. I jumped to conclusions and thought you were a spoilt millennial still living with your parents, trying to find out what you wanted to do, and now I see that you did have a career, albeit one you didn't like, I assume?' She left the question hanging, but as he didn't say anything she blundered on, digging the hole deeper. 'There's not many people your age who live at home.' Shit, his eyes narrowed. In a rush she added, 'Of course then I realised I could be talking about me. I was living with my m—, with Mirren until she died. And I'm not doing exactly what I want job-wise either.' He relaxed back into his chair. She'd saved it.

'Yeah, look at us. Losers both of us. Early thirties, no partners, no career prospects.'

Kate bristled. Perhaps her attempt to dig herself out of a hole was too convincing.

He leaned forward. 'Maybe I'm being presumptuous and you do have a partner.'

Kate drained her glass and put it on the coffee table. 'Time for me to go to bed.'

He reached out and took her hand. 'I was teasing you, Kate. Stay. Have another glass of wine, talk with me some more.'

Her hand tingled where he'd touched it. 'It's late.' She stood up.

'Of course, goodnight, Kate.'

Two hours later, she was still awake going over and over their conversation. Had she imagined the attraction between them or was it wishful thinking? She also worried about what was going to happen the following day. Would Brenda Taylor even turn up? The room was too hot and she threw off the duvet. It made no difference. Sleep eluded her. Kate lay in the bed, her mind filtering the day's events until she could have screamed. At last, when the sun was rising, she fell into a fitful sleep.

TWENTY-EIGHT

Glasgow?

ALEX WOKE the next day feeling like someone had beaten him up during the night. It was a moment or two before he remembered the meeting with Kate Fallon and Brenda Taylor that afternoon. Fuck, he turned over, hoping to grab a few more minutes of oblivion but his stomach churned in a way that couldn't be ignored. He also had to do something about his mother. She was becoming harder to deal with. Damn, was he coming down with something? Christ, he hoped it wasn't his depression returning. He'd had periods of depression off and on since Mairi's disappearance but it was some time since the last bout. He didn't have time for that now.

He drove to work, his mind on other things. At the first set of traffic lights he missed them turning to green, only coming to when the car behind him hooted and overtook him, the driver doing a 'dickhead' sign as he passed. He stalled the car and by the time he was ready to go, the lights had changed. It was one of those days.

At work, he skim read his messages to see whether the post-mortem had been done on Donald Morton yet but there was nothing. Disappointed, he turned to the report he needed to finish by tomorrow afternoon, but first he had to arrange some care so he could bring his mother home for a few days. Enough to give him some peace of mind.

'How much?' His voice was loud enough to attract the attention of several officers in the room. He glared at them and they put their heads down and returned to what they were doing. Lowering his voice he said, 'I'll get back to you on that.'

He scribbled some figures on the notepad in front of him, added them up and sighed. It cost four thousand a month for the care home. The sale of his mother's house was paying for this at the moment, but the money wouldn't last forever. He couldn't believe what he'd been quoted for full time care at home. Time to phone the social worker.

For once, Beth was in when he phoned. She was usually out and difficult to get hold of. He started to outline his plan, but she interrupted him as soon as he mentioned bringing his mother home for a few weeks.

'I'm going to stop you right there, Alex. Surely you remember the OT's report?

'What's that?

'The occupational therapist's report? You remember, when your mother moved into the care home, we looked at all the options including her staying with you.'

His memory of the report was vague. That time had been so stressful, what with the Julie Campbell affair and the added tension caused by his mother's illness and the attacks on her carers. 'It was a difficult time for me,' he mumbled. 'I don't recall the details.'

Beth was very patient, he'd give her that. There wasn't a hint of annoyance as she went through it with him. 'The bottom line is, the OT said your flat was completely unsuitable.

For a start there's the stairs at the entrance to the close. Yes, there's a stair-rail, but at the time of the assessment your mum was only able to manage five steps unaided. She'll probably have deteriorated by now but even if she hasn't, there's the two flights up to your flat. The OT felt, and I quote, *Mr Scrimgeour's flat is not in the least suitable for anyone with Alzheimer's and/or the physical difficulties that his mother has. She would effectively be a prisoner in the flat as she would need to be carried up and down stairs. Mrs Scrimgeour has wandered from her bungalow four times in the last month. If she managed to get out of her son's flat when left alone, there is a danger of her falling down the steep steps in the close. As Mrs Scrimgeour has osteoporosis this is to be avoided, as a fall could result in a broken hip that could render her immobile.'*

Shit. It was coming back to him now. Along with the relief he'd felt at the time. He couldn't believe he'd forgotten. 'So, you wouldn't recommend it then?'

'Absolutely not. She's in the best place.'

'Yesterday she hit one of the carers and accused her of trying to kill her.'

'Listen, Alex. You're paying a great deal of money for her care. They need to sort this out. Do you want me to speak to them?'

'No, no. They're going to arrange a case conference. In fact, I'm surprised the manager hasn't phoned you yet.' He said his goodbyes and put down the phone. He hated doing this, but he was going to call in a favour.

Alex phoned Gordon, his pathologist friend from school, and explained the problem. 'Is there any way the PM on Donald Morton could be brought forward?'

'Jesus, Alex. We're up to our balls in dead bodies here.'

Alex grimaced at the image. 'It's related to what I told you earlier this month. You know, about deaths in care homes. I spoke to Mr Morton's daughter last night. She's adamant that her father was physically fit. She'd seen him earlier in the day and he was fine.'

'Ah right. I thought the name was familiar. Hang on a second.' There was a rustling of paper. 'Yes, I know the case you're talking about. The GP for the home wasn't happy, told us to be extra careful doing this one. Bit of a cheek, I thought. Anyway, it's next on the list. I'll let you have the results as soon as I know. I take it the daughter's on board?'

Alex exhaled. 'Absolutely. Thanks, mate. I owe you one.'

While he was waiting for the results, he decided to phone the home's GP. He'd only met the man once, when his mother had an infection. As was usual these days he had difficulty getting through. The receptionist would have made a great guard dog.

'Is it an emergency?' she asked repeatedly. 'If not, you'll have to make an appointment with the doctor.'

He tried explaining, but she wouldn't listen until exasperated, he said, 'Look this is a police matter. I need to speak to Dr Barr now.' That did the trick.

'Mr Scrimgeour, how can I help you?'

Alex outlined the situation succinctly.

'Right, well I was worried about Mr Morton's death because frankly he was as fit as anyone is at the age of eighty-nine. Physically, that is. I honestly thought he'd live to be a hundred. He was a fell runner, you know. Still does, sorry, did park runs most Saturday mornings with his son-in-law.'

'Really?' Alex couldn't imagine walking five kilometres at such an advanced age, let alone running.

'Oh, yes. Pleased as punch he was because he could still do them in under forty minutes. Couldn't tell you what day of the week it was, but ask him his personal best time from twenty years ago and he'd have it off pat.'

'Was that the only reason you were suspicious?'

Silence. 'Dr Barr, are you still there?'

A heavy sigh. 'To tell the truth, I've been worried for a wee while now. Not enough to raise a red flag, but enough to feel uneasy. Unfortunately, I was on sick leave in June when there were three deaths. If I'd been there I would have asked for PMs but the deaths had been signed off by the locum and by the time I got back all three of them were cremated.

'I see. Well, we should know soon enough. Thank you for your time.' Alex rang off.

Before he knew it, it was almost time for the meeting with Kate Fallon and the Taylors. Alex wished he'd never mentioned meeting Kate Fallon to Pamela. He'd been taken by surprise when she'd spoken to him yesterday. Off his game. Now he was stuck with this. What if he had been wrong about Robbie Taylor? Perhaps he'd been responsible for sending an innocent man to jail, for hounding him to death. He went over the evidence in his mind. It was true that it was mainly circumstantial once you took away the confession. Christ, it had been a blow when Taylor stood on that stand and pleaded not guilty. His lawyer claimed he'd been forced into confessing. Thank fuck for tape recordings; there was no way anyone could listen to the interviews and claim he'd pressurised Taylor. He had to admit though that he had feared a not proven verdict. But the evidence about the blood on the Babygro and the stupid explanation given by his wife, the way she was so obviously lying, was another nail in his coffin. No, it was impossible that he'd got it wrong. The man was guilty as sin. He knew it and Pamela knew it too. She was right to get this out of the way and get the Fallon woman off their backs.

There were also the anonymous emails to consider. If he was right and they were to do with Taylor as he suspected, then someone definitely had an axe to grind. Their origins must lie somewhere in the Taylor family. It had to be Jamie. He was a wee kid when his sister disappeared. He'd be in denial about his father's guilt. Word on the street was that he idolised his father and that he was shaping up to be as big a thug as Taylor had been. Alex had invited him along to get his DNA tested also, to try and nip this campaign in the bud. He'd had three emails now, and last week another dog turd had been pushed through his letter box. That was two now. God knows how they'd got into the close of his tenement building. Probably said they were the postie. No matter. He'd gone round his neighbours – like he should have done after the first time – and asked them to double check before allowing anyone in. That was one good thing about living where he did. People cared. And the thought that they might get something similar through their letter box was enough to make them vow to be very careful about who they buzzed in. Come to think of it, he hadn't had any post since. Maybe they were being a wee bit too wary.

Kate Fallon arrived on time and he asked the civilian on reception to show her up. He got up as she entered the room. 'Thank you for coming,' he said.

She nodded, her lips tight. Perhaps she was regretting this.

'Can I offer you some tea, coffee?'

'No, thank you. Is Mrs Taylor here yet?'

'Not yet, I've asked her son to come in as well.'

She paled. 'Oh, right. Why?'

'As I said to you yesterday, we always suspected her of being involved or at the very least of knowing what her husband had done. I'll be very surprised if she agrees to this test. I thought that having Jamie here might persuade her, although of course he had nothing to do with it.'

'So, is this a sort of entrapment then? If she doesn't agree, she's automatically guilty?'

'No, no. I... I want you to be reassured. To see once and for all that you are not Danielle Taylor. If we don't get Brenda's DNA we might get Jamie's. From what you've said he's convinced that your mother took his sister, so he'd be daft to pass up this chance.'

Kate opened her mouth, but before she could speak his phone rang. Alex picked it up. 'Send them up.'

Jamie came in first, didn't knock, pushed the door so hard it banged off the wall. His mother followed, unlit fag trailing from her fingers. 'What's this all about then? What's this evidence you've got?'

Alex explained. She and her son listened carefully. When he'd finished speaking, Mrs Taylor got up from her chair. 'No way, man. No way are you taking our DNA. This is a trap, isn't it? You get our DNA and before I know it, we're in the frame for something we didn't do.'

'I assure you, Mrs—'

'Did you not hear me? No fucking way. Get to fuck.'

Alex glanced at Kate. Her face was expressionless. He tried again. 'This is a chance to clear your husband's name.'

'Aye right.'

'He's right, Ma. This is our only chance.' Jamie leaned forward in his chair. 'I've been wanting this for months. You always said—'

'Shut the fuck up. What do you know, you moron? Face it, son, your sister's dead. And no way is this one related to us.' She indicated Kate with a nod. 'The size of her. For fuck's sake.'

Kate blushed. 'Your son is tall.'

Brenda shot her a venomous glance. 'You're not my daughter. Believe me, a mother knows.' She got up. 'Come on, Jamie. We're out of here.'

'No. I'm staying. I knew I was right in thinking this Muireann woman was behind our Dani's disappearance. I mean, was it a coincidence that they both vanished within days of each other? When I read those articles about her own wean having died, I knew I was on to something.' He was pleading with his mother now, who was standing rigid, hands by her side. 'Please, Ma, I want this sorted.'

'Is it because you want to be reunited with your sister, or is it the money you're after?' asked Kate.

'What the fuck you talking about?' Jamie's face was bright red.

'How much was it again?'

'Shut up! I never... I...'

'Oh, forget it,' said Kate. 'Let's get this over with.'

'What's this?' said Alex to Kate. 'What do you mean?'

Kate shook her head, her lips pursed. 'It doesn't matter.'

'See, Jamie. What did I tell you? It's a set up. You know

they've been after you for years. Give them your DNA and you'll be banged up before you know it.'

Jamie sat back in his chair, arms folded. 'I've made my mind up. I know that woman took our Dani and this is our chance to prove it.'

Mrs Taylor's face contorted. 'You'll regret it, son. You'll see. Dani's dead and that's all there is to it.' She tugged at his arm, but Jamie didn't move. 'For fuck's sake, Jamie. This is a trap.' When he refused to look at her, she stormed out of the room. 'Suit yourself, but don't say I didn't warn you.'

It was several seconds before anyone spoke. Alex broke the silence. 'Shall we do this then?' He took the kits out from a drawer and told them what would happen. It was over in seconds.

'When do we get the results?' asked Kate.

'I'm not sure. I'll email you as soon as I have them.'

Jamie stood up. 'I'll be off, then.' He turned to Kate, 'You coming?'

Before she could answer, Alex spoke.

'If you don't mind, Ms Fallon. I'd like to ask you a couple of questions. You're free to go, Mr. Taylor.'

Taylor scowled as he left. The door slammed behind him.

Once Alex was sure he was out of earshot, he asked Kate if Jamie had been blackmailing her.

She looked close to tears. No doubt the vitriol coming from the woman she thought might be her mother had upset her. 'It's nothing,' she said. 'A nasty phone call to my dead mother.'

Alex pressed her but she wouldn't say anymore. 'I'd better go,' she said. 'Train to catch.'

Alex stared out of the window and watched Kate leave the building. Jamie Taylor was nowhere to be seen, which was a relief. He didn't want him to accost her. After a few moments, a car drew up and Kate got in. No doubt it was one of the Fallon people. She'd be safe with them. He looked at the DNA tests. He hoped for Kate's sake as well as his own that they showed no relationship between her and Jamie Taylor.

TWENTY-NINE

Glasgow

THE REPORT, when it came, was to the point. Donald Morton had died of a heart attack. There was no trace of anything suspicious on the body, no bruising or other contusions. Nor were there any signs of heart disease. Nothing to go forward on except for one thing, a pin prick under the hairline, suggesting an injection. Alex picked up his phone.

'So, Gordon, this pinprick then, what could it indicate?'

'He'd been having Botox injections?'

'But that wouldn't kill him, surely?'

'I was joking, Alex. Botox, it freezes the muscles, makes you look... Oh, never mind. No, someone was trying to hide something so we've asked for advanced toxicology testing. Meantime, you'd better get someone along to question staff and visitors at that home. Because someone is up to no good.'

Alex called his team together and gave them a quick outline of what he knew so far. 'We have little to go on at this point, so any questions, refer them back to me. I want you to find out who was on duty yesterday, the dates of the last four deaths and who was on duty then. Also, who visited on those days? And I want all visitors, laundry collectors, TV repair men, posties. Anyone who was in that place. I need a volunteer to stay here and find out about the wills of those who are recently deceased – go back six months. Who benefitted from their deaths, that sort of thing. There's some well-off people live in that home. Mark, I need you to coordinate it all. I can't be involved, for obvious reasons. But I'll be waiting here, gnawing my fingernails.'

He kept Mark back for a final word. 'I didn't want to say in front of the others, but my mother may be in danger. She claimed someone tried to inject her with something yesterday. It's likely all in her imagination, you know what she's like, but I don't want to chance it. Can you make sure someone keeps an eye on her?'

'Yes, of course. But...'

'I'll be along later. I wanted to take her home but my flat isn't suitable. I'm going to try to get her in somewhere else for respite until we know for sure whether there is someone out there killing people, but meantime...'

Mark nodded and turned to go.

Something was wrong, Mark wasn't his usual cocky self. 'Hang on a second. Everything OK with you?'

'Sure.' He didn't look at Alex.

'What are you not telling me?'

Eye contact at last. 'I got a text message from Suzanne yesterday.'

Alex half rose from his chair. 'What? I hope you ignored it and deleted it. She's trouble and you know it.'

Mark shook his head. 'I don't know what to do, boss. She says she's pregnant. Says it's due next month.'

Alex sank back down in his chair. 'Oh, fuck. Oh fucking hell. What...' He tailed off, at a loss what to say. 'Right, we'll go for a drink after I've seen my mother and you can tell me all about it then. But what the actual fuck, Mark. What the actual fuck.'

———

It was after seven when Alex arrived at the nursing home. He'd almost made it safely past Ms Jenkins' office when she called out to him. 'Mr Scrimgeour, a word, please.'

Christ, it was like being back at school. He turned, cursing under his breath.

She ushered him into her room and told him to take a seat. When he did, she remained standing, her arms folded. 'What is this nonsense? Why are all these police officers here? It's upsetting the clients.'

'They won't be here much longer, I imagine.'

'What evidence do they have that Mr Morton's death is suspicious?'

'I'm not an active part of this investigation, but even if I was, I couldn't discuss cases with you, as you know.'

She sniffed. 'But you're here anyway.'

'To see my mother.' He kept his voice level. 'How has she been today?'

'You don't usually come two days running. Here to keep an eye on your officers, are you?'

She was deliberately riling him. 'You haven't answered my question. How is my mother?'

'Quiet, subdued. You'll be pleased to know that the care assistant won't be pressing charges.'

He nodded, non-committal. 'Well, I'd best make a move.'

His mother was asleep. He sat with her a while and then set off to find Mark. The residents' lounge was being used for questioning. Mark was in the middle of an interview, so Alex waited until he had finished.

'How's it going?'

'OK, I think. Two more to go, then we'll have finished interviewing everyone here. We have the names and dates of death of the last six people to die here and a list of people who visited the home on those days.' He indicated a sheet of paper, which Alex picked up.

'Want to go for that drink now?'

Mark looked round the room. 'We'll be finished in about fifteen minutes, I reckon. Can we go to your flat? I don't want anyone to overhear anything.'

'Sure. Meet you there in half an hour. I'll order a couple of pizzas and pick up some beer.'

It was more like an hour before Mark arrived. They ate quickly, Mark chatting about what he'd found out so far, saying there had been quite an overlap with people there on all six days. 'I think we can rule out anyone external. The laundry gets picked up on a Tuesday and only two of the deaths are on a Tuesday. We can also rule out people on nightshift because none of the deaths happened during the night, which is unusual when you think about it.'

'Is it?'

Mark nodded, his mouth full. When he'd swallowed his food, he said, 'Yeah, in general most deaths occur between three a.m. and four, apparently.

Alex wasn't convinced, but it wasn't worth arguing. 'So, do we have a definitive list then?'

'I think so, but I'll go over it again tonight when I get home.'

Alex noted how flat Mark's voice was when he mentioned home. 'OK. Put that aside for the moment. What are you going to do about Suzanne?'

Mark slumped back in his seat. 'Fuck knows. Take out a contract on her?' He held his hands up. 'Joking, joking. Fuck, Alex I don't know what to do.'

'What are your options?'

Mark closed his eyes. For a moment Alex thought he was asleep. He wouldn't blame him if he was. This was a terrible dilemma to face. Mark stretched and said, 'I've done nothing but think about this since I got the text.'

'What did it say?'

Mark rummaged through his jacket pocket and brought out his phone, which he passed to Alex. 'See for yourself, the code's 1234.'

'Original,' said Alex. 'You'd better change that to something more secure.'

'Shit! You're right. Karen could get into it at any time, but then if I do change it, she'll suspect something's up.'

'So delete the text then.' Alex had opened the phone and read it aloud. 'I've thought long and hard about this, Mark, but in the end, I've decided it's the right thing to do. I'm pregnant with your child, a boy. I'm sorry to land this on you but I thought you had the right to know. I don't want anything from you, don't worry. You won't hear from me again.'

'What am I going to do?'

Something had been niggling Alex since Mark had told him about the text message and it finally clicked. Christ, he was slow today. Alex frowned. 'This doesn't add up. I thought your affair with her ended before her sister died last year. She can't still be pregnant if that's the case.'

Mark blushed. He didn't look at Alex.

'Oh, for fuck's sake, man. It didn't end then, did it?'

'It was a one off, I bumped into her in town one day and we ended up going to her flat. It was only that one time.' Mark's voice took on a pleading note. 'What the fuck am I going to do, Alex?'

Alex shook his head. 'You are one fucking idiot.' He drank the rest of his beer and opened another bottle. For a few moments he said nothing.

'Well, as I see it, you have several options. First, you ignore it completely. Delete the text, block her number and forget about it. Second option, as the first, except you tell Karen about it. Otherwise, it's a ticking time bomb.' He stopped.

'Go on, you said there were several options.'

Alex sighed. 'You could arrange to meet her, see what she wants. Because she wants something, Mark. That's for sure.'

'I can't see her, I don't trust myself.' Mark was picking at one of his cuticles, peeling the skin away. It started to bleed. 'Shit,' he said. 'Do you have an Elastoplast?'

Alex fetched one from the bathroom and handed it to him. 'If only every problem could be sorted out so easily.'

'I know.' Mark wrapped the plaster round his finger. 'I don't suppose...'

'No,' said Alex.

'You don't know what I'm going to say.'

'Yes, I do. You were going to ask me to act as an intermediary.'

'Fuck! They're right to call you scary Scrimgeour. How did you know?'

Alex tapped his nose 'Secret of the trade.'

'Seriously though, would you?'

'Look, I wouldn't know where to start. I'd be a lousy go-between.'

'I don't want to beg.'

'Don't then.' Alex was tetchy. The last thing he needed was someone else's problems.

Thank fuck, Mark took the hint. 'I think I'll delete the text and block her.'

'Tell Karen first. It'll be worse if you don't and she finds out.'

'How would she find out though?' huffed Mark. 'You're the only person I've told. No one else knows a thing.' His voice sharpened. 'I can trust you, can't I?'

He was gracious enough to look ashamed when Alex glared at him. He got up to go. 'I'll get a taxi from Shawlands Cross, pick up the car in the morning. These fucking Belgian beers are too bloody strong. See you tomorrow.'

After he'd gone, Alex tidied up the mess left behind. He was tempted to act as a go-between in spite of what he had said to Mark. Apart from anything, he wanted to see for himself what the attraction was, what hold she had over a man who, to his mind, had everything. He'd met her during the investigation. She was attractive enough, but in Alex's opinion, not a patch on Karen. The man was a fool.

The following day it was all go from the minute he got into work. Alex had gone through Mark's notes and now he wanted to have a look at the wills of the deceased. As soon as he started going through them, one name jumped out at him. In both cases the wording was similar. 'Finally, to the wonderful carer at Rosebank Nursing Home who has cared for me so diligently, Shahida Ahmed, I leave the sum of £10,000.' His heart was beating fast as he picked up the phone to speak to the lawyers who had drafted and executed the wills. Ten minutes later, his heart had calmed down and he sat bemused, mulling over what he'd been told. In both cases,

Shahida had refused the money. Still, it was worth having a word with her. He told Mark to ask her to come into the station for questioning. He trusted his team but he also wanted to observe the woman for himself while Mark and another officer did the interview.

———

The young woman sitting across from Mark and Ryan twiddled with her hijab, adjusting and readjusting it. She didn't look at either of them. Watching through the glass from the next room, Alex could see she was terrified. Why?

'Ms Ahmed, can you tell me why you didn't accept these gifts?'

'It wasn't my place.' Her voice was barely audible.

'What do you mean?'

'That's what the text messages said. That I would do well to refuse the money, that it wouldn't look good if I took it.'

'Did you get messages in both cases?'

'Yes. I was so upset when Mr Connelly died. He was such a lovely man. So interesting to talk to. Most of the residents have dementia as you know, but he was all there. I was astonished when I got the letter about the inheritance, but before I got the chance to reply I got the first message.'

'Do you still have it?'

She stared at him for a few seconds before whispering, 'Yes'.

'Can I see it, please?'

She didn't answer but instead rummaged through her handbag before handing him an iPhone.

'You'll need to open it for me.'

'Of course, sorry.' She keyed in her password, searched

through her messages and handed the phone back to him. 'Some of the language is a bit...'

Mark studied them for a few seconds. 'Is it all right if I show these to someone else?'

'Go ahead.'

Mark brought the phone through to the room where Alex was observing and handed it to him. 'It's pretty bad, sir.'

Understatement if ever there was one. The language was vile. Both sexist and racist, and Alex's hackles rose as he read through the thread. He handed the phone back to Mark. 'Find out if she has any suspicions about who sent them.'

Mark went back into the room and continued the interview. 'Who sent these, do you know?'

Shahida shrugged. 'I imagined it was one of the family, but I have no proof. Or it could be someone who works at the care home.' She looked away. 'I made a stupid mistake.'

'Oh?'

'Yes, I told one of the other care workers that Mr Connelly had left me some money and she spread it about. Some of the comments I got were awful, accusing me of sooking up to residents in order to get money from them. I had already decided to turn down the money before I got the texts.' She half smiled at him. 'I'm a medical student, Detective Sergeant. I can't afford to have any rumours concerning my conduct floating about. I was horrified when a second resident left me money and immediately wrote to the lawyer saying I wasn't going to accept it.'

'Was there any link between the two people who left you money?'

'Oh yes. They were best buddies. Honestly, they were such lovely people.' A tear coursed down her cheek. 'I miss them both so much.'

Something in the timbre of her voice disturbed Alex. He rang through to speak to Mark.

'I think she's the woman who phoned me about the three deaths in Rosebank. She sounds familiar. Ask her about it.'

'Ms Ahmed, you phoned us a few weeks ago, didn't you? About the number of deaths in the home.' Mark waited for her to answer.

She was no poker player. She looked away. 'I don't know what you're talking about.'

'What made you suspicious?' His voice was low and unthreatening. 'You need to tell us.'

She gave in. 'It was Mr Connelly's death. I saw him a few hours before he died. He was fine. And three deaths in a fortnight. It's too much, even for a care home.'

This was a blind alley. Alex didn't believe for a second that Shahida Ahmed had anything to do with Donald Morton's death. But someone did and he was determined to find out who.

THIRTY

Glasgow

THE MEETING with the Taylors had shaken Kate. For one thing Brenda Taylor's refusal to have her DNA taken was suspicious. Kate couldn't believe it when Scrimgeour had suggested she might be reluctant. She'd thought Brenda would welcome the opportunity, but she was more concerned with being set up than with possibly being reunited with her daughter. She was, it had to be said, a very unpleasant woman. Now Kate had an anxious wait for the results.

The drive to Central Station had been uncomfortable. She hadn't felt like talking and Aodhan too had been quiet. He dropped her off near the station. 'Don't be a stranger, Kate. No matter what the DNA says, we'll always think of you as family.'

A tear rolled down Kate's face. 'I've made a mistake, haven't I?'

'No, you did what you thought was right. First of all, you have a right to know who you are. I find it hard to believe that my sister may have kidnapped a baby, but...' He brushed a bit of fluff off his trousers. 'Secondly, if there has been a miscarriage of justice it has to be righted. Even if it is very painful for our family. So no, I don't think you've made a mistake.'

Kate got out of the car. She wasn't as sure as he was, but to say so would be insensitive in view of the fact that she had set this in motion. They said their goodbyes with both promising to meet up soon. As soon as Kate had settled on the train she went to the toilet and burst into tears. What had she done?

It was after midnight when she got home. In spite of all her worries, she slept well. When she woke up, she felt better. Whatever the result of the DNA testing was, she'd deal with it. Mirren's live for the moment attitude was, after all, ingrained in her bones. She was working from home, but first she intended to go through the box of papers that Aodhan had given her.

She opened the old suitcase that Margaret had put them in to transport them. There were a lot of sketch books of varying sizes, which she put aside. First of all, she wanted to have a good look at the paintings. There were about twenty, all of them watercolours, some unfinished.

The ones dated before Caitlin was born were light, happy paintings, usually of the sea. Kate searched for the mermaids that Aodhan had said were Mirren's trademark. They were hard to find but eventually she tracked them all down. Some were beside her signature, others were part of it, attached to one of the letters, and yet more were tucked in amongst the waves. The paintings were beautiful, and Kate planned to put some up as soon as she was able. They'd make a lovely group if hung together. She pictured them framed in slim grey to match the grey-green shades of the sea.

A few of them were darker. The sea in them was wilder, murkier, and the land too looked more desolate than in the others. These were all painted around the time of Mirren's disappearance. In the foreground of one of them was a seagull with its beak wide open, squawking at a raven. The two birds looked odd together. Kate had read somewhere that a raven symbolises death in art. Maybe seagulls had a meaning too. Perhaps Mirren meant it as a personification of herself fighting back against death and despair. The meaning of her name was 'of the sea', and a herring gull was certainly a sea creature. But perhaps she was reading too much into it.

She put the paintings aside and pulled out one of the sketchbooks. It was full of drawings. Some were of a man, handsome, relaxing in a chair by a fire. Kate studied them. Tommy, most likely. Others were self-portraits that made Kate catch her breath. Mirren had been so beautiful when young, her eyes large in her tiny face. She looked at the dates and they were all from 1968, so Mirren would have been a student at art school then. One in particular was captivating. She was gazing straight at the viewer, a knowing look in her eyes, her hair long and tousled. Her essence captured in a few lines. Kate would love to see it framed but wasn't sure if it was good form to tear pages out of a sketch book.

Kate put it back in the suitcase; the rest could wait until later. She needed to get on with what she had to do today. She opened her laptop, logged in and started to work. She was in the middle of updating one of her first-year lectures when the doorbell rang. She cursed the interruption and thought about ignoring it. After the fourth ring she got up and answered the door.

When she saw who it was she folded her arms. 'I told you not to come round again.'

Jack held out a bunch of pink roses and gypsophilia, hand tied with twine. 'What do you want?' she said.

'To apologise.'

'I wasted over a year of my life waiting for you to leave your wife. You didn't then and you won't now. I don't care. I've moved on, Jack, and you should too.'

'But, I... I love you.'

'No, you don't. You love the idea of having a mistress. The lack of responsibility. The feeling of being young again that it gives you.'

'I've told Vicky about you, about us.'

Kate shut the door on him and went back into the living room. This was a complication she didn't need. He was hammering at the door, calling out to her. Kate put her hands over her ears but the drumming didn't go away. She looked out of her window. Two neighbours had come to their doors. She'd have to let him in.

Kate cracked first. 'What did she say?'

'She told me to leave.'

'So you thought you'd come to me. The soft option.'

'Well, yes.' He gave her the lopsided grin she used to find so charming.

'Jack, I've moved on. As you already know, there's someone else. So, no. Go back to Vicky and your child. How can you contemplate leaving him?'

His mouth turned down. 'So it's true then?'

'Yes, I met someone recently. Someone decent, someone who likes me. Someone who isn't fucking married.'

They glared at each other. She was lying, of course, but he didn't know that. She wanted him out of her house. Their session of mutual hatred was broken by more knocking at the door. 'For fuck's sake,' she muttered as she went to answer it.

The woman at the door was instantly recognisable. That pert prettiness. The straight bob, carefully coloured with caramel and cream highlights, the slight figure, so dainty, so different to Kate, who was at least twenty centimetres taller and ten kilograms heavier. She felt like the literal elephant in the room compared to Vicky. Vicky's eyes were cornflower blue, a shade Kate had never seen in real life. Contact lenses, she'd bet her life on it. She was in no mood for this and nodded towards the living room. 'He's in there. Take him home.'

Vicky's head retreated. She'd come ready for a fight. She gave Kate a sidelong look as she marched into the house. 'So, this is your slut?' she shouted at Jack.

Kate kept her mouth shut. She was not going to get into a slanging match with her. Not now, not ever. Jack's head was in his hands. 'Well?' demanded Vicky.

'She's not a slut,' he muttered. 'I love her.'

Vicky turned to Kate. 'And you, I suppose, love him.' Her eyes glittered. Definitely contacts.

Kate broke her silence. 'Nope. I've told him. I feel nothing for him. I want him out of my life. So, take him away, please.'

'Well, this is a fine mess we're in,' she said. She sat down and Kate's heart sank. She had work to do.

Vicky turned down her mouth. 'I want an explanation.'

'Jack,' Kate appealed to him. 'Jack, please go. You have a wife and—'

'Didn't stop you before, did it?'

'No,' Kate agreed. 'And I was wrong to let it go on as long as I did. I should have put an end to it when I found out about you.'

'Hmm,' she sniffed, unimpressed. 'And when did he tell you about the little detail of already having a wife?'

'He didn't. I saw you both in John Lewis.'

She swung round to face her husband. 'You bastard! You told me she knew right from the start. That she chased you until you gave in.'

He had seduced Kate, pursuing her with flowers and gifts of books, but she kept that to herself. Vicky screamed at him again and he stood up.

'We should continue this elsewhere,' he said.

Kate didn't move, didn't say a word. She wanted them both out of her house. Vicky stayed where she was, not prepared to budge. Kate was shaking with hunger. It was hours since she'd had breakfast. She left the room and went into the kitchen. Jack followed her.

She cut herself a slice of bread. 'Get her out of here.'

'Are you sure it's over?'

How many times did he need to be told? She'd told him it was over three times and yet he was still snivelling on about it. Where once she had seen the man of her dreams, now she saw only a nuisance, a fly buzzing round, irritating. 'It's over.'

'If you're sure,' he tried again.

'I. Am. So. Fucking. Sure.'

He squared his shoulders. 'Fine. Well, I have a child to consider. So, yes, you're right. My family need me.'

Kate looked down at her shoes and counted to ten, hoping he couldn't see she was struggling not to laugh. 'It's the right thing to do.'

She stayed in the kitchen and finished making a sandwich, trying not to cram it in her mouth, and failing because she was so hungry. After a few minutes they left, slamming the door behind them. Kate heard another muffled shout and shrugged. At least they'd gone. She went into the living room and logged back on to her laptop. She was in the middle of a lecture preparation when the doorbell rang again.

It was her next-door neighbour, Mrs Golightly, a misnomer if ever there was one, as she weighed about ninety kilos. 'Is everything all right, dear? I heard shouting.' She craned her neck to see past Kate into the cottage.

Kate moved to block her view. 'Fine, thank you.'

'It sounded as though someone was upset.' She was not going to let this go.

'As I said, everything's fine.' Kate smiled at her. 'Is there anything else? I'm working from home today and I have a lot to do.' Mrs Golightly was of the generation who didn't understand the concept of working from home. Mirren had had to be firm with her about not popping in for a cuppa, as she put it, but she'd persisted nonetheless, appearing at the door with all sorts of excuses.

'Well, if you're sure.' She moved away from the door and Kate tried to keep her relief hidden. But she wasn't finished. 'I'm sure I heard swearing and I know you'd never swear...'

No, you fucking don't, Kate wanted to say to her. *You know nothing about me.* She put on her best puzzled look. 'Perhaps it was something on the radio.'

'Oh no, I saw them leave. She was shouting *slut* and other profanities. I wanted to check you were all right.'

Kate's first impulse was to shut the door in her face, but the woman was a neighbour and she had to remain on good terms with her. 'Friends of mine, going through a bad patch. I'm very sorry it disturbed you.'

'Oh. Well, as long as you're all right. I promised your mum I'd look out for you.'

That was the last straw. She'd stayed well away during Mirren's illness. Other neighbours were kind, bringing flowers and casseroles, but she never once came to the door. Kate's smile was condescending, 'Of course. And thanks for being so understanding about my friends. *You* know how it is with men. They're all the same, aren't they? Can't keep it in their pants.'

Bullseye. Mrs Golightly's husband was a notorious womaniser.

'I... what? My Jeremy would never...'

'Of course not,' said Kate, in a voice as smooth as Mr Golightly's patter. 'I was talking in general terms. Mr Golightly's such a homely man. You're made for each other.' Her fingers were crossed behind her back. 'Now, I really must go. I have a conference call in ten minutes and I need to get prepared for it.'

Mrs Golightly went then, casting a puzzled look over her shoulder as she closed the garden gate. She knew she'd been insulted but hadn't worked out how. Kate closed the door before she caught on.

Kate prayed that was the last she'd see of Jack. She could have cried with frustration; the amount of time she'd spent moping over him, the hours she'd wasted waiting for him to call. She should have listened to Mirren. She had known a bad lot when she saw one. Kate went back to work. Never again, she vowed. Never again.

THIRTY-ONE

Buckinghamshire

THERE, in her inbox, was the email she both feared and longed for. As she stared at it, she realised dread was her principal emotion. All she wanted to do was hide from it. She called Laura to ask if she'd come round.

'I'm at work,' Laura said.

'Of course, I'm sorry. I shouldn't have asked.'

'Look, I'll come over at lunchtime but I can't stay long. I have a case conference at two p.m. in Slough.'

'Could you, Laura? That would be great.'

Kate put down the phone feeling better. The email was burning her eyes, so she closed her laptop and planned what to do. It was impossible to do any serious work while that time bomb was ticking away, so she settled down to weeding the garden.

There was something soothing about kneeling close to the earth, Kate thought. She loved the smell. She loved the way the earth looked as the space opened up underneath the roses when she plucked out the weeds. The roses were particularly good this year. Kate thought back to March when Mirren had cut them back, telling her to pay attention.

'Look, you have to find an outward facing bud and cut there. Cut it at a slant and it will encourage an open-centred shape.'

Kate had nodded as if she understood but she wasn't taking in any of it.

'Kate, pay attention. I won't always be here, and if you don't prune them properly, they'll weaken and eventually they'll die.'

It was too close to the bone. Mirren was getting weaker every day. Kate wished she was able to prune her to give her strength, but all she could do was stand by and watch her fade. Now, as she tended to Mirren's garden, she appreciated what a treasure it was. How it lived on after a person's death with so much of their personality in it. The hours flew past, and at half past twelve she tidied up and went inside. Laura was a few minutes early. Kate knew she was lucky to have a friend like her.

Kate made tuna mayonnaise sandwiches with salad and a pot of tea. They ate their lunch without saying much, both lost in thought. When they finished, they went through to the living room.

Laura handed the laptop to Kate. 'Are you ready for this?'

She swallowed and took it from her. It took ages to open. It was like getting exam results, no, worse, because at heart Kate had always known she'd passed. This wasn't the same at all. With this she didn't know what she most feared. She clicked on the email and started to read. The words didn't make sense and she turned to Laura. 'I don't understand.'

Laura looked over Kate's shoulder to read the email. 'It's

negative,' she said. 'There is no match between you and Jamie Taylor.'

Was it possible to feel both relief and disappointment at the same time? It shouldn't be, one ought to cancel out the other, but it was exactly what Kate felt. 'Right,' she said. 'Right.'

'Are you OK?'

'I think so.'

Laura looked at her watch and swore. 'Sorry, I really have to go. Will you be all right?'

'You go. Thank you for being here, Laura. You're the best.'

Laura hugged Kate and she hugged her back, not wanting to let go.

Once Laura was gone Kate made herself a strong espresso and read the email again. She still didn't fully understand, it was too scientific for her, but the final sentence was clear. 'This test shows there is no familial connection between the two samples given.' It was not entirely good news, she decided – she still had no idea who she was and she hadn't the least idea about what to do next – but she was delighted for the Fallons. They'd be so relieved. Kate was desperate to hear Margaret's voice, with its soothing warmth, or Aodhan's, with its gruff sincerity. She picked up her phone. Conor answered.

'Is your dad there?'

'Sorry, no. They've gone out for a walk. It's a nice day here. It's "taps aff" all round.'

'What?'

'Taps aff. The sun comes out and all the men take off their shirts and t-shirts.'

'Oh, I see,' said Kate.

'Will I do instead?'

She hesitated. She had wanted to tell them herself, but the

need to speak to someone was overwhelming. 'It's good news,' she said. 'For you and your family. I've got the results back and there's no connection between me and the Taylor family.'

'That's a relief. I'll not lie to you, Kate. My parents have been so worried about all this. They've had a few sleepless nights. The Taylor family are bad news. Jamie has links to a notorious gang. Dad was petrified they'd find out we were related to Muireann and come after us.'

Kate was shocked. She'd known they were worried but this sounded worse than she'd thought. And they'd been so good to her too. Scrimgeour had had a hardness in his voice when he'd told her to leave well alone. She should have listened to him.

'Are *you* all right though?' asked Conor.

Her defences were down. 'What do you think?'

'Want to talk about it?'

'How long do you have?'

'As much time as you need.'

'That's very kind,' said Kate.

'I mean it. This must be so hard for you.'

They talked for over an hour. Kate felt like she'd known him for years, he was so easy to talk to. 'You've missed your vocation,' she said as they neared the end of their call. 'You should have been a therapist.'

Conor laughed. 'I'll tell the parents you phoned,' he said. 'And any time you want to chat, phone me.' He paused, 'Actually, I'm coming down to London next weekend if you'd like to meet up. If you're free.'

She didn't want to seem too keen. 'I'll need to check my diary. When exactly were you thinking of?'

'The Sunday?'

'Hang on a second.' Kate put the phone down and counted

to twenty before picking it up again. 'Sunday's great,' said Kate. 'Where would you like to meet?'

'I can come out to see you if that helps. You're not too far from London, are you?'

They agreed that Kate would pick him up at the local train station late Sunday morning. They'd go for a walk then back to her cottage. He'd text her the exact time of his train. She put her phone away and returned to work, humming. Roll on Sunday.

THIRTY-TWO

Buckinghamshire
_____

SUNDAY ARRIVED. Kate was going to make supper for Conor so she looked out one of Mirren's recipe books. Mirren had been a superb cook, and as well as having huge numbers of cookery books she also made up recipes of her own. She settled on Mirren's version of Malaysian chicken, a one pot fried rice concoction involving lots of spices, chicken and vegetables.

Conor texted her at half past ten. His train would get in to Gerrards Cross round about noon. Kate swished round the house to make sure everything was in order. It looked lovely. Mirren had collected lots of different pieces of furniture over the years, all of it second hand, all of it good quality. It was dated, older than the fashionable mid-century brands that millennials went for, but Kate didn't care. She loved it and it looked especially good in the sunshine. It gleamed, the wood nourished by the beeswax that Kate had used.

A short drive and she was at the station. Now the train was due she was shaking, unsure if she was doing the right thing in inviting him to her home. Another venue would have been more neutral. Too late now to change her mind, and they had a whole day to get through as well. Perhaps she'd imagined the attraction between them. She breathed deeply and tried to calm down. For heaven's sake this wasn't a date. He was practically family!

When he arrived, the atmosphere was uncomfortable at first. His accent sounded stronger in amongst all the southern drawls. It wasn't until they reached the pub that they began to relax. After they ordered sandwiches and drinks – a pint for him and ginger beer for Kate – he launched into a speech.

'We were worried about you, Kate. About what you'd got yourself into with the Taylors. It was such a relief when you told me about the DNA results. You're well out of it.'

Kate didn't feel it was over though. She'd had an email from DI Scrimgeour on Friday, which said Jamie hadn't taken the news well and had accused the police of fiddling the results. He had ended the mail by advising her not to meet Jamie if he asked. She'd paled at the thought of seeing him again. No way would she agree to meet him and she emailed Scrimgeour to thank him for letting her know.

'You're very quiet. Are you all right?'

The last thing Kate wanted was to discuss her fears about Jamie. She'd brought all this on herself and she was determined to enjoy her time with Conor, so she mumbled something about being tired. He frowned, but let it go.

'What are you going to do now?'

'Nothing. I don't think there's anything else I can do.'

'Dad said he'd speak to the police again for you. He has several contacts. There might be other children who went missing at that time.'

Kate shook her head. 'I doubt it. Two babies, both girls, going missing in the west of Scotland? The papers would have been full of it.'

'Yes, we've been thinking about that. Maybe Muireann stole the baby, you, from somewhere else, somewhere in England.'

It was possible. But Kate didn't want to go there. She had to make peace with not knowing who she was. The brush with the Taylor family had left her wounded, and she worried about going through the whole thing again and maybe finding out horrible things. 'I don't know, Conor,' she said.

'Or adoption. Maybe you were adopted as an older child, maybe your date of birth was the same, by coincidence, or maybe she pretended...' He tailed off. 'I'm not helping, am I?'

Kate nibbled her sandwich. 'Not really.' She changed the subject. 'Let's talk about you. Why are you visiting London? Seeing friends?'

He blushed. 'I have an interview. Tomorrow.'

'That's great. What's the job?'

'It's not for a job. It's for a Master's degree in international relations.'

'Wow. Even better.'

His face lit up. 'Do you mean that? The whole family is on my back, telling me I'm mad, doing another degree, using up all my savings. And in London to boot. They know how much I hated it last time I lived here.'

'Which university is it?'

'LSE.'

Kate was impressed. It was a difficult course to get on to, popular across the world and in high demand. 'You must have a pretty good degree,' she said.

'First in economics and politics.'

Kate took another bite of her sandwich. 'Honestly, Conor. That's brilliant. I'm sure they'll offer you a place. When is your interview?'

'Two o'clock tomorrow. I've actually been offered a place; the interview is for funding. It would be great to get the funding but in any case I've saved enough to pay my fees and to keep me for a year. It's worth a shot anyway.'

Kate changed the subject. All her questioning was making her feel like an auntie, so she told him about the walk she'd planned. 'And then, if you want, if you have time, then we'll go back to mine and I'll make you something to eat.'

'That would be great. I'd love to see where you live. And my dad wants to know all about Muireann's cottage. He's so pleased to have found out what happened to her, you know? And to see where she lived. He said it looked very nice, but you —' He stopped, embarrassed.

'I wouldn't let him in, kept him on the doorstep.' Kate finished his sentence. 'In my defence, it was very late.'

'I know. Mum gave him hell for that. *You did what? Went round at eleven o'clock at night? You're lucky she didn't pull a shotgun on you.*'

Kate laughed. 'Your mum and dad are very welcome to visit at any time. And I'd be delighted to show you round. Take photos if you like, to show them.'

The walk was beautiful. The fields were full of wild flowers, and Kate astonished Conor with her knowledge of the various species. In turn, he impressed her with his ability to identify birds from hundreds of metres away. It was only when he called out, 'Kingfisher! Over there. Quick,' that she realised she was being had.

She punched him on the arm. 'We're nowhere near a river. That was a sparrow. Even I know that one.'

The afternoon passed quickly and soon they were back at Kate's cottage. She gasped as she parked the car. 'The door's ajar. I didn't leave it like that.' She jumped out.

'Wait, you don't know whether anyone's in there.'

Kate stopped dead at the doorway. Of course, it could be a burglar, and here she was assuming it was Josie. Conor joined her in the tiny hallway. There was barely room for the two of them. 'I don't think there's anyone here,' Kate whispered. 'But in case there is, there's a brush in there.' She pointed to the cupboard under the stairs.

'A brush? You expect me to sweep them away?'

His expression was so comically indignant that despite everything Kate giggled. 'It's better than nothing, no?'

He side-eyed her. 'If you say so.' He fetched the brush and pushed in front of her. 'Ready?'

They barged through the living room door, but there was no one there. Nor in the kitchen. Kate swallowed. They'd have to go upstairs. Thank goodness Conor was there. They listened for the slightest sound to betray the presence of someone else and made their way upstairs. Nothing. Kate went to her bedroom and pushed open the door. She nodded towards the wardrobe and Conor opened it. Nothing. It was the same in the bathroom and in Mirren's old room. Only Mirren's study/work-room remained. It was in a terrible state. Papers were strewn everywhere, as were her precious materials for her wall hangings. But there was no sign of any intruder.

'What a mess!' said Conor. 'Is anything missing?'

Kate shrugged. 'Who knows?' She bent down to pick up some papers but Conor told her to leave them.

'You'll need to call the police and report this. They'll want to test for fingerprints,' he said.

'You're right. I'll call them after we've eaten.'

All the excitement of the day had vanished. Kate was desolate. She hated that someone had been inside her house. It had always been her safe haven, but now... She led the way downstairs.

'Let's have a drink before I start making the meal.' In truth she was no longer hungry, but it gave her something to do and helped take her mind off the mess upstairs. She was uneasy. It seemed so targeted, as if the person knew something about her, knew where papers were kept, knew how important Mirren's embroidery was to her. Her mind returned to Josie. She hadn't heard from her since their argument. She hadn't returned the keys, nor had Kate changed the locks. But she wouldn't dare come back, would she? Kate remembered little comments Josie had made since Mirren's death, about her being 'loaded'. Perhaps she thought there was cash in there. It was where Mirren kept her money, but Kate had gathered it all up and banked it while she was ill. Josie was always broke, or so she said. She lived beyond her means. Her upbringing in an upper middle-class family had led her to believe herself entitled to a certain standard of living. For as long as Kate had known her, she'd borrowed money from Mirren that she never returned. First thing tomorrow she would phone a locksmith.

They opened a bottle of Pinot Grigio and had a glass before Kate started to cook. There wasn't much to do, as Kate had prepared everything before leaving in the morning. As they were about to eat there was a knock at the door. Kate sighed and got up.

It was Jack. Kate was about to tell him to fuck off when she spotted the woman in police uniform beside him. He frowned a warning. 'I'm sorry to disturb you, but one of your neighbours reported that your door had been left open all day and they thought you might have been burgled. Can we come in?'

She stood aside and let them in. Conor came out of the kitchen. A look of wounded betrayal flitted across Jack's face. What a nerve.

'Sit down,' said Kate. 'Yes, it looks as though someone has been in here, but I'm not sure if anything is missing.'

The woman spoke now. 'I'm Constable Jennifer Harrison and this is Sergeant Mathers. They got in through the front door, is that right?'

'I don't know. We only got back half an hour ago and we were going to eat before doing all the checks.'

'It looks as though the front door was jemmied,' she replied. She looked at Jack with a raised eyebrow. 'Isn't that right, Sergeant?'

Jack was glaring at Conor, who was oblivious, thank goodness. 'Eh? Oh yes. It's definitely damaged. Can you show me the rest of the house, please?'

This was the last thing Kate needed. Her meal was congealing next door. 'Only one room shows any signs of disturbance. Upstairs. My mother's old workroom and study.'

'Can I see? You stay here, Constable. Check downstairs in case anything's been missed.'

Jack followed her upstairs. As soon as they were inside the study, he closed the door. 'So, that's your new man, is it? Didn't take you long?'

Kate ignored him. 'As you see, Sergeant, the room has been thoroughly searched. I'm not sure anything is missing but it will take me time to confirm that.'

'How could you?'

Kate wasn't going to engage with him. 'Well, if that's all. I was in the middle of a meal.' The door opened and Conor came in. 'Everything all right here?'

'Yes. Sergeant Mathers is on his way out. He got what he came for.'

Conor raised his eyebrows at her bitter tone. They went downstairs, where Jennifer was waiting. 'Shall I phone for forensics, Sarge?'

Jack said nothing for a few seconds. 'What? Oh, yes. Of course.' He turned to Kate. Someone will come out – tomorrow morning at the earliest – to get fingerprints. In the meantime, don't touch anything in the room upstairs.'

'OK, well thank you for coming.' They took the hint and left. Kate watched them go down the garden path. Jennifer's voice rang out in the still, evening air. 'You OK, Jack? You looked a bit—'

Jack interrupted her. 'I'm fine. Waste of my fucking time.'

'But didn't you ask to come on this call? That's what Fred said.'

They got into the car then and Kate didn't hear any more. Shame. She'd been enjoying Jack's squirming responses. She went inside and back into the kitchen where Conor was already reheating the food. 'Bit of a back story there, if I'm not wrong?'

'You don't want to know.'

'Ex-boyfriend?'

Kate looked at him. Time to tell him the truth. 'Yep. It was a bad relationship. He was married.'

'Oh, I'm sorry.'

'Nothing to be sorry about. I'm well out of it.'

Conor served the food and they sat down to eat. When they finished, Kate offered to make coffee and then run him to the station.

'Are you sure you'll be all right on your own?' said Conor. 'I hope I'm not out of line here but I could stay if you like. Sleep on the sofa.'

It was a reassuring thought. 'If you really don't mind, that would be great. And no need to sleep on the sofa, I'll make up Mirren's bed.'

Kate was relieved at the thought of him in the house. A little part of her was also pleased that it meant more time together. She'd really enjoyed their day together.

THIRTY-THREE

Buckinghamshire

Noises from downstairs woke Kate to the mouth-watering smell of bacon. Conor must have popped out to the shops. She jumped out of bed, pulled on her dressing gown and ran downstairs. Conor was by the stove.

'That smells good.'

'Sit down and I'll get you what, tea? Coffee?'

'Coffee, please.'

'Do you want an egg with the bacon?'

'Toast will be fine.'

As Kate waited for her breakfast she hummed under her breath, happier than she'd been for months. It was so good to have someone here with her, someone to share things with. But of course, he'd be gone again in a few hours.

'This has been lovely,' he said. 'I hope we can keep in touch.'

'So do I,' said Kate. 'Your whole family has been brilliant, made me feel so welcome, even if I am the cuckoo in the nest.'

Conor laughed at that. 'I'll phone for a taxi.'

'Don't you dare. I'll run you to the station.'

Two hours later, and he'd gone. Kate was working from home. She'd wait for the fingerprinting to be done before starting on the task of clearing up Mirren's study. The police officer arrived at noon. First, he took her fingerprints, for elimination purposes. Then the questions started.

'Who else has been in the room?'

'My mother,' said Kate. 'It was her room, so her fingerprints will be everywhere.'

'Can we speak to her?'

Kate kept it brief. 'She died in June.'

'I'm sorry for your loss.' The young PC said it as if he meant it. 'Is there anyone else who's been in here? Sergeant Mathers mentioned a young man.'

'He didn't touch anything in the room and he'd never been in the room before yesterday.' Kate hesitated. 'There is one other person, a friend of my mother's, Josie Turner. She spent a lot of time with my mother so...'

'Fine, we'll take her details before we leave, and perhaps if you could let her know we'll be in touch, that would be helpful.'

Kate left them to it and washed her hands several times to get the ink off her fingertips, but it was surprisingly resistant. She decided to phone Josie later, as she needed to get on with cleaning the room.

The room was a complete mess when they left. Black powder everywhere. The room looked dreadful, as if no-one had cleaned it for years. She ran downstairs and fetched cleaning materials. The floor was wooden, not carpeted like the rest of upstairs, thank goodness. She wouldn't bet on getting that powder out of a carpet. After an hour of cleaning there was progress. All the stained surfaces were clean and polished, papers were piled up and the materials were folded, ready to be put away again on shelves. Kate did that first as it was the easiest. She knew she wouldn't be able to make as good a job of it as Mirren had. Although Mirren hadn't cared much for housework, she'd been obsessive about keeping her workroom in order, the order they were in, and everything was colour matched. But she tried her best and the end result was acceptable if not brilliant. It would do for now, anyway, until she made a decision what to do with it all. Perhaps a local school or art class would want them. Kate didn't. Mirren had tried several times to get her interested, but she had no imagination, no real creativity. She could manage a simple embroidery kit but that was it. Her efforts at the sort of art that Mirren did were so poor that eventually Mirren admitted defeat. 'I always hoped you'd take after me,' she'd said. 'Always hoped you'd be artistic.'

She turned to the papers and began to sort them. It was wrong to keep putting it off, and now was as good a time as any. There were bills and bank statements from years ago. Kate had read somewhere that you only need to keep the last five years of bank statements and two years of utility bills, so the older ones could go. She got the utility bills into order first. She'd already had the bills transferred to her name so the ones in Mirren's name could be shredded. She was aiming for a clutter-free life. Bank statements next. They went back to 1993. The year after Mirren disappeared. Kate was disappointed. She thought maybe there might have been something there from before. She picked up the one nearest. Bloody hell, she thought, things were a lot cheaper then. The weekly shopping at Budgens was under twenty pounds. Kate's last trip there on Saturday cost her sixty-three pounds.

She was about to put it on the shredding pile when a familiar name jumped out at her. Josie's. She studied the statement and then picked up another and another. There in black and white on the first of each month, fifty pounds into the account of Josephine Turner.

It was a lot to take in. Every statement she picked up was the same. Dozens of them. Why had Mirren paid out so much money to her friend? She looked in the pile for a more recent one and gasped. Two hundred and fifty pounds in January 2010. She kept looking. The payments stopped round about the time of her diagnosis. Kate was baffled.

Downstairs, she found her mobile and looked for Josie's number. 'Dahhling,' Josie drawled as soon as she heard Kate's voice. 'Will you ever forgive me for my little mistake? I'm so sorry if I upset you.' The infamous qualified apology.

'There's no if about it, Josie. You did upset me, but that's not why I'm calling. Why was my mother paying you money every month for the best part of thirty years?'

Silence. 'Josie. Are you there? I want an answer.'

'I... we had an arrangement.'

'What the fuck are you talking about?'

'Don't swear, darling. It's so vulgar.'

'I'm not your fucking darling and I don't give a flying fuck *if* you find it vulgar. Tell me the truth.'

'Such emotion, darling. It's so bad for you. It'll give you wrinkles. Well, if you have to know, I might as well tell you. Mirren owed me money.'

'For twenty-five years! I don't believe you.'

'It's true. I lent her the money for the deposit on that little house you have. Must be worth a fortune now.'

Kate's self-righteous bubble burst. She hadn't thought of that. She'd been expecting blackmail, something more sinister.

Scenes from the past had rushed in on her, when Mirren had been less than pleased to see Josie. Once they'd hidden behind the sofa when she was at the door, two conspirators giggling. Not long after, Josie acquired a key.

'You need to return your key.'

'Of course. I'll pop it through the letterbox.' She was lying but it didn't matter. The locksmith was booked for tomorrow.

'Right, well then. I have to go. Good-bye.' Kate went back upstairs, furious. She'd keep the statements as proof of payment, but first she was going to add up exactly how much had been paid to Josie over the years, and she needed to find something about how much was paid for the house.

Josie had been paid a total of over thirty thousand pounds over the years. It started off at fifty but went up bit by bit until the last five years, when Mirren had been shelling out three hundred pounds to her each month. Thirty thousand pounds sounded a lot for a deposit in the 1990s, but Kate had no idea how to find out how much the house had cost. She continued to search.

Hours later, and she'd found nothing, but at least the bank statements were in good order. For now, she had no option but to accept Josie's word for it, but she was far from convinced. It didn't add up. The increase in payments started at a time when Mirren was earning well for the first time. Coincidence, or had Josie seen it as an opportunity to squeeze more money out of her? Kate wasn't going to let this go.

THIRTY-FOUR

Glasgow

CONOR PHONED her from the train later that evening, to say he'd got the scholarship. Kate was delighted and told him so. 'I hope we'll keep in touch when you move down here,' she said.

I hope so too,' said Conor. 'Maybe you could help me look for a flat.'

'If you tell me what areas you're considering, I'll keep an eye open.'

They chatted on for over an hour until Conor swore, 'Damn, I'm about to run out of battery.'

After they rang off, Kate hugged herself. She had a good feeling about him.

The next morning when she was at work, the phone rang and she answered it quickly, hoping it would be Conor, but it wasn't. She knew immediately from the southern accent. Fuck. A cold caller. Her voice took on an officious tone. 'Who is this?'

'Miss Fallon. This is the police. We have a couple of questions about your break-in last week. Is this a good time to talk?'

Kate glanced at her watch – twenty minutes before the next class. 'I have ten minutes,' she said.

'That will be fine. Now when our officers called round the other evening there was a Scottish gentleman present, is that right?'

Her bristles were rising. 'That's correct, yes.'

'A Jamie Taylor?'

Kate looked at the phone and shook it, as if that would help her bewilderment. 'Ms Fallon? Are you still there?'

'I... um, yes.'

'Is that the name of your gentleman friend or not?'

'It is not.' The words came out in an indignant burst.

'Do you know a Jamie Taylor?'

'Why?'

'Answer the question, please.'

'I have met him three times very briefly and spoken to him on the phone once or twice. Or, I should say, he spoke to me.'

'And when you met him was that at your home?'

'He appeared at my house one evening. I didn't let him in. I barely know him and he turned up uninvited.' Kate suspected where this was going. 'Why are you asking?'

He got to the point at last. The police must get special training in the ways of obfuscation. 'Fingerprints found at your home were run through the national database and a match was found with those of Mr Taylor. Did you know he was a drug dealer when you met him?'

'Not at first, no.'

'Did he come to your house to deal drugs?'

Her hand was cramping, she was clutching the phone so tight. Jack was behind this, she'd swear to it. 'Is Sergeant

Mathers there?' It was a stab in the dark but it reached its target.

The policeman stuttered, taken by surprise. 'I... yes, he's right here.'

She imagined Jack, red faced, signing to him that he wasn't there. 'I'd like to speak to him.'

There were a few muffled words before Jack came on. Kate exploded. 'You must have been wetting yourself finding a drug dealer's fingerprints in my house. You thought they'd been left by...' She stopped. She was not going to tell him Conor's name. 'By my friend.'

'I have to investigate everything thoroughly. So if he's not your friend, why are his fingerprints in your bedroom?'

'It's not my bedroom, as you well know. It was my mother's workroom. If Jamie Taylor's fingerprints are there it's because he broke in.'

'You've already said you know him. Why would he break in?'

'I don't know, do I?'

'Come off it, Kate. You must know. You were scared enough before when he came to your door, so scared you called out to a neighbour to call the police.'

Shit. She was going to have to explain. 'Look,' she said. 'It's complicated.'

'Complicated,' he repeated. 'What's that supposed to mean? You were in a relationship with him?'

'No, I was not in a relationship with him. I thought... I thought he was my brother.'

'But you're an only child.'

'That's what I thought.'

She'd silenced him. There were voices in the background,

asking him questions. He came back to her. 'I'll send someone round to take a statement.'

'No—' she protested, but he had already hung up.

When she opened the door an hour later, he was there alone. Thank goodness. Kate didn't want a stranger hearing this story. 'Well?' she said.

He sighed. 'Kate, there's no easy way of saying this, but this guy is no good. He's into drug dealing, he's done time for GBH. His father was done for the murder of his own daughter and killed himself in prison. Why would you think he's your brother?'

'I already know his background. He's not my brother.'

'Go on.'

She had to tell him, though not the whole truth. She couldn't tell him she had suspected Mirren of kidnapping her. 'It appears I was adopted. And that family were a possible match for my birth family.'

'But they're not?' He relaxed.

'No, definitely not.'

'How can you be so sure?'

He was a police officer. She should have known there would be questions, but it didn't make her resent them any the less. Especially as she was making things up on the spot. 'The... um adoption company made a mistake.'

'Adoption *company*? What the hell are you talking about?'

'Agency, I mean agency.' Fuck.

'Kate, what's really going on? Is this bloke harassing you? Because if he is, I...'

'Everything's fine, Jack. He must have come to the house, and when I wasn't in he took the opportunity to have a look round. Nothing's missing so I want it dropped.'

'That's not up to you or me, I'm afraid. If there's enough

258

evidence to charge him, then that's what will happen.' He stood up. 'I know you're not telling me the truth, Kate, and I could have you charged with wasting police time.'

'It wasn't me who called the police,' she reminded him. Her hands trembled and she sat on them so he wouldn't notice.

'I won't charge you, don't worry. If you want to talk about it, you know where I am. It's a lot for you to take on, finding out you're adopted like that. Are you sure you're OK?'

That was the Jack she fell in love with, the one who sounded like he cared, but she was not going to weaken. 'And what would Vicky have to say about it if I took up your offer?'

'This is a police matter, Kate. Confidential. She wouldn't know anything about it.'

'Jack, go. I'm fine, really.'

She didn't move for ten minutes after he'd gone. What the fuck had Jamie Taylor been doing in her house? Money, she decided. He must have been looking for money, started upstairs and got disturbed before he found anything. She hoped he was on his way back to Scotland. It made her very uneasy to think he'd been rummaging around in her house.

THIRTY-FIVE

Buckinghamshire

KATE PUT her worries to one side. She had too much to do to take time out to fret over that lowlife. She finished her work for the day and brought out the box of Mirren's art to go through. Four of the paintings were set aside for immediate framing. There was an excellent picture framer nearby, and she'd take them in the next day on her way to work. The other paintings she put away for the time being. There was nowhere obvious to hang them, but she didn't want to lose them. She'd stack up the sketch books on her bookshelves. There were more than fifty of them, mainly A5 size, so they'd take up the greater part of a shelf. They would need to be catalogued, perhaps by date. From what she'd seen, Mirren had been rigorous in dating her paintings, and Kate imagined she would have done the same for the sketch books.

She found the one she'd already looked at, and sure enough it was dated April – September 1968. Mirren had written the dates on the frontispiece, and Kate checked another to see if it had the same dating system. It did. She was going to go through them all with the aim of putting them in chronological order.

Once she'd done that, she'd label them on the outside and then make a list on her computer of what each one contained. It was a daunting task but she reckoned she'd enjoy it. She poured a glass of wine before starting.

With Nina Simone playing in the background, she settled down to work. It was easier than she thought to sort them. She resisted peeking inside. That was a task for another day. But when she found one marked June – December 1991, she had to look. She turned the page tentatively, frightened of what she'd find. The first few sketches looked as though they'd been drawn in a medical waiting room. Mirren must have taken her sketch book with her on ante-natal appointments. There were rows of women in various stages of pregnancy. How did they feel about being drawn? Did they know? There were several pages of this; she must have intended doing a painting of the scene, as there were notes of how she could change the composition to make it better. Kate turned the pages and caught her breath.

Mirren had sketched then painted scenes of childbirth. Kate's first thought was that it was of Mirren's own experience, but the women depicted were all different. She must have got permission from the women to be there. She examined one more closely, and sure enough Mirren had written down the woman's name and age. *Shabana 24, first child, Tahir born 13th September 1991*. Shabana's face was contorted with pain. Beside her a woman, her mother judging by her age, gripped her hand tightly and mopped her face with a flannel. On the next page, Shabana was holding her baby close to her chest while a nurse cut the cord, and on the next, she was feeding the baby while her mother looked on. There was such tenderness in these sketches that Kate wanted to cry. Her mother would never be beside her while she gave birth.

Overwhelmed, she leafed through the next few pages. There were more, similar in style. Perhaps Mirren had thought of exhibiting them, although according to Aodhan, her husband had more or less stopped her painting by then. Maybe it was her way of chronicling her pregnancy. The dates were in chronological order, so Kate skimmed through them until she reached the first of October. Sure enough there was a self-portrait – she must surely have done these from a photograph – among others. Her husband was there in one, and in another there was what must be her extended family. Kate recognised Margaret, heavily pregnant with Conor. These would have to be given back to the family – they should have them – but she'd also like to find out who the other women were. They'd surely love to have their pictures.

Kate put the book aside and went downstairs to get another glass of wine. Back upstairs she continued. The next few pages held drawings of Mirren's baby: *Caitlin aged two days; Caitlin's first bath; Caitlin aged five days*. Kate was so engrossed in the beauty of these that she didn't expect what came next, though she should have known by the very fact that the Caitlin in these sketches was getting older: *eight weeks three days; ten weeks two days; twelve weeks*. Kate cried out when she turned the page and found another drawing. It was unbearable. There was nothing to say what it was, no date, no name, but nothing was needed to tell her she was looking at a drawing of Caitlin's coffin. That inside that stark white box lay the destruction of all of Mirren's hopes and dreams. She broke down.

It was more than an hour later before Kate was composed enough to carry on. There were no more drawings. Only words. Page after page filled with tiny writing, so cramped it was difficult to read. Kate thought perhaps she ought not to read it but she was compelled.

. . .

Today I went to see the therapist for the first time. They've all been on at me for months to see a counsellor, my parents, husband, friends. They tell me it's not natural to grieve so much, that I should be trying harder. I don't know what they mean. How can you grieve too much for a child? What do they want from me? Smiles, nodding like an imbecile as if nothing has happened. They want me to be quiet. They can't cope with the howling wreck I've become. All snot and tears and rage. It's all right for them, with their stupid ignorant mediaeval beliefs. The other day Mammy told me she's in a better place. They all say the same, singing from the same fucking hymn sheet. The Good Lord only takes the best for Himself. I don't believe in their God but if I did, I'd hate him for what he's done.

My therapist has asked me to keep a diary. I don't see the point. But she says it will help me process my grief. 'But what if I don't want to process it?' I asked. 'What if I want to grieve, if I believe I should never stop grieving?'

She has a habit of not looking at me when she's talking. Or rather, she looks at me but avoids eye contact. Her gaze rises above my forehead, as if she's talking to my hairline. It's disconcerting. I raise my eyes, trying to catch hers, but they're elusive. 'You must understand, that grieving is a process we all go through. That we must go through. There are five stages.' Her voice is expressionless. She could be reading from a text. Not a very interesting one, a telephone directory perhaps. 'First, we have denial. Our first reaction is numbness. Where is the meaning in life, how can we go on? In this stage, life makes no sense to us because we are so shocked. Getting through the day is an effort. Why is this the case? Well, it helps us cope and makes survival possible. It is nature's way of letting in only what we can handle.'

I pick at a thread on my skirt, pulling at it until the hem starts to unravel. 'And what's the evidence for this?'

Her eyes flicker, searching for an escape route. 'It's a well-known theory, from the work of a woman called Kubler-Ross.'

'A theory is nothing. It's hypothetical until you provide evidence to support it.' I've scored a point but she doesn't miss a beat.

'Does this not resonate with you?'

My head goes down again. I haven't the energy to argue.

'The second stage is anger.' She leaves a long pause. She's waiting for me to speak, but I'm not going to make things easy for her. The clock on the wall ticks as she waits, but I'm too good for her. I stare at her pale face. Patsy, her name is. It suits her. Pasty Patsy. She stares back, her gaze still not on target, still grazing my eyebrows. Tick, tock, five minutes to go. She sighs. 'It is my belief and that of your family, that you are stuck at this phase. Until you work through it, you will never move on.'

I glower at her. To her credit she doesn't flinch. 'It would be very helpful,' she says, 'for you to keep a journal of your feelings. Be honest in it. We will discuss it next time.'

I'll keep the diary and she'll find out how angry I am. What she doesn't know is that I don't want to move on. I want to move back, to a time when I was happy. But that's not going to happen, is it? And no matter what they all say, memories are not the same. If I hear one more person say I have my memories, I swear, I'll fucking kill them. A memory, you idiots, is not the same as a person.

Well, rant over. For today. At least I've done my homework, that'll please the family, make them think I'm beginning to 'process' things.

Kate put down the sketch book. It was dreadful to read. She felt as if she was there with Mirren going through her grief.

Mirren's parents sounded as though they had no real under-standing of her grief, and as for the therapist? From the look of things, she ought never to have worked in counselling. There was no sign of any empathy in the interactions with Mirren, no sign of any sort of human feeling. Kate steadied herself with another gulp of wine and read on.

She told me writing would make me feel better. Why doesn't anyone understand that nothing is going to make me feel better? Ever. Except oblivion.

I am angry. All those times when I argued for the parents to keep their child. I'd fight for resources: a place in daycare, a home help to come in and help with the housework, a place in a special project where well-meaning people like myself would show hapless young girls how to play with their baby. Why did I not see how hopeless it was, that it would take a miracle to compensate for the lack of care these girls had had themselves from their own parents? An unbreakable cycle. There was that young woman, Linda, who I met in hospital after the birth of Caitlin. She hadn't known she was pregnant. How she laughed, 'I went for a shit – couldn't pass nothing and thought I was dying. Half an hour on the jacksy and there it was, another fuckin wean.' She was nineteen and already had three children, all of them in care. I was forty-one and had only the one.

The maternity hospital where I was had small rooms for four people. The other patients were all right except for one or two. I didn't want them to learn what I did for a living. I was worried when I recognised one of Linda's visitors as a former client. I lowered my head and prayed for the first time in years.

My luck was in. A huge argument started between her and Linda and security was called. The sister, as she turned out to be, was escorted from the hospital and told not to return. Linda turned to me.

'She's a right fuckin bitch, that one.'

'Oh,' I said, careful not to give her any encouragement. I didn't want to engage with her any more than I had to. But she had no social skills, no boundaries, and so launched into a barely coherent diatribe. The 'bitch' wanted her wean as she'd already had hers taken off her.

'I was going to give her up. The last thing I want is another fuckin wean, but no way is she getting her manky hands on anything of mine. I'd kill the wean first.'

My head raised at that and I glared at her. 'You're not serious.'

She looked back, her eyes dead. 'You're a right stuck-up cow.'

'Fair enough.' I got up out of bed and pulled the curtain round my bed. Didn't make any difference, she carried on ranting and calling me names. It wasn't pleasant.

So, yes. I am angry that people like her have their child and I don't. I am angrier than I have ever been in my life. And no, Patsy. It isn't helping the least to write down my feelings. If anything, it stirs everything up. Another appointment today. What a waste of time. I gave her my diary to read. While she was looking it over, she gave me a rating scale about my feelings.

Question One: on a scale of 1–10, how angry are you? With 1 being not at all angry and 10 being as angry as you've ever been. What a stupid fucking question. As if there's a score for my fury, it is infinite.

Question Two: on a scale of one to ten, how sad are you? Are you fucking serious, Patsy?

Question Three: what would need to happen for you to move down one place on the scale? This one got me, I admit. The only thing that would work was to have another child to love, and that's not going to happen. Those endless years of trying for a child, six miscarriages and then the fluke that resulted in our beautiful daughter. And after that, the blow to end it all. An emergency hysterectomy. So it would take a miracle to move me down one place on the scale.

I put the questionnaire down and sneaked a look at Patsy to see how she was taking my journal. Not well by the look of things. Probably didn't like my description of her. Tough. She asked me to be honest and I was. She caught me staring at her and nodded towards the paper in my hand.

'Finished, have you? That was quick.' Icy voice. I shook my head and continued.

Question Four: where would you like to be on the scale? And so it goes on. Jesus Christ – give me patience. Another child though. The thought makes me feel better, not much it's true, but the seed is germinating. A child. Not that anyone could replace what we had lost but nonetheless. Perhaps adoption is an answer.

Kate stared at the words. At last. Something to show she'd considered adoption. This was the answer she needed. She read on, hoping to learn more.

I mentioned it to Tommy last night, asked if he'd ever consider it. He looked at me with those eyes that have become so sad. In a few short words he destroyed me forever. 'You're too old, sweetheart, and so am I. The oldest they'd consider is thirty-eight. After that you're past it.' I walked out then, went up to the park. I was in a daze, my last hope gone. I hated him so much I wanted to kill him. So unfair when all he does is worry about me. He worries about me all the time. I'm too thin, too quiet, too angry, too sad. All of those and more. I don't care, I want to die. I failed to protect the one thing that mattered. Our daughter is gone, after a span on earth barely longer than the wisp of smoke that spirals up from my cigarette. That's another thing. I've taken up smoking again. After all those months of abstinence.

Above me the clouds were the sort of charcoal grey that heralds heavy rain. I pulled my jacket tight. Tommy's right. I am getting thin. Three months ago, I struggled to do up the zip, now it flaps round me. It started to rain. One drop followed by another followed by thousands. Within a minute I was soaked, the rain pushing its way through the so-called waterproof material to drench my shoulders and neck. I put my head down and walked, not seeing the figure coming towards me with a pram.

'Muireann! How are you? Managed to escape without the baby? Lucky you.'

Lucky me. Am I lucky, Patsy? Unlucky more like. Is it bad luck that my baby died or did I bring this on myself? Are you one of those people who say senseless things like 'what goes around comes around'? I always want to spit when I hear that, that and 'what's for you, will not go by you.'

I didn't stop, pushed my way past and ran down the hill towards the main road. The woman – she was an acquaintance, I knew her from work – called after me, 'What's wrong with you?' I thought everyone knew by now. I was crying so hard I couldn't see and I ran out onto the road. A car screeched to a halt, stopping inches from me. I stood there unable to move as an angry man berated me. 'I'm sorry,' I managed, my voice a croak. He must have realised there was something up because he withdrew, muttering under his breath about 'crazy women'. I wanted to be invisible, to disappear. To be free of the people mumbling ill thought out condolences. To be free from Tommy pressing food on me, free of my family with their concerned glances and whispered briefings behind doors – how has she been today, did she go out at all, has she eaten anything?

When I got home the house was empty. A blessing. Mammy keeps coming round at odd hours, to check on me. I can't stand it. If it was up to me, I'd stay in bed all day, burrow into the bedclothes and sleep. I'd dream of Caitlin, have time away from the harsh reality of life. But they won't let me be.

Yesterday Tommy suggested it was time to go back to work. Do you believe that, Patsy? I work in child protection. I'll never work in that area again. When I go back to work, I'll have to get a transfer. Work with old people maybe. I enjoyed that when I was a trainee. God knows why I went into child protection. All that abuse, for trying to protect the most precious thing in the world.

Kate stopped reading. Mirren's grief was so raw, it was unbearable. She must have suffered terribly. She closed the book and got up from where she was sitting on the floor. The rest would have to wait for the coming days. She got ready for bed – it was well past eleven now – and slid under the duvet to lie awake for hours going over what she'd read.

THIRTY-SIX

Buckinghamshire

KATE WAS EXHAUSTED from the emotional maelstrom of reading Mirren's diary and woke late. There was only time to shower and grab a cup of coffee before setting off to work. It was the first day back for the students and they'd be there early, keen to get started. She arrived with five minutes to spare, enough to set up the power point presentation.

The students were restless. Up at the back a little group chatted between themselves and Kate spotted several scrolling through their phones. She didn't blame them. The subject matter was dry – copy editing – and although she usually made it interesting and amusing with anecdotes about bloopers that escaped editors' notice – *Statistics show teenage pregnancies drop off after the age of twenty-five,* that sort of thing – she couldn't be bothered today. At last, the tortuous hour ended and she was free to escape to her room where she worked until lunchtime without a break. She had another lecture at two p.m. so she picked up a tuna sandwich from the cafeteria and ate it at her desk. It was dry and left an unpleasant metallic after-taste. She was desperate for the afternoon to be over so she could return to the sketch book with its insights into Mirren's life.

It was eight o'clock before she got home. Once she'd eaten, she fetched the sketchbook and resumed reading.

Tommy was late coming home from work again. 'You're late,' I said.

His tone was flat when he responded. 'You noticed.'

He needed something from me, a word or a gesture to show I cared. He looked sad, worn down, but I didn't have the energy to respond.

'What's for tea?'

I shrugged.

He opened his mouth as if to remonstrate with me but thought better of it. 'I'll go out and get a fish supper. Do you want anything?'

'No.'

He walked over to me and took my hands in his. He looked at them closely, felt the bones of them. 'What have you eaten today?'

My mind was empty. Food, what was that? At last, I managed, 'Toast... I had toast.'

'You're lying,' he said. 'You've had nothing to eat. You're killing yourself. You're surviving on nothing but coffee and fags. You have to eat. You have—' He broke off and turned away. 'Oh, what's the point? Do what you like. I'm off to the pub.'

I wanted to stop him, to try to offer him comfort, but I was empty. He was late to return home. At midnight I went to bed, knowing I wouldn't sleep. I lay on my back in the double bed and waited until I heard him stumble in. He made his way upstairs muttering and I turned on my side to feign sleep.

'I know you're awake.'

I said nothing, trying to steady my breathing, hoping he'd be fooled into thinking I was asleep.

'We can't go on like this,' he said. 'We've lost a child, now we're losing each other. I can't bear it.' He waited.

I counted out the seconds. I reached fifty-seven before he spoke again.

'Is there any future for us? Is there any hope left?'

My mouth was dry, my tongue stuck to the roof. I couldn't answer even if I'd wanted to.

'I'll take that as a no then.'

After trying to sleep and being unsuccessful, sleep was now the only thing my body craved. Why didn't he go away? A few seconds later, I heard him sigh and he left.

I overslept. The light filtering into the bedroom was bright, the sun high in the sky. I turned over, desperate to return to my dream where Caitlin was alive, playing on a sandy beach, squealing with delight as waves splashed over her feet. It was fantasy, nothing more. She had never played on a beach and she never would. I didn't even have memories. How many memories do you make in twelve weeks and one day? Not a lot. Those I do have are vague. The difficult labour, the forceps delivery, which had been an invasion rather than an intervention as the young doctor had called it. Then turning away as they'd tried to put Caitlin into my arms. I didn't feel the rush of love everyone claims hits them. That came later. Now, with the dream slipping away, I tried to remember everything about those first few hours, but it was hopeless. Maybe Caitlin sensed I didn't immediately love her, maybe that's why she left. I do have memories, of course I do. But there are so few of them and they mostly involve crying, and struggling to feed... but there were good times too. Oh, God. Bending over her as she lay in her pram and cooing and the twitching of her cheek as she attempted her first smile. Mammy said it was wind but I knew better. It was a smile, tentative, unsure, but a smile nonetheless.

There was nothing for it but to get up. I didn't want Mammy to see me still in my nightclothes. She's taken to calling round at odd times, trying to catch me out. I looked at myself in the mirror. My hair was fine. No need to shower. Who was I kidding? My hair hung in lank strands around my face, forming greasy clumps.

The next few pages were similar. There was no sign of any improvement. Only the heart-breaking details of a life without the longed-for child and the meetings with her counsellor with whom she had a terrible relationship. Her descriptions of the counsellor grew ever more vitriolic until one day she wrote that *Patsy has given up. She's passing me onto another counsellor*.

It wasn't a surprise. Mirren's diary entries showed that Patsy had little empathy or understanding of what Mirren was going through. She was more concerned about getting through the programme she had developed. There were no signs of the unconditional positive regard counsellors are supposed to show clients. Mirren ended the entry with a note that a Ms Josephine Turner was going to be taking over from next week.

Kate read the name again. It must be a coincidence. Turner was a common name. And Josie and Mirren were friends. Kate's earliest memories included Josie. She was sure it was against professional ethics to be friends with a client, even if they were no longer receiving counselling. It was late and she was exhausted, but she had to know. She picked up the book and continued reading.

I met the new counsellor today. All very posh and ladylike. Looks like she has a poker up her arse. She's English, from Sussex she told me. She's less pushy than Patsy. Told me to take my time, that I was in a safe space and if I didn't want to talk I didn't have to. Oh the relief! She was comfortable with the silence, didn't feel the need to interrupt my thoughts, didn't ask me how I was feeling today. Of all the questions Patsy asked, this was the worst. It was no better than what my family does, but she was getting paid for it. I asked if I should continue keeping this diary that Patsy was so keen on. 'Will you read it?' I asked. 'Only if you want me to,' she answered. I liked that reply. It made me feel as though I was in control.

Kate stopped reading. It *was* Josie who had taken on the role of counsellor. It had to be. It was too much of a coincidence otherwise. Kate had a bad feeling about this. Perhaps there was nothing sinister in it. Perhaps it was all above board. But one thing was certain. Josie knew more than she had told Kate.

THIRTY-SEVEN

Glasgow

Two WEEKS since the meeting with Kate Fallon and Alex couldn't stop thinking about her. It had been a relief when the results proved there was no familial link between her and the Taylors. Part of him was sorry she hadn't found resolution, but it was no surprise to him. That baby was dead; he'd known from the minute he'd met Robbie and Brenda Taylor. Perhaps if her remains were ever discovered they'd find evidence to make it clearer what had happened. Brenda Taylor knew all right, but she'd never break her silence.

He'd emailed Kate after the results came through, but other than a brief thank you she hadn't replied. He'd thought of emailing again but couldn't think of a good enough reason. She had got under his skin right enough. He understood why. She was determined to trace her family. He was desperate to find out what had happened to his daughter. When his ex-colleague had come to him with that story of a friend whose sister had disappeared all those years ago and whose daughter now suspected her of kidnap, his heart leapt. Then the blow. The disappearance of her mother, Mirren, a funny name like that, had happened at the same time as Danielle Taylor's kidnapping. Eleven months too early for it to be Mairi.

He should put it behind him, but their meeting had brought back all those memories, memories he'd suppressed for twenty six years. He hadn't set foot in Jordanhill since the day he handed the house keys to the estate agents not long after Sandra killed herself. The house had sold quickly to a couple who were thrilled to get it, dry rot or not. He'd moved to a rented flat in Hyndland and stayed there for a few years. Now he lived on the Southside in a tenement high up on Camphill Avenue with a view over the city. It had been nearer his mother. Now there was only a shadow of his mother left.

He looked round his living room. He called it minimalist, but in truth it was barren. The flat was far too big for one person, but he'd given up any hope of finding a woman to share his life with a long time ago. After Sandra had killed herself, he'd had a couple of relationships but they didn't last long. He didn't trust the women and they'd sussed it out. He no longer cared. He had the bare minimum for a comfortable life. There were two sofas and a coffee table in the room. And a television of course, large enough to watch in comfort but not so big it was absurd. The furniture was lost in the space, which was twenty-two foot by eighteen, but on the plus side the sound from his expensive music system was uncluttered. He'd gone for the best. A local firm, one of the best in the world. Paid them to download his entire collection onto digital. He would never tell anyone what it cost. There were no books lining the wall, no shelves full of CDs or vinyl. Once it became clear that streaming wasn't just another fad, he had downloaded his favourite books to his Kindle and rid himself of the rest, going day after day to the Oxfam second-hand bookshop in Victoria Road. He'd intended to take his CDs and records to a shop in the city centre to sell, but when he phoned to find out how much he'd get, he was so disappointed at the lowly sum, they too went to charity. Cancer Research this time. The woman in the shop had been overwhelmed when he'd gone in with the first boxful. Effusive in her thanks. After the tenth she barely acknowledged him when he came through the door.

There were times when he wished he hadn't been in such a hurry to offload them. He had the space after all, and the lack of personal possessions screamed out to the few people who visited him, how empty his life was.

Over the past few years, he'd developed a taste for classical music, nothing too obscure. He searched through Spotify, put on a Beethoven sonata, the *Pathétique*, and sat back on the brown leather sofa. The music washed over him; he wished he'd continued with the piano lessons he'd had as a child, but peer pressure was too much when he was a teenager and he'd given up. Maybe one day he'd take it up again, buy himself a piano. A baby grand would look great in this room. His mind wandered back to Kate Fallon again. Poor girl, she must be so upset. Was there anything he could do to help? Perhaps she had been taken from somewhere else. Maybe he could look into it, ask around other police forces. As if he didn't have enough work to do. Shit. They were getting nowhere with the investigation into Rosebank. Alex was desperate to move his mother somewhere else, but as yet her social worker hadn't managed to come up with a long-term alternative. He'd arranged respite care for her in another home but she'd caused so much fuss that he'd had to return her to Rosebank after two days. He'd been reluctant to let her go back there but what could he do? Nowhere else had space for her so he had to content himself with visiting her every day, which was hard, but until he was sure they had the murderer he had no alternative.

The following day he went in early to work. He wouldn't waste police time on this search, but he'd do a little every day, for half an hour. His first attempts drew a blank. The only other baby who had disappeared at that time was a boy. Two days old, he had been taken from a hospital in Southampton round about the same time as Danielle. Alex had a vague memory of it. It had happened three days after Danielle was reported missing, and the Southampton police had been keen to liaise, but they were well on the way to building a case against Robbie and it came to nothing once they'd got his confession. In any case, that baby had been found a couple of weeks later. He had been taken by relatives of the father from whom the mother was estranged. Alex looked further afield, in Europe. As he waded through the data that came back to him, it struck him that he knew nothing of what went on in other countries crime-wise. It was safe to assume that other countries knew as little about Scotland's high-profile cases. Very few of the missing children he read about were babies, and they were mostly abducted by a family member, usually an estranged father.

This was getting him nowhere. Although he tried to stick to cases that were relevant, it was hard not to get drawn into the misery outlined in these pages. He was tired and grumpy and felt soiled by reading the sordid details, whether it was a father who kidnapped and then murdered his own children in custody dispute cases or paedophile rings who kept young children in a cage and starved and raped them. Was this what had happened to Mairi? Please God, no. When he thought about her, he always imagined her having been taken by someone who had sold her on to a childless couple desperate for a child. A couple who would love and cherish her. It was his only comfort. Anything else was too horrific to contemplate.

At last, he came across something of interest. A six-month-old baby girl had disappeared along with her pram outside a shop in Lille, France. The mother had wanted to take the pram into the shop, an exclusive and expensive boutique, but the shopkeeper refused and so she left the baby asleep in the pram, coming out to check it every ten minutes, or so she said. The third time she checked, both the pram and the baby were gone. The boutique was in a busy street, but there was no CCTV coverage and no witnesses. In spite of a nationwide search, no trace of the baby or the pram was found. He noted the child's name and checked on Google to see what speculation there had been in the press. There was nothing to be found in the British press, leaving only the French papers, and he didn't speak French, not well enough anyway. He copied and pasted the texts into Google translate and read through the stilted passages that resulted.

An hour later, he was convinced he had enough to justify contacting Kate. It all added up. The baby, Aurelie Dupont, was roughly the same age. Close enough not to raise suspicion if Muireann Fallon tried to pass her off as Caitlin. If they'd had electronic passports in those days then there would be a record of her having travelled to France. But they didn't become available until 2006. He tried to keep his excitement under control, but it was hard. First things first; he needed Kate's phone number. He picked up his iPhone and called Tommy Finlay. Ten minutes later, he had Kate's number, having first phoned Aodhan Fallon. He was careful not to say anything too positive. 'No, nothing important. I'd like another wee chat with her, that's all. Make sure she's OK after that meeting with the Taylors.'

Before he phoned her, he thought carefully about what to say. He had to strike the right note, stay downbeat. He keyed in her number.

'Hello?' She sounded suspicious.

'Ah, yes. Is that Kate?'

'Who's calling, please?'

Her posh accent grated on him. 'It's Alex Scrimgeour—'

'Oh, right. How can I help you?'

'I wondered... I mean, it's unlikely to lead anywhere, but do you have clothes or toys, anything like that from when you were a baby?'

'I don't think so, why?'

'Well, there are databases of missing children. They might help to find out who you are.'

'I don't understand. Are you going to help me find out what happened?'

'Well, I wouldn't say that. I thought... well, it's a possible avenue that hasn't been explored.'

'Why are you doing this?'

Why was he doing this? The question took him by surprise. He didn't know what to say. 'I... I don't know. I lost my family years ago, so you see, I thought we had something in common.'

'Are you coming on to me?' She sounded amused.

'What? No, of course not. I'm twice your age.' The nerve, coming on to her indeed.

'I'm sorry. I'm just teasing you. And I really am sorry you lost your family, that's terrible.'

'Ach well, it's a long time ago now. So, do you have anything?'

'Not that I know of, but there are old suitcases in the attic. I think I remember Mirren saying there were old baby clothes in there. I'll have a look.

'I'll give you my phone number. Get back to me if you find anything relevant.' He waited to be told it was a waste of time, but again, no outburst. He recited his phone number to her and finished the call. Well, he'd tried, hadn't he?

THIRTY-EIGHT

Buckinghamshire

WHAT ON EARTH was that all about? Why was Scrimgeour trying to help all of a sudden? Kate put the phone down and returned to what she was doing. She'd look in the attic at the weekend but was pretty sure there was nothing to be found in those cases.

She couldn't settle, though. It troubled her. Why the sudden interest? She phoned him back, but it rang out. No voicemail, nothing. It was unreasonable, but she was still annoyed at the reception she'd got from him in Glasgow. Fair enough. She'd rattled his cage with accusations of miscarriage of justice. And she'd been in the wrong. She'd stirred up the hornet's nest that was the Taylors. Fuck. She was going to have to look in those suitcases now. They wouldn't wait.

It was years since she'd been in the attic. There was a Ramsay loft ladder, which she pulled down with difficulty. As far as she remembered, there was a light in the attic. When she reached the top of the ladder she leaned inside and scrabbled for the light switch. Thank goodness the bulb was still working. She didn't fancy going into the attic without it, although it was safe enough; Mirren had it floored years ago. She hauled herself up and looked around. It was cluttered with more boxes than she remembered. Mirren rarely threw anything out. She pulled one towards her and looked inside. Books. She'd need to look through these and sort them out. Another was full of CDs. Hadn't Mirren got rid of these when Kate persuaded her to use Spotify? There were a dozen or so of these boxes and Kate baulked at the thought of going through more stuff. No sooner was one thing ticked off her list but another popped up. She spotted the suitcases she'd been thinking of in a corner and edged towards them. Kate was sure they contained clothes from when she was a young child, because she remembered Mirren telling her. Mirren had made most of her clothes when Kate was a child, only stopping when she reached the age of about twelve and Kate nagged her into buying stuff from New Look and H and M. She'd wanted to be the same as everyone else by then. As teenagers do.

There were two suitcases. Kate took a brief look inside. Sure enough they were packed with clothes. Kate hauled them down the ladder, or more accurately let them slide down and climbed down after them.

She opened the smaller one. They were dresses from when she was at least six years old. She resisted the temptation to go through them, to sit with them in her lap and remember her childhood, and so she stuffed them back in again, grateful the moths hadn't got to them. She turned to the other suitcase. It was old and excellent quality, made from brown leather and lined with pink silk. The kind of thing people turn into coffee tables these days or use as props. Mirren had bought it in a charity shop. She was always snuffling around in them, looking for bargains or old dresses to use in her projects. Where they lived was a wealthy area and there were always bargains to be found.

This was more promising. The clothes were smaller, though none were small enough to be for a baby. They were all toddler size or bigger and looked as though they were home-made. Kate was putting them back when she noticed one of them had a label. It was in French and she took it out and put it aside. It was smaller than the rest of the clothes – the label said 12–18 months. She didn't think it would lead anywhere but she'd phone Scrimgeour later and let him know. The rest of the things went back in the attic.

Josie was yet to get back to her. It was over a day since Kate had phoned. She hadn't left a message as Kate wanted to see her face when she told her she'd been rumbled. She'd gone through every one of the sketch books and there was nothing more of interest. Kate felt as though she was about to make a break-through, but everything was conspiring against her to stop it happening. It was time to phone Josie again. This time she answered.

'I need to see you,' said Kate.

'Hello, Kate, nice to hear from you.' There was no mistaking the sarcasm in her voice.

'I don't have time for this, Josie. I have to speak to you.'

'What about?'

'You can come round here or I'll come to yours.' Kate waited for her to refuse or brush her off but Josie invited Kate over. 'I'll make you lunch. Get some decent food into you.'

Kate wasn't going to rise to the inference that she was not capable of feeding herself but instead told her she'd be there in half an hour. She went upstairs and got the relevant sketch book. She was on the point of leaving the house when her phone rang. Scrimgeour.

'You rang?'

'Yes. I've looked through the suitcases. There's lots of children's clothes but only one baby dress.'

'Is that all?' He sounded disappointed.

'Well, it's a French make. It must have been a present. My mother never bought me clothes until I was a teenager and certainly never French ones.'

For a moment there was silence on the other end of the line. When he spoke again there was an air of suppressed excitement in his voice. 'I'd be grateful if you'd take a picture and email it to me. Along with any information you have. The brand, the exact size. Anything unusual about it.'

'What are you not telling me?'

Once more it was a few seconds before he replied. 'I don't want you getting your hopes up,' he said. 'I've been looking through cold cases and there's one in France. A baby was taken not long after your mother disappeared. A fortnight or so. It's likely to be a coincidence, but I'll follow it up once you get the information to me.'

Kate's mouth was dry. She was on the verge of tears. Was this it? Was the mystery about to be solved? 'Can you tell me more?'

'At the moment, no. I'm sorry. If you send those details to me, I'll get back to you as soon as possible. But I warn you. It may take a long time.'

Kate tried not to get too excited about this development but her hands shook as she laid out the dress on the kitchen table and took photographs of it from a number of different angles. She composed an email to Scrimgeour and included a description of the dress: It's blue with a white collar. There are daisies embroidered on the front. It is 100% cotton. The brand is French – *L'enfant chic*.

She'd looked it up. It was a French company, on the go since the 1970s when the proprietor decided to create *un marque qui est aussi chic comme les mamans*. It didn't look as if the designs had been updated since that time. They were all very pretty but impractical, and Mirren had never bought Kate anything so, well, girly. Her childhood clothes were beautifully made, but they were made to last and to shrug off stains. Kate looked at the prices and knew for sure Mirren hadn't bought it. Over a hundred euros for a dress! She returned to the email, checked it and pressed send.

THIRTY-NINE

Buckinghamshire

KATE WAS HALF AN HOUR LATE. Josie greeted her with a sour look when she answered the door.

'I'm late, I know,' said Kate before Josie had a chance to remonstrate. She was furious with herself for not being on time. She was the one who should be full of righteous indignation.

She sat down to a perfectly prepared chicken and avocado salad. Josie knew how to cook, Kate would give her that. She and Mirren used to go to cookery classes together and would make interesting meals. They made small talk as they ate. Kate didn't mention the keys. There was no point. The locks had been changed. Let her find out if she dared try again.

Josie lit a cigarette, a real one this time, and sat back in her chair. 'Well, my darling. Spit it out. What's so urgent that you have to speak to me immediately?'

Kate brought out the sketchbook and pushed it across the table to her. 'This is partly full of drawings Mirren did before her baby was born. It's also a diary of sorts.'

'You mean before you were born.'

Kate stared at her. She'd been Mirren's therapist. She knew Caitlin was dead. 'When I was going through her papers, I found a death certificate.'

'And?'

'It was in my name.'

She laughed. 'Well, that's not possible. You're not dead, are you darling? Pretty good looking corpse if you are.' She didn't look at Kate as she stubbed out her cigarette in the saucer she was using as an ashtray. She gathered the plates together to wash them up. Everything about her oozed guilt.

'What do you know, Josie?'

She tried again to divert Kate, mumbling about making coffee. Kate thumped the table with her fist, making her jump. 'I know she had a baby called Caitlin, same as me, and that the baby died when she was three months old. She went to see a grief counsellor, Patsy, who made her keep a diary. This.' She lifted up the sketchbook and waved it in front of Josie's face. 'Here she makes a note to say that Patsy has transferred her to another counsellor.' Kate opened the book and pointed, her finger jabbing the page as she spoke. 'Josephine Turner. That's the name of her new therapist. It was you, wasn't it?'

'Turner is such a very common name,' Josie drawled. 'It always annoyed me when I was growing up.'

'Turner is common, but combined with Josephine? I've checked. There's around a hundred people with that name on the electoral role. Twenty-two of the relevant age. Out of sixty-six million people in the UK.'

'Darling, you're confused. I'm telling you. It's not me.'

'I looked at your LinkedIn profile, Josie. You've had an interesting career, haven't you? It was a mistake uploading such a detailed CV, because there it is for 1986–1992. Grief Counsellor in Glasgow Therapeutic Services.'

Josie crumpled. In an instant she was ten years older. It was a few moments before she spoke. 'I always knew I should have deleted that profile when I retired.'

'What do you know?'

'Nothing, honestly, darling. I knew nothing about you until I bumped into her by chance in Gerrards Cross about six years later. She told me she'd adopted you.'

She was lying. Her default position. 'My date of birth is the same as Caitlin's. My name is the same. Would you do that to an adopted child?'

'A coincidence?' she tried.

'Oh for fuck's sake. I'm not an idiot. All those payments to you. You were blackmailing her, weren't you?'

'For goodness' sake, darling. Why would I blackmail her? What possible reason could I have?'

'I don't know! Maybe she stole me, and when you met her you sussed it out and saw your chance to make a little bit of extra money.'

She shook her head. 'What an imagination. Any other crazy theories?'

Kate was desperate now. 'Or, I don't know... maybe she had an arrangement with someone, an illegal adoption...'

She wouldn't meet Kate's gaze. 'That's not how it was.'

'So, tell me how it was, then. Let's hear your side of the story. But I'm warning you, Josie, my bullshit detectors are on full alert.'

'You're right. I did take over from Patsy as Mirren's counsellor. She was known as Muireann then, of course. She was in a dreadful state. Suicidal. Patsy was inexperienced and I was her supervisor. It was obvious they didn't have a good relationship.' Josie stood up and started walking around the room. 'I felt obliged to step in. And Patsy was relieved to be shot of her.' She paused. 'Mirren was in a bad way when I took over.'

'So you came in as her saviour?'

'Not exactly. But I did have more experience and she responded to me. She told me things, things about her relationships with her family and her partner.'

'What things?'

'Tommy was jealous of her talent. She'd had to give up full-time painting because of him, retrained as a social worker. She resented him for that. And the relationship with her parents was poor. They didn't approve of her life choices, of the fact that she was living with a man fifteen years older than her and they only really came round when she had Caitlin.'

It all tied in with what Kate already knew.

'She had seen Caitlin as a chance to start anew, build her relationship with Tommy and parents and when she died... well.'

'Go on.'

'It was obvious she had to get away from them all. Tommy, her parents, even her siblings, who she was fond of but who were all married with children. A constant reminder of what she didn't have.'

It made sense. 'You helped her disappear.'

She looked at Kate over her glasses. 'More than that. I saved her life.'

'Go on,' said Kate again.

'She'd gone to stay in Troon. On an impulse I went to see her. She wasn't there.' Josie fiddled with her necklace. 'I had nothing better to do so I went down to the beach. It was dusk when I got there. She was wading into the water.'

'What?'

'I ran after her and pulled her out, dragged her to my car.

She was in a terrible state, drunk, begging me to let her go. We drove back up to Glasgow and I spent the night sobering her up. In the morning I called in sick and we drove to the Highlands. I had a small cottage there, miles from anywhere. The nearest village was Achiltilbuie. It was my retreat from the rat race. I hoped I'd be able to move there one day, but it was never to be. Mirren lived there for the best part of a year.'

'But her family... They were desperately looking for her.'

'We didn't see anything about that. As I say, miles from anywhere.'

'You must have known they'd be looking for her—'

Josie interrupted, her voice harsh. 'It was what Mirren wanted. To be free of her family.'

Kate found it hard to believe she would have been so heartless, yet she'd lived in England for all those years, only a few hundred miles away, and not once had she contacted them to let them know she was all right. Kate thought about what Josie had said and her mouth dried up as she took in the implications. 'You said she lived there for about a year. So, she didn't disappear in June 1992 like everyone thinks?'

'No, she did not. It was eleven months later.'

'But surely she would have been recognised? From photos in the papers.'

'Darling. This was thirty years ago. There was no world wide web. Email had not long been invented. It was much less difficult to disappear then than now. And in any case, there was little press interest once the police decided she was dead.' She sat down at the kitchen table, opposite Kate, and took her hand. 'Believe me, she was desperate to get away. I offered her the cottage, rent free. It suited me to have her living there. It kept out the local wildlife and meant that any leaks, things like that, were dealt with immediately. I'd visit from time to time – it was my getaway after all – and she got better bit by bit. Over time we became friends. Or at least I thought we did.'

'What do you mean?'

'She disappeared. One weekend I went up there and she was gone. No note, nothing. I asked in the village, which was a good four or five miles away. They knew her because she walked there once a week to stock up on food. Filled up a ruck-sack and walked back.'

'She walked four miles to get her shopping?'

'And back. You need to read Dorothy Wordsworth's diary, darling. She and William would walk seven miles and back to Keswick, over the hills, to get their shopping. In all weathers. The walk to Achiltilbuie was nothing in comparison, along a road. From time to time she was lucky and got a lift back.'

Kate's idea of a walk to the shops was a fifteen-minute stroll. An eight-mile return journey to pick up bread and milk sounded like torture to her, and as for wandering in the Lake District hills – that was something you do on holiday. Josie continued with her story, relating how Mirren had apparently taken the first bus one morning to a hotel where she picked up another bus to Inverness. There she got on the bus to Glasgow, but after that the trail went cold. Josie relished telling Kate how upset and betrayed she felt when she discovered Mirren had gone.

'So, did you really not see her again until you moved down south?'

'No, from time to time I thought about contacting her family, to let them know she wasn't dead, but I was bound by confidentiality. It was best not to.'

She was being disingenuous here. Surely she could have phoned them anonymously to let them know Mirren was safe?

She'd already gone against professional ethics by getting so involved with a client, but Kate said nothing and let her talk on.

'She wasn't pleased to see me. I was really upset by that. All those months of free accommodation and she didn't as much as leave a thank you note. And then years later, there she was in the fishmongers in Gerrards Cross.' She rubbed the crease in her forehead, trying to smooth it out.

'What did she say?'

'Well, she was embarrassed, darling, as you might imagine. Didn't want to let me know where she was living. And of course there was you. She told me she had adopted you through a private agency. I believed her, why wouldn't I?'

She was lying. Her eyes avoided Kate's. 'The thing is, Josie. I don't believe you. I think you sussed out immediately that there was something off. You knew she couldn't have adopted me legally, she was too old. You saw a way of exploiting a vulnerable woman and so you blackmailed her.'

'How dare you!'

'Josie, over the years she gave you thirty thousand pounds. You told me it was the deposit on the house. Well, I contacted her lawyer and she told me what Mirren paid for the house, how much was mortgage and how much deposit. Her deposit was ten thousand pounds, Josie. Ten thousand, not thirty.' Kate's face reddened as she got into her stride. 'And there's two other little details that don't tie in with your story. Firstly, she bought the house three years before you say you met up with her again. But secondly, and this is the clincher, she was paying you from 1993. I have it in black and white in case you've forgotten. In her bank statements. So you're lying. It wasn't several years before you saw her again. You must have tracked her down.'

If Kate's face was red, Josie's was puce. 'You always were

trouble. I told Mirren whenever she complained to me about you.' She smiled. 'Oh yes, didn't you know? She was always complaining about you. About you not having a man, not getting on with things and giving her grandchildren. Never-ending it was. I said to her, well what do you expect, you don't know where she came from, do you?'

'Give it up, Josie. This attempt to pit me against my mother is pathetic. She never said those things to you.' Kate stood up. 'Stay away from me. Do you hear me? I never want to see you again.'

As she walked out the door, she heard Josie shouting, 'You never replaced Caitlin, you know that. You were always a disappointment. Always.'

Kate's anger had gone. She'd always disliked Josie. What she hadn't known was how much Josie resented her. Tears came to her eyes and she blinked them away. She'd had great hopes for Scrimgeour's French connection. Well, that was another avenue closed off. She'd have to phone him and let him know that everyone's assumptions about when Mirren disappeared were wrong.

FORTY

Glasgow

ALEX GLANCED AT HIS EMAILS. He was due in court in thirty minutes. Not enough time to deal with anything serious, but he scanned them anyway. Kate Fallon's name caught his eye. She certainly hadn't hung around. He opened it up and began to read. Good, there was a brand name. That was sure to help. He'd contact the French police tomorrow and see if they had a note of the make of dress the baby was wearing. He clicked open one of the photographs. It was blurred and hard to make out. No matter, there were another two. He opened the next one and blinked. It wasn't possible. His heart jerked uncomfortably and he swallowed, not believing his eyes. He enlarged the photo to get a better view. Alex forwarded Kate's email to his personal one.

'Are you all right, Alex?' The police officer sitting across from him gave him a worried look.

He pulled at his shirt collar. Had it always been this tight. Beads of sweat appeared on his forehead. He thought he might be sick. 'I... um. No, I'm not feeling great, no.'

'You should go home, mate. I'll go to court instead of you.'

'I ought to be there for the verdict. I led the case.'

'I know, but... honestly, mate. You look terrible. I'll clear it with the boss. Do you need a lift or anything?'

He was out of his seat. 'No, thanks. I'll be OK. It's a migraine, that's all.'

Behind him his sergeant muttered, 'The bugger must be ill, never heard him say thanks before'.

'I heard that,' he shouted back at him, giving him the finger as an added bonus. The banter made him feel slightly better. Well enough to drive home, at any rate. He got into his car and breathed deeply. He was imagining things, had to be. It wasn't possible.

Back home, he looked out the old biscuit tin where he kept photos. He rarely looked at them. It only led to tears and a heavy drinking session. He'd kept every photo they'd ever taken of Mairi. Nowadays people had thousands of photos stashed on their phones and computers, shared on social media, stored in the cloud. But when Mairi was a baby, you had to get photos developed from a film. Digital cameras were relatively new and still quite expensive. So there were few photos to rifle through. He cast aside the ones of her as a very young baby. They mostly had Sandra in them and he had debated with himself whether to keep them or not. He should have dumped them. He never looked at them. They brought back painful memories of a time when he was happy, when his wife loved him and he had everything to look forward to. He paused when he reached ones of when she was about six months old. They'd called her the monster muncher because she was growing so fast. Her arms were chubby with folds of fat over her wrists. They'd disappeared by the time she was a year old, shortly before she was taken.

Where were the photos he wanted? They must be here.

There were three of them, all taken on the same day. Ah, got them. He laid them out on the kitchen table and studied them.

It had been a long, hot day. They were on holiday in France. He'd wanted to go to Spain, the Costa del Sol, where he could get a fish supper if he so wished. But Sandra said no, as she did to the majority of things he suggested. She insisted on France. He'd had to admit her choice of Honfleur, a little fishing town in the north, had been a good one. He'd missed his fish and chips, but the restaurants round the quay made up for it with their Menus du Jour. Fish stew had been a revelation.

They'd been walking in the back streets when she spotted it. A little boutique selling children's clothes. There were signs posted across the window, the print large and red. SOLDES. He sighed. They'd be here for hours. No point in putting up a fight though. She'd only huff.

'You go on in,' he said. 'I'll wait out here with Mairi. We'll be fine. There's a bench over there in the shade.'

She skipped into the shop and he sighed, hoping whatever she bought wouldn't be too expensive. The holiday was costing more than he'd bargained for. The exchange rate was abysmal and everything was dearer here anyway. She was in there for half an hour. Chatting to the owner in fluent French, no doubt. One of the reasons she insisted on coming here instead of Spain.

She was carrying what looked like a full carrier bag when she came out. It was paper, not plastic. An expensive shop then. She sat down beside him and sighed. 'Fancy a coffee?'

'A beer would be nice. Let's go to one of those places round the old quay.' They stood up. Alex nodded towards the bag. 'What did you get?'

'Couple of dresses. I'll show you when we get our drinks.'

'How much?'

'It was a sale. They were reduced.'

This was Sandra's standard answer when she'd spent too much. He shook his head. 'Right.'

Sandra took his arm and squeezed it. 'Come on, Grumps, cheer up. You're on holiday.'

Definitely expensive. She rarely touched him these days. Once they had ordered their drinks, a beer for him, a diet coke for her, he held out his hand. 'Let's see them then.'

They didn't look any different from the standard stuff she bought from Next and Marks and Spencer. He didn't say so though. It would only cause a fight, so instead he nodded and agreed that they were very pretty.

'My favourite is this one.' She spread out a blue cotton one on the table. 'It's been hand-embroidered, look.' She pointed to daisies on the front bodice.

'How do you know?'

'How do I know what?'

'That they've been embroidered by hand. They look as though they've been done by machine to me. Too perfect.'

Her face fell. 'Do you think so? Have I been had for a mug?'

He'd laughed. 'I'm having you on. Do you think I'd know the difference between them? No, it's lovely, really.' He softened. 'The exact colour of her eyes, of your eyes.'

———————————

It was the same dress. He'd swear to it. He sat for an hour with the photographs and a magnifying glass. Mairi had been wearing it when she'd been taken. Did this mean Kate Fallon was his daughter after all? He didn't see how she could be. The woman who'd raised her had faked her death long before

Mairi's disappearance. He pushed away the feeling of hope rising in him. Mairi was dead. He'd long reconciled himself to that. But yet, the dress. From a French boutique mind, not a supermarket or a chain store. A coincidence? Perhaps the stolen French baby had the same dress. No, that was impossible. He already knew she was four months old when taken, so the dress would have been too big for her. Hope bubbled up in him once more. But what was he going to say to Kate?

FORTY-ONE

Buckinghamshire

THE REVELATION that Kate had been taken a year later than she thought had shattered her. She'd put too much faith in this French connection. Christ, so many disappointments. Too much time and energy had been wasted worrying about who her birth family were and how she came to be with Mirren. Josie said she was adopted. Perhaps she was. What did it matter anyway? It was time to leave well alone and get on with her life. Mirren had loved her and looked after her, and Kate had loved her. That was what mattered. Not who passed on their genes. She'd tell Scrimgeour to stop looking, that she was happy as she was. Better still, she'd tell him she'd found her adoption papers. That would put an end to it. Stop all this hope.

The phone rang but she let it to go to answer phone. It was Scrimgeour. His voice was hesitant; he wanted to talk to her about the photograph of the dress she'd sent. Kate sighed; might as well get it over with. She crossed the room to pick up the phone.

After the usual greetings they both spoke at the same time.

The usual dance of *on you go, no you first* until in a gap he managed to tell her that he had contacted the French police and was waiting for their response. He ended by saying, 'I'm sorry I don't have more definite news for you.'

'I have though,' said Kate.

'Go ahead.'

She told him about Josie and how Mirren had been hidden for the best part of a year. 'So, you see, it isn't possible that I am that French baby. I'm sorry you've wasted your time.'

He was breathing heavily as if he had asthma or had been running. 'Do you know when your mother actually disappeared?'

'I don't know the exact date, but perhaps Josie knows. The thing is though, Inspector, I don't think I want to take it any further. After all, what good could come of meeting my parents after all this time?' She couldn't bring herself to tell the lie she'd prepared about finding the adoption papers. There had been too much lies and deception already.

His voice sounded far away. 'Please, could you find out the exact date? I have... There's a possibility...' He tailed off.

'You're not making sense,' said Kate. He sounded ill. He asked her again to find out when Mirren disappeared from Achiltilbuie and if Kate was sure she was heading for Glasgow. Kate didn't want to do it because it meant speaking to Josie again, but he'd put himself out for her so she agreed and told him she'd phone back as soon as possible.

As usual Josie was infuriatingly vague. 'The date? Oh darling, I have no idea. It was summer or maybe late spring. Yes, that's right, late spring. May.'

Kate struggled to keep the irritation from her voice. 'Do you have the exact dates though? Do you keep diaries, anything to help you remember?'

A long pause, 'I'm thinking, darling. Trying my best.' Another pause. 'There *was* something out of the ordinary. It was her birthday. I had decided to go up and surprise her. Found out she'd taken the bus to the Summer Isles hotel where you transfer to—'

'It doesn't matter how she did it.' Kate cut her short before she launched into one of her interminable rambles. 'Mum's birthday was the twelfth of May. Are you sure it was then?'

'No, it was the eleventh. I went up there on the twelfth but she'd left the day before. Definitely. I remember the woman in the post office telling—'

'Thanks, Josie, that's been helpful.' She hung up.

Scrimgeour answered on the first ring. He sounded strange, stuffed up, as if he had a cold. She was about to ask him how he was when he said, 'Well?'

What a rude man. 'According to the friend whose house she was staying in, she left on the eleventh of May. She took the first bus out of town to a hotel, I think.'

'The Summer Isles hotel?'

'Yes, I think so. Apparently, it's a long journey back to Glasgow.'

'Aye, it is. You have to go all round the houses.'

Kate smiled at this. It was one of Mirren's favourite expressions.

'Is she sure about the date? I mean, how does she know it was then when it was so long ago?' He was abrupt, barking out the words at her.

'She's sure.'

'Aye, but how?'

'Because she went up there for my mum's birthday, and when she asked where she had gone, the woman in the post office told her she'd taken the first bus out the day before.

Mum's birthday was the twelfth of May, therefore she left on the eleventh.'

'So, she's your mum now, is she? A woman like that who takes someone else's wean.' The words were vicious. It was like he was taking it personally.

'I'm sorry?'

'You call a bitch like that your mother?'

'Wait a minute. I'm not sure what's going on here, but she brought me up. I loved her. She was all I had. This is very hard for me you know – after all we don't know for sure what happened – and it's unprofessional slandering her like that.'

He was breathing heavily into the phone. He sounded distressed and she didn't know what to do.

'Aye, you're right enough. Unprofessional. Sorry.'

Kate had never heard anyone sound less sorry, but she murmured, 'OK'.

'Eh, right. I've got things to be going on with now so...'

'Wait a minute, don't hang up. What's going on? As I said, I'm not sure I want to go any further with this. It's upsetting my mother's family, the Fallons, and they've been so kind to me, accepted me as one of their own.'

'You said you wanted to know who you were.'

'That was before I met the Taylors. Maybe I should leave things as they were.'

'Right, OK then.'

'Hello? Are you there?' He'd cut her off. Unprofessional, rude, coarse. Kate didn't like him one little bit.

———

Alex looked at the phone in his hand. He hadn't handled that well at all. Antagonised her, if he wasn't mistaken. His heart was beating so fast he thought he was having a heart attack. He looked at the fancy Apple watch he'd treated himself to on his last birthday. Fuck, his pulse was more than one sixty. You'd think he'd been running a marathon. He took a deep breath and another and sat down, trying to relax. A glance told him it was working. Down to one twenty. Not good but not in the danger zone either. Another five minutes of visualising a beach and it would be back to normal.

He jumped up and went over to the window. It was a typical August day in Glasgow. Overcast, threatening rain. He leaned his forehead on the glass. Of all things, he'd never imagined this day. Never allowed himself to. Sure, there had been times in the first year after Mairi's disappearance when he'd hoped he'd discover what had happened. Put the whole thing behind him. But this? He'd never let himself think she was alive. That all these years after her disappearance, she'd come back into his life. Fully formed. An adult human being with thoughts and beliefs all her own. One that answered back. He shouldn't have called that woman a bitch. That was a mistake. Though it rankled. Kate calling her Mum. She wasn't her mother. That woman had destroyed his life by taking what wasn't hers.

He walked back to the sofa. Christ, he couldn't keep still. He paced across the floor. Had she destroyed his life? Really? Sandra had destroyed their marriage by sleeping with Jimmy. If Mairi hadn't been taken by that woman, Sandra would have left him for Jimmy anyway – everyone always said she was too good for him – and taken their daughter with her. So he'd have lost Mairi either way. No, no, he wasn't going to think that way, didn't want to excuse what she'd done. It was wrong, wrong, wrong.

He sat down, put his head in his hands and wept. He

hadn't the slightest idea what to do next. One part of him thought he should let it be. Kate had made it clear she didn't want to know who her real family were. What was it she'd said? She didn't want to upset her mother's family. What about him? What about his sorrow? It was like little pieces of glass cutting into his heart when he thought of those words. He wasn't going to let it go though. It was too hard. He had to act on this information, but how? Best to sleep on it, not do anything rash that he might regret.

FORTY-TWO

Buckinghamshire

KATE WAS HALFWAY through revising a lecture when the computer pinged with an incoming email. It flashed up with Scrimgeour's name. She was inclined to delete it without reading – that remark about Mirren had stung her, not least because it was true – but when she tried to return to work she knew she would get nothing done until she had read it. She opened it. It was lengthy. What on earth did he want now? Had he disregarded her wishes and gone ahead and looked into disappearances round about the 11th May 1993? She read it through.

Dear Kate,

I hope you don't mind me using your first name but in the circumstances, I don't feel it's inappropriate. I have attached a photograph. Please look at it before you read on.

She frowned, what on earth? She clicked on the attachment and it opened. It was a photograph of a very young child sitting up in one of those big prams that used to be fashionable but had all but disappeared now. Kate had no experience with young children, so it was hard to put an age on the child, but at a guess she'd say fifteen months, maybe more. She was wearing a sunhat and a blue dress with a white collar. Kate caught her breath and looked closer. It was the double of the dress she had found in the attic. Was it possible that the child was her?

The name of the girl in the photograph is Mairi and she was taken from the garden of the house where she lived, on the 11th May 1993. Her empty pram was found in a nearby park later the same day. Her mother blamed herself for her disappearance and killed herself a few weeks later. The dress she's wearing in the photograph is what she had on the day she was taken. As you have no doubt noted, it is identical to the one you found in your attic. Given this and the fact that we now know Muireann Fallon disappeared on 11th May I think there is enough evidence to suggest that you are Mairi. Enough anyway for the case to be re-opened. As Mairi's father I have asked for this to happen as soon as possible.

Kate read the last sentence over and over. It didn't make sense. Surely this wasn't true. This man might be her father and this was how he told her? He was a sociopath. He had to be. There was no emotion in there whatsoever. She read on.

A DNA test will show beyond any doubt whether what I suspect is true and I would ask that you come to Glasgow as soon as possible to arrange this. I know you had your DNA tested recently but I have already checked and it has been destroyed, as is protocol. It usually takes three or four days for results to come through, but I've asked for them to be fast-tracked. It would be good if you could stay on in Glasgow to receive the results and I hope this doesn't inconvenience you. I'm sorry to have disregarded your wishes to abandon the search for your birth parents but I believe that it is in both our interests to clear this up once and for all. I look forward to hearing from you.

Alex Scrimgeour.

And that was that. No term of endearment, nothing to say he wanted to find his daughter. It was as cold a letter as she'd ever seen. She read it again in case she had missed something, but no, on second reading it was worse. One of her parents was dead, the other a fat old man who didn't care about her.

Dead. If these were her parents, she'd never get to know her mother.

It was unbearable. She wanted to write back and tell him to fuck right off but she refrained. Like it or not, the man was right. They needed to know for sure.

Her head was bursting. She had to talk to someone. The obvious person to phone was Scrimgeour, but she was too upset, so she phoned Margaret. Conor answered, but it wasn't him she wanted. She wanted the calm mothering of an older woman. She cut him off in the middle of his greeting. 'Is your mum there?'

'Oh, do you not want to speak to me?'

Kate was unable to say anything. There were tears running down her face.

'Are you all right, Kate? My parents are away for a few days. Can I help?'

'Can we FaceTime? It will make this easier.'

'Of course.'

Half an hour later, he had the whole story.

'You have to speak to him,' he said.

'I don't want to.' The tears started again. 'You heard what the email said. It was cold and... oh, I don't know. It's not what I imagined. There was no emotion in it.'

'Look at it from his point of view. His daughter's been gone for twenty-six years. He doesn't know for sure you're his daughter so he has to keep it professional for the time being.'

He had a point. 'I suppose so.'

'Get the DNA test done. The sooner the better because you'll worry about it otherwise.'

'Do you think that's the right thing to do?'

'Yes. I do. Shall I book you a flight?'

'No, no. It's fine. I'll sort myself out.'

'Come and stay with us again.'

'No, I'll book a hotel. I need to do this on my own. But I'd love to meet up once everything's... you know, out of the way.'

She booked a room in a city centre hotel and a flight for the next day. She sent an email to the cheeseburger saying something urgent had come up and she needed to take unpaid leave. In return she received a curt message agreeing to her request but also asking her to come and see him on her return. She felt sick. She tried to pre-empt the informal warning that was undoubtedly coming by thanking him wholeheartedly and reminding him she wouldn't miss any classes. There was no reply. She'd made things worse. Finally, she composed an email to Scrimgeour. It was brief and to the point.

. . .

Dear Alex,

I will be in Glasgow tomorrow from noon and suggest we meet at a mutually convenient time and place to get the DNA testing done. I am staying at the Radisson Blu hotel in Argyle Street. I have arranged to be in Glasgow until the results come through.

Best, Kate Fallon

He replied immediately, suggesting they meet at the hotel. He'd ordered a test from a local lab used by the police.

FORTY-THREE

Glasgow

HE WASN'T sure it was the right thing to do but he had to speak to somebody. He had very few real mates to turn to. After his wife's infidelity he was unable ever to trust anyone again. Mark, his DS, was the closest he had to a confidante. But Mark had his own troubles. All he could talk about was his ex-lover and how she could blow his life apart. Alex didn't have a lot of sympathy for him. After all, he'd brought it on himself. No, it had to be his mother. If he was lucky and it was a good day, she'd listen and he could pretend that she was taking it in. If it was a bad day... fuck knows.

The car park was busy when he arrived. Relatives were still worried about the murder of Donald Morton and the fact that it had not yet been solved. Some were campaigning to get the place shut down but there was such a shortage of care places that most people had no option but to keep their loved one here, like he had. There was an unspoken consensus that everyone would visit as often as they could. The killer would have to be crazy to try anything when there were so many people around. Alex hoped they'd get a result soon but the fact was the trail had gone cold.

His mother beamed when he came into her room. 'Alex!' A good day right enough.

'How are you, Mum?' He bent down to kiss her cheek.

'Oh, you know. Aches and pains. How are you and Sandra?'

He sighed. Not such a good day after all. Maybe he'd better not say anything. 'I'm fine.'

They chatted for fifteen minutes before she dropped off to sleep. He wondered if he'd ever get used to the way she was now. She hadn't been the same since Mairi disappeared. She'd doted on her, her first grandchild. When Mairi had vanished, she'd gone into a terrible depression and for a while she turned to drink. Up until then she'd been as respectable as they come. Church of Scotland every Sunday, bridge parties in her bunga-low, volunteering in a Cancer Research shop when she retired from her job as a nurse. The disease had kicked in for sure when she was in her late seventies. She was eighty-eight now.

'I may have found Mairi, Mum. Do you remember her?' He didn't wait for the reply, which wasn't forthcoming in any case, but continued. 'I was so sure it was that bastard Taylor behind it, but no, turns out it was a local woman. Can you believe it? Her baby had died so she took mine. She's dead now but if she wasn't, I'd kill her.' He stopped to control himself. 'Mairi's a grown woman, posh. Kate's her name now. And she won't hear a word against the woman who stole her. Got herself all pally with the bitch's family. Where does that leave me, Mum? Where does that leave me?'

His mother woke up. He saw at once she was frightened. 'Who are you? Jean, Jean, there's a man in my room.' Her hands flapped about her, pushing him away.

He grasped them both, held on tight. 'Mum, it's me, Alex. Your son.'

She calmed down as she sometimes did when he was firm with her. If only that worked every time. 'So it is. Silly me. I must have been dreaming.'

They talked for a few more minutes before he got up to go. When he leaned over to kiss her cheek, she said, 'Don't be too hard on her.'

'Hard on who?'

'That poor woman. She'd lost her child. Grief does awful things to people, changes them. Look at me.'

He stared at her. 'Yes,' he said. 'It does terrible things.'

This had happened before. Out of nowhere she'd said something completely coherent and unlike her usual ramblings. He didn't understand why it happened. Nor did the doctors. Paradoxical lucidity they called it. One warned him it often happened not long before death. That was a year ago. And as for not hating the woman who stole his child. Impossible.

He was exhausted. He needed to get home and go to bed. It had been an emotional day. First though he needed to use the toilet. He decided to use the one in the en suite instead of the visitor's one, as that meant passing Ms Jenkins' room. Every time she saw him now, she nagged him about the murder enquiry. At least it had stopped her going on about how difficult his mother was.

He was towelling his hands dry when he heard the door to the bedroom open. Shit, visitors weren't supposed to use the residents' en suite shower rooms. He thought quickly and filled the tooth mug with water. He'd tell whoever it was that his mother had wanted a drink of water. When he went into the room, however, Ms Jenkins was standing over his mother, needle in hand.

'What on earth are you doing?' he shouted. He rushed over and removed the needle from her hand before taking out an evidence bag and securing it.

Ms Jenkins glared at him. 'What the hell are you doing? I'm giving your mother her insulin dose.'

'What insulin dose? She isn't diabetic.'

'She was diagnosed yesterday. I forgot to tell you.'

He wasn't fooled. He'd seen the panic in her eyes as he'd bagged the evidence. 'Ms Jenkins, I am arresting you on suspicion of the murder of Donald Morton. You do not have to say anything. But, it may harm your defence if you do not mention when questioned something which you later rely on in court. Anything you do say may be given in evidence.'

'I want my lawyer.'

'You can make one phone call when we get to the station.'

Back at the station he told Mark what had happened. 'You'll need to question her. I can't because I can't take the risk of her lawyer using my links to Mum to scupper the case. I'm going to see if I can get this fast tracked for analysis.' He showed Mark the syringe. 'She says it's insulin, but we'll find out for sure soon enough. Her lawyer should be here soon.'

When the lawyer arrived, Mark took her into one of the interview rooms. Ryan was there with him, and once more, Alex found himself on the other side of the two-way mirror, a passive observer. After Mark had taken her details, the interview started.

Unsurprisingly, she answered 'no comment' to every question. Alex sighed. This was getting them nowhere. She maintained that Alex's mother had been recently diagnosed with diabetes. The first thing Alex had done when he got back to the station was to check with Dr Barr, the GP for the home.

'Diabetes? No, your mother is definitely not diabetic. Her blood sugars are excellent. Jenkins may well be telling the truth about the insulin though. An overdose can kill you, though it is not as easy to do as people think. You have to use a lot on an adult. Anyway, it doesn't matter for your case against her, as there was absolutely no reason to inject your mother with insulin.' He rang off.

The results came through quickly. Alex called Mark through as soon as he got them.

'Well, we've got the means – potassium chloride, same as was used to kill Donald Morton, and we've got opportunity, seeing as I caught her with the syringe, but what the hell is the motive?'

Mark was as much at a loss as he was. 'No idea, and she's saying nothing.'

'Fuck's sake. Well, I can speak to the PF but I'd prefer more evidence.'

The next morning, Alex took a look at the file. Charmaine Jenkins, date of birth 31st March 1988, address 42 Beech Avenue, G46. Alex stared at the address. Beech Avenue. He'd heard of that. Where the fuck was it? He brought up Google Maps on his phone.

'Got it! Mark, do we have the search warrant for her house yet?'

'Yes, there's a team on their way.'

'Get in the car. We're going too. Have to make sure we do a thorough job.'

It took them twenty minutes to get to the address. The area was all too familiar to Alex from June 1992. He stared at Brenda Taylor's house as they drove past. It had new windows and one of those white plastic doors he hated so much. Not far now. If his hunch was right...

There were two names on the doorplate of her house. C. Jenkins and J. Taylor. He looked at Mark and grinned. 'I think we've found her motive.'

The house was empty when they broke in. But there was plenty of evidence, including two notebooks where Charmaine Jenkins had detailed all her plans.

Her face paled when Mark threw the notebooks on to the table. Alex wished he could be in the interview room too.

'Anything to say about these before I start going through them?'

She turned her head to the side, refused to look at him. Her lawyer frowned.

'OK, fair enough. We'll start with this one. For the purpose of the recording, I am showing Ms Jenkins a small black notebook. Inside the notebook are cuttings from newspapers about the disappearance of four-month-old Danielle Taylor in 1992. Any comment?'

'No comment.'

'Further on in the book there are newspaper cuttings about the disappearance of Muireann Fallon in June 1992. There are also various sums of money mentioned. One sentence reads:

20k at least. More if possible.' He showed the page to Jenkins. 'Any comment?'

She shook her head.

For the purpose of recording, could you please speak up?'

'No fucking comment.'

Mark and Ryan continued in this vein for fifteen more minutes. Alex watched as Jenkins got more and more agitated. They were not far from breaking her, he was sure of it.

It was the second notebook that did for her in the end. Ryan started reading from it. A murderous to-do list. It was highly incriminating. 'Things to do: Find out how to get potassium chloride. Kill a couple off before Scrimgeour's mother – hide her death in plain sight. Find out where Fallon lives now and get the bitch. Get as much money as we can from her and then kill her.' He put the notebook face down on the table. 'Handy for us that you wrote it all down. Is this your handwriting or that of your partner, Jamie Taylor?'

For a few long seconds she said nothing. Alex would swear later he could see the cogs working behind her eyes.

'It's Jamie's writing,' she said at last. 'It was all his idea, all of it. He's not been the same since he started his own investigation into Dani's disappearance. You've seen the cuttings. His mum showed them to him last year. He became obsessed with the idea of finding Muireann Fallon and Dani and eventually he did.'

'How did he find her?'

'It was sheer luck. He was getting nowhere, couldn't understand it because Muireann is such an unusual name. So he googled it, found out it was Irish and looked up its meaning on a site about Irish names. There he found out that the English equivalent is Mirren. He tried Mirren Fallon and eventually found her on an electoral register in the south of England. She must have lied about her name to the authorities or maybe she changed it by deed poll. It didn't matter. He'd found her. Can I have a break?'

They stopped for half an hour to give her some respite. Alex was desperate for them to get back in and continue the interview. 'Get back in there, before she clams up.'

Alex almost felt sorry for her. She seemed to have diminished in size over the past few hours. Her hair, normally sleek and shiny was lank and greasy and the shadows under her eyes looked like ink stains. Mark switched on the recorder and carried on with the questioning. 'What was your motive for attacking Mrs Scrimgeour?'

'Jamie had it in for Scrimgeour. Blamed him for his dad's death. First he was going to get Fallon, then that bastard detective. He just went on and on at me. It was never-ending. I wish I'd never mentioned that Scrimgeour's mother was in the home. Should have kept my fucking mouth shut. Soon as I told him, he never gave up. *When does he visit? Is it definitely him?* Every fucking day he was on at me, even when the home was under investigation. He's as much to blame as me. I didn't want to kill the others. I thought we should just do her, but no, he had to go for some fancy plan. It was meant to protect me, in case anyone ever worked out that we were partners.' Her lawyer was desperately trying to get her to stop incriminating herself but she ignored him.

'And who were the other people you killed?'

Something switched on in her brain, 'No comment,' she said.

They had what they wanted. The motive, the means, the opportunity. She'd been charged with the murder of Donald Morton and attempted murder of Elizabeth Scrimgeour. Taylor had disappeared but it was only a matter of time before they got him too. There was a warrant out for his arrest.

Once home, Alex poured himself a large Laphroaig. He deserved it, needed it. He was delighted that they seemed to have a cast iron case, but he was heartbroken for the others who had been murdered before the attempt was made on his mother. There was no evidence that she had killed anyone other than Mr Morton but Alex was convinced that Donald Morton hadn't been the first. They'd never know though. At least they'd got them on one count. They'd made it all too complicated. If they had just gone ahead and killed his mother, they might have got away with it.

One whisky led to another. His hands shook as he thought about how close his mother had been to being a murder victim. He wasn't an idiot, he knew she wasn't going to live forever but he wasn't ready to lose her yet.

With two large whiskies in him he felt a little better although he still had a difficult day ahead of him tomorrow. Would any good come of this? If Kate Fallon wasn't his daughter, he had upset them both for nothing. And if she was, what then?

FORTY-FOUR

Glasgow
———

KATE WAS WAITING for him at the reception of her hotel. He stared at her from a distance, trying to spot anything that linked her to him or Sandra. She had a look of Sandra, now he thought about it. Around her mouth. She had his height, but apart from that he saw no resemblance. The DNA test weighed heavy in his jacket pocket. He hoped they could go up to her room to use it. It was too public in here.

Kate looked up and waved. He moved towards her. She stood up and they shook hands. His were clammy; too late he wiped them on the sides of his trousers.

'I thought we'd go to my room. It will give us more privacy.'

'Yes,' was all he said. He thought she rolled her eyes as she walked towards the lift. He wished he had better people skills. They'd got off to such a bad start. He cringed when he thought of the email he'd sent her. What had he been thinking? Well, he was paying the price for it now. 'Good journey?' he asked. She didn't reply. There were others in the lift so he said no more. At the fifth floor they got out and she walked briskly along the corridor.

Once they were in the room, she offered him coffee, which he refused. 'Let's get this over with.' It was the wrong thing to say. Her face closed up and she nodded. He opened the kit and gave one of the swabs to her, before scraping the inside of his mouth.

'What now?' She handed her sample over to him. How blue her eyes were, but were they the same shade as Mairi's? He couldn't recall.

'The lab is five minutes' walk away. Perhaps you'd come with me while I drop it off and then we could have lunch?'

She couldn't have looked more surprised if he'd asked her to an orgy, but she agreed and they set off up Buchanan Street to find the lab. She waited while Scrimgeour spoke to the receptionist. When he'd finished, she asked how long the results would take.

'I've called in a favour. It should be done in two days, one if we're lucky.'

'Of course, sorry. You already said.'

The restaurant he'd chosen was lovely; she'd give him that. It had once been a bank and was lushly decorated. A waiter showed them to a booth, which gave them a little privacy. Scrimgeour recommended a Negroni. Apparently the restaurant was famous for them.

'Sparkling water,' she replied. It was hard enough without drink making it worse. Scrimgeour ordered the same and the waiter left. She picked up a menu and looked at it in silence. She settled on a Caesar salad with grilled chicken.

'No starter?'

'A salad will be fine, thanks.' She sounded like a sulky

teenager. This was a mistake. She should have said no to lunch. Now she was stuck making small talk with him for at least an hour. More, probably. This didn't look like the sort of place where you picked up a quick bite to eat. Her stomach twisted at the thought.

Over lunch he thawed and asked about her life, what she did, where she lived, whether she had a partner. Kate avoided the last question and concentrated on telling him about her work. He was interested, which was good, she guessed. The police were often antagonistic towards journalists, and it would have been the last straw if he'd started to disrespect her job. He asked intelligent questions, which she enjoyed answering, and then moved on.

'Sounds as though you loved writing. Why did you move into lecturing?'

Kate chased the salad leaves around her plate. Rocket. She hated rocket. It shouldn't be allowed anywhere near a Caesar salad. She gave up and stabbed a piece of chicken instead. 'Oh, you don't want to know. Let's talk about you. Did you always want to be in the police?'

'Don't change the subject.' He was smiling; it transformed his face. Kate relaxed and talked about the difficulties of breaking into journalism. She wanted to know more about him, though, and was on the point of asking him when his phone rang. He answered and listened, his face serious. 'I'll be there in twenty minutes.'

He gestured to the waiter for the bill and paid up. 'I'm really sorry, Kate. I'll have to go. Work, you know.'

'Of course. No problem.' She was half disappointed, half relieved. 'You'll let me know when the results come in?'

'Of course.'

She sat on for a while after he left, trying to sort out her feelings before she went back to her hotel room and got ready to meet Conor and his family for dinner.

———————

Dinner was strained. The Fallons were struggling with the possibility of finding out that Mirren did in fact steal Kate after all.

Towards the end of the meal, Margaret pushed aside her plate. 'Do you think he'll stop you from seeing us?'

Kate was touched that she was worried by the possibility. 'I don't think so, no.'

'But if Muirrean did take you, and you are friendly with us, don't you see how that will look to him? It would be so hurtful.'

Kate thought carefully before speaking. 'Well, he's old enough and wise enough to know that we're not responsible for the actions of our relatives. If Mirren did take me then that was her doing, and hers alone. And if he is my father then he'll want what's best for me, and being part of your family means a lot to me.'

The mood lightened after that and they shared more memories of Mirren. More than anything Kate wished she was here with them.

———————

The two day wait for the results was over in a flash. The Fallons kept her occupied every minute so she didn't have time to brood. Hill walks, visits to museums, shopping (Laura was right about this) and eating out until she was fit to burst. Only when she was alone in the hotel room did she get the chance to think about what was to come.

Scrimgeour arrived at the hotel earlier than agreed, but she was ready and waiting. Her stomach was in knots as they went into the lab. On the way there, he told her that one of the technicians would go through the results. 'It's a favour,' he explained. 'We, the police that is, use this lab a lot.'

Kate would have preferred to be on her own but she didn't say so.

The receptionist showed them into a small room. A young woman came in and got to the point. 'It's positive,' she said. She talked about markers and statistical evidence, but Kate was in shock, unable to take it in. When the woman stopped, Kate stared at her until Scrimgeour got up. He took the report and thanked the young woman. Once outside he turned to Kate. 'What now?'

'I... I don't know.'

'How do you feel?'

Jesus! How did she feel? Sick and scared, that's what. She put the question back to him.

'Honestly? Well, I'm pleased, of course I am. I never allowed myself to hope you were alive...' He turned away from her so she was unable to see his face, but not before she caught a glimpse of tears.

It was too much. 'I'm sorry, I have to go.'

'Where?'

'I'm meeting friends.'

He reddened. 'Huh, from the Fallon family, no doubt. They're not your family though, are they? I'm your family, like it or not. And from the looks of your face, you don't like it.'

Kate took a step back from him, shocked at the venom in his voice. 'It's none of your business who I'm meeting.'

His face fell and he stuttered an apology. Kate softened,

remembering what Margaret had said about how he must feel. 'Look, phone me tomorrow. I just need some time to take it in.'

Alex nodded. 'Aye, you're right. I'm sorry . I'll phone you tomorrow.'

They said goodbye. Kate looked down Buchanan Street, trying to gather her thoughts. She couldn't take it in. She'd lied about meeting friends, the Fallons but it was too soon for her to have an intimate one-to-one with her father. Her father. Jesus.

Her hotel was only a few minutes away. She'd look round the shops first, maybe buy something for Laura, and then go back and think about what to do next.

FORTY-FIVE

Glasgow
_____

ALEX WATCHED Kate stride down Buchanan Street, her ponytail swinging from side to side. He'd done everything wrong, shouldn't have said anything against the Fallons, because face it, man, they were her real family. He was an unwelcome surrogate. He was lightheaded from the revelation that Mairi was alive. Kate, he'd have to learn to call her Kate. Funnily enough it had been one of the names on their list, but they'd dismissed it because one of their friends got there first. He was glad she had a name he liked. Christ, she was alive! After Sandra's betrayal and subsequent suicide, he'd never allowed himself to hope. He'd shut down his emotions in the year after her disappearance, done all the grieving he could. After that he'd retreated into himself. Never let anyone get close. Truth be told, he didn't know how to be happy any more.

Alex followed Kate into Frasers. He wasn't stalking her or anything, but he didn't want to let her out of his sight. He feared that given half a chance she'd get right back on a plane to London and he'd never see her again. So he was going to keep her in view for the time being. She was at the handbag counter, but her heart wasn't in it. One by one she picked them up and let them drop again. A man nearby stared at her, looked her up and down like a piece of meat. He had a baseball cap on so his face wasn't visible but there was something familiar about him. No doubt he was a ned Alex had lifted in the past. He hated men like that, who saw women as objects. He watched until he was sure the man was well away from her. His daughter. He'd never thought he'd say those words again. Kate continued her tour of the ground floor of Frasers. The man who'd been staring at her had disappeared. Alex had to go, he had to trust she'd still be there the next day. It would take time for her to get used to the idea of him as her father.

Alex was halfway up Buchanan Street when it dawned on him who the man in Frasers reminded him of. Jamie Taylor. The same colouring, the same height, the same mean look. Fuck, it *was* Taylor. He started to run.

———

Kate was in a state of near fever. What was she doing in this shop looking at Mulberry handbags she didn't want and couldn't afford? She should be at the hotel, phoning the Fallons, arranging to meet them, telling them her news. Oh Christ, what would this do to them? She turned on her heels. She was on the point of leaving the shop when she became aware of a figure standing nearby. A man. Shit, it was a security guard and she had a six hundred pound bag in her hand. She hurried back to the counter and put it down. What the hell had she been thinking?

Back at the hotel, Kate called the lift and stood in a dream, waiting for it to arrive. Her eyes were lowered and she took no notice of the other people waiting beside her. The lift stopped at the fifth floor and she got out and walked to her room. There were footsteps behind her but she thought nothing of it. She passed the card through the reader and the door opened. She fell into the room, pushed from behind.

Damn his weight. He ought to have gone on a diet years ago. This was what came of no longer being on the beat. You got fat. His breath came in short gasps; a couple of neds shouted *gaun yersel granddad* as he passed. He didn't have the energy even to give them the finger. The hotel was in view. Was that Taylor going in? He gave one last sprint.

There was no sign of the bastard at Reception. Had he imagined it? No, it had definitely been him. He stood at the door, wheezing, trying to catch his breath. A couple going out asked if he was OK and he nodded, unable to speak. He had to check her room. He moved towards the lift but the boy on Reception was there before him.

'Excuse me, Sir. Are you a guest?'

'Police.'

'ID, please.'

'Fuck's sake.' Alex fumbled in his pocket and thrust it in the boy's face. 'You come with me. You got a master key?'

The boy nodded.

'Right get in. I'll explain on the way up.' Alex bundled the boy into the lift in front of him. 'My daughter's in danger. She's on floor five, room... oh for fuck's sake, what's her room number?' Tears of frustration filled his eyes.

'Is she tall, with a ponytail?'

'Yes, yes! That's her.'

'Room 515. She picked up her card a few minutes ago.'

Thank fuck. The lift stopped and they got out. 'Come on, let's get going.'

As they ran towards the room, they heard shouting. Already several people were standing outside. One of them was hammering on the door. Alex pushed through them, shouting to the receptionist for the master card. He fumbled with it. 'It's not working.' There was a thump in the room and the noises stopped.

'You're putting it in the wrong way. Give it to me.'

Alex stood back and let the receptionist open the door.

Kate scrambled to her feet to find Jamie Taylor behind her, slamming the door. They faced each other, glaring. 'What the fuck do you think you're doing?'

'Just want to have a wee chat, I reckon you owe me.'

'I owe you nothing.'

'OK, maybe not you personally, but that fucking bitch who stole you does and now she's dead, you've got all her money. I'm sure you'll want to share it with your family. With me.'

'Jamie, I'm not your sister. You know what the results from the DNA test said. We are one hundred percent not related. DNA doesn't lie.'

'Doesn't it? It does if you're a corrupt polis, and that bastard Scrimgeour is as bent as they come.'

She'd get nowhere going over the same stuff. It was none of his business but she said it anyway. 'I know who my father is.'

That confused him. 'What? Who?'

'It doesn't matter.'

'Ach, you're a lying cunt, like the rest of them.'

'It's true.'

'Rubbish, you don't believe that. Your so-called mother, she took you cunt our garden. You're my sister. This is just a ply to get me off your back. Well, too bad, doll, I'm going nowhere.' He sneered at her. 'Don't you see? That polis, he's controlled everything. Just like my ma said he would. He's even fucking holding my wife on a murder charge and he's after me too.'

What the hell was he talking about? Alex hadn't said anything about this. Kate held her hand up. 'Stop it. I'm not your sister. I don't owe you anything. I'm sorry you lost your sister but it's nothing to do with my mother. She disappeared long after everyone thought. She was hiding in a cottage in the Highlands and the best part of a year later, she resurfaced in Glasgow and stole me. I was a year old when I was taken. I've met my...' she stuttered over the next word, '...father and had a DNA test. We got the results today and it's one hundred percent certain.'

Jamie's face paled. He slumped down onto the bed, his head in his hands. 'I don't understand. Fallon didn't take Dani? Well, who the fuck did then?'

Kate didn't reply. It would only make things worse if she said what she was thinking.

'I don't believe it,' he said. 'Prove it. When were you taken and from where?'

'It was May the following year. I was taken from a garden in Jordanhill, I think it's called.'

He was very still. 'That polis scum lived in Jordanhill. I mind my ma talking about it. Fucking posh cunt. So, Scrimgeour's your father?'

Christ, she should have said nothing. The change in his voice was terrifying.

'That *cunt*. That fucking cunt is your father!' He was shouting. His face red with rage. 'My ma kept all the cuttings.

He blamed it on my da. The papers couldn't get enough of it. The poor polis who convicted a child killer and then had his own wean taken. Bastard. Any other cunt would've admitted he'd got it wrong and allowed the case to be re-opened, but no, not him. He went on and on about how my da had arranged it all until the whole of Glasgow believed he was behind it. He was in the fucking jail. How the fuck could he have done it from there?'

Kate glanced at the door. In her initial panic to get away from him when he ambushed her, she had moved to the other side of the room. Now she was trapped. She wouldn't get past him easily.

'Scrimgeour. He killed my da. He decided my da was guilty and the fucking jury believed him. And now here's his daughter in front of me, a stuck-up bint if ever there was one.' He looked her up and down, appraising. 'Oh, we could have fun here. No doubt about that.' He stood up and moved towards her. She dashed towards the door, but he was too quick for her and in an instant had her on the floor. He straddled her, holding her wrists tight. She froze.

'You'll regret the day you ever came to Glasgow,' he said. 'I've hated that bastard Scrimgeour for years because of what he did to my family. It would have been good to have had my sister back, but hey, seeing as you're not, we can play instead. And what a bonus, this will really get to him.'

Kate knew what he had in mind. She also knew what to do, thanks to the self-defence classes Mirren made her do before she moved to London. His arms were at a forty-five-degree angle holding her wrists, so she wriggled up between his legs so they were nearer ninety degrees, which was ideal for what she planned. She lifted her hips high and used her thighs to push his body forward. This unbalanced him and he released her wrists to stop himself falling on his face. At the same time Kate moved her arms down to the side of her body. She held his torso tight and placed her face against his chest so he couldn't get an arm near her throat, then seized his right arm, rolled him over and pushed him to one side. The crack as his head hit the side of the minibar made her wince, but she didn't wait to see if she had done him any harm. She jumped up and ran to the door, getting there as it opened to reveal Scrimgeour and a whole bunch of strangers. 'What kept you?' she said and burst into tears.

FORTY-SIX

Glasgow

It wasn't what he was expecting to see. He'd thought the worst. Taylor was a big man, like his father before him, and he reckoned Kate was in trouble, but it was Taylor who was out cold on the floor.

'Did he hurt you?'

'No. He was trying to but I knew what to do.'

'What, I mean how did you know what to do?'

'M—, I mean Mirren...' She stopped and looked him in the eye. 'I'm sorry, Alex, but she was my mum. It was terrible what she did to you and my birth mother and I still find it hard to believe she did it, but she loved me and I loved her. So yes, I will call her Mum.'

It hurt him to hear this, Christ how it hurt, but he nodded and said, 'What did she do?'

'She made me go to self-defence classes before I went to university in London. She was worried about me being alone in the city. I hated them but she insisted, and when she had her mind made up, well, she was hard to say no to.'

'Thank God she did. Are you all right?'

She looked at her wrists. 'I bruise easily so these will be pretty colourful tomorrow, and I pulled a thigh muscle when I was making my moves, but other than that, fine. Better than him anyway.' She nodded at Taylor, who wasn't moving. The receptionist was feeling for his pulse. For a few heart-stopping moments, Alex feared she had killed him, but then he announced he'd found it. 'I'll call an ambulance,' he said.

'And the police,' added Alex.

He stayed with her while she made her statement to the officers who attended. Taylor came round while they were doing so. 'She assaulted me, she's a fucking mad cunt, needs to be locked up.'

The paramedics arrived, checked both of them and pronounced them fine. Taylor was arrested and charged with assault following a witness statement from the occupant of the room next door, who had seen him push her into the room and heard them shouting.

'That's not the only crime he'll be charged with,' said Alex as Taylor was hustled out the door.

'What do you mean?' asked Kate. 'He said something about you arresting his wife for murder? Is it something to do with that?'

'Yes, I caught her trying to kill my mother and their house was full of evidence that they'd been plotting to kill her for some time. They were also planning to blackmail your... erm, Mirren. You should know that once they'd got money from her, they were going to kill her. All because he was obsessed with the idea that his father was innocent.'

Kate shook her head. Christ, what a horrible man Taylor was.

'Are you OK? It's a lot to take in.'

'Is your mother... I mean, my grandmother... is she going to be OK?'

'She has Altzeimer's, so she'll never really be alright but physically she's fine.' Alex stood up. 'I should go,' he said.

'No, don't. Stay and talk. Tell me about you, about my mother, my grandmother. About you. Tell me everything.'

He'd been talking for an hour when Kate remembered she was supposed to have contacted the Fallons. 'I ought to let the Fallons know what's happened,' she said.

Alex's face closed and she added, 'They'll be worried. I'm going to text to let them know I'm all right and then I'm going to order dinner and I hope you'll join me.'

He tried to hide it but she could tell he was pleased. Kate took out her phone. There were several missed calls from Margaret and she texted her, telling her the results of the DNA test and promising to be in touch the next day. Alex looked at the room service menu while she was doing that and they ordered two burgers and chips.

'Would you like wine?' he asked. They ordered a bottle of Merlot and waited for the food to arrive. Kate was starting to understand what it must have been like for Alex. He was bitter, but who wouldn't be after what he'd gone through? It sounded as though he'd loved his wife, her mother, very much. It must have been devastating to find out that she'd betrayed him with his best friend. He had lost everything.

'What was she like, my mother, I mean?'

He chewed his food for a few seconds before answering. 'She was lovely. Clever, full of fun. She doted on you.' He talked on for a few minutes about how much she'd loved Kate, how besotted they'd both been. 'You know, it's great to remember the good times we had. For so long now all I've done is dwell on the... well, you know what the guilt did to her. She couldn't live with it.' He stopped. 'I blame myself. I was too hard on her. People make mistakes and she paid dearly for hers. We all did.'

'What happened to the man she was having an affair with?

'He lost his job. His wife divorced him. Last I heard he was working down south. He'd started his own security firm.' He drained his glass and filled hers up before pouring himself another. 'To tell you the truth I haven't thought about him for years. And I'd be happy never to hear of him again.'

Alex was exhausted. Talking about the pain of the past had drained him and he yearned for bed. but instinct told him to keep going. It was going to be slow, but he thought he saw the beginning of a thaw. Never one to hope, he nonetheless allowed himself to fantasise for a second about having a relationship with his daughter. Her voice interrupted his thoughts.

'You're tired. You should go.'

Perhaps it was the drink, perhaps it was the emotion of the moment, but for the first time in years, Alex Scrimgeour allowed his true feelings to show. He reached over and took her hands in his. 'Kate, I've waited a long time for this. Sleep doesn't matter to me now. You do.'

She smiled in return and he thought his heart was going to burst out of his chest.

FORTY-SEVEN

Buckinghamshire

Three months later

THE PAST MONTHS had been challenging. Kate often thought about the saying, blood is thicker than water. She wasn't so sure. We are formed by the people around us, those who bring us up and if we're lucky, nurture us. She was moulded by Mirren Fallon, who was a powerful personality full of love, full of life. Mirren in turn had been made by *her* family, and it was to them that Kate turned when life was difficult. She couldn't believe her luck. She had found a complete family, the one she'd always wanted. She'd kept Conor at arm's length although the attraction was very strong, scared that a relationship between them might ruin the family dynamic. Now he was in London though, things were different. Perhaps she'd let him get closer to her. Everyone was happy. Except Alex Scrimgeour.

Alex, the birth father she never knew she had. It was tough getting to know him. He'd opened up that first night but not since. Kate knew he found it hard that she was so close to the

Fallons. It was early December; he would be arriving shortly for the weekend and she dreaded it. She wanted to get on with him but Christ, he wasn't an easy man.

Alex got off the train and looked around for Kate. She'd said she'd be there to meet him but there was no one on the platform. He made his way out to the front of the station and leaned against a wall to wait. She'd been reluctant to see him this weekend but he'd insisted. He wanted to share his worries about her case. All along he'd thought the timing of Muireann's trip to Glasgow was off. He'd once gone to Achiltilbuie by bus and it had taken forever, but maybe that wasn't the case in the 1990s. A few days ago, he'd sought out the relevant timetable. It took eight hours to travel by bus from Achiltilbuie to Glasgow. The bus left at eight, so you wouldn't get to the centre of Glasgow until four p.m. Add on another thirty minutes to get to Jordanhill and there was no way she could have taken Mairi, who was reported missing at two forty-three, according to the case notes. Yesterday he'd got the piece of footage he'd asked for from the case file in the archives. A clip from the CCTV in Mothercare taken on the day Mairi disappeared. It was a long shot. Despite it being shown on the news several times, no one had come forward to identify the woman, and it was far from clear that she wasn't an innocent customer. But it was unusual for a child that young not to be in a pram, and the woman did, as the original witness had stated, look shifty. Alex wanted to discuss this with Kate to see what she thought.

He brought up the subject after dinner, breaking the silence that was threatening to drown them. She frowned. 'What does this mean?'

'Perhaps everyone's right about this not being in Mirren's character.'

She said nothing for a few seconds, then, 'I knew Josie wasn't telling me everything.'

'Josie. That's the woman whose house she lived in when she disappeared the first time?'

'Yes, she was a friend of Mum's. Bled her dry for years.'

'What do you mean?'

'Mum was paying her money. Had been for nearly thirty years. Comes to over thirty thousand pounds.'

Alex whistled. 'That's a lot of money. I think we need to go and see this Josie, but first take a look at this.'

Alex took out his phone and played her a video clip. It was blurred. 'What is this?'

'It's from the day you were taken. It was the only lead we ever got. CCTV footage from Mothercare in Sauchiehall Street. I'll send it to your email and we can watch it on your laptop.'

It was clearer on the bigger screen. Clear enough for Kate to see it was definitely not Mirren. Too tall. She watched it over and over until her eyes didn't focus any more. 'I think that's Josie,' she said at last. 'The way she's holding her head looks familiar.'

'You sure?'

'I... I don't know.'

Alex put down his glass of wine. 'Right, here's what I suggest we do. I'll contact the local police in Achiltilbuie and get them to see if anyone remembers Josie or your mum.'

'Do you think that's possible?'

'You never know. It's a small place and people don't move around much. There may well be several people there who remember Mirren.'

The next day he spent hours on the phone to Scotland. By five o'clock he'd got it pretty much sussed out and they started to plan their attack.

Josie was not an early riser so they turned up on her doorstep at seven a.m. She opened the door bleary eyed and yawning. 'What do you want?'

Alex stepped forward. 'A little chat.'

'It's the middle of the night. Come back later.'

As Kate thought, their early appearance had put her on the back foot. Josie moved away from the door and they took their chance and pushed their way in.

'Nice place you have here, Miss Turner.'

She scowled at him. 'Who are you?'

'Oh sorry, Josie. I should have introduced you. This is my father, Alex Scrimgeour. Mirren took me from his garden the day she left Achiltilbuie. I thought you'd like to meet him. He's a detective with Police Scotland.'

It was almost funny the way she paled. She bit her lower lip and rallied. 'At this time? When I don't have my face on? Bring him back later and we'll all have a little drink to celebrate, darling.'

'No, we want to talk now. Don't we, Kate?' Alex brought out a file of papers that were yellow with age and waved them in front of Josie. 'Bus timetables here. Tells us the times of the buses from Achiltilbuie to oh, all over Scotland. Turns out it's a bit out of the way.'

She was beginning to wake up. There was suspicion in her eyes. 'I know it's out of the way. I used to own a house there.'

'How long does it take to get there from Glasgow? As a matter of interest.'

She yawned. 'It's been a long time. I sold the house years ago. Look it up on Google.'

He nodded. 'I've done that all right. It takes five hours give or take fifteen minutes.'

'There you are then. You know already.'

He carried on as if she hadn't spoken. 'The first bus left at eight o'clock, is that right?'

'If you say so.'

'That gives Mirren enough time to get to Glasgow to kidnap my daughter, who was taken before half past two.'

'I suppose.'

'You suppose wrong. A car would get you there in time but a bus won't. There is no possibility that Muireann could have got to Glasgow in time to take Mairi.'

Her eyes darted from side to side. 'I must have got the date wrong.'

'Mmm, I wonder. What would you say if I told you that no one in Achiltilbuie remembers Muireann getting on that bus, that what they do remember is you coming up and taking her away. They also remember you having a baby with you. A baby you said was your niece. Muireann was popular with the locals. They liked her. They were shocked when I told them what she was supposed to have done.'

'What locals? They're all dead now or demented.'

He scratched his nose. 'Really? It was twenty-six years ago, not sixty. There's plenty of people around remember Muireann, and you too. They're not as complimentary about you though.' She flushed. He carried on. 'I'll tell you what I think happened. I think you told Muireann you could arrange an adoption. It would cost her though. A lot of money. Money she didn't have but you could lend her. The early nineties, that was when all those awful stories came out about orphans in Romania. You told her you'd arrange to adopt a child from there. You didn't know what age or sex because you never know with these foreigners, eh? Can't trust them.'

'This is rubbish, I don't have to listen to this.' Josie rose from her chair. Alex caught her hand.

'Sit down, I haven't finished.'

She sat down, arms folded. Her lips were pursed; what a mean little mouth.

'So, you set this up. You knew my wife, not well, but you'd sussed out what was going on with her and her lover. He'd come round in the afternoons when I was at work and she'd leave Mairi in her pram in the garden, thinking it was safe. It couldn't have been better. Mairi was seventeen months old, a little younger than Caitlin would have been, so Mirren could use her papers when you were unable to produce official papers from Romania.'

'I have no idea what you're talking about.'

'You lived in a tenement flat near to us. Our garden was visible from your front window. I asked someone to check yesterday. It was a risk, but you took it. No doubt you would have had an explanation if you'd been challenged, but the only person who saw you was an old woman with failing eyesight, and that got us nowhere.' His voice was acid with the memory.

Josie didn't look at either of them. She nibbled at a cuticle.

'After you took Mairi, you drove into town to buy her clothes and other necessities. You then drove up to Achiltilbuie with Mairi to surprise Muireann on her birthday. After that, I can only guess at what happened. Did Muireann know where her new baby came from? What happened when the promised papers did not materialise? I think she knew there was something off, but she chose not to go to the police.'

Josie's voice was so quiet Kate hardly heard it. 'She didn't know.'

'What?'

'She didn't know. I told her the papers had gone missing. She had Caitlin's birth certificate. Your daughter was big for her age, she could pass for a nineteen-month-old child. It was simpler that way, I said.'

Alex closed his eyes and sighed. 'And she agreed?'

'She had no choice. It was either that or go to the authorities. She thought Kate was Romanian. With no papers the local authority would take over. Mirren had enough experience of social work to know it wouldn't end happily, so she used Caitlin's birth certificate. She had registered her in her name because that's what she and Tommy had agreed.'

'But her father's name would be on the birth certificate,' Alex said.

Kate shook her head. 'Only on the full certificate. The short form doesn't name the parents.'

'So when she registered you at nursery, at school, she showed them the short version and they accepted it. They badgered her for few months but eventually forgot and,' she shrugged, 'once you're in the system it's easier. By the time you're in secondary school, no-one's going to ask for a birth certificate that should have been dealt with years ago.

Alex stared at the wretch in front of him. She had stolen Mairi, had good as admitted it, but why? He didn't understand. He asked her over and over, but all she said was she'd wanted to

help Mirren. Perhaps she did, but she had also benefitted finan-
cially from it. At least thirty grand and then there were the
amounts she 'borrowed' and never paid back. He arrested her
and contacted Police Scotland to make arrangements for her to
be taken north for further questioning. Whether the Procurator
Fiscal would agree they had enough evidence to charge her was
another matter.

He didn't know what to think about Mirren. Josie claimed
she hadn't known, but she must have had suspicions. She'd
been an intelligent woman from all accounts, and the story
Josie had told her was thin. At night when she was alone,
Mairi sleeping peacefully, obliterating the memories she had of
her real parents, she must have wondered where she came
from. Perhaps she didn't want to know and had deluded
herself into thinking she'd rescued a child from being tied to a
cot in a filthy Romanian orphanage. The papers had been full
of them at the time. There were documentaries showing list-
less babies without the energy to cry, lying motionless on bare
mattresses. When Mairi had arrived in her arms, how had she
reconciled the lively baby she had been with those shells of
humanity? He sighed. He'd never know and he had to let it go
if he was ever going to have a relationship with Kate. Now he
knew Mirren wasn't behind the kidnapping, his bitterness was
fading.

They waited in Josie's house until she was taken away to a
local police station to await her fate. Once she was gone, they
made their way back to Kate's house.

'Do you think Mirren knew?'

Alex thought for a moment before replying. 'I think she
must have suspected. She was a social worker, she'd have
known about the effects of neglect. You were a happy,
contented baby. And chubby! You've seen the photos.' He

laughed as she made a face. 'I don't see how she could look at you and confuse you with an abandoned child.'

'I'd been snatched from my pram. I'd have been upset. Separation anxiety.' She was clutching at straws.

'It's a long way from a baby crying because she wants her mummy to one who has been disregarded and ignored from the time she was born.' He made sure to hide the rancour he felt.

She looked into flames in the log burner. 'I know. Can you ever forgive her?'

He chose his words with care. 'Forgiveness is complicated. It depends what you mean by it. If you mean can I forget or condone what she did, then no, I don't forgive her. Nor do I believe that what happened to her is an excuse for what she did.'

'She was bereft.' The words were a plea.

'As was I when you were taken. It doesn't mean you then hide what is wrong.'

'As she may have done.'

'Yes. But there's another way of looking at forgiveness. It can be a considered decision to let go of any feelings of anger or retribution towards someone. Now I know she didn't actually take you, I *am* less angry. I have started to let it go. And I can't have vengeance, as she's dead.' He saw she was going to object and hurried on with his next words. 'Not that I want it. It's enough to have you back in my life. So, yes. I forgive her.'

They sat in front of the log burner. This time last year, Kate and Mirren were planning her funeral. She had just received her diagnosis. Mirren would have been horrified at all this coming out after her death, whatever her part in it. Kate wasn't as sure as Alex that she did know she'd been stolen from a loving family. She wouldn't have gone along with that. And now Kate thought about it, one of the charities she left money to was one that worked with Romanian orphanages. Kate was sure she had believed the story Josie told her. Mirren had been a trusting sort of person.

Kate had to accept she'd never know for sure and move on. She wanted Alex to be in her life, and now he'd forgiven Mirren for what she might or might not have done, it was a real possibility. She put another log in the burner and smiled at him. 'You did a good job today.'

He raised his glass of beer to her in a salute. 'So did you. It was a brilliant touch going round so early. She didn't have a chance.'

'She didn't,' agreed Kate.

'We make a good team, you and me.' His voice was shaky.

Kate raised her own glass and smiled. 'I think you might be right.'

Acknowledgments

First of all, a huge thank you to Rebecca Collins and Adrian Hobart at Hobeck Books. I couldn't ask for better publishers. Thanks are also due to Sue Davison for copyediting *The Deception*. I am astounded by the level of attention to detail she has and really appreciate this. Thank you too, to Jayne Mapp for designing the wonderfully atmospheric cover. It is exactly what I had in mind for *The Deception*.

I am very lucky to have the support of two writing groups. Thanks to the Glasgow University editorial group: Ailsa Crum, Alison Miller, Ann Mackinnon, Clare Morrison, Griz Gordon and Heather Mackay and thanks also to the Glad Group: Ailsa Crum, Alison Irvine, Bert Thomson, Emily Munro, Emma Lennox Miller and Les Wood.

Finally, my family, and especially my husband Martin, are always there when I need them. Thank you.

MAUREEN MYANT

About the Author

Maureen worked for over 25 years as an educational psychologist but has also worked as a teacher and an Open University Associate Lecturer. She is a graduate of the prestigious University of Glasgow MLitt in Creative Writing course where she was taught by Janice Galloway, Liz Lochhead, James Kelman, Alasdair Gray and Tom Leonard among others. She also has a PhD in Creative Writing. Her first novel *The Search* was published by Alma Books and was translated into Spanish, Dutch and Turkish. It was longlisted for the Waverton Good Read Award and was one of the books chosen to be read for the Festival du premier roman de Chambéry. Her second novel, *The Confession*, was published by Hobeck Books in 2022 and introduces DCI Alex Scrimgeour. In an earlier incarnation it was shortlisted for a Crime Writers' Association Debut Dagger.

Maureen has been a voracious reader since the age of six when, fed up with her mum reading Noddy stories to her, she picked up her older brother's copy of Enid Blyton's The Valley of Adventure and devoured it in an evening. She hasn't stopped reading since and loves literary fiction, historical fiction, crime fiction, psychological thrillers and contemporary fiction but not necessarily in that order. Her favourite book is *The Secret History* by Donna Tartt and go-to comfort read is *Anne of Green Gables*.

Maureen lives in Glasgow with her husband. She has three grownup children and six grandchildren who love to beat her at Bananagrams.

🐦

Hobeck Books - the home of great stories

We hope you've enjoyed reading this novel by Maureen Meant. To keep up to date on Maureen's fiction writing please do follow her on Twitter.

Hobeck Books offers a number of short stories and novellas, including *You Can't Trust Anyone These Days* by Maureen Myant, free for subscribers in the compilation *Crime Bites*.

- *Echo Rock* by Robert Daws
- *Old Dogs, Old Tricks* by AB Morgan
- *The Silence of the Rabbit* by Wendy Turbin
- *Never Mind the Baubles: An Anthology of Twisted Winter Tales* by the Hobeck Team (including many of the Hobeck authors and Hobeck's two publishers)
- *The Clarice Cliff Vase* by Linda Huber
- *Here She Lies* by Kerena Swan
- *The Macnab Principle* by R.D. Nixon
- *Fatal Beginnings* by Brian Price
- *A Defining Moment* by Lin Le Versha
- *Saviour* by Jennie Ensor
- *You Can't Trust Anyone These Days* by Maureen Myant

Also please visit the Hobeck Books website for details of our other superb authors and their books, and if you would like to get in touch, we would love to hear from you.

Hobeck Books also presents a weekly podcast, the Hobcast, where founders Adrian Hobart and Rebecca Collins discuss all things book related, key issues from each week, including the ups and downs of running a creative business. Each episode includes an interview with one of the people who make Hobeck possible: the editors, the authors, the cover designers. These are the people who help Hobeck bring great stories to life. Without them, Hobeck wouldn't exist. The Hobcast can be listened to from all the usual platforms but it can also be found on the Hobeck website: **www.hobeck.net/hobcast**.

Other Hobeck Books to Explore

Silenced

A teenage girl is murdered on her way home from school, stabbed through the heart. Her North London community is shocked, but no-one has the courage to help the police, not even her mother. DI Callum Waverley, in his first job as senior investigating officer, tries to break through the code of silence that shrouds the case.

This is a world where the notorious Skull Crew rules through fear. Everyone knows you keep your mouth shut or you'll be silenced – permanently.

This is Luke's world. Reeling from the loss of his mother to cancer, his step-father distant at best, violent at worst, he slides into the Skull Crew's grip.

This is Jez's world too. Her alcoholic mother neither knows nor cares that her 16-year-old daughter is being exploited by V, all-powerful leader of the gang.

Luke and Jez form a bond. Can Callum win their trust, or will his own demons sabotage his investigation? And can anyone stop the Skull Crew ensuring all witnesses are silenced?

Her Deadly Friend

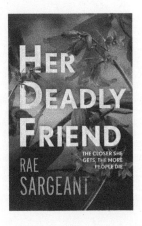

The Suspect
Bullied by Steph Lewis at school, then betrayed by her lover, Amy Ashby still seethes with fury.

The Stalker
When both women are stalked by a figure from their shared past, danger threatens.

The Detective
Now Detective Inspector, Steph follows a tip-off to her old rival. She had vowed never to see Amy again. But that was then.

The Deaths
Murder rocks the city, and all Steph's leads point to Amy. But is Steph obsessed with a schoolgirl vendetta or closing in on a deadly killer?

Pact of Silence

A fresh start for a new life

Newly pregnant, Emma is startled when her husband Luke announces they're swapping homes with his parents, but the rural idyll where Luke grew up is a great place to start their family. Yet Luke's manner suggests something odd is afoot, something that Emma can't quite fathom.

Too many secrets, not enough truths

Emma works hard to settle into her new life in the Yorkshire countryside, but a chance discovery increases her suspicions. She decides to dig a little deeper...

Be careful what you uncover

Will Emma find out why the locals are behaving so oddly? Can she discover the truth behind Luke's disturbing behaviour? Will the pact of silence ever be broken?

Blood Notes

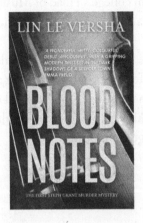

Winner of a 2022 Chill With A Book Premier Reader's Award!

'A wonderful, witty, colourful, debut 'Whodunnit', with a gripping modern twist set in the dark shadows of a Suffolk town.' EMMA FREUD

Edmund Fitzgerald is different.

Sheltered by an over-protective mother, he's a musical prodigy.

Now, against his mother's wishes, he's about to enter formal education for the first time aged sixteen.

Everything is alien to Edmund: teenage style, language and relationships are impossible to understand.

Then there's the searing jealousy his talent inspires, especially when the sixth form college's Head of Music, turns her back on her other students and begins to teach Edmund exclusively.

Observing events is Steph, a former police detective who is rebuilding her life following a bereavement as the college's receptionist. When a student is found dead in the music block, Steph's sleuthing skills help to unravel the dark events engulfing the college community.

Be Sure Your Sins

Six people. Six events. Six lives destroyed. What is the connection?

Detective **Melissa (Mel) Cooper** has two major investigations on the go. The first involves six apparently unrelated individuals who all suffer inexplicable life-altering events.

Mel is also pursuing a serial blackmailer but just as she's about to prove the link between this man and the six bizarre events, she's ordered to back off.

So why are her bosses interfering with her investigations? Who are they trying to protect? And how far will they go to stop her?

The answers come from a totally unexpected source.

Also by Maureen Myant

The Confession

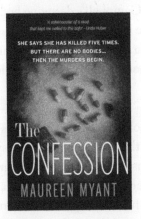

**2001 SHORTLIST TITLE FOR A CRIME
WRITERS' ASSOCIATION DEBUT DAGGER**

'Superb. Fast-paced and intense. *The Confession* is
a rollercoaster of a read that kept me nailed to the

sofa. A truly original premise and an addictively intense plot.' Linda Huber

'Maureen Myant blends Scottish police procedural with dramatic domestic noir, flips the mix upside-down and dishes up an original, readable helping of psychological thriller.' Rachel Sargeant

A house on a quiet street on the southside of Glasgow. Neat, terraced homes with manicured lawns and pruned trees. Not the sort of place that reeks of decay or where dead bluebottles pile up on a windowsill.

When the police break in, there's a surprise in store for them. They find Julie Campbell's decaying body at her desk, her laptop open beside her. She's a well-liked, respectable woman. On the laptop is a confession – to five murders. There's one major problem though – only one of the victims she names is actually dead.

DI Mark Nicholson is persuaded by his boss DCI Alex Scrimgeour that the confession is a fantasy, and to drop the case, but Mark senses there's more to it than meets the eye. As he delves further, the darkest of secrets are revealed, and everyone around him is dragged into a vortex of fear, danger and murder. No one is beyond suspicion as *The Confession* becomes a murderous reality.

The Search

In Czechoslovakia, 1942, Jan's father has been summarily executed by the Nazis. His mother and his older sister Maria have disappeared, and his younger sister Lena has been removed to a remote farm in the German countryside. With Europe in the throes of war, the ten-year-old boy embarks on a personal journey to reunite the family he has been violently torn from. The experiences he goes through and the horror he faces during this desperate quest will change his life for ever. While examining the devastating effects of war on ordinary families, *The Search* provides an exploration of fear and loss, and of the bond between parents and children. Riveting, moving, at times disturbing, Maureen Myant's debut novel will haunt its readers for a long time after they have put it down.

9 781915 817167